THE SWITCH

Olivia Goldsmith is the bestselling author of *The First Wives Club*, *Flavor of the Month*, *Bestseller*, *The Switch*, *Young Wives*, *Bad Boy*, *Insiders*, *Uptown Girl*, and *Wish Upon a Star*. *The First Wives Club* was a major Hollywood film, starring Goldie Hawn, Bette Midler and Diane Keaton. Olivia Goldsmith died in 2004, aged 54

By the same author

OLIVIA GOLDSMITH

The Switch

HarperCollins*Publishers*

HarperCollins*Publishers*
77–85 Fulham Palace Road,
Hammersmith, London, W6 8JB

www.harpercollins.co.uk

This paperback edition 1999

First published in Great Britain by
HarperCollins*Publishers* in 1998

ISBN 0 00 776814 1

Typeset in Perpetua by Palimpsest Book Production Limited,
Polmont, Stirlingshire

Printed and bound in Great Britain by
Clays Ltd, St Ives plc

ACKNOWLEDGEMENTS

Amy Fine Collins for helping with the idea

Cindy Adams

Paul Mahon for not being there when I needed him the most

Linda Grady for her continued support and comments

Richard Saperstein for getting it and buying it for New Line
   Cinema

Lenny Gartner for the islands, the support and the earrings

Marjorie Braman for the great edit and 'Marjorie Moments'

Beaver Hall for the gnawing, lodging and tail slapping

Leonida Karpik for knowing how to sell my books

Anthea Disney for laughing at my jokes

PART 1

Bait

Sylvie stood for a moment in the cool, dark hallway. It was the only dim place in the house and, though Sylvie loved the light — in fact, had fallen in love with the house for its light — she always found the comparative darkness of the hall a welcome contrast. She told herself that she really had too much to do to stand still here, one hand on the simple carved mahogany of the banister. She put her thumb on the comforting place where the curve of the wood had been worn flat by years of other thumbs. You don't have time to linger here, she told herself sternly. But despite her admonishment, just for a moment, she would enjoy this quiet. She listened to the tiny creaks the old house made and the comforting tick of the wall clock, then forced herself to pick up the cup of tea she'd left on the sideboard. The jasmine smell filled her head.

Sylvie began to walk down the hall but, as always, glanced first into the dining room, then the living room opposite before moving down the hall toward the music room. Oh, she loved her house. It wasn't large by Shaker Heights standards — just a center-hall colonial with only three bedrooms. But visitors, once in it, were always surprised by the grand dimensions and dignity of the house. Each of the downstairs four rooms was exactly the same size: all of them were large, light, airy rooms with ten-foot ceilings and long, high windows. Bob, at one time, had suggested they sell the house and buy a bigger one, but Sylvie had been aghast and had steadfastly refused. She didn't need a guest room — guests stayed next door at her mother's or camped out on the music room sofa. She didn't need a family room: *all* the rooms downstairs were for the family.

Sylvie knew how lucky she was, and she didn't take her good fortune for granted. Bob sometimes laughed at her for her little habit of checking each room. 'Do you think they're going away?' he'd ask. Or 'Are you looking for something?' he'd inquire. 'Not *for, at,*' she'd tell him. She was looking *at* her home, a place she had created slowly, over time, with Bob and the children. And she never wanted to be complacent about it.

Now Sylvie knew more surely than ever that she'd been right to not even consider selling the house. Perhaps in the old days they'd been the smallest bit cramped, but what would they do now with a larger place? Without the twins at home, the two bedrooms upstairs did stand empty, yet the rest of the house seemed to enfold and protect her. It was not a house too big for a couple, and perhaps someday when Sylvie was used to the idea that the children were gone she could turn one of their rooms upstairs into a proper guest room. Maybe she'd make a den for Bob out of the other. Then he wouldn't have to leave his paperwork all over the desk in the corner of the dining room, though lately he hadn't used it much, or at least kept it much neater than usual.

Sylvie moved down the hall to the music room, carrying her cup of tea before her as if the luminous white china could light her way like a lamp. She had only a few minutes before her first lesson and turned into the music room to see the usual organized clutter of sheet music, *Schirmer's Piano for New Students* piled beside *A Hundred Simple Piano Tunes* and *Chopin's Sonatas*. Her gray sweater lay across the bench of the Steinway, but nothing — ever — sat on its beautiful ebony lacquered top. Sylvie felt a little shiver of pleasure as she walked into the room. There was a touch of fall in the air and she closed one of the long windows. It was too early for a fire but, with the approach of autumn, she knew that soon the time she liked best in this room, the time when she gave lessons and played while apple wood burned in the grate behind her, was just ahead. Though she certainly missed the twins, this season was always a good time for her; September, when the children had begun school and she'd gone back to her full routine of piano lessons. It felt as if the year was beginning. Students returned from their summer holidays. Sylvie remembered that Jewish people actually celebrated their New Year about now. It made sense to her.

No reason to be sad, she told herself. No empty nest syndrome here, just because the children were no longer at Shaker Heights Elementary or Grover Cleveland High. Her daughter, Irene — Reenie to the family — would settle in at Bennington, and her twin brother, Kenny, already seemed perfectly happy at Northwestern. So, Sylvie told herself, she should settle in and be happy too. She was about to celebrate her fortieth birthday and was planning a treat. Bob had asked what she wanted and she'd finally decided. After all, she wanted romance. She had everything else.

Sylvie stopped for a moment, sipped her tea, and reflected on how many marriages in their neighborhood had failed. She and Bob were one of the lucky couples. They were happy. They loved each other. But she had to admit that sometimes she felt . . . well, Bob was always so busy. She'd expected he'd have more time once the kids were gone, but it was only she who had more time. He had filled up his agenda with campaigning, men's club meetings, and business. But now

Sylvie would help him take the time so they could discover themselves as a couple once again. She herself could focus a little more on Bob. Men liked that, even men as evolved as Bob. She'd already ordered some nice nightgowns from Victoria's Secret. She'd make romantic dinners. She'd bought three bottles of champagne and had them hidden in the old refrigerator in the garage, waiting for a spontaneous moment to reveal one with a flourish and let Bob pop the cork.

Sylvie smiled to herself. She wanted to lie in bed with Bob in the morning and talk and giggle instead of letting him jump up, shower, and shave by half past seven. She wanted to sit out in the backyard in the coolness of the October evenings, wrapped in a blanket with him beside her, gazing up at the stars. She wanted to spend a Sunday morning poking around a flea market, sipping coffee from a Styrofoam cup held in one hand with Bob holding the other. She looked around at her lovely room and smiled with anticipation.

Sylvie had always felt sorry for women who had to work outside their homes. She had been so very lucky. Lucky to meet Bob as early as she had, lucky that he had come back to Shaker Heights and had seamlessly become part of her family. She was lucky that the twins were both so healthy, so smart, and had never been in any real trouble. There were no financial problems. Bob had given up his music to become a partner in her father's car dealership, and that had provided well for them. Bob seemed to have done it willingly, though it always caused Sylvie some regret. There was no doubt in her mind that he had been the more talented musician. Perhaps his talent had actually made it easier for him to give up music as a profession; Sylvie didn't mind teaching and wasn't troubled by the knowledge that she was almost – but not quite – good enough to tour. Her talents had been exaggerated by a loving family. Juilliard, at first a startling comeuppance, had been a pleasure — once she realized that she didn't really have the stuff it took to be a concert pianist.

But she had become a good teacher, and she enjoyed teaching. For her it was not a fallback, the boring trap that serious musicians were so reluctantly forced into. She loved bringing music into people's lives and found that she also liked the glimpses into their lives that the lessons afforded her. Sylvie was a woman who enjoyed the process, and for that she was grateful. She actually enjoyed teaching scales, just as she enjoyed playing them. She liked the orderliness of building one week's lessons upon the next, and the slow construction of a musician, week by week, as a student mastered fingering, timing, and sight-reading until the thrilling moment came when music burst out in apparent effortlessness. Sylvie treasured those moments when, almost invariably, students looked up from the Steinway keyboard dazzled by their own ability to bring forth a waterfall of sound, to recreate the ordered noise that Handel, Chopin, or Beethoven had first composed.

Oh, she was lucky all right. Lucky with her material possessions, with her family, and with her ability to be satisfied. She had, thank goodness, none of her brother's constant dissatisfaction, or Bob's restlessness, which Reenie seemed to have inherited. Sylvie and Kenny were more alike. But then, she had never had to give anything up, to sacrifice anything as Bob had. She had gotten to keep her music *and* her family. She'd gotten to have it all — a good marriage, good kids, a house she loved, a career she cared about. And if Bob sometimes seemed a bit absent, if he ignored her just a little or took her for granted, they could fix that now — now that they had the luxury of this time together.

7

She looked at her watch. Honey Blank, her next student, was late. Typical. Sylvie heard a noise in the hall and stepped out there again. The mail came sliding through the post slot in the front door. Maybe there was a letter from one of the children. Kenny would be bad about writing, but Reenie might take the time to send a note. Sylvie knelt to pick up the pile. The usual bills, some catalogues (soon the pre-Christmas deluge would begin), and a card from her sister. Ellen was always early with her birthday greetings. Sylvie opened it. '*Forty but still fabulous*' it said on the front, with a photo of a wizened old woman in frightening makeup. Thank you, Ellen, Sylvie thought. Older but still passive aggressive, I see. Sylvie shrugged. There was a postcard from Reenie. Sylvie read it quickly. Good. It seemed as if Reenie was settling in. She had signed it '*your daughter, Irene,*' the formality of which made Sylvie smile.

But it was the Sun Holidays brochure that lit up her face. This was what she'd been waiting for. She felt as if she and Bob needed to rekindle the lamp, the light that had always been at the center of their relationship. And now, with the children gone, there would be time. Here, in her hand, was a ticket to romance. It was up to her. She had always been the spontaneous one, the one who created their adventures.

The phone rang and Sylvie took the mail to the hall table.

'Are you in the middle of a lesson?' Mildred, Sylvie's mother, began almost every phone conversation that way.

'No, but Harriet Blank is due over any minute.'

'Lucky you. The only woman in the greater Shaker Heights – Cleveland area with no social boundaries whatsoever. After her, do you and Bob want to come over for dinner?'

'No thanks. I've defrosted chicken.' Bob loved Mildred,

8

but he got enough of Jim, Sylvie's father, on the car lot most days. As she listened to her mother, Sylvie finished sorting through the mail.

'Your father is barbecuing,' Mildred told her.

'Well, that *is* an inducement. I haven't eaten charcoal since July Fourth. You know, Kenny says Grandpa's burgers are carcinogens. Something about free radicals.'

'The only free radical I know about is Patty Hearst,' Mildred snapped. Sylvie giggled while she opened the Sun Holidays envelope. It was the glossy brochure she'd written away for. She unfolded it, her heart beating a little faster. The photos were like gems, glowing deep sapphire and emerald in the dimness of the hallway.

'I thought I'd do your birthday dinner on Thursday,' Mildred continued, 'in case Bob was taking you out someplace fancy on Friday.'

The only place she wanted him to take her was Hawaii, Sylvie thought. 'He hasn't mentioned it. I'll ask him.'

'Maybe it's a surprise.'

Oh no! 'No surprise parties, Mom. I mean it,' Sylvie warned. 'It's bad enough being forty. I don't need the whole cul-de-sac gloating. Not to mention Rosalie.' Just the thought of her ex-sister-in-law made Sylvie shiver. She held up the brochure. There was a picture of a guest room showing a canopy bed hung with white. She and Bob, tanned, lying under the canopy . . . Well, she couldn't tan but she could turn pink and put her arms around him and . . .

'Sylvie, are you moping? Not that I'd blame you, with the twins gone. It's hard that both children had to leave at once. For me, I had six years to get used to Ellen, Phil, and then you leaving . . .'

'I'm not moping. I'm happy.' Sylvie clutched the brochure

9

and dropped the other mail into the basket. 'I've got to get ready for my lesson.'

'All right, dear. Call if you change your mind.'

There was a tapping on the glass of the French door. Mrs Harriet Blank – Honey to her friends, if she had any – was standing at the back entrance. 'You have a lot of leaves in the pool,' she said as she stepped into the room. 'You should get one of those automatic pool sweepers.'

'Nice to see you too,' Sylvie said mildly. 'It's been a long summer.'

'I practiced *every* day,' Honey assured her, as defensive as Sylvie expected her to be. The lazy students always were. Honey took off her sweater and laid her bag on the armchair. She moved toward the bench, but paused and looked intently at Sylvie. 'I saw you at L'Étoile, out by the lake, last week with Bob. You did something great to your face . . .' Honey took an even closer look at Sylvie, '. . . *that* night, anyway. I thought maybe you had a face-lift over the summer. You know, Carol Meyers did. She looks awful. Stretched. I hear she went all the way to Los Angeles for it. Waste of mileage. Anyway, you looked great – at L'Étoile—'

'Bob and I haven't been out to dinner for months,' Sylvie said mildly. 'Not since Bob started campaigning for the Masons' grand vizier or whatever the boss is called.'

Honey made a face of disbelief. 'Are you lying or did you forget?' she asked.

'I wouldn't lie about being with my husband,' Sylvie said, laughing, 'or about a face-lift.' She touched the part of her neck that had just begun to go a little crepey. Lately, when she glanced in a mirror, she sometimes saw a shadow of her mother's face. God. She pushed the thought from her mind. She was letting this woman get to her. And Honey was such a ditz. She was too vain to wear her glasses most of the time, even when she drove. But . . . 'When was it?' Sylvie couldn't help but ask.

'Last Tuesday.'

'We were home,' Sylvie said. Then she remembered that Bob had been late on Tuesday. But not very late. 'We were both home,' she emphasized.

'Come on. You were there,' Honey insisted. 'The two of you were flirting like crazy. That's why I didn't even say hello.' Her voice drifted off. 'You guys looked so romantic,' she murmured.

'That proves I wasn't there,' Sylvie said, relieved. 'In Shaker Heights, husbands don't flirt with wives – at least not with their own.'

'It was you.' Honey paused. 'Only your face was somehow . . . up. And you had only one chin.' Honey examined Sylvie's face again. 'You didn't seem to have a wrinkle. And you were tan.'

'Honey, I *never* tan. Not since I was born. I turn red, crack, and peel. My mother can verify that.' Honey was a pain. 'Shall we?' Sylvie asked, gesturing to the keyboard.

Honey leaned closer to Sylvie, still examining her face. 'Well, you were tan two weeks ago. Did you buy that thing on QVC with the tape and the rubber bands? That temporary face-lift thing?'

'No, but I once did get the thigh master. It's still under my bed. Want it?' Sylvie smacked her right leg and gestured for Honey to sit at the bench. 'Obviously, I never used it.'

Honey seemed miffed by Sylvie's response. They settled down to some finger exercises. It was clear that Honey *hadn't* been practicing. Slowly they moved through the lesson. Somewhere near the end of the tiresome hour Sylvie thought she heard Bob's car. She wanted to finish up quickly with Honey and present her new plan to her husband, but she was too professional to do it. She merely glanced over at the Hawaii brochure, propped at the edge of the music holder, and smiled.

At last the session was over. Sylvie gave Honey a new assignment and walked her to the French doors. What a day! The autumn air refreshed her, the crisp underscent of apples combining with that of drying leaves. Sylvie took a deep breath, then patted the sheet music she had handed Honey and raised her eyebrows, the strictest she ever got with an adult student. But subtlety was wasted on Honey. They said good-bye. Honey took the sheet music, looked up at her, and moved her hand to her own eyebrow, lifting the skin into a wrinkle-free arch. 'If a person is going to look *that* good, even for one night, I think it's really mean not to share how you did it with a friend,' Honey sniped.

'I share all my musical tips with you, Honey,' Sylvie said. 'Here's my best one: practice.' Gently she pushed the door closed and turned to join her husband.

2

Bob wasn't at his desk or in the living room. Sylvie checked the kitchen, flipped over the chicken that was sitting in its marinade, and sighed. Bob must have already slipped upstairs.

Sylvie was halfway up the stairs herself before she realized that she had left the travel brochure down in the music room. Honey, Sylvie admitted reluctantly, had flustered her. She turned around, bounded down the stairs, got the brochure, and doubled back. Now she could hear the sound of the shower in the master bath. That was what she'd been afraid of ! It meant that Bob was probably going out again this evening. The chicken would be wasted. Damn it! Sylvie didn't want to have to put off this conversation, but she didn't want to be forced to sandwich it in between Bob's ablutions and his departure.

Since Bob had begun to talk about becoming the grand panjandrum of the very secret Masons he'd been so busy. Why did he even want the position? It didn't pay anything and it couldn't really be any fun. Walking around in aprons, or whatever they wore, and singing secret songs seemed so unlike Bob. And why he needed to shave, change, and dress up for a smoke-filled room was also beyond her. He'd become more vain lately – she didn't remember him ever bothering to shower and shave before Rotary, even when he was the president of that. Well, for all she knew, it was a Masonic rule or something. Sylvie got to the bedroom door, paused, and nervously smoothed her hair and then smoothed the brochure in her hand. It was time for a change. She'd just *have* to make Bob see that. Charm and quirkiness worked with her husband. She stopped for a moment at her bedside table and took out a roll of adhesive tape. She smiled to herself as she walked through the bedroom. She'd get his attention.

Sylvie marched aggressively into the bathroom. The steam pushed up against the door, then up against her body with a wet force. She couldn't stop herself from looking at the place on the wall where, months ago, the paint had begun to peel. She wished, for the hundredth time, that Bob would remember not to turn the hot water up quite so high – but he never did. Acceptance was just a part of marriage. Sylvie shrugged and walked over to the glass shower wall.

Through the mottled texture of the glass she could see Bob's body, but the glass seemed to turn him into what looked like animated blots of color – kind of like the way technicians electronically scrambled guilty people's faces on television when they were being interviewed against their will. Sylvie stared. Pointillistic Bob. Then she picked up a hand towel and wiped down the glass. She'd be cute and quirky. Jauntily, Sylvie pushed the brochure up against the shower wall and, despite the moisture, used the adhesive tape to secure it there.

'Hi, honey. I have a surprise.'

'Your lesson over?'

Sylvie could see that the white dots topping the pink dots of Bob's head had just about been washed off the animated figure that was her husband. Which meant that the shampooing was over and that he could safely open his eyes. She tapped the glass. 'See what I brought you,' she said. She watched as he moved closer to the glass. He bent, suddenly, almost against

14

the textured partition and his face clearly emerged. Very wet, but recognizably Bob's nice-looking face. Close to the glass the wavering images didn't blur. Sylvie knew he was close enough to see the brochure.

'Show and tell?' he asked casually.

'Show and go,' she responded, trying to be cute.

But then, to her disappointment, cuteness failed. His head disappeared again. He became a Seurat painting: Tuesday in the Shower with Bob.

Sylvie felt her jauntiness drop like a wilted leaf from a tree. No. He *had* to pay attention. She tapped the shower stall again. 'Bob! Look! There haven't been colors like this since the seventies.'

He was fumbling for something on the corner shelf. 'Beautiful. What is that? Something like Hawaii?'

'Good, Bob. It *is* Hawaii.' For a moment she felt hope surge, but then realized he wasn't even looking. She'd have to try again. 'You see those two people snorkeling? Isn't it weird how they look just like us? They could *be* us, Bob.' Sylvie paused for his reaction. Then, to her dismay, she saw more white animated dots appearing at the top of her husband's wavering form. He was shampooing twice. That was *truly* unusual. Bob never read the directions on any product or appliance, not since she'd met him. When did he ever read the instructions on the shampoo tube? Since when did he soap up *twice?*

The steam was taking over. Sylvie took the brochure down. Already its crisp new feel had begun to be transformed by the bathroom dampness. The pictures now sagged across the double-page spreads. For a moment the sag was echoed by the sag of Bob's little belly, which emerged first from the stall, followed by the rest of him, only to be quickly wrapped in the special bath sheet he liked to use. Then, swaddled, he turned and inserted his arm into the shower, shutting off the water at last. The silence seemed startling to Sylvie, who felt more than a little bit forlorn. Perhaps Bob noticed, because he turned and gave her one of the big bear hugs that he was famous for. Just as she started to relax into it he dropped his arms, turned to the sink, and took down his razor and can of foam.

'You hear from the kids?' he asked casually.

'Nothing from Kenny, but Reenie sent a card. She says she wants to change her major again.'

'No more French poetry?' Bob asked, spreading the foam along his right cheek and stretching his neck up in that way men did before they patted the cream on their jowls. Sylvie wondered if shaving had some age-defying quality – Bob's neck looked more taut than hers did, though he was already forty-four.

'She feels she has to major in post-Communist Russian studies.'

'*Has to*? That seems like something no one *has* to do,' he said as he pulled the razor down his cheek.

As always, Sylvie felt she had to spring to the defense of their mercurial daughter. Temperamentally Reenie and Bob were so similar that sometimes Sylvie had to run interference. 'She's been thinking about it a lot. I admit she's a little at sea right now.'

'Well, she better move up to an A, or a B plus at the very least,' Bob punned. He flashed her a quick smile. His teeth seemed yellow against the unusually white-white of his foamy beard. It gave him an almost unpleasant wolfish look. Sylvie thought of the phrase 'long in the tooth.' 'She has to get a scholarship by next year is what she has to do,' Bob continued.

The razor sliced another path through the foam. 'First she had to pick the most expensive school in America. Now she *has* to study irrelevant recent history. You can't even make a living with a degree in irrelevant *ancient* history.'

'The two of us felt we had to major in music,' Sylvie reminded him.

'Yeah. It sure helped me in my career,' Bob said, his voice heavy with sarcasm. 'When I'm giving a test drive, I know all the classical radio stations.'

Sylvie didn't like the tone of this conversation. Bob seemed distracted and cranky. Normally, he was an indulgent father, a loving husband. Feeling a little desperate, Sylvie leaned forward and taped the buckling brochure to the mirror, beside the reflection of his now almost shaved face. It was hard to get the tape to stick to the wet glass.

Bob ignored the thing and rinsed the razor. 'It's not the seventies or eighties anymore,' he said. 'Reenie has to begin thinking responsibly. Realistically. Do you realize the kids are older now than we were when we met?'

'They're too short to be that old,' Sylvie told him.

He laughed and used one hand to pinch the nape of her neck, giving her the tug that connected deep inside her. Sylvie smiled into the mirror at him and started to gesture to the brochure, but he pulled his hand away and bent over, rooting around in the cabinet under the sink. 'Bob, when we finished Juilliard, we were going to travel around the country in a painted bus. And play music wherever we felt like it. Why didn't we do that?' Sylvie asked. Her voice, she realized, sounded plaintive. Where was quirky? Where was jaunty?

Bob was slapping his face with an aftershave. 'Two reasons,' he said. 'We were a decade too late and we had a life instead.'

'Bob. About Hawaii. For my birthday I'd really like to—'

'Oh no! A trip? Now?' He turned away from the mirror. 'Come on, baby. That's out of the question. We have the new models just jamming the lot. Your father's talking about an advertising push, and I'm flirting with the idea of this political thing. Anyway, with two tuitions . . . we just can't.'

'It's not expensive,' Sylvie gabbled. 'Not at this time of year. The season hasn't begun yet. There's a package deal. And I have money saved from lessons.'

'Hey! Pay for your own fortieth birthday present? I don't think so.' He bent to her cheek and kissed her. His aftershave smelled of lime, unfamiliar. 'Anyway, I already got your present for you. I brought it home tonight. Want to see it?' He dropped his towel, pulled on his briefs, stepped into his slacks, and looked around for his belt. Sylvie handed it to him. As he threaded it through his belt loops, Sylvie watched the brochure slide slowly down the wet mirror and settle in a pool of water on the vanity.

Bob, his shirt on, gave her another bear hug. 'Hey! Come downstairs. Don't worry, I haven't forgotten your upcoming big day. Four decades! And you don't look a day over forty.' She smiled weakly at him. He took her hand. 'So, come on down and see your reward.'

Sylvie slowly followed Bob as he led her downstairs, through the kitchen, out the back door, past the rose bed and her row of double zinnias, over to the driveway. The light was beginning to fade, and his car — his obsession — was parked in front of the garage.

'You're giving me Beautiful Baby for my birthday?' Sylvie joked mildly. If Bob had a choice between losing his car or his prostate, he'd probably keep the two-seater. It was a perfectly restored BMW, a 1971 XS200. But what in the world had he gotten for *her?* Her heart fluttered for a moment. Bob's car was tiny, but there was enough room in the glove compartment for a jewelry box.

'You know my birthday isn't until Friday. Shouldn't we wait until then?' Sylvie asked. She felt guilty that she'd had ungracious thoughts about Bob. He really was thoughtful.

'Come on! You seem a little down. I want you to enjoy this as soon as possible. Use it on your birthday.' Bob pressed the remote to open the garage doors. As they swung up, he turned on the lights.

There, illuminated by the overhead fluorescent, was a new BMW convertible. A huge red bow was stretched across the hood. A car? Bob put his arm around her. 'Happy birthday, honey,' he said. 'Kids are gone. Time for a toy. Enjoy yourself.'

Sylvie looked at the sparkling silvery-paint-and-shiny-chrome object. 'You took away my sedan?' she asked weakly.

'Don't worry about a thing. Already detailed and in the previously owned lot.' He gestured to the convertible. 'Isn't she a beauty? Isn't that better than a trip to Hawaii?'

Sylvie reluctantly nodded. She should feel grateful and excited, she told herself. Even if the family did own a BMW dealership and she got a new car every couple of years as a matter of course. This one *was* special. She knew Bob couldn't keep the new convertibles on the lot. So why did she feel so . . . disappointed? She looked up at Bob. 'Thank you,' she said, trying to muster some enthusiasm. She failed. 'It's really extravagant. It's great,' she said, and she heard the flatness in her voice. God, she hoped Bob didn't. She wouldn't want to hurt his feelings.

But Bob didn't seem hurt. He patted the leather of the seat. 'You'll love it as much as I love mine,' he told her.

Sylvie doubted that, but she managed a smile. 'Look, I've got to go,' he continued. 'We'll take the car out for your birthday, okay? Maybe we'll drive up to the lake. Eat at L'Étoile. We haven't been there in a long time.'

'Sure. Okay.' Sylvie paused. What was it? Oh. 'That's funny, because when Honey Blank came over today—'

Bob had pulled out his car keys. 'Honey Blank? That piece of work? Can you tell me in four words or less?' he asked. 'Or, better, save it for later. I really have to go.'

'Never mind. I'll tell you when you get home,' Sylvie agreed. What difference did the coincidence make? Barely a conversation point.

'I might be late. I won't wake you.' Bob got into Beautiful Baby and started her up. For a moment Sylvie saw him there as a stranger, a middle-aged man with a bit of a paunch sitting in a sports car built for the very young.

'I wouldn't mind if you did wake me,' she told him, hoping he'd get the hint, but he had already begun backing out of the driveway. He waved as he pulled into the cul-de-sac and then accelerated. Sylvie watched him go. She stood for a moment in the twilight, the ugly fluorescent shining out of the garage behind her making the macadam under her feet look purple with oil.

'Well. That's impressive.'

Sylvie looked up. God, it was Rosalie the Bitter, her ex-sister-in-law. Not right now, Sylvie thought. It wasn't that Sylvie didn't love Rosalie and feel sorry for her. She even took her side over her own brother's, but Rosalie *was* difficult.

'A new car?' Rosalie asked. 'I can't even get Phil to fix my transmission. And he's in charge of the service department.'

Sylvie had long known there was no way to have a conversation with Rosalie. Everything was a complaint or an attack. Though she'd wound up with the house, alimony, and healthy child support, Rosalie still felt cheated. Of course, Sylvie had to admit, Rosalie had been cheated on. Even if Phil was her brother, Sylvie thought he'd gotten what he deserved. But she couldn't help wishing Rosalie didn't live right next door.

'Have you been jogging?' Sylvie asked, partly to change the subject and partly to just say something. Rosalie was in shorts and the kind of industrial Nikes that cost in the three figures. Sylvie pressed the garage button to close the door. Rosalie, thin as a rake, ignored the question. It seemed to Sylvie that she'd displaced most of the energy she'd used nagging Phil and now used it to exercise with. Rosalie jogged, lifted weights, taught aerobics, and even attended a yoga class in downtown Cleveland. Maybe, Sylvie thought, she should give Rosalie her thigh master. Not that she needed it.

'You know how lucky you are?' Rosalie demanded. 'Do you know?' Rosalie looked around at the flower beds, the lawn, the house. 'A new car in your garage, two nice kids in college, *and* a husband in your bed.' Rosalie shook her dark head. Sylvie turned away and started for the back door. She felt sorry for Rosalie – her three kids argued or ignored her, had dropped out of school and out of work. But Rosalie never stopped complaining. Now she followed Sylvie across the slate patio. Rosalie the Relentless. 'Forty isn't easy for any woman. But if anyone has it easy, you do,' Rosalie was saying. 'You're lucky. You've always been lucky.'

Sylvie got to the screen door, opened it, and slipped in.

Then, she very deliberately locked the button. 'You're right, Rosalie,' Sylvie said through the screen. 'I'm lucky. My life is a paradise.'

And she shut the back door.

3

Sylvie had put the top down on her new car although there was a chill in the air. It was wasteful to drive with the heat pumping and the top off but she was doing it. What the hell. She'd be self-indulgent. She was almost forty. Live a little!

The groceries she'd just bought were arranged neatly in four bags across the backseat and, as she took a sharp turn, she glimpsed them in the mirror. They shifted but didn't spill. Before the children had left she used to have to fill the backseat and the trunk of the sedan with groceries – Kenny and his friends ate like horses. Now four bags and a dollar tip to the box boy was all it took to fill the backseat and restock the larder at home.

She took a curve much faster than usual. The wind whipped at her hair. It was odd there was so much air, yet she couldn't seem to breathe. Somehow all she could manage was shallow breaths. Maybe she should take a yoga class.

Last night, after choking down a solitary dinner of overdone chicken, she'd waited for Bob. He'd come in after midnight and he hadn't wanted to talk. Sylvie didn't push it. Instead, she'd lain awake most of the night, sleepless and confused. She had——

Out of nowhere a car pulled out of an almost hidden driveway on her right. Sylvie moved the wheel and the convertible swerved responsively. A van was in the oncoming lane. The slightest touch brought her car back, long before the van was a real danger to her, but she was shaken. So were the groceries. Sylvie had to admit that the convertible was beautiful to drive, but she didn't want it. It was wrong somehow. It felt all wrong.

What's wrong with *me?* Sylvie thought. Most women would give up their husbands for a car like this. Or, for that matter, give up their cars for a husband like mine. And I have both. Rosalie is right. I'm very lucky. I should be grateful. She began her litany. I'm healthy, I love Bob, he loves me, the kids are fine. It's a beautiful sunny day, and the leaves are just starting to turn. This unease she felt, this nagging sense of dissatisfaction, wasn't like her. Sylvie felt ashamed at her unhappiness, but it was still there, right under her breastbone. She braked for a red light, the car gliding smoothly and effortlessly to a stop.

The steering wheel under her hands was wet with sweat. The feeling that had been building in her, lodging in her chest, now moved into her throat and blocked it. She tried to swallow and couldn't do it. It didn't matter anyway – her mouth was so dry there was nothing to swallow. Either I'm going crazy or something is really wrong, she thought as the light turned green. A horn blared behind her. The driver hadn't even given her a minute. She accelerated. All at once she was swept with a surge of anger – of rage – so complete that she had trouble seeing the road. She looked in the rearview mirror at the old man in the big Buick behind her, gunned the motor, and flipped him the bird.

God! She'd never done that before in her life. Road rage? What was going on?

She realized that it was more than not wanting this car. Bob hadn't thought of her when he took it off the lot. It was a reflexive gift, not a reflective one. He hadn't reflected, thought, for one moment about what she might want. He took her for granted. He hadn't listened about Hawaii either. When was the last time he *had* listened? Sylvie didn't want automatic gifts, no matter how luxurious. She didn't want to be taken for granted. She didn't want to be ignored by Bob. There was so many things she had that she *didn't* want, she felt almost dizzy and nearly missed the left into the cul-de-sac. She jerked the wheel and the new tires squealed making the turn. She drove slowly on Harris Place, the street she lived on, where her mother had the big house with the white columns and where her brother had lived in the Tudor before he'd divorced Rosalie. The few other houses on Harris were all traditional, well-designed and maintained. She drove past the beds of vinca in front of the Williamsons' and the row of gold chrysanthemums unimaginatively lined up along Rosalie's fence. Everything appeared so right, but this foreboding, this sense that it was wrong, became insupportable. She still couldn't breathe. It was as if the open top of the car let the entire weight of the universe in to crush her. Her house, the house she loved, loomed up.

Sylvie made a sharp right and felt the wheels of the BMW effortlessly move over the curb. She drove the car calmly across her own side lawn and, when she reached it, through the flower border, right over the zinnias. She felt an icy stillness as she proceeded onto the back lawn and engineered a carefully calculated right turn, avoiding the slate patio. The aqua rectangle of the pool was right before her and, without slowing down, she headed for it, the car, like a homing device, moving toward the concrete edge of the eight-foot diving drop. As the front wheels spun out into empty space, just before they took the plunge into the turquoise water, Sylvie was able to take the first deep breath she had taken all day.

* * *

'Sylvie! Sylvie, baby! Are you okay?'

Mildred had been rehanging the bedroom curtains and had looked down to see the L her daughter made in the lawn as she had done this crazy thing. Now Mildred stood at the edge of the pool. She couldn't swim – never had – but she'd jump in to attempt to save her daughter if she must. Mildred was relieved then to see that Sylvie's head had broken through the leaf-strewn surface of the water. Sylvie, a good swimmer, breaststroked gracefully over the trunk of the car and across the pool, still holding on to her purse. Her shoes had fallen to the bottom, but the shorts and blouse she had on felt surprisingly heavy, pulling her down. Still, Sylvie managed to move through the cold water to the ladder.

Mildred was panting, one hand against the ladder rail, the other hand on her heaving chest. 'You frightened me,' Mildred said. There was a scream from the other side of the property and Mildred started and turned her head. Sylvie, still in the pool, couldn't see but knew whose voice it was. 'Oh god,' Mildred muttered. 'I know *she* never washes her curtains, so what's her excuse for seeing this?' She squatted down to get closer to Sylvie and extended her hand to help her. 'Your ex-sister-in-law is waving to you,' she said.

Climbing the ladder, Sylvie turned and saw Rosalie's dark head over the pickets of the north fence. 'Trouble in Paradise?' Rosalie yelled.

Mildred, ignoring Rosalie, carefully helped her daughter out of the pool. 'Why did you do that?' she asked.

'So I'll remember where I parked?'

'Are you being flippant with your mother?'

Sylvie opened her purse, oblivious to the water that poured out, and dropped in her car keys. She snapped the purse shut.

The noise it made, like a tiny sedan door closing, did not sound as solid as usual. 'Flippant?' she echoed, distracted. She was a little dazed, but at least she could breathe.

'Sylvie, you do realize you've just done a very strange thing? If you don't, it's even stranger.'

Sylvie turned to look at the scene behind her. Three nectarines and a head of lettuce were now floating on the top of the pool. The car glinted up from the bottom like a silver fish lying under aspic. *What had she done?* And why had she done it? She put her hand up to her eyes to wipe away the water streaming down from her hair, only to realize there were also tears rising over her bottom lids. What had she done? Was she crazy? 'I just want Bob to notice me,' she admitted in a whisper.

Mildred nodded, then opened the door to the outdoor cabinet that Bob had always laughingly called 'The Cabana.' Oh, he was a card, Bob was. Sylvie shivered in the cool autumn air as she watched her mother take out two faded beach towels. 'Sylvie, sweetheart,' Mildred said, 'men don't notice their wives. A new blonde in the neighborhood, yes. A sports car, absolutely. But after forty-six years of marriage, just ask your father what color eyes I have.' Mildred looked deep into her daughter's own eyes. 'Give it up, Sylvie.' Mildred wrapped one of the towels around Sylvie's shoulders and handed her the other one. 'For your hair,' Mildred directed. Rosalie had thrown her left leg over the fence. 'What can I do?' she hollered.

Exasperated, Mildred raised her own voice. 'You can move out of the neighborhood, Rosalie. You've been divorced from my son for three years.' Rosalie had almost managed to breach the fence. Sylvie knew Rosalie was lonely since the divorce and with her kids away, but though she tried to feel for her,

27

Rose was shameless in her interfering with the family. She wouldn't sell her house or leave the cul-de-sac; she wouldn't stop snooping and gossiping and showing up uninvited. After her settlement from Phil had left him broke, she still insisted he had secret funds. And that everyone was better off and had more resources than Rosalie.

Now Rosalie the Resourceful got her right leg over the fence and jumped into the yard.

Rosalie made a beeline for the pool and stared into it. 'Holy shit! I heard it but I didn't see it.' She squatted down, looked at the car, and grinned. 'Is this gonna be covered by the warranty?' she asked. She reached out and grabbed the lettuce, floating near the edge of the pool coping, and brought it over to Sylvie. 'God, you're a mess,' Rosalie said as she surveyed Sylvie, who was dripping like a defrosting freezer. Rosalie held up the lettuce. 'Salad, anyone?' Mildred snatched it from her. 'What's happened to you, Sylvie?' Rosalie asked. 'I mean, aside from the dunk? I couldn't see you in the dark last night, but you look awful. You looked so much better the other day when I saw you with Bob leaving Vico's. He was driving pretty fast but I could have sworn you'd lost weight. I thought you'd lost weight,' Rosalie said doubtfully, looking at the wet clothes clinging to her sister-in-law.

'I wasn't with Bob in his car the other day,' Sylvie said. 'He moves too fast.'

'He was putting the moves on you, all right.'

'Go home, you loon,' Mildred snapped and began propelling Sylvie away from the scene of the crime. Sylvie knew Mildred felt sorry for Rosalie, just like she did, but still, the woman was brash and insensitive. That's why she'd been such a perfect match for Phil, and it had broken Mildred's heart when they split up.

'I wasn't in Beautiful Baby,' Sylvie called over her shoulder. Did all of Cleveland spend its free time sighting her in places she wasn't? Next she'd be seen with Elvis.

'You'll have to continue this little chat later.' Mildred turned her back on Rosalie and guided Sylvie gently but firmly into the house to the music room. She locked the French doors behind them and sat Sylvie down on the bench.

Rosalie, outside, tried the door handle.

'I haven't ridden in Bob's convertible in years. I'm not totally crazy,' Sylvie told her mother.

'Evidence to the contrary,' Mildred said, and took the towel from around Sylvie's head. 'You need a touch-up at the roots,' she added.

'I'm letting them gray and grow in,' Sylvie said.

'Then you *are* crazy,' Mildred told her daughter.

'Why? Bob didn't even notice when I changed the color.'

'Well, he'll notice this,' Mildred predicted, looking at the pool.

'My god. How will I tell him?' Sylvie felt her stomach lurch.

There was a banging on the window. Rosalie was pointing to the door lock. 'As if,' Mildred sniffed. Sylvie looked at the poor locked-out woman. But she just couldn't cope. She needed comforting now, and some calmness. Rosalie was too self-involved to offer that. For some reason, imagining Rosalie alone in her house next door made Sylvie lonely herself. Well, she realized, she *was* lonely. Even with her mother here beside her. She gestured for Rosalie to go away. Rosalie paid no attention.

'Maybe I am nuts,' Sylvie said, and nearly sobbed. 'It's pathetic to be so hurt because your husband is ignoring you. I just can't figure out if he always did and I didn't notice

29

because the kids were around or if he's ignoring me in a whole new way.'

'Oh, Sylvie,' Mildred sighed. 'This is all so normal and predictable. I did the car thing too, back when your father was still running the lot. Maybe not as dramatically, but every time we had a big fight, I'd rear-end somebody.'

'You did? What did you tell him?'

'That the brakes failed, and that's back when they were still calling it "the ultimate driving machine."'

'So it's hereditary?' Sylvie asked. 'Being crazy?'

'From your father's side.'

Rosalie began rattling the door. Mildred turned and surveyed her. 'Isn't it strange? She seems to think it's accidental that she's excluded,' Mildred observed to Sylvie. 'Just remember,' she added, 'I didn't like her while she was married to Phil.' She turned her full attention back to Sylvie. 'But I admit my son unhinged her. Poor thing. *She's* crazy by marriage.' Mildred sighed. 'Phil could make any woman nuts. Not like Bob.'

Sylvie felt the towel between her and the bench turning sodden and stood up.

'We better go upstairs,' Mildred told Sylvie. 'If she can't see or hear us, Rosalie will get tired and go home and the neighbors won't hear her banging to get in. Otherwise this will be all over town by dinner.' Sylvie nodded, though it would be all over town by dinner anyway. Mother and daughter moved together from the brightness of the music room into the darkness of the hall. Mildred sighed deeply as she shepherded her daughter up the stairs. 'Maybe the family business made all the rest of us crazy. But I thought you and Bob were immune.'

They got to the landing, where a picture from Reenie and

Kenny's tenth birthday party hung. Bob had been dressed up as a bagel, the twins' favorite treat at the time. 'Remember how much fun Bob used to be?' Sylvie asked.

'Fun? No. Intense, yes. Fun, no.'

'Yes you do,' Sylvie urged. 'He was such a great dancer. And he was always playing the piano.' She lowered her voice. 'The music in him has died.'

Mildred gave her a little push and propelled her up the rest of the stairs, still carrying the head of lettuce. 'Oh, please, Sylvie! Those artistic dreams always die. There's not a chiropractor in Shaker Heights who didn't think, at one time, he had a novel in him.'

Sylvie shook her head, unutterably sad. They entered the bedroom. It was all so pleasant – the bed had an antique headboard she and Bob had bought and refinished together years ago. She'd found the chest of drawers at a Cleveland thrift shop and had painted and decoupaged it. The quilt had been her grandmother's. It was a room with a lot of history. So why did she feel so desolate? Sylvie stood there and dripped on the floor. Mildred unbuttoned the back of Sylvie's blouse and began helping Sylvie off with her wet clothes. Sylvie felt absolutely limp.

'I don't know. I thought after the kids went off to college that . . .'

'. . . the two of you would . . . yeah, yeah, go on cruise vacations, dance until midnight.' Mildred pulled at the wet blouse, dragging it over her daughter's head, then caressing her wet hair. 'Just like your father and me,' she said. She shook her head. The gesture made Sylvie feel somehow bereft. 'Where you got the idea that marriage was supposed to be romantic is beyond me,' Mildred said. 'You certainly didn't get it in my house.' Sylvie knew her mother was trying to cheer her up, but jokes were no comfort — if Mildred *was* joking.

Mildred turned Sylvie around to look at her. 'Listen to me: you want excitement? You want affection and devotion and some nights out in the spotlight?'

Sylvie nodded her head.

Mildred brushed her hand tenderly across her daughter's cheek. 'Then take my advice: raise show dogs.'

4

Sylvie sliced the rescued head of iceberg lettuce into four quarters and then took two of them and halved them again. She wondered if being submerged in the pool had poisoned the stuff. She'd removed the outer leaves and then washed the lettuce for almost ten minutes. Was it enough? Sylvie shrugged. What the hell. If chlorine in the pool didn't kill you when you got a mouthful of pool water, she supposed it wouldn't kill her husband when it was spread on a vegetable.

Bob had come home while she was showering. She'd come downstairs, neatly dressed and her hair freshly blown dry, but he had been on the phone in the dining room. For that she was grateful, because it gave her a few moments to prepare for her confession. When moment stretched into a tense half an hour, she went into the hallway looking for him, only to hear the shower running upstairs. She shrugged and began preparing dinner, mentally rehearsing what she could possibly say.

She looked at the lettuce. She didn't care for it, not really, but no matter how hard she tried, Bob had never graduated from iceberg to mesclun greens or even Bibb. Sylvie reached for the balsamic vinegar in the cupboard on the right. She was almost out and took a moment to jot that down on her grocery list. Then she glanced out the window at the pool. Because the kitchen was slightly above ground level she could just look into it and see the BMW's right fender and part of the trunk. God! She was nuts. Well, she'd done what she'd done. Bob would probably kill her, and she probably deserved it. She was a whining, spoiled, ungrateful woman. He, on the other hand, was an excessively clean man. At last she heard Bob coming down the stairs and, on an impulse, she flipped on the pool light. He entered the kitchen, sat down at his place at the table, and picked up the glass of white wine she had already poured him.

It was funny, Sylvie thought, how she could do some things automatically. How, despite this sense of everything being askew, she could manage to pull the salmon steaks out of the broiler and nestle them on the plates next to the broccoli. She looked at Bob, sitting there clean and damp, sipping his wine and going through the mail, seemingly calm and content. Her heart swelled. He was still so handsome. What was her problem? Maybe he didn't notice her, maybe he did take her for granted, but he was a good husband, a great father, a good provider. He loved her. She glanced out the window again at the illuminated pool. She restrained a shudder and put the dinner plate in front of her husband, sitting down opposite him.

'Mom wants to know if you'd like to come to a birthday dinner at their house.'

Bob had picked up his fork and speared a piece of the salmon. He looked across the table at her. 'Whatever you want,' he said, his mouth full of fish. He went back to the mail.

Sylvie stared at the top of her husband's bent head. You could live with someone for two decades, sleep with them, do their laundry, bear their children, and then look up one moment and see them not as a perfect stranger but as a very, very imperfect one. For a moment Sylvie stopped regretting that she had driven the car underwater and wished instead she had driven it over her husband. Out of nowhere that same feeling of rage hit her again. Why?

Well, she thought, for one thing, her birthdays had always been special. They were a day to rejoice. For Bob's birthday she always made his favorite dinner: pot roast, potatoes, and red cabbage, even though the stink of the cabbage always made her queasy and hung in the air for days after. He liked angel food cake and she'd never failed to make one for him. She always had at least one funny gift, and one he really wanted. For the twins' birthdays, every year, she'd made *their* favorite foods – and because Kenny loved fish sticks and Reenie liked glazed ham she had to serve two dinners. She'd never failed to bake her special angel food cake. She'd worried over gifts. She'd written (and saved) birthday poems every year, taken pictures of each event and put them in the special birthday album she had. Photos of all of them, on each birthday for nineteen years. Why was it only now she realized she wasn't in the book on her birthdays?

But, she reminded herself, men knew nothing about celebrations and gifts, though she'd tried to teach Bob. On the first birthday she had spent with him, when they'd been married less than five months, he'd given her a toaster oven. Sylvie had opened the package, laughed, and then waited for her real gift. The oven, though, had been her real gift. She hadn't spoken to him for almost two days and then, in an explosion of tears and anger, had had to explain that she wanted something *personal*, something romantic and meaningful, as a gift between them. He'd never made an error as egregious as the toaster oven again, but he'd still never quite gotten it about gifts and birthdays. Sylvie didn't like to feel selfish or ungrateful, but she had to believe that twenty years of training could yield something more insightful, more meaningful, more imaginative than a car she didn't want and a shrug of his shoulders for her fortieth birthday.

But maybe she was wrong. Maybe all he was trying to do was make her happy and doing it in the best way he knew how. The convertible – nothing she cared about and nothing she needed or wanted – might, to Bob, be the equivalent of an emerald ring with a loving engraving within. Might. Just possibly.

Sylvie looked across the table. 'Bob, I did something terrible today.'

He didn't put down the Ace Hardware flyer he was reading. 'Terrible? You never do anything even remotely bad. What did you do, play "Für Elise' in quarter time? Come on, kid, tell me about it.' He put down the flyer and glanced at her. 'But I'm running late again so tell me in four words or less.'

Sylvie looked out the window again. She couldn't help but stare at the car in the pool. It was an eye magnet, glowing like a grape submerged in aqua Jell-O. God, I must be insane, Sylvie thought. Maybe I'm more upset about my birthday than I think. She vamped for time. 'I hate it when you give that four-word order,' Sylvie told Bob and then took a deep breath. 'Let me ask you this: how long does it take a submerged BMW to rust?'

'Huh?' Bob, his mouth now full of broccoli, stopped chewing for a moment and furrowed his brow.

She had his attention. 'Okay,' she said. 'In four words or less: drove car into pool.'

Bob managed – just barely – to swallow the broccoli. Sylvie wondered idly whether she still remembered CPR, just in case the vegetable got caught in his throat. 'What? . . . why the hell? . . . are you kidding . . . ?' he choked out.

Now he *was* listening to her. Not about Hawaii or her

birthday, but about the car. Now, however, *she* didn't want to talk. Did he still want it in four words? Sylvie counted on her fingers. 'Felt bad. Turned right.'

Bob put down the fork and stood up slowly. Sylvie realized that this was the first time she'd seen him move slowly in months. Lately he was always in a rush, always on the go. 'Your car? Our pool?' he asked. It seemed that he could talk in four words now too. Silently, Sylvie nodded. She watched him move slowly, like a sleepwalker, to the kitchen window and look out. It was getting dark earlier and twilight had fallen. The blue corner of the pool and the glinting car within it glowed. Bob stood absolutely still at the window, his back to Sylvie, his hands spread wide and as flat as two flounders against the countertop. It was very quiet in the kitchen. Sylvie could hear the ice maker growl on. Bob continued to stand there, his back to her. 'Why in the world would you do a thing like that?' he asked, his voice full of wonder. 'That's nuts.'

Sylvie hung her head. All at once her anger deserted her and she felt like a preschooler, as wrong and needy as Kenny had ever been on his worst day. 'Maybe I just wanted us to have something to talk about,' she managed to whisper.

Bob turned away from the window, but only for a minute. He swiveled his head back as if he were unable to tear his eyes away from the unnatural panorama. 'We have plenty to talk about: Kenny, Reenie . . .' he paused, obviously stuck, '. . . Hawaiian brochures,' he added lamely.

Sylvie lifted her head. Bob was obviously mesmerized; she could see the willpower it took him to force his eyes from the window. His voice was hoarse, either with broccoli or emotion. 'A BMW underwater. It's so . . . so wrong,' he said. In the light of the kitchen, she could see that his face was registering shock. 'I can't even imagine how I would feel if that was Beautiful Baby.'

'I'm not as close to my car as you are.'

He didn't even notice her sarcasm. 'But why, Sylvie? Why? I know you're . . . spontaneous. You know . . . Lucy Ricardoesque. Maybe sometimes a little . . . well, flaky. But this is not the kind of thing that happens to us.'

Sylvie looked up at him with tears in her eyes. 'Bob, I don't feel like there is an "us."'

'Don't be silly. We're married. That's as "us" as you can get.' Bob crossed the floor, leaving the window and its shocking view. He gave Sylvie another quick bear hug. Then, taking her hand, he led her out the back door, into the soft darkness of the yard. How long had it been since they had held hands? she wondered. She couldn't remember the last time. He led her across the patio and onto the lawn.

The sky hadn't turned inky yet, but the hedges and shrubs had. The back garden was now fifty shades of indigo. When she and Bob had bought this property, the yard had been a huge forlorn lot with nothing but a scrawny Norfolk pine and an ugly border of chrysanthemums. Since then they had done so much together. In the last fifteen years the bushes and evergreens that she and Bob had planted had grown into an encircling shelter. And her flowers had thrived. Sylvie looked up.

There was only one star overhead. That dot of light and the lunar glow of the white impatiens in the border were the only touches of light in the darkness – except, of course, for the Technicolor glow in the center of the yard. The turquoise and silver of the pool and the car drew them to it.

Bob stood beside her at the edge of the pool, looking down at the sunken convertible. To Sylvie its sleek, metallic-gray chassis looked like the corpse of a shark. 'You did't lose control of the steering?' he asked. 'Nothing went haywire?'

'No,' she told him. Nothing but me, she thought.

'But how could you have an accident like this?'

'Bob, it *wasn't* an accident . . .' She was about to launch into the stuff about her feelings, about gifts, about attention, when he spoke again.

'I understand,' he said.

'You do?' She could hardly believe it. Somehow her gesture, extreme as it was, had gotten through to him. 'You really do?' she asked.

'Sure.'

Sylvie felt a flood of relief wash over her. Then Bob spoke again.

'You know, Sylvie, this has been a time with a lot of adjustments for you. Your birthday. Both of the kids gone. I mean, maybe it's time to think about some medical help.'

'Medical help?' she echoed. 'What do you mean? Psychiatrists?'

'No, no. I mean, not yet. Not unless you feel you need one. I just think maybe you're a little moody, a little down. Maybe it's time for that hormone replacement therapy. Maybe you should see John. Have a checkup.'

'Have you been watching the Lifetime channel secretly again?' Sylvie snapped. 'Bob, this isn't about my estrogen levels. It's about our communication. Or lack of it.'

Bob was staring again at the pool bottom. 'Jesus! Did Rosalie see this? Does your dad know? Well, all of Shaker Heights will be talking about this over granola and prune juice tomorrow morning.'

'Who cares?' Sylvie demanded. 'I only care about what *we* talk about. Or don't. We don't talk.'

Bob turned to her and took her shoulders in his hands. They were warm against the cool autumn air and she shivered. 'Look. I'll talk to you about whatever you want to talk about,' Bob said, his voice as soft as the night. Sylvie took a deep breath, but before she could begin Bob continued, 'I just can't do it now. I have to get to this meeting. Tomorrow night though, over dinner, we'll talk about whatever you want. I promise. It's your birthday. It's your night.' He took her elbow and moved her away from the pool edge. 'I'll take care of the car. Don't worry about a thing. Then the weekend is coming up. We'll talk some more. But, Sylvie,' he paused. 'You make an appointment with the doctor. It can't hurt.' He had propelled her across the slate and was opening the screen door. He helped her up the steps as if she were an invalid but then closed the door from the outside. 'I've got to go,' he said. 'But don't worry. We'll talk.'

Sylvie pressed her hand against the screen that was shutting her in as she'd shut Rosalie out. She began to tell him . . . well . . . to tell him *something*, but Bob had already swung around into the darkness and was gone. There was something, or a lot of things, out there more important to him than she was. She'd never talk to him again. She promised herself that. Then, in the harsh light of the kitchen, Sylvie dropped her hand, turned away from the door, and began clearing her untouched dinner from the table.

5

Bob Schiffer drove his car down Longworth Avenue and pulled into
the Crandall BMW lot. The sun glinted off the cars. It was a
perfect day, but Bob felt uneasy. Well, worse. How long could
he get away with this? Sylvie was upset and his girlfriend, well,
she was pressuring him. Roger, from maintenance, waved as
Bob pulled past him into the special parking space he had
reserved for his car. She purred to a stop and he switched off
the ignition and patted the dash. 'You're beautiful, Baby,' he
said to the car, which was how Sylvie had given it the name.
He got out of the car and carefully closed the door. If he
left her in the sun for any length of time he covered her,
but he'd had a roof built over this spot so that her perfect
paint wouldn't fade.

The Crandall BMW car lot was on the edge of Shaker
Heights. Jim Crandall, Sylvie's father, had started the business
almost thirty years ago when Beemers ran unbelievably behind
Mercedeses in status and sales. He'd struggled for years, first
against Detroit and then against Japanese imports. Finally,
when he'd welcomed his son and son-in-law into the business,
his days of glory had commenced. Now the lot spread over
an entire block on Longworth Avenue and Jim was as proud
of the neat landscaping, lush grass, and pristine building as
he was of the healthy bottom line. Bob knew that Jim found
his own son, Phil, a disappointment. He also knew that Jim
thought of him as a son rather than a son-in-law. And Bob,

whose own father had died when he was twelve, looked on Jim as a father. And, why not? After all, he spent more time with Jim than Sylvie did. The old man could certainly be a pain in the ass at times, though.

Now Jim was crossing the lot, his white hair glaring in the autumn sunlight. So was he, and talking before he was close enough for Bob to hear. 'Let me get this straight,' he was saying. 'She drove the car right into the pool?' Jim asked. He'd asked the question several times already last night and this morning over the phone.

Bob nodded. 'Into the pool, Jim.'

'Wasn't she looking where she was going? And why was she driving in the backyard?'

'That, indeed, is a legitimate question. But what is the answer?'

'Insanity,' Jim barked. 'Not that your mother-in-law can drive. She's had more fender benders than a demolition derby. Well, Sylvie didn't get it from my side of the family. Crandalls can all drive.' Bob forbore to mention the several accidents Jim had been in. 'You making the arrangements?'

'Yeah. I'm on it. So I guess we're canceling the commercial shoot?'

'No. In fact, I got an idea. Let's use the car in the pool as part of the commercial.'

Bob looked at his father-in-law. 'Is a wet Beemer an inducement to purchase?' he asked. 'I mean, it's not like the old Volkswagen beetle. Believe me, Jim, this car is not floating.'

'Hey. We don't shoot it *in* the water. We shoot it in the air. When they're lifting it out. Hell, even Phil can think of the patter. Christ knows he's good with bullshit.' Jim turned around and started back toward the office. 'Me, I'm playing golf this afternoon. You can get me at the club if you need to.'

Jim was in what he called 'semiretirement,' but one of the problems was you never knew at which moment he was in 'semi' and which moment he was in 'retirement.' Bob shrugged. This morning appeared to be the former and would therefore be a killer. They were in the process of doing inventory, preparing for the special promotion, shooting a commercial, and now, as if that weren't enough, he had to keep an eye out for Jim *and* take care of Sylvie's little . . . mishap. He shrugged and pulled his phone out of his sports coat pocket. He punched in a number. It was busy. He hated that. It was almost the millennium. Hasn't everyone heard of call waiting? Bob sighed and began to dial another number. He was a man with a lot on his mind.

'A crane. That's right, a crane . . . because it's in the pool, that's why . . . Please don't make me say it again.' Bob had finally gotten through to the wrecking company. He was at the farthest end of the lot, overseeing Sam Granger and Phil, who were going through the inventory. It had been a busy morning, except in terms of sales. Now a woman, middle-aged but attractive, was idly wandering among the gleaming cars, a row behind Bob. Normally he would approach her, but she had the look of a browser, not a buyer. Despite the risk, Bob motioned to Phil. 'Why don't you handle her?' he asked. Phil nodded and moved toward the woman. Since Phil had been put in charge of service he relished selling opportunities. Bob just hoped Phil didn't take his suggestion literally.

Since his divorce, Phil blamed everything that was wrong in the world on women. The fact that he'd caused the end of his marriage by continuously cheating on his wife never entered his mind. Lately he was also slightly delusional, assuming every female was interested in him in a carnal way. Bob looked at his brother-in-law. He was still sort of good-looking, despite his receding hairline, his paunch, and his questionable taste in clothes. Yet he saw himself as Ohio's answer to Brad Pitt. This was a guy who would order a hamburger at lunch and, when the waitress asked how he wanted it, would leer and insist her question was a double entendre. 'How do I want it?' he'd repeat, nudging Bob, who'd squirm with embarrassment while the bored waitress stared out over the parking lot. Invariably, after the girl left, Phil would begin his excited whisper. '*You* heard her. It's not like I started it. *How do I want it*? Why doesn't she just give me the key to her place? I tell you, they can't leave me alone.'

The woman was looking at the sticker price of a sedan. She was squinting in the sun. Phil looked over at her. 'Did you see that?' he asked Bob.

'What?'

'The way she stared at me, checking out my package,' Phil cried hoarsely. Sam Granger snorted. Bob rolled his eyes. Phil was a danger to himself and others. Rosalie the Horrific might have been a witch, but she'd certainly had her hands full with Phil.

'Phil, behave,' Bob warned. 'Take it easy or I'll tell your father on you.'

'Hey! She better take it easy. The laws against sexual harassment cut both ways, ya know.'

'Control yourself, Phil. Try to sell a car.' Bob's cellular rang and he pulled it out. He moved away from Sam Granger and put the phone to his ear. 'Hello. Bob Schiffer. Oh,' he said. He lowered his voice. 'Hi, Cookie Face. I can't talk now. No. Really. I can't.' Bob looked around. Phil was leaning up against the sedan, talking to the poor female prospect while Sam had disappeared into the front seat of a model a row away. 'Come on, honey. You know this isn't a good place for me to talk,' Bob murmured into the phone. He laughed out loud. 'Sing? If I can't talk, how can I *sing*?' She always made him laugh, but after four months he still wasn't sure if it was intentional or accidental. That was part of her charm. Now he listened to her request. 'But *you* called *me*. The song makes no sense if I sing. No. Of course I do. All right, but then I have to go.' Bob began to hum into the phone, then tried for a Stevie Wonder voice. 'I just called to say I love you . . . I just called to—'

When he was tapped on the shoulder, Bob must have jumped eight inches straight off the ground. John Spencer, Bob and Sylvie's best friend, was standing behind him. 'Gotta go . . .' Bob hissed into the phone. 'No. Not now. And be sure to get the crane there by one o'clock,' he added in his normal authoritative tone, then flipped the phone closed and slipped it into his pocket. He turned to John as casually as he could and gave him a big bear hug. 'Hey. How ya doing?'

John wasn't buying it. 'Why, you sneaky, slimy bastard. Bob the Saint . . .'

Bob opened his eyes wide and tried to make a blank face. He wasn't sure it was working and when John raised his brows upward Bob felt his stomach tug downward. 'What? It was Sylvie,' he protested.

John shook his head. 'Maybe I'm just a general practitioner, but I'm not stupid. You, Bob? Come on. You're no player. What the hell is going on?'

'Nothing,' Bob said and sounded to himself like one of the twins when they were eight years old. He looked at John's doubting face. 'Okay,' he admitted. 'Something. But nothing

45

important.' He bit his lip. 'I don't want to hurt Sylvie. You don't either, do you?'

John looked him in the eyes. 'I won't tell, if that's what you're asking, but I won't lie. She's my friend too. She was my girlfriend before she even met you.'

'I know. I know. You remind me of that all the time. But this is . . . just a temporary thing.'

'So? Temporary but indefensible.'

Bob, trapped, knew he had no defense. 'Well, Phil did it,' he said, sounding like one of the twins when they were ten.

'Great response,' John snorted. 'Let's not forget that Phil is a delusional penis with a man attached. And he wasn't married to a Sylvie.'

Bob looked away, ashamed. John's wife, Nora, had died almost three years ago, and if their marriage hadn't been perfect then, it was now, enshrined in John's memory. Since then John had thrown himself into his practice and into his avocation – Little League coach and professional widower – but in Bob's opinion, he took a certain amount of pleasure in wallowing in his bereavement. Plus, there were always so many Shaker Heights women dropping off casseroles and inviting him to be the extra man at their dinner parties that his life wasn't anything close to the living hell he depicted it as.

But mine could be, Bob thought. It could if I lost Sylvie. And he had been meaning to end it with the girl. He just didn't know how. He had never had an affair before. Best to come clean. 'You're right. You caught me,' he admitted. 'I don't know what I'm doing. One day I'm a nice guy, the next I'm a Kennedy husband.' He paused. John looked skeptical, as if he doubted Bob's sincerity. 'Wait. I'm worse. I'm dead dog meat.' John raised his brows. 'No,' he corrected himself. 'I'm dead dog meat with maggots.' John nodded. 'Can we talk about this while you drive me to my house?' Bob asked. 'I don't deserve to sit behind the wheel of Beautiful Baby.'

'Vehicular morality wasn't the first concern I had.'

'Please. Will you drive me?'

'No problem. I can't get enough of that dead dog meat smell in *my* car.'

They got into John's three-year-old sedan, which Bob had sold him after using it as a showroom model. He'd given John a real deal on it. They drove off the lot. It was time for Bob to recoup a little. After all, John was only a doctor, not a judge.

'Don't tell me you never did it. With all those women patients! With all those females who worship you. Swear on Nora's memory that you didn't.'

'Not with a patient. Never.' John maneuvered the car into the passing lane.

'Ah. With someone impatient! Come on. Come clean. You were human too!'

John hesitated. 'Only once,' he admitted.

'I knew it! See. No one is perfect.'

'Okay. Okay. But I was loaded. No excuse. I was on a business trip and it was with a pharmacologist, not with a patient. I regretted it immediately.'

'Afterward, that's easy. I always regret it afterward too.'

'Yeah, but it was a decade ago. To this day I regret it. Nora's dead almost four years and I still feel really bad about it.' Bob patted John on the shoulder. John came out of his reverie. 'Just look at your brother-in-law.'

'God. Do I have to?'

'I mean, look how he ruined his life. His ex-wife hates

47

him, his children are turned against him. And he can't afford a meat loaf sandwich.'

'But he had an excuse: he was married to Rosalie.'

'What does that mean?'

Bob gave John a look. 'Rosalie pushed him into infidelity. Me, I just slipped. I never meant for this to happen,' Bob admitted. 'This girl was just there, all pink and naked.'

'She was pink and naked right when you met her?'

'Well, no. But, I could tell she wanted to be . . . Hey. Come on. You think I *want* to lie to my wife?'

John's voice finally became sympathetic. 'No, buddy, I don't.'

'In its way, my position is its own kind of hell,' Bob said mournfully.

John nodded. 'I've been there.' Then, for a moment, John became distracted by a racing green 530i that passed them on the right. 'Nice model,' he commented.

'Forget it,' Bob told him dismissively. 'It's not for you. A vinyl interior. If you're going to trade up, trade up for the best.' John nodded his agreement. He pulled back into the right lane. There was a truck ahead of them. John should have passed it too. Bob hated sitting in the passenger's seat.

'You know, Sylvie is too good to risk losing.'

'I know.' Bob sighed gustily. 'Let's face it. Men are pigs.'

'The worst form of human life,' John agreed.

'Slime . . .' Bob figured he'd change the subject while he could. 'So, you seeing anyone?'

John shook his head. 'You know I haven't been able to see anyone since Nora passed away . . . Maybe it's the guilt over that . . . episode.' He reflected for a minute, his eyes on the road. 'This month we would be celebrating our twentieth anniversary. I ignored her more than I should have when we were married. During med school, and my internship, and then building my practice. Jesus. Men *are* stupid.'

'Yeah,' Bob agreed. 'But women are crazy.' John stopped for an amber light that Bob would have slid through. God, he was a cautious driver. Cautious about everything, in fact. Bob looked over at his pal, who now seemed very depressed. 'You know, I didn't realize your anniversary . . . well . . . that has to be hard for you.'

John nodded. 'It's not easy. A guilty conscience is never easy to live with.' He gave Bob a look. 'Know what I mean?'

The light changed. John just sat there staring ahead at nothing, or something only he saw, some flashback from an earlier time. Bob pointed to the green light and John blinked, then accelerated. 'Look, I know I *should* stop,' Bob admitted. 'And I'm going to. As soon as I find an opening.'

'Those openings are tricky,' John said dryly.

Bob gave his friend a boyish punch on the shoulder. 'Hey, enough. I take your point. Today my job is to make *you* feel better. It's time for a change. You're going to trade your car in for a newer, shinier model. It's exactly what a man needs when he's contemplating his own mortality. And I'm going to give you an unbelievable deal. As a tribute to Nora.' He paused. 'But I do need a little favor.'

John shrugged. 'It's yours.'

'Can you make an appointment to see Sylvie? Casually, but as a professional. Talk to her?'

'To what end?'

'Put her on hormones or something? She's just not herself. Frankly, I'm worried.'

'What? Hormones? Why? Anyway, I'm not a gynecologist.

49

And they'd want to run blood work first. You know, I don't hand out powerful drugs as if they were candy corn.'

'Look, I didn't mean to insult you . . .'

'Anyway, what's wrong with Sylvie? *You're* the one who's sick. Sylvie is fine. We both know that.'

'Fine? Would you say that if you knew she drove her new car into our pool yesterday?' Bob's cell phone rang. He pulled it out and flipped it open while John, openmouthed, stared at him. Bob wished he'd keep his eyes on the road.

'Yes?' Bob snapped into the phone. 'Uh-huh. Right. The crane goes to my house. Yes. Through the yard, into the back. How else could it get over to my pool?' He sighed deeply. 'Please don't make me explain it again.' When Bob hung up, he looked over at John to see him shaking his head.

'She drove the car into the pool?' John asked. They were both silent for a moment as John drove – too slowly – through Highland Heights. 'And you think this affair isn't affecting Sylvie?'

'Sylvie doesn't know anything about it,' Bob said vehemently.

'Come on, Bob. Even if she hasn't heard about it – yet – Shaker Heights is a small town. Anyway, haven't you ever heard of the subconscious? Sylvie must know something is wrong. Not to mention the girl. She may have called Sylvie, for all you know.'

Bob's stomach clenched and a nasty taste of bile rose to his throat. 'I told her not to even talk about Sylvie, much less talk *to* her.'

'Well, I hope she's good at obedience,' John said. 'Aside from all this, if the Masons find out, you'd get drummed out, or whatever they do to a shamed Mason.'

'Who cares? The Mason story is just a cover-up to give

me an excuse to go out at night. God, I'm an asshole. No, I'm the world's *biggest* asshole.' Bob stared out the window. 'Think of the biggest asshole in the world. Now raise it to the power of ten. That's me. I am a thousand assholes.'

'Don't be so grandiose,' John told him. 'You're just a common garden-variety adulterer. I see them every day. Your dick is running the company right now. I might as well be talking to it.'

Bob nodded morosely. 'You're right.' He looked down at his crotch. 'He's the C.O.O.' He sighed. 'You know what I wish? I wish I could get him off the board of directors. Or just cut it off. Or better, I wish it would just fall off. It's ruining my life.'

John snorted. 'Bob, eunuchs are not happy guys.' He swerved around the corner and Bob instinctively pressed his foot down where the brake pedal should be on the passenger's floor.

'I'd like to see the research on that,' Bob said as John turned the car into the driveway.

As John and Bob pulled up to the house, the whole cul-de-sac looked more like a derailed circus train than a suburban street. 'Looks like my brother-in-law is in charge,' Bob said. Phil, gesturing madly, looked as if he were either teaching parallel parking or directing the crane.

'Well, good luck with him. And, Bob . . . think about what I said. Your life is becoming unmanageable.'

'No it isn't. But as God is my witness, I'm ending the . . . you know,' Bob promised John. 'Sylvie deserves better. The poor girl deserves better.' He looked at his pal. 'Do you think I'll ever forgive myself?'

'Somehow, Bob, I think you'll manage,' John said and laughed. 'Kiss Sylvie for me. If you don't, maybe I will.'

Bob got out of the car. Vans, a couple of trucks, and the crane were scattered over the sidewalk and lawn. People milled around. Confusion reigned. Bob headed for the backyard, stopping to bear-hug everyone in his path. Phil was by the pool already, yelling, looking up at the convertible, which was being lifted by the crane. Bob stared up at the suspended car doubtfully. Perhaps his life *was* unmanageable.

6

Today would be a full day for Sylvie. Not only did she have back-to-back students, but then she also had to try and get Bob to talk with her about why she decided to transmute her car into an amphibian. Blessedly, that wouldn't come until tonight. Now she just had to try to concentrate on Lou, her oldest student. He was sitting at the piano blundering through 'You Don't Bring Me Flowers Anymore' as if this were his fifth lesson. Actually, it was closer to his fifty-fifth. Lou had been taking lessons twice a week for months now – not that he got any better or more enthusiastic. Lessons were by doctor's orders. John Spencer had sent Lou over to Sylvie, so she couldn't say no. Since Lou had retired, he was having a hard time. For Sylvie, listening to him play wasn't easy either, but she always tried to encourage him. Now Lou missed two notes, stumbled on the sharp, and paused to look up at her. 'I can't do it,' Lou stated and dropped his hands into his lap, utterly defeated.

'Yes, you can,' Sylvie reassured him, and approached the piano.

'No. I can't do it. And this is my last shot at life.'

'You remembered to take your medication today, right, Lou?' Sylvie asked.

'Yes. And if I'm this depressed on antidepressants, what's the use?' Lou said, shrugging.

Sylvie caught a glimpse of something or someone flash by

the French doors. Oh, please, not Rosalie, she thought. Sylvie put a hand on Lou's shoulder to try to comfort him. Then she saw something else flash by. This time, Sylvie looked up in time. There, strategically positioned in her backyard, was a crew of construction workers trying to direct a large piece of equipment around the hedges. What? Turning her attention back to Lou, she forced herself to encourage him. 'C'mon, Lou. Look, all men have trouble with transitions: from single to married, from couplehood to family. It's tough to have your kids leave home. It's tough to go into retirement. But change is a joyous part of life.'

'Yeah? So how come there are no joyous songs about menopause? You wait. You'll play a different tune then.' Lou sighed, then started to move his fingers over the keys as if to play. Sylvie was sure that he was going to do a bit better when, instead, he fisted his hands and began to pound the piano keys.

Gently but firmly, Sylvie lifted his hands off her precious Steinway and closed the lid. 'Lou, have you thought of taking a trip?' Sylvie asked, rubbing his shoulder.

'I'm too old,' Lou said. 'And besides, who wants to die on a strange mattress?' He sat, immobile. Sylvie moved back to the window. Without even trying to talk him out of his stupor, she watched the activity brewing in her backyard. After a time Lou opened the piano, began to play, and caught the melody of the song for a moment. Sylvie thought of Bob. He didn't send her flowers anymore either, she thought, and leaned up against the door frame.

The classical piece, a Schubert sonata, was being played far too quickly. Sylvie winced, but continued looking through the French doors. Now there was a crane poolside, along with a milling crowd of cameramen setting up for some kind of shoot. Would her drowned car make the local news? Sylvie turned away and looked back at her twelve-year-old music pupil, who was playing frantically. Too much Ritalin.

'Slow down. It isn't a race, Jennifer.' Jennifer looked up. You could see that though she tried to hide it, she was totally crushed by even this slight criticism. Jennifer already excelled at gymnastics and tennis, and was the leader of the girls' swim team. No wonder she rushed. She had a lot to do, and she tried to do it all perfectly.

Sylvie focused on the girl, leaving the growing pageant at the window and putting her hand on the girl's shoulder, trying to gently explain. 'Play it as if you were falling in love for the first time,' Sylvie suggested and sat down at the piano. She played the Schubert dreamily, and the yearning and romance of the piece came through. Sylvie herself fell under the sonata's spell. '*Feel* it, Jennifer.'

'I don't know what that love stuff feels like.' Jennifer sat, as solid as a packed laundry sack.

'You will,' Sylvie told her reassuringly. Looking at Jennifer's doubting face, she continued: 'Love heightens the senses and makes you do things that are *so* surprising,' she lowered her voice, 'and feel so-o-o good. You'll be amazed. But you have to go slow then too.' Then, as if she were waking up from a dream, Sylvie realized how inappropriate she was being. To cover her slip she smiled brightly, a teacher-to-pupil face. 'Don't worry, Jennifer, you'll feel it after your first kiss.' Sylvie got up from the piano and went to look out the window again at the activity around the pool. 'Try it again,' she encouraged.

'I've already been kissed, like, three times,' Jennifer told her, still defensive. Then she began playing the piece again, almost as maniacally as before.

Sylvie turned back to her. 'Maybe you just need a better kisser,' she suggested. Jennifer giggled, perked up, and actually slowed down. Good. Poor kid. Sylvie wanted her students to enjoy their lessons, and Jennifer had talent. She just needed the capacity to enjoy it. The girl finished the piece and Sylvie made it a point to praise her. Meanwhile, when she glanced back, her backyard had become even more of a circus.

'Come over here and take a look,' Sylvie told the girl. Jennifer and Sylvie both peered out the window. The crane, tearing the hell out of the lawn, was poolside. Men with hard hats were gesturing, one of them obscenely. 'How did your car get in there?' Jennifer asked, sounding awed.

'I don't know. Maybe it wanted one more swim before winter.'

Jennifer giggled, until her mother, Mrs Miller, appeared on the walk outside the French doors and stepped in to join them. She was the kind of suburban matron who not only had to have her children do everything, but always had to know everything herself. 'Sorry I'm a little late,' she apologized, but it didn't sound like she was sorry. 'There's a lot of confusion in your driveway. How did the lesson go?' she asked brightly.

Jennifer tore her eyes off the crane and looked up at her mother. 'She told me I had to get kissed better. Like, maybe with tongues.'

Mrs Miller opened her eyes wide and turned to Sylvie. Great, Sylvie thought. She shook her head. 'No, Jennifer, I did not say that. I didn't give specifics,' Sylvie reassured Mrs Miller. 'We were talking about tempo, actually.' She raised her brows and lowered her voice. 'I'd also suggest you monitor her television.' Jennifer's mother, pacified, took her daughter by the arm and left.

Sylvie walked out into her yard. People were all over. Phil was yelling at a guy with a video camera. She felt as if it were some kind of foreign film and she was in it. 'What *is* all this?' she asked her brother.

'We're shooting today's commercial here.'

'Here? In my *yard?*'

'Yeah. I rerouted the crew. We'd been scheduled to shoot one on the lot, but this is better. Now we're just waiting for Bob to get ready.' Phil laughed and looked over toward the garage, where Sylvie was surprised to see her husband having his hair combed by a woman. 'He's becoming the Harrison Ford of car ads,' Phil smirked. He looked back at her. 'It's a hell of a thing to do to a Z2,' he told her. 'But Pop thinks it's a stroke of luck that you couldn't control yourself. Women drivers.' Phil shook his head again.

Then Bob approached. Sylvie just looked up at him and his professionally combed hair. He smiled back sheepishly. 'Hey, Bob, you—' Phil began but, klutzy as always, he tripped over a cable, then looked around to see who he could blame it on. Of course, Sylvie saw, he noticed the only woman on the crew, a pretty woman with freckles and auburn hair. 'Hey! Red! Is this the way you hope to get a good-looking guy?' he shouted. 'Try taking out a personal ad.' Sylvie cringed. Phil peered at Bob. 'Makeup! We need makeup.' The woman Phil had just dissed picked up her makeup box and moved toward them.

'Well, I'm sure she'll do a great job now,' Bob said to Phil, smiling again at Sylvie. She said nothing, just moved away as Bob was prepped and fussed over.

'Okay, okay, listen up. A star is born,' Phil yelled to the crew.

My brother is an ass, Sylvie thought. She watched as Phil hunkered down to talk to Bob. 'You know what we need here. The usual bullshit. Sincerity until it hurts.' Phil paused in his directorial overdrive. He'd obviously seen what Sylvie just had – Rosalie's face popping up over the fence. 'Get that head down out of the shot or we're going back to court!' he shouted.

Rosalie disappeared. Poor Rosalie. She'd always been loud and insensitive, but no woman deserved Phil. Sylvie looked back at Bob, who'd been powdered down and was now being led to his mark. Phil handed him the script. Bob was used to doing all this, but he looked nervous. Sylvie watched him. Somehow, he looked different. It wasn't just the makeup. She approached him.

'Sylvie, I know that you—' Bob began.

From behind, Phil interrupted. 'Got your lines down?' he asked.

Bob gestured toward the script. 'I don't think it's—'

Phil, the half-pint Quentin Tarantino, was in his glory. When they were shooting a commercial, he got himself confused with an *auteur*. 'Come on. No temperament,' he said to Bob. 'And people: let's get this the first time or die,' he called out. Sylvie saw one of the crew members roll his eyes. She blushed for her brother. Meanwhile, Bob turned to the camera.

Was this, then, all the attention she got after doing something as crazed, as outrageous, as dunking her car like a doughnut? Had Bob, before he'd even spoken to her, before he'd had a chance to . . . before *she'd* had a chance to – well, to talk – digested this bold act of hers? Had he processed it in his own way, turned it to his advantage and already moved on, leaving her frozen here, unable to move?

Somehow Bob had managed, literally overnight, to turn her discomfort, her confusion and pain, into an advantage, or at least an ad. No wonder he'd been president of the Rotary and head of the Chamber of Commerce!

Sylvie stood, frozen, while Phil the director signaled for Bob to start. But then Sylvie broke out of her trance and began walking toward her husband. Rosalie, along with another neighbor and a few kids, had come from her side of the fence and joined the crowd around the shot.

'Rolling,' the cameraman called out. 'Speed.'

Bob began to speak his lines. 'Why would I put a BMW in a pool? To prove to you—'

'Bob?'

'Great, Sylvie! You blew a take!' Phil cried. 'You know we're working here.'

'Bob?' Sylvie repeated, ignoring her brother. 'You didn't put the car in the pool.'

'No. I know that, Sylvie. I'm just reading the script.'

Phil got between the two of them and shook his head. 'Even my own sister acts like a woman.' Phil signaled to the crew to begin again. 'Sylvie, move out of the frame. Okay, people, let's take it from the top. Rosalie, move back. No one wants that face in their living rooms.'

Rosalie flipped Phil the bird and stalked away.

Sylvie, who felt like doing the same thing to her brother, ignored him instead and looked only at her husband. 'Bob, do you think I did this to improve car sales?'

'No.'

'Oh, come *on!*' Phil smacked his own thigh. If he'd been von Sternberg he'd have used a riding crop. 'Are we playing twenty questions, Sylvie?' Sylvie just stood there.

Despite his brother-in-law's impatience, Bob did, to his

credit, keep his eyes locked with hers. 'I thought you must have been upset about something,' he admitted.

'Have you thought about what, Bob?'

Phil smacked his own forehead, but not as hard as Sylvie wanted to. He pointed to his watch. 'This is not the time for a tender marital moment.'

Sylvie kept the laser look on her husband. 'What, Bob?' Sylvie repeated, ignoring not only Phil but all the now silent staff and neighbors crowding her yard.

Phil, a desperate look on his face, glanced at the watching crew. Then he grabbed his sister's hand. 'Hey, how about you be in the commercial with Bob?' he asked in the false, cheery voice of a desperate clown at a children's birthday party gone wrong. He regrouped and then continued in a tone that sounded apologetic. 'Women buy cars.'

'No . . . really. I don't want to—' Sylvie tried to pull free.

But Bob grabbed her other hand. 'Come on! Wasn't it you who wanted us to be spontaneous? Just kick off your shoes so they don't get wet,' he told her. 'We're only shooting from the knees up.' He pulled her into the shot, hugged her, and then grabbed the nape of her neck. Bob tried to point her at the camera.

Sylvie was about to pull away when she looked down and saw that Bob's own pant legs were rolled up, his socks and shoes off. She stared down at his bare feet. She couldn't believe it. She stiffened and once again she found it hard to catch her breath. Bob's hand on her shoulder became suddenly unbearable. 'Sorry. No. I can't,' she said, horrified, and pulled away.

'You *can't*? Come on, Sylvie. Since when do you have stage fright?' Phil asked. He grabbed her hand.

'No. It's not that. I forgot. I have to go.' Sylvie pulled away again.

'Where?' Bob wanted to know. As if he had any right.

'I just have to go. I need to . . .' Sylvie felt tears welling up in her eyes. She couldn't think, couldn't lie, couldn't stay. She couldn't bear for Bob to touch her, for them all to be looking at her. She felt exposed, humiliated. 'I have to . . . go get a pedicure or something,' she said and bolted.

7

Jim, Sylvie's father, was sitting in his wing chair, his feet on an ottoman, watching television. Mildred was deadheading her African violets. She noted that the pot on this one was cracked. She made a mental note to glaze another one at the pottery shop she owned. She looked over at her husband, seeing what the world saw. Jim was still good-looking, but he'd mellowed into a slightly overweight, grandfatherly type, the kind of man who could sell oatmeal on television. In fact, at the moment he had the television on, the remote in his hand. He was watching a PBS documentary on Dunkirk, or maybe it was Anzio – one that he'd probably seen a hundred times.

'Mildred. Look at this.'

'Please. Change the channel. You're making me nervous,' she told him. 'I hate it when you say, "Honey . . . the Nazis are on." As if I care.'

'I thought you wanted to see them lose again.'

'Jim, I'm not interested. Women don't want to watch World War II unless Gary Cooper is an officer in it. Why don't you give *me* the remote? There's an Angela Lansbury rerun on.'

He waved her away, then realized she was teasing. 'You know, we've been fighting about television since it was invented,' Jim commented.

Mildred laughed. Jim put his arm out but before he could hug her, gunfire broke out. He looked back at the screen and only patted Mildred's back. Mildred had hoped for more and, anyway, she didn't like to be patted. Never had. It felt . . . condescending. There, there, old girl. She turned to go back to her deadheading. Just then the doorbell chimed. Jim, of course, didn't move, so Mildred went to the door and opened it. Sylvie was standing there, disheveled, out of breath and clearly upset.

'My god! Sylvie! What's happened? Another car incident?'

Sylvie shook her head and tried to talk, but no words came out of her mouth. Looking in both directions, Mildred drew her into the foyer. No use sharing the latest bizarre family behavior with the entire neighborhood, not to mention Rosalie the Mouth. 'Take a deep breath. There. Now another,' Mildred directed. 'Okay. Talk.'

'Bob's having an affair,' Sylvie finally managed to gasp.

The two women stared at one another for a silent moment. Mildred then shook her head. 'Not Bob. I admit my son is crazy, but not my son-in-law. We took him into the business *and* the cul-de-sac . . .' She paused. 'How do you know?'

'He's never home. He forgave me about my car too easily. Did you see the crane he's got in the backyard? He and Phil are using it to shoot a commercial. Daddy told them to.'

'I'm not surprised,' Mildred murmured.

'Mom, don't you see? Next he'll even let me drive Beautiful Baby. Something is *definitely* wrong. And . . . people are saying they saw us out together. But it's always some place *I* haven't been to.'

Mildred, her heart beginning to flutter in her chest, forced herself to take on the practical aspect that Angela Lansbury used in *Murder, She Wrote*. 'That's nothing. Circumstantial,' she said dismissively. 'You still haven't given me anything definitive.'

Sylvie burst into tears. 'He's gotten a pedicure.'

'A pedicure! My god!' Mildred took her daughter into her arms. Sylvie wasn't just paranoid. 'Was it a professional pedicure?' Mildred asked, giving her son-in-law the benefit of the doubt.

Sylvie nodded and wiped her nose on her sleeve. 'He's been stabbing me with those pointy, deadly, fungoid toenails for twenty-one years. And now, just when he's ignoring me, they're short and shell pink.'

'He had a *professional* pedicure?' Mildred repeated, outraged. 'He was dying to get caught,' she muttered.

Sylvie began crying on Mildred's shoulder. 'I know he's sleeping with a younger woman.'

Mildred rocked Sylvie in her arms, but managed to shrug. 'Of course it's a younger woman! Do you think men cheat on their wives because they miss their grandmothers?' Mildred glanced toward her husband. Jim was still in the living room and the GIs were still eating lead on the beach. He was entranced. If a sociopath with a can of acid and a butcher knife had been at the door, Mildred would be blinded and gutted at this very moment while Jim waited for a commercial break to channel surf. Men! What were they good for? 'It's your daughter,' Mildred called out to him.

'Hi, honey. Want to watch the Nazis?' Jim called back, his eyes still glued to the screen.

'No, dear. We're going to have a little chat instead,' Mildred told him. She wasn't sure if he heard or not, but since he didn't move she figured he didn't need any further communiqués from the front. Mildred took her daughter's arm and led her upstairs.

'Where are we going?' Sylvie asked, still wiping at her eyes with her hands, just the way she'd done when she was small.

'To cry our eyes out for two hours. You're getting into bed and I'm bringing you a heating pad. Then we'll talk.' Mildred led her into the bedroom, made her sit on the bed, then knelt and took off Sylvie's shoes. 'Lie down,' she said, and Sylvie did. Mildred drew the chenille spread up over her and tucked it under her shoulders, just the way she liked it.

Sylvie awoke in her old canopy bed. Everything in the room was dated: teenager circa 1967. The house was a big one, and Mildred had left the children's rooms just as they had been. There was a shelf of Barbie dolls still on display and a blue Princess phone. The light was fading outside. Mildred was sitting in the dimness on the bed beside Sylvie, who sat up slowly and stretched. 'What time is it?' she asked.

'Time to stop dealing with suspicion and start looking for facts,' Mildred told her.

'Is the crane gone?'

'The crane, your car, your brother, and Bob. They're all wet and they're all gone,' Mildred said. 'The coast, as they say, is clear.'

Sylvie threw the blankets off and stood up.

'Where are you going?' Mildred asked.

'Next door. Back home. I have some research to do.'

Sylvie was sitting in the dimness of her dining room ensconced behind Bob's desk. In all their years of marriage, she'd never even glanced at open mail on it. Now every pigeonhole and drawer was emptied. She'd even lifted up the blotter, to look under it. She had bits of papers, cards, and receipts spread out around her on the desk top and the dining room table. It had grown dark outside but Sylvie hadn't bothered to turn on the lamp. She didn't need to survey any more of this. What she had in front of her was not just a paper trail of betrayal but a sort of First-Time-Do-It-Yourself-Adultery-Kit. Her hands were shaking, but she hoped she had the strength to shoot Bob when he came in the door – if only she had a bullet. Or a gun to shoot it with.

She wouldn't aim for the heart or the head – she was enraged but not deranged. She didn't want to go to prison. She would only shoot him in the legs, both of them. Then he'd hurt a little bit, but not the way she did. After he bled and cried for a while, he could drag himself behind her to his damn car and she'd drive it while he bled all over the upholstery. They could go to John, who would discreetly take out the bullets. After that, she'd leave Bob. Maybe she'd start her life over in Vermont with Reenie or alone in New Mexico. She had always wanted to see the desert. A nice adobe house, tumbleweed, and a dog. No, two dogs. Golden retrievers, and both of them female. She'd do a Georgia O'Keeffe thing and maybe, when she was ninety, some young man would come to her, too, and she'd be ready to try again. But not before.

Sylvie got up and went through the darkened hall to her music room – the only place where she could find comfort. In the darkness she sat down at her piano and began to play. The liquid glissando of Mozart's Piano Concerto No. 17 filled the room. She'd played this piece at Juilliard, for a recital. Bob had been there. She remembered his face as he'd congratulated her afterward. They'd made love for the first time that night. He'd adored her then. She'd played well, but now – alone in the darkness – she knew she played better. Her fingers fumbled a few times, but her feeling, her timing, and the heart of the music was better, truer.

When she heard the door open she started, dropping her hands. The shock of hearing the music ending abruptly gave her the energy to turn around to face her husband. She felt her heart thump painfully against her breastbone. But it was only Mildred, standing there in the music room doorway, carrying a sandwich on a plate.

'You haven't eaten anything,' Mildred said. 'You have to keep up your strength.' Sylvie turned on the lamp, wordlessly stood up, took her mother by the hand, and led her down the hallway. At the dining room door Mildred surveyed the room, took in an audible breath, and put the sandwich down on the other end of the cluttered dining room table.

'You want proof?' Sylvie asked. 'I have it. In spades.'

'So you don't want the sandwich. You want a pistol,' Mildred said. 'Where's Bob now?' she asked, picking up one of the pieces from exhibit A.

'He left a message. Supposedly he's working late and then going to a special Masons' meeting tonight. But there is no special meeting. I checked with Burt Silver's wife. And there was no Masons' meeting yesterday.' Sylvie sat back down at the desk. 'I knew something was different,' she said. 'It wasn't just the usual, routine, taking-me-for-granted Bob. It was the new, improved, making-a-fool-of-me-cheating Bob.' Sylvie lifted up a crumpled slip of paper. 'Look at this,' she said.

Mildred crossed the room and took the receipt. She scrunched up her eyes and held the bit of paper out but still couldn't read it without her glasses. 'What is it?' she asked.

'An American Express receipt from Weiner's Jewelry.'

'That thief. You shop there?'

'*I* don't. *I* don't buy jewelry. But *somebody* bought a necklace there.' Sylvie's voice became high with sarcasm. 'Who could it be? Wait! Look! The receipt was signed by Bob.' She turned away from her mother.

'Maybe it was a pair of cuff links. You know how he likes cuff links.'

Wordlessly, Sylvie handed her the store sales record. 'No cuff links,' she said. 'A necklace. And trust me, Bob hasn't worn beads since college.'

Mildred looked at the transaction record and then looked at her daughter. She sat down heavily at the head of the table. In Bob's chair. 'Maybe the necklace is for you. For your birthday.'

'I got my present. Remember?'

'Well, it could be for Reenie. When she comes home for Thanksgiving.'

'Don't try and justify my husband's actions,' Sylvie said. 'It was sent to an M. Molensky.'

'M. Molensky? Is that the name of a girlfriend?' Mildred asked. 'Sounds like an accountant.'

Silently, Sylvie handed Mildred another receipt. 'Save your breath. Read it and weep.'

'Switzer's?' Sylvie nodded, put her hand to her mouth, and stifled a sob.

Mildred made her way over to her daughter, the final proof of her son-in-law's infidelity still clutched in her hand. 'Oh, honey, I'm so sorry . . .' Mildred looked down and whistled at the amount at the bottom of the bill of sale. 'We're talking some serious lingerie,' she said.

Sylvie was crying full force by now. 'And I wear cotton panties I buy myself,' she sobbed.

Mildred sighed. 'Don't men know anything about discount

malls?' she asked. She stroked her daughter's hair. 'One of the main differences between men and women is that we brag about how little we paid for something. They brag about how much.'

'That's not one of the main differences,' Sylvie said grimly. She gestured to the papers and cards. 'Women wouldn't be so dumb as to make calls to their lovers in Cleveland from their home in Shaker Heights. And that's not all, Mom. When I went through the American Express bills there were dinners, lots of them. No wonder people said they saw me around town. They were expensive too. *And* he tipped twenty-five percent.'

Mildred nodded her head. 'A dead giveaway. Men tip big to make up for other things that might not be.' Mildred lifted two other receipts. 'So you didn't go to Vico's?'

'No. But Rosalie thinks I did.'

'What was *she* doing there, anyway?' Mildred wondered.

'She's dating some guy with nine toes. He probably took her. Anyway, are you convinced?' Sylvie asked.

'Oh yes,' Mildred said. 'I'm optimistic, not stupid.' She shook her head. 'I'm so disappointed in Bob. So what now?'

Sylvie had wondered the same thing herself. As she had gone through the pile of proof, she'd moved from disbelief to fear to denial and all those other phases that Elizabeth Kübler-Ross had described as the stages of accepting a death, because what Sylvie had been through was not just Bob's desk but the death of her marriage and the end of all her future dreams. In her heart, buried somewhere deep under her optimism and blindness, there had been a core feeling that had told her something was wrong although she had refused to listen. There, at Bob's desk, she had had to not only face this reality but decide what she was going to do about it. She had known immediately that she couldn't pretend, that she couldn't excuse it, nor could she doubt that it had happened.

'Sylvie?' Mildred's voice was gentle. 'So what now?'

'Well, before I decide, I want to show you just one more thing,' Sylvie said, and the tears in her voice were laced with bitterness. She pulled out a small package from the bottom of Bob's desk and handed it to her mother. Mildred looked down at the condom in her hand.

'Well, at least he was having safe sex.'

'The only safe sex Bob can have is with *me*,' Sylvie said. 'And that hasn't happened for fifty-six days.'

'You're counting?' Mildred asked. 'It's a bad sign if you're counting.' She sighed. 'My god, if I counted the last time your father and I—'

'Mother, please!' Sylvie stood up and gathered all the evidence, throwing it into a large envelope. Then she crossed the room.

'What are you doing?' Mildred asked. 'Where are you going?'

'Upstairs to pack.'

'Pack?' Mildred echoed as her daughter disappeared into the hall. 'Oh no, Sylvie. You mustn't do that.' She ran up the stairs after her daughter. 'I already have one ex-in-law on the cul-de-sac. You can't leave the house.' Sylvie was already in her bedroom, and by the time Mildred got there she had thrown an opened suitcase onto the bed. In fact, she had already thrown some of her cotton underpants into it. 'Sylvie, don't do it. This is where your life is.'

Sylvie opened the closet door, took out a blouse and a suit – a Karen Kahn she hadn't worn since the twins' eighth-grade graduation – and threw them into the bag. 'What life? This is not a life. It's a sham. I have to go. I'm married to a man who not only cheats and lies but also has his toenails buffed.' She knew she was as angry at herself as she was at Bob, because some part of her had suspected something and another part – the stupid part – had refused to acknowledge it. Sylvie picked up the little lamp on her dressing table, unplugged it, and threw it into the suitcase.

Mildred put the lamp back. 'You won't be doing much reading for a while, I think. But if you were to pick up a book, may I suggest *A Week in Firenze*? Camilla Clapfish is such a good writer. She knows everything about middle age.'

'No. I'll be too busy calling lawyers,' Sylvie said bitterly. 'You know, I'm actually glad I found out. I'm strong. I'll survive. I'll become a lawyer or a forensic psychiatrist, or marry a senator. No. I'll *become* a senator – a thin one. I'll pass a bill tripling import duties on foreign cars. Then Bob will be sorry.'

'So will your father.'

Sylvie ignored her mother. 'This was a man I used to trust. My only regret is that I did the laundry before I left.'

Mildred moved across the room, opened Bob's leather jewelry box, and rattled it like a cocktail shaker. 'This is a man who used to have very organized cuff links,' she said. Then she opened the box, took out one of each of the good cuff links, and put them in her own pocket. 'That will drive him bananas. Listen, Sylvie. You're angry. You're hurt. Take my advice: act out. Spend money. Scream. Cry. Have an affair if you have to. Make *him* pay emotionally. But hold on to your marriage.' She looked intently at her daughter. 'I know Bob. Your husband is a man who likes order and routine. Most men do. And you give him that. Not some bimbo named M. Molensky. Perhaps he's taken what you give him for granted, but he needs it. Just let this blow over.'

Sylvie turned her back to her mother, added a couple of bras to her suitcase, and then threw in a framed photo of the twins. Mildred watched, shook her head, and opened Bob's shirt drawer. All of his sports shirts, back from the laundry, were starched, folded, and arranged meticulously by color. He was a nut about his shirts. The dress shirts had to be hung in the closet facing the same direction. Mildred took out the cardboards, pulled off the collar forms, and stirred them as if they were a stew. 'Sylvie, put your clothes away,' she commanded.

'Mother, you have no idea how I feel. I couldn't possibly get back into this bed and sleep with Bob.'

'Oh, be realistic!' Mildred snapped. 'You're not going to be doing any sleeping for weeks anyway. Look. I admit this is a shock. I admit it's awful. But I don't believe it's ever happened before. I know Bob. So do you. Why believe it will ever happen again? You're not the only one who's facing your mortality, you know.' Mildred pulled open Bob's bedside table drawer, took out his carefully rolled socks, and began mismatching them. Then she rerolled them and threw them back into their accustomed place. Meanwhile, Sylvie added a photo album to her cache and was about to put in the Christmas cactus when Mildred sat down on the edge of the bed. 'Sylvie, where are you going to go?'

'Mom, times have changed. Women don't just put up with this behavior. They don't stay anymore. I want to confront him, I want to punish him, and then I want out.'

'Listen to me, this feeling will pass. Don't run. And Sylvie, don't point the finger at Bob.'

'I want to point the finger! And I want him to hurt like I do.' Sylvie picked up the phone.

'What are you doing?' Mildred demanded.

'I'm making an appointment.' Mildred tried to pull the phone away but Sylvie wouldn't let her. 'I'm in hell. Why shouldn't he be?' Sylvie asked. Then the phone was answered by the lot receptionist. Sylvie, with an effort, managed to speak in a sweet voice. 'Betsy? Mr Schiffer, please . . . Oh, fine. They're both fine . . . He's not? Oh . . . Off the lot? . . . No. No message.' Sylvie slammed down the phone, and in a second she had gathered her things, ready to leave.

'What, the finger in person?!' Mildred asked.

'Yes! I'm not wasting this rage. Can I borrow your car?'

'Listen. The two of you have history. That's worth something. You have a past and maybe a future. You point the finger at him he gets mad, then deaf.'

Sylvie picked up the suitcase. 'Your thinking is so out-of-date.'

'Out-of-date my buttocks,' Mildred croaked. 'You think, Sylvie. Think hard. Do you know what you want? A future like Rosalie the Bitter?' Sylvie just shook her head, grabbed her purse, and left the room. 'Where are you going?' Mildred cried, then followed her daughter.

'I've called a taxi. I'm going over to the lot, confronting Bob, and then I'm leaving him.' Sylvie was down at the bottom of the staircase. 'And I'm taking back my old car to do it.'

'Oh, no,' Mildred moaned. There was a honk from outside and Sylvie opened the door, waving to the driver. She picked up her suitcase. 'Please . . .' Mildred began, but her daughter had already walked out the door and down the walk to the waiting cab.

8

Sylvie hadn't taken cabs often. Shaker Heights was the kind of town you drove in, and even when they went to the airport, she and Bob preferred to drive and leave their own car in long-term parking. The taxi that was now waiting outside was all blue — the beaten-up exterior, the vinyl interior seats, the dirty floor mats, and even the ineffective pine-shaped deodorizer hanging from the windshield. Well, blue matched her mood, Sylvie thought as she got in. Since the driver didn't even offer to help with her bag, she threw it in the backseat herself. Might as well get used to doing everything for myself, she thought.

'Where to?' he asked.

'Longworth Avenue. Crandall's car lot.'

'No problem,' the driver said. She could only see the back of his neck and a strange hat he had pulled down. It was blue too, and shaped like a mushroom with seams. The cab took off and Sylvie leaned forward.

'Let me ask you a question,' she said. She tried to catch his eye in the rearview mirror. 'Did you ever cheat on your wife?'

'Not that I can recall,' the driver said. Sylvie raised her brows.

'I think if you cheated you'd be able to recall it,' she spat.

'Maybe not if I was very, very drunk,' the driver said.

'Not that I drink. Anymore. 'Course, I'm not married anymore either.'

Sylvie directed the driver past the main entrance of the BMW
lot and onto the side street off Longworth. Sylvie asked the
driver, after lambasting him for most of the ride, to try and
not be obvious. She got out of the car and, perhaps out of
shame, he handed Sylvie her bag, obviously relieved to be
rid of her. She fumbled with her purse. She wasn't exactly
sure how to tip. The ride had been awful, but so had her
behavior and, after all, he had gotten her there and taken
her abuse as well. She handed him the fare and fished out
another two dollars. 'This is for calling you a scumbag,' she
told him. 'I'm sorry.' She reached into her bag and took
out another two dollars. 'And this is for referring to you
as a "hopeless asshole." I'm sure you're not hopeless.' She
paused for a moment, remembered something, then handed
him a five. 'And this is because you said I'm still pretty.'

The driver smiled. He was missing a bicuspid and the teeth
he had didn't seem worth keeping. 'Hey, thanks, lady.' As he
started to pull away, leaving Sylvie in the middle of the empty
street, her mother's car pulled up, Mildred at the wheel.

'Don't argue. Put your suitcase in the backseat and get
in,' Mildred commanded. Sylvie had last heard that tone
of voice when she was in the seventh grade and, to her
own surprise, she responded automatically and did exactly
as her mother told her. Once in, Mildred rolled up the
window and turned to her daughter. 'Okay. You want to
confront Bob?' Sylvie nodded her head and held up the
envelope full of proof. 'Foolish girl. If you have to confront
someone, I say you confront the *girlfriend*. Throw *her* out
of town.'

'Mom, this is not about two women fighting over a man. This is about Bob lying and making a fool of me.'

Mildred sighed, shook her head, and then laboriously managed a three-point turn. As she braked for the stop sign at Longworth, they simultaneously spotted Beautiful Baby zipping by.

'Oh my god!' Sylvie cried. 'I'll bet he's going there. To her.'

Mildred pulled out and began to follow him. 'We can't get right behind him,' she said. 'Do you know where she lives?'

'Across the bridge. Cleveland. 1411 Green Bay Road. That's where the negligee went.'

Mildred snorted. 'I bet there's no green and I bet there's no bay,' she said. 'I think that's the section beyond the airport. Condos,' she sniffed, as if it were a dirty word. They drove in silence for a while. Grimly, she clutched the wheel and stared ahead at Bob's distant tail-lights. Mildred kept a car between her own and Beautiful Baby. As they left their Shaker Heights neighborhood, the houses got smaller and the traffic more congested. But Mildred never lost sight of Beautiful Baby.

'Hey, you're good at this,' Sylvie marveled.

'There's a lot of things I have experience with.' Way ahead Sylvie saw Beautiful Baby pull off the road.

'Look!' Sylvie cried. 'Bob's stopped. Does he have car trouble? Or is he having second thoughts?' They slowed down. 'It's a roadside stand. What does he want?'

'Isn't it too late in the evening to buy vegetables?' Mildred asked. 'Who needs emergency eggplant?' she demanded, and after Bob pulled out she drove up and pulled her car over.

Sylvie opened the window. 'What did that guy just buy?' she demanded of the man at the stand.

'A couple a dozen roses. You interested?'

Sylvie screamed, closed the window, and Mildred burned rubber. The car sped off, Mildred pushing to catch up with her son-in-law.

'An adultery flower stand. Of course it's open late,' she muttered.

'Flowers! I don't get flowers!' Sylvie said.

'Déjà vu,' Mildred said, half to herself.

'Bob never cheated before.'

Mildred was silent, knuckles white, peering out over the steering wheel. 'I wasn't talking about Bob,' she said at last. Sylvie looked at her. What? Something about the set of her mother's mouth, the jutting of her shoulders, gave Sylvie the clue.

'Daddy? Daddy cheated on you?' Sylvie couldn't believe it. 'Not Daddy.'

'No. Just one of his body parts.' Mildred paused, embarrassed, then tried to explain. 'You remember what happened when your brother hit puberty?' Sylvie shrugged. 'Well, maybe Phil isn't a good example. He's never *left* puberty. But with most boys . . . they . . . their heads and their penises . . . peni . . . separate. It's natural. Still — with the exception of your brother — it's only for a time. They unite when the guy falls in love. He wants to use his thing to start a family. That's how it was with your father and me.'

'Please, Mom. There are limits. Don't talk to me about Daddy's . . . thing.'

'You don't understand. It was *our* thing. Freud was right: women *do* want a penis, but they want it attached to their man. When you kids were growing up, your father and I shared his . . . thing.' Sylvie made an 'Eeee-euu!' face. She *definitely* did not want to hear about her parents' sex life. But

77

as she looked over at her mother she saw that Mildred was smiling to herself. 'Anyway, just about the time that Daddy was Bob's age, his penis and his mind separated again. And out of nowhere, it turned on me and took your father out with the bookkeeper.'

'Oh, Mom. I'm so sorry.' Sylvie stared ahead into the gathering darkness at Bob's tail-lights. Her daddy had cheated on her mom. She'd never even known it, never suspected. It put her father in a whole new light. He was now a member of The Opposition, just another man. Sylvie was flooded with a sadness so sharp that she had to push her nails into the flesh of her palms to distract herself and make it more bearable. And then she took her eyes off the road and Bob's car to glance at her mother's profile again. She'd thought she'd known everything – or almost everything – about Mildred. How many other secrets had Mildred not revealed? How much pain had she gone through? And she had never let on, never leaked it to her children. 'It must have been terrible for you,' Sylvie whispered.

Mildred nodded. 'It was a god-awful year, but I had only two choices: to wait it out or to leave. Remember, we didn't have much money then. And I had three children. What could I do? Wait tables? I retained my dignity by staying.'

Sylvie bit her lip. Maybe, she thought, she shouldn't be so quick to judge her mother or discard Mildred's opinions. Shy for a moment, Sylvie peeked over at Mildred again. Her mother was a strong woman. She had been through a lot and she had managed to keep a family, a husband, and a home while she created her little business in the community. Who was Sylvie to judge that? She focused on the road ahead and saw Bob's blinking directional. Sylvie yelled and pointed. 'He's turning – he's turning!'

'I saw,' Mildred said grimly.

Sylvie couldn't help but wonder, if years before, Mildred had followed Jim just this way. But Sylvie didn't want to inquire and didn't want to know. She did, however, need to know her mother's strategy. 'So what did *you* do?' she asked as they took the corner. 'You just waited it out?'

'Heavens, no!' her mother said and took her eyes off the road for the first time, giving Sylvie a quick but piercing glance.

'Mom, putting up with this kind of behavior for me is not possible,' Sylvie protested. 'It's old-fashioned.'

'Are you calling *me* old-fashioned? Even before they invented the word, I knew how to be proactive,' she paused. 'Look, I made a cash deal with the bookkeeper. Why do you think I couldn't afford to get my legs waxed for two whole years? A cash deal. How nineties is that?'

'I'm not buying anyone off, Mom.'

'Hey, how much do you love him?'

'Who? Bob? Not at all, now.'

'Oh, really? Think again. Imagine you're at my funeral . . .'

Sylvie shuddered. 'Don't be morbid. I don't even want to *think* about that.' She was actually shocked by her mother's remark. What would she do without her mother?

'Okay.' Mildred agreed. 'You're at your *father's* funeral. Whose shoulder are you crying on?'

Sylvie stopped to think. 'Bob's,' she admitted.

'I rest my case.'

Both cars drove onto a street filled with condo apartments. It was one of the developments built fifteen years ago – quickly constructed, cheaply made 'town houses' with paper-thin walls and fake Palladian windows with snap-on muntins. The whole tacky thing had been painted an ocher color in some misguided attempt to make the place Italianesque but the paint was faded and chipping and the faux Tuscany look didn't work in Cleveland. Sylvie imagined stewardesses, dental hygienists, and hairdressers living alone in each of the warren of apartments. Yes. And divorced piano teachers, she added. Like me. Then Bob pulled over into a reserved parking spot.

'He has his own parking place?' Mildred asked, outraged.

'Big deal, his own spot,' Sylvie said dismissively. 'The point is, it's outside. He parks Beautiful Baby *outside* for her! He wouldn't do that for me.' Then Sylvie saw what Bob had parked next to: a car exactly like her own (recently drowned) BMW. Another silver Z2 convertible! Sylvie shrieked as quietly as possible. 'She has my car! He bought her the exact same model. No wonder I sank it.'

Mildred, with a look of determination, drove past both vehicles and parked down the block. 'Now don't—' she began but Sylvie didn't hear the rest because she'd already gotten out to spy on Bob, making sure, though, that she couldn't be seen.

Bob approached a walkway and turned up it. Sylvie got as close as she safely could, trying not to cry or trip in the dark. Bob turned around and she hid behind a tree. He turned up the branch of the walkway that led to 1411. She saw him ring the doorbell of a ground-floor apartment. A woman answered the door and, although Sylvie couldn't get a good look in the light spilling out from the door, she saw that they embraced and that Bob was let in. Sylvie gestured to Mildred, still in the car, who then pulled it up beside her. Sylvie got back in. Mildred drove next to Bob's parking spot.

Sylvie got out of the car, followed by Mildred. She looked at the silver BMW convertible, exactly like her own. She peered in the window on one side, Mildred's head right beside hers, their noses pressed up against the glass.

'I've *got* to smash it,' Sylvie said.

'Control yourself. Divorce for a woman is not a pretty picture,' Mildred repeated to her daughter.

'Times have changed.'

'Not enough. Look at Rosalie. She's dating a man with nine toes. She dreads summer coming and having to go to the beach with him.'

'I'm not Rosalie,' Sylvie said defiantly. 'I hate Bob. He should never have done this. And I'm going to make him sorry he has.'

9

What do you wear to confront your husband's mistress? Sylvie wondered. And did you even call them — those women — 'mistresses' anymore? Was she his girlfriend? His lover? The other words that came to Sylvie's mind were ones she wouldn't call anyone, not to their faces. Though, she thought, once she looked at M. Molensky's she might.

Sylvie was in her convertible, now as good as new again — except for the mildew smell. She was full of determination. Sylvie was bothered by the odor but her mission in progress was even more troublesome. She'd had two days to think this all through, to stew and settle and then stew some more. She must be goulash by now, she figured. She pulled her car up to a spot just beyond 1411 Green Bay Road, got out, and smoothed the black slacks and blue sweater set she was wearing. Then, tucking her purse under her arm, she marched up the walk to the condo entrance. At the doorway she lifted her arm, ready to pound on the door. But, all at once, her bravado left her and she pulled her hand back. What was she doing? This wasn't between her and M. Molensky, whoever *she* was. This was between her and Bob. Despite her mother's advice and her own hatred of violence, she should go back to the lot, find her husband, and tear his goddamned pink toenails off. She felt another surge of anger, turned around, and began to walk back to her car. Then she saw something that made her stop in mid-step and catch her breath. It was the convertible, the one just like her own birthday gift.

She realized, all at once, that she would have to actually kill Bob. But first, before she had to spend the rest of her life in the Betty Broderick wing of the Ohio State penitentiary, out of curiosity alone she might as well confront this M. Molensky. Sylvie spun around and stalked back up the walk. She approached the doorway for the second time and was about to bang on it until it crumbled away and her fists bled, but then, at the last minute, she knocked softly.

It took a little while. She heard some noise inside, a shuffling and a rattling. She knocked again gently. 'Who is it?' a voice called out at last.

'The exterminator,' Sylvie replied in a husky voice, and she didn't feel the slightest bit of guilt about the lie. It wasn't a lie. She felt ready to rub out this insect.

The door opened and a woman stood behind it, obscured by the comparative darkness of the living room. 'I didn't call for you,' M. Molensky – if she *was* M. Molensky – said. 'Life is sacred. I don't want to harm living things. I mean, since my stepdaddy died, one of those bugs could be him. I *want* him to live as a bug.'

Sylvie pushed her aside and stepped into the shaded interior. 'Actually, I'm Mrs Schiffer and I'm looking for a rat. Does the name ring a bell?' It must have because M. Molensky retreated behind the door.

'You're married to Bobby?' M. Molensky asked from her spot in back of the door. 'And you're an exterminator?'

Was she kidding? 'Yes and no,' Sylvie told her. M. Molensky was holding the knob so Sylvie couldn't pull it away. 'It was a ploy so we could talk and then I could kill you. Or him.'

'I didn't know he was married,' the girl whined. 'Ignorance is nine tenths of the law.'

'No. That's possession,' Sylvie corrected.

'I don't have any drugs here. Not even grass!' the girl protested. Then she stepped from behind the door, though she was still in its shadow. All Sylvie could see was that she was wearing a tiny robe in some cheesy material that clung. It was white with little roses on it and showed a lot of leg. Sylvie could see her legs were good, even though her feet were stuffed into big terry cloth slippers. M. Molensky took a step and then another out of the comparative darkness of the corner by the door. Then Sylvie saw her face, while the girl, for the first time, lifted her head up and looked directly at Sylvie. For a long moment they stared at each other, face to face.

'My god!' Sylvie gasped. She was staring at her own face – but not. It was her face as it had looked a decade ago. The same wide forehead, the same even brows, the same blue eyes – though M. Molensky's might be a slightly darker blue. But the shape was the same. The only real difference was the ten years of wrinkles missing on the girl's face. Sylvie stared at M. Molensky's nose. It was Sylvie's nose, straight and long, narrowing just a little in the middle before the nostrils flared. But again, though the nose replicated her own, the girl was missing the lines that, on Sylvie's own face, ran from the outside of each nostril to the outside of her mouth. 'Marionette lines' Sylvie suddenly remembered they were called.

And their mouths! Sylvie felt hers pucker into an O of surprise as she watched M. Molensky's do the same. It was the eeriest feeling Sylvie had ever experienced, like watching herself in a mirror – but a mirror from ten years ago. They stared at one another, wordless and horrified. M. Molensky was seeing what she would become, and Sylvie was seeing what she had been. Sylvie stared at the girl's chin. Yes, she had once had a jaw that taut, a chin that smooth. It hadn't been so long ago. But time and gravity had softened everything. Instinctively, Sylvie moved her hands to either side of her face and, resting them against her cheeks and temples, she stretched the sagging skin up, giving herself a momentary face-lift. At the same time, her twin opposite raised her own hands and dragged her eyes and cheeks down. Bob, his betrayal, and her rage flew out of Sylvie's mind. All she could see was the work of Father Time. She looked not at what she had, but at what she had lost.

The younger woman's eyes mirrored her own horror. In their blue depths Sylvie could see a fear as acute as the one she was experiencing. Why? Here was a girl who still has her youth and beauty. A girl, Sylvie suddenly remembered, who also has my husband, at least part-time. Yet, looking at her, it was obvious that she was as shocked and horrified as Sylvie. 'I looked like you once,' Sylvie whispered. 'Just like you.'

'And I'm going to look just like you,' the girl whispered back and, letting go of her face, she burst into tears. She threw herself onto a chair and after a minute or two gestured that Sylvie should also sit down. Since Sylvie's legs were shaking, it seemed like a good idea. 'Momma always said each of us had a twin somewhere in the world,' the girl said, sobbing. 'Then she used to say she hoped mine had more brains than I did.' She looked up, wiping her eyes. 'I'll bet *you* went to college,' she said, resentment in her voice. Sylvie nodded. 'See? I have these kind of psychic feelings about those things. I'll bet you finished. *And* you're a Pisces.'

'Right on the first, wrong on the second,' Sylvie answered

automatically, still staring at her doppelganger, sprawled in the chair across from her. 'I'm a Virgo.'

'That would have been my next guess,' the girl assured her, nodding her mane of blonde hair. 'Anyway, you probably have Pisces rising.' She had more hair than Sylvie, and it was very blonde. Was it natural? Sylvie wondered. But the face . . . it was just unbelievable.

The girl, meanwhile, was staring at her. Sylvie didn't have to be a psychic to know what she felt or the tragedy that all women experience. Sylvie realized that her feelings of loss were decimating, but this girl's feelings of dread were just as acute. We're in a no-win in our relationship with old Father Time, Sylvie thought. And it was no accident that he was a man. A mother wouldn't treat her daughters like this.

Finally the girl stood up, turned her back, and walked through the room. Sylvie followed her, peeking at the apartment of a mistress. There was a little too much pink, too many knickknacks and figurines, not enough real furniture — a brown carton served as an end table — but there were two dozen long-stemmed roses in a vase. They made Sylvie wince. Meanwhile, the girl had disappeared down a short hallway. Sylvie followed her through the bedroom — the bedroom, Sylvie reminded herself, where her husband had cheated on her — and into the bathroom. M. Molensky was staring into the mirror, her face again pulled down, aged by her hands.

Sylvie stood beside her. 'The wrinkles just crept in, like an invisible hand that wiped across my face,' she said. 'One day I stopped squinting when I looked in the mirror and saw what was really there.' She looked at the young woman's perfect, dewy skin. 'What moisturizer do you use?'

'Quince cream and super-blue algae. I swear by it.' She reached for two jars and held them up.

'I used to . . . I used to look in the mirror at you,' Sylvie said quietly.

'And someday . . . someday I'll be looking at . . .,' the girl continued softly, but glanced away and didn't finish the sentence.

Sylvie turned from the mirror and looked directly at her rival. The light here was strong and white. Everything was mercilessly exposed. The two women circled each other, getting closer and closer. They studied each other's faces: eyes, wrinkles, skin, hair texture. Everything. The most important thing on their minds was this incredible twinship, how much they looked alike. Bob had been pushed right out of Sylvie's head for the moment. Then, 'Did he tell you we were doubles?' Sylvie asked.

'No. He said I was one of a kind,' the girl wailed. 'This is really spooking me out.'

'I bet he doesn't even see it.'

'I bet you're right. I know *all* about this because it's my own personal nightmare. But backward. You know, sometimes your dreams can tell you what your future is. Like my cousin Ray, he used to have this dream about a chain saw. And he would have it, like, all the time. And in the dream he'd cut off his leg with the chain saw.'

'And did he?' Sylvie asked, fascinated but revolted.

'No,' M. Molensky admitted. 'He just wouldn't go near chain saws. I guess because of the dreams. It was kind of like a phobia with him. But I'll bet if he did, he *would* have cut his leg off. Anyway, I've got this kind of, like, phobia too.'

'You're afraid of chain saws?' Sylvie asked.

'No. That was my cousin. *I'm* always scared a man is going to discard me for somebody newer and shinier. I call it the John Derek syndrome.'

Sylvie was dizzy, both with the shock and the endless spirals of this girl's logic, or lack of it. 'I thought he was an old actor, not a syndrome,' she said.

'He's both. Remember how he started with Ursula Andress, then traded her in for that . . . you know. The one with the shoulder pads . . . the one with the Greek boyfriend who won't marry her . . .'

'Linda Evans?' Sylvie asked.

'Yeah! Anyway, she looked *just* like Ursula. And *then* he wound up with Ten. Afro braids. You know, Bo. They're all the same, only younger and younger. Clint Eastwood's women all looked just alike: that freckled, sandy-haired thing, till this wife. Not even pretty. Johnny Carson did it, too. Remember? They even had the same name: Joanna, Joanne, Joan, Joanna, Joanna.' She paused and lowered her voice. 'My theory is he did *that* because he was scared he'd yell out the wrong name in the middle of the night.'

'But this isn't Hollywood, it's Shaker Heights,' Sylvie protested.

'Hey, it's an epidemic all over the country! Trump did it in New York. Marla for Ivana. And now I hear he's got an even younger one. She looks *just* the same.'

Sylvie was dumbfounded. The girl's looks, her stream of consciousness conversation, the strange surroundings all seemed surreal. Next she'd see a melting clock. 'Where did you come from?' Sylvie asked.

'The sky . . . I'm a stewardess. I mean, a flight attendant. I met Bobby on a flight.'

She remembered her anger. '*Bobby*! He lets you call him *Bobby*?' Sylvie asked, outraged.

The girl ignored her question. 'I really didn't know he was married.'

'Yeah. Like you asked,' Sylvie retorted bitterly.

'. . . he didn't even have a wedding band tan line,' M. Molensky said, trying to explain. 'Don't ask. Don't tell. That was my motto even *before* the army stole it from me.'

Sylvie couldn't help but take a good look at the way this little piece of work was put together. She might be an inch or two taller than Sylvie, or perhaps it was just her willowy thinness that gave the illusion of it. And that hair! 'I'll bet you were a cheerleader,' Sylvie, jealous, said accusingly.

'Do you have psychic tendencies too?' M. Molensky asked.

'Excuse me?'

'Well, you're close. I was a majorette,' she said proudly.

'What's the difference?' Sylvie snapped back.

'Hey, there's a *big* one, especially in the uniforms . . . sometimes I like to dress in uniforms,' M. Molensky admitted.

'Oh, I'm sure you do. And what do you do, then? Play sex games with my husband? You know, like The Pilot and The Stewardess.'

'Actually, he prefers—'

Sylvie raised her hand, arm extended, palm facing the girl, before she could hear more. 'Talk to the fist,' she said, clenching her hand. She didn't want to know details, at least not now. 'So this isn't the first time that you were involved with somebody else's husband?' Sylvie asked, her voice turning bitter. 'Don't you know how wrong adultery is?'

'I don't commit adultery!' M. Molensky said defensively. 'I'm not even married.'

'Don't you think about the women who are? The ones married to the Bobbys?' Sylvie demanded. 'How what you do makes other women suffer?'

'No.'

'It never occurred to you that you were making somebody's wife suffer?' Sylvie asked, her voice raised high in disbelief.

'You think *I* don't suffer? Like *I* don't spend Christmas and Valentine's Day alone? Like *I* don't always get my presents from Bobby late?'

'Presents?' Sylvie shrieked. '*Presents?*' She refrained from smacking the girl, but it took all her willpower. Instead, she reached toward the mirror and, desperate to express her fury, she smeared M. Molensky's image with a handful of the quince cream. M. Molensky's eyes opened wide. (Sylvie couldn't help but notice they didn't have a single crow's-foot.) Then, in retaliation, M. Molensky smeared over Sylvie's reflected face in the mirror. Images blurred with the grease, they turned to face one another directly.

'You're the lucky one, you know,' the girl said. 'I don't have the comfort or security of a legalized relationship. And that's because I don't have anyone in this whole wide world to count on.'

'What about your family?'

The girl walked away from Sylvie. 'What family? My mother left me on Santa Claus's lap when I was four.' She shrugged. 'Well, sometimes I do write to my brother, but he's not great at answering. He's probably real busy at the rehab.' Her tone sounded happier as she told her woes; then she continued, 'So, as you can see, *I'm* the karmic victim here.'

'No, *I'm* the victim. How can you talk about karma? *You're* stealing my husband.'

There was total quiet as the two women stared at each other.

'It's probably because of something you've done in your previous life. Like, I grew up in Presidential Estates Trailer

Court probably because of being a Chinese empress in a previous life.'

What? The girl made no sense. 'You sure you weren't a concubine?' Sylvie asked bitterly.

'I don't think you can be reincarnated as a vegetable,' M. Molensky said matter-of-factly. 'Look, I don't want to fight with you. Can't we work something out? Like with kids. Joint custody. I could get him a couple of nights a week and vacations.'

'Vacations!' Sylvie yelped and thought of Hawaii. 'You're not going *anywhere* with my husband! And . . . and . . . neither am I,' she admitted.

'Oh yeah? . . . Well, Bobby asked me to go to Mexico.'

Sylvie stopped dead, absolutely stunned. If that were true, her mother was wrong. This wasn't just some bimbo who could be bought off. It wasn't just sex if Bob was willing to travel with her. 'He wanted to take you to Mexico?' Sylvie asked, then turned away and walked to the window, her back to the girl to prevent her from seeing this agony. She stood silent, hurt at her core. If she moved, she felt she'd crack.

Sylvie felt a hand on her shoulder. 'It was only because we went to this Flaming Fajitas restaurant,' the girl said, her voice soft. Her sympathy was worse to Sylvie than anything yet. 'It was a spur-of-the-moment idea,' she continued. 'I don't think he was really serious about going. I mean, I've never seen tickets or reservations. And say, hey! Who wants to lay out in the sun and ruin their skin?'

Sylvie went to the mirror and tried to see herself more clearly but her reflection was obscured by the quince cream. It made her look misty, à la Katharine Hepburn shot through Vaseline in the 1960s. In the smear beside her the girl looked misty too, not that *she* needed a filter. 'I hope I looked as good as you do when I was your age,' Sylvie said.

'I'm sure you did. I can't believe how nice you are! Once before I was accidentally with someone's husband and she came over and broke all my lamps.'

They turned away from the mirror and looked at one another.

The girl still stuck out her hand to shake. 'By the way, I'm Marla.'

Sylvia recoiled. '*Marla?* As in . . .'

'Yeah. I used to love the name. But then she got dumped.' This Marla heaved a deep sigh.

'I'm Sylvie.' Sylvie extended her hand. Marla took it. There was a moment of real bonding between them – until Sylvie focused on another vase of roses.

'Are those also from . . . ?'

'I'd rather not say,' Marla admitted.

All at once it was way too much. '*I* want to be the one who gets the roses!' Sylvie cried out. 'And I want him to romance me. I want to be treated like a . . .' She paused. 'Like *you*.'

'Well, I wanna be you!' Marla said. 'You think it's easy, holding in my belly pooch forever? Ever since I was born I've wanted to be a wife.'

'Oh, really? You're looking *at* a wife. Does this look like a happy person to you?'

'No,' Marla admitted.

'When you're married, you don't even get kissed on the mouth!'

'When you're single, you have to smell good twenty-four hours a day,' Marla retorted.

She was infuriating. Sylvie suddenly realized why she had

come here in the first place. 'I want you to stop seeing him,' she demanded.

'Try and make me,' Marla said, sounding half her age. Sylvie wondered for a moment what that would make her. Fourteen? Sixteen? 'You can't tell me what to do.'

'No, but I can tell Bob that this affair is over.' Sylvie saw the fear rise in the girl's eyes. She pressed her advantage. 'Do you think he's going to give up his children? Do you think he's going to give up the house? And his job?' Sylvie narrowed her eyes. 'My father still owns the car lot. If he's fired . . . well, men his age end up working part-time in the Wal-Mart automotive supply department. *Without* medical insurance. And, believe me, with his cholesterol, he's going to need medical soon enough.'

'He'll stay with me,' Marla said, though she not only looked frightened, she sounded it. 'He loves me. He'd give up everything. You just don't remember what that feels like.'

Tears sprang to Sylvie's eyes. The blow was so dirty that she almost backed down, but then her anger welled up. She could fight dirty too. 'You think so, huh? I'll tell him you said that. I'll tell him you called me. That you told me *I* had to give *him* up.' Sylvie put on an exaggerated sad face. 'I'll be distraught and fragile and so, so hurt. You'll be the one who looks like the demanding witch.'

Marla's eyes opened wide. 'But *you* came to *me*!' she gasped.

'That's what *you* say,' Sylvie sneered. 'Who do you think he's going to believe? His innocent wife of almost twenty-one years or a woman who has slept around?'

'I'm the rubber, you're the glue. That goes double for me,' Marla said. Her arsenal was not full of big guns. Sylvie, all at once, actually felt sorry for the girl. This wasn't what she'd meant to do.

They collapsed onto opposite sides of the bathtub ledge like depressed bookends. Sylvie, looking across at the mirror, wondered how either of them could win.

10

Sylvie had driven back from 1411 Green Bay Road and gone directly to the mall where her mother's shop was located. Her hands had shaken so badly on the short ride that she'd had to pull over to the side of the road twice. Cars whizzed by her but she didn't see them.

Over and over, the thought that had kept running through her head was that Bob, or anyone, might never make love to her again. The romance, the loving, maybe her entire sex life had ended for her some time ago and she hadn't even known it. What an idiot I was. What an idiot I am, she thought and remembered the Hawaiian brochure. What had Bob thought when she'd virtually begged him to go? She actually blushed with embarrassment, though she was alone in the car. She'd been pathetic. What exactly had Bob been thinking while she was busy pitching a romantic adventure? Going with Marla Molensky instead?

Breathing became impossible. She was too shocked. She'd been replaced and the worst part was she hadn't even known it. Twenty-one years of dedicated service, now over. At least in the corporate world they had the courtesy of giving you a pink slip and a watch. She felt as if she'd been kicked all over. Imagining Bob touching her younger twin, the more perfect Sylvie, hurt so much it was intolerable. And what had the neighbors, her students, her friends known? She remembered Honey's comments, her sightings all over town. Sylvie couldn't bear to think about it. She wouldn't or she'd go crazy.

More than anything else, though, she was upset and hurt by Bob's charade. He was the person she trusted more than anyone else in the world — except for her mother — and he had tricked her, deceived her, and made her look like a fool. However scatterbrained that girl was, Sylvie had to admit that she herself was far more stupid.

When she got to the mall, she parked like a madwoman, unfairly swooping into a spot ahead of a blue Toyota and selfishly straddling the line so that no one would be able to park beside her, at least not without taking off her goddamned car's door handles. Well, let them. Let them take the tires and the hubcaps and the rest of the goddamn car, too. The woman in the Toyota gave her a dirty look, but Sylvie, usually so sensitive, didn't even blink. She wasn't having a shoe emergency here at the mall. She needed her mother. She strode across the parking lot and through the door of her mother's store — Potz Bayou. The pottery shop — living up to its punny name — was decorated with New Orleans-style wrought iron. Fake Spanish moss hung from the ceiling. All the shelves were lined with every imaginable unpainted ceramic article, from the tiniest demitasse cup to huge punch bowls.

Suburban matrons were clustered together at long tables busily painting glazes onto mugs and bowls. Two shop girls, Cindy and another one, a new one, were bent over, assisting a customer. 'Hi, Sylvie,' Sandie Thomas called out.

For a panicky moment Sylvie thought she'd have to stop and gossip, something unthinkable. What would she do if she couldn't find Mildred? She'd burst into public tears in front of all these women. Oh, screw them, she thought. This isn't about them. Then, thank the lord, her mother came out of the kiln room, wiping her hands on her apron. Sylvie stalked across the shop. 'Did you have another daughter that you put up for adoption?' she demanded.

Several of the women turned and stared, their conversations momentarily halted by what looked like a better drama. Mildred opened her eyes wide and gestured with her chin toward the back. As if Sylvie cared if people overheard her. As if Sylvie cared about *anything* right now. The hell with it all. If the kiln was on and her mother was firing, Sylvie would be more than willing to stick her head into it.

But Mildred took her wild-eyed daughter by the elbow and led her to the tiny office in the back of the shop. 'What *do* you mean?' she asked, sounding exasperated.

'I saw her. Mom, she looks just like me, only she's much younger.'

Mildred shrugged. 'You didn't expect she'd be like you, but older, did you?' Then she put her arm around Sylvie. 'I'm so sorry, baby.' She opened the back door, which led to the service area. She turned and called out to the shop floor, 'Cindy, could I please have that big planter on the third shelf for my daughter?'

Sylvie stepped away from her mother as if she'd lost her mind. 'Mom, I know glazing is your life, but this is no time for ceramics. I can't paint now.'

Cindy appeared, holding a large pot, and handed it to Mildred.

Cindy looked over at Sylvie, obviously curious. 'Thank you, dear. I think Mrs Burns needs you now,' Mildred said, dismissing her and looking back at her daughter. 'A nice girl, but nosy.' She handed the pot to Sylvie.

'Mom, I'm not going to do ceramics.'

'Not *do* them, *throw* them.' Mildred gestured out the door into the parking area and the brick wall. Sylvie looked from the planter to her mother's face. 'It will make you feel better. Not much, but some. You can't keep all the anger inside. It'll make you sick.'

Sylvie blinked and then, with a fury she didn't know she had, she hurled the pot against the wall. It exploded into thousands of shards that fell onto the blacktop and bounced. For a moment – just a moment – she felt totally at peace. 'I *do* feel a little better,' she admitted. But then the turmoil returned. 'Cindy, three more planters, please,' Sylvie yelled.

'And bring a broom,' Mildred added, then lowered her voice. 'Do you think you're the first one to have this type of therapy? When I found out about that thing with your father and the bookkeeper . . . well, that's when I got into ceramics in a big way. It was incredibly soothing to break all that crockery and have your dad pay the bill. He always asked what I was doing with the stuff, since I never brought it home.' Mildred laughed. 'I told him I was sending it to your aunt Irene. And look – now I'm in the business.' She patted affectionately the sign over the back entrance. 'I love what I do. I have a staff, and I make a nice profit.' She raised her brows. 'Plus I bank every penny. I could buy out a hundred bookkeepers now.'

Mildred looked at her daughter. 'I know this is a shock to you – and to me – but you have to hold yourself together. You're not alone.' Mildred gestured to the bustling shop. 'See Sandie over there? Just last year she smashed eight complete place settings of dinnerware before she started painting.' Mildred handed another bowl to Sylvie and then patted her on the back. 'Don't throw your shoulder out,' she said. 'Put your whole body into it with the next one.' She paused. 'So, how much did you offer her?'

Sylvie shook her head. 'Mom, she can't be bought off. This is not about money.'

Cindy arrived, carefully juggling the three huge pots. 'I'm afraid there's a chip on one, Mrs Crandall,' she said.

Mildred smiled at her. 'That's all right, dear. We'll work around that.' She waited for Cindy to, rather reluctantly, remove herself to the front of the store. She shook her head. 'That girl always senses domestic tragedy. What she manages to overhear in this shop isn't just the *Days of Our Lives*, it's the nights too,' Mildred said loudly. Then she lowered her voice. 'You didn't offer her enough.'

'Mom, you don't understand. She's not a bookkeeper. She's some New Age space cadet. But she's my twin. She looks exactly like me. Except she's got less mileage. She's a replacement part. Well, more like an entire new model.' Thinking of the girl's face, Sylvie took the top pot and threw it with all her might against the wall. It smashed into slivers with a satisfying pop, but it wasn't enough. She picked up the next one and hurled that too. The destruction was satisfying, but still not enough for Sylvie to get sufficient air into her lungs. 'I can't breathe,' she told her mother.

'Yes, you can,' Mildred assured her. 'You can and you will. Think of it as Lamaze. You'll breathe all the way through this.'

Sylvie shook her head, looked away from the shards and back to Mildred. 'I'm not going *through* this, I'm getting *out* of it. But first I want to make Bob feel as shattered as that.' She pointed to the pile of debris. 'As shattered as I feel.'

'So you're going to break up your marriage, not just these pots? Over Bob's dumb mistake?'

'It's not a mistake. And *she's* not dumb. She's addled. She's weird and maybe amoral, but she's not mercenary.

She's looking for a husband. And she wants mine. She knows *exactly* what she's doing.'

'Well, you have to admire her for that. Knowing what you want is the first step in getting it,' Mildred said. 'I'm not sure you know what you want yet.'

Sylvie almost began to cry again. 'Oh, yes I do. I want Bob to ache for me. I want *him* to feel rejected, and used up. I want *him* to be deceived and feel like a fool. And I want to be able to breathe again.'

Mildred handed her daughter another pot. 'Will this make you feel better? It's the last one I have.'

Sylvie shook her head and put the pot down on the counter. 'No,' she said, 'it's chipped. What's the point? Once things get old or damaged or imperfect, who wants anything to do with them?'

'Now I feel a victim of your sarcasm,' Mildred sniffed. 'Sylvie, you're only forty. You don't even subscribe to *New Choices*, let alone *Modern Maturity*. You're lovely, not an old soup bowl. I'd like you to try now to calm down.'

'You know what *I'd* like? I'd like to be able to breathe again, and think,' Sylvie said. 'I do have to calm down to do that. I have to really take this all in.' She paused. 'I don't think I actually want to kill Bob, but I don't want to see him with this replacement. You know, if I could have one wish it would be to make my husband fall passionately in love with me. But I don't want Bob the way he is today. I mean, I don't care about his paunch or his hairline. I want the old Bob. The Bob who was passionate. Who adored me. I remember how good that felt. I want him back, and I want him to love me more than he ever did.'

'What are you saying, Sylvie?' Mildred sputtered. 'That you wish you were Bob's mistress instead of his wife?'

'Yes. Well . . . no, not exactly,' Sylvie lied. It was shaming to admit it, but right now that *was* part of what she wanted. Of course, she also wanted to see Bob hang from a meat hook. But after he was punished, then what? 'She's the one who's getting all the affection. She's the one who gets flowers and gifts. Meanwhile, I'm the one who's hanging his shirts up, defrosting chicken, and writing to the kids.'

'That's a wife and mother's job description.'

'Well, I want a promotion.'

'But you need some quiet time. Sylvie, every woman here has husband trouble. That's if they *have* a husband. If they don't, they have boyfriend trouble, or they're lonely. Half of the ones with husbands are bored by them or can't stand them. Or they ignore them. The other half are being driven crazy because *they're* ignored – or they're suspicious. Nobody has it easy.' Mildred looked out the office door at the crowded shop. 'It makes for very good business. You may not be able to cope with your marriage, but you can glaze a hell of a tureen. I feel like I'm providing a community service.'

Mildred began to sweep and sighed. 'Time moves on, Sylvie. We grow and we change. Some things we lose. Others we gain. I can tell you I don't miss menstrual cramps, but sometimes . . .' She paused and put down the broom. 'God! What am I yammering about? Go home, sweetheart. Take a nap. You'll feel better. Then call me. I'll come over. We'll talk some more.'

In the car Sylvie's thoughts whirled. Her mother hadn't understood about Marla, about their twinship, but who could? You had to see the girl to believe it. In an odd – very odd – way Sylvie thought that perhaps she should feel complimented. Bob hadn't picked a Spanish señorita with black hair trailing down to her hips. If I lightened my hair, Sylvie thought, and I lost a little weight . . . If I got rid of these bags under my eyes . . . Well, she wouldn't do that to please Bob. She'd much rather poison him. If only he'd eat a meal at home.

Despite her mother's advice, the idea of being in the same house with Bob made her dizzy. How could she not manage to kill him, or keep her mouth shut after meeting his mistress? Because despite her hurt, despite her outrage, despite her confusion, deep down Sylvie felt that there was something she wasn't quite grasping that was at the very center of this. Something more important than the simple issue of her injured pride and her husband's egregious betrayal. There was something that could be learned, but it kept flickering at the edges of her thoughts. She couldn't bring it into focus.

What did she really want? her mother had asked. Sylvie had thought, only a few days ago, that she had everything she wanted. And she'd been deceiving herself. Life was too precious to waste in a dream state or pursuing a goal you didn't really desire. What *did* she really want and, once she knew that, how could she get it?

11

Sylvie lay flat — well, as flat as she could with the mounds that her breasts and her stomach made — on the single bed in Reenie's room. She couldn't bear the thought of going into her own bedroom or touching her bed — the bed she had slept on all these years with Bob. But she had to lie down somewhere because she simply didn't have the strength to stand up for another moment. She stared at the ceiling and felt time pass over her. That is what had happened: time had passed over her and, as it did, minutely, bit by bit, day by day, it had washed away her youth and her freshness and her options and her courage and left behind this thing she had become. She moved one hand to her hip — it took all her energy to do it — and felt the fleshiness there. The last time she'd been to the mall she'd had to buy a size twelve pair of slacks. The saleswoman had assured her they were 'European cut' but Sylvie knew she had thickened.

Yet, she told herself, it was natural. She was aging, just like everyone else on the planet. Including that . . . that . . . New Age bimbo. Someday (well, probably in about eleven years) that poor addled tramp will have thickened too. The nice definition between her rib cage and her waist would smooth out into a flat line. And her butt would sag.

Yet, until then, it seemed that Bob preferred her to his own wife. Tears began to fill Sylvie's eyes, but she blinked them away. She was too angry and too shocked to cry. Yet she was vindicated. She wasn't crazy, or oversensitive, or paranoid. Even her mother had been wrong. Bob *was* ignoring her. No wonder he hadn't noticed when she changed her perfume or wore that new nightgown. No wonder he hadn't tried to make her feel guilty about the car in the pool. He was putting something inappropriate into something inappropriate himself. And no wonder he had given her the car in the first place. When you had a car lot, a car was the easiest gift in the world to give. He'd given one to his mistress. Sylvia wondered who else he had given cars to. Their dry cleaner?

She also wondered when was the last time Bob had really noticed, really thought about her? She clenched her fists. This nightmare was the kind of thing that happened to other people, other less fortunate women. It happened to Rosalie, but she had always been . . . well, shrewish. It happened to women who chose obvious Lotharios for husbands. It happened to Sandie Thomas. But it didn't happen to her. She'd been a really good wife. She hadn't ignored Bob to focus on the children. She hadn't nagged. She'd been interested in his hobbies. She hadn't let herself go – much. For God's sake, she'd gone fly-fishing with him three years in a row. And she hadn't just kept his home, she'd also kept their musical life going. She'd taken him to concerts, they'd played duets. This kind of thing *did not happen to her*. She wasn't stupid, she wasn't blind, and she wasn't a victim.

But it had happened.

It had also happened to her mother.

Sylvie felt as if she were sinking into Reenie's mattress, as if she weighed not just a dozen pounds more than she should but a thousand, or a million. She felt as if she could sink right through the mattress and the box spring, through the floor, down into the basement, and then, her density increasing, right down to the center of the earth. She was sure she would never be able to stand up again, much less walk.

But when she remembered that moment – that shock of seeing her own more youthful face staring at her from inside that woman's apartment – Sylvie had to admit that this was not just the usual dalliance. Even now, she would swear that Bob had never cheated on her before. Even now, with her heart and her belly and her fists and her thighs all feeling heavier than an imploding star, she had to admit that in selecting Marla Molensky, her younger twin, Bob hadn't been completely rejecting her. Well, he'd been rejecting her, Sylvie Schiffer, but he'd selected her, or something very like her. He'd selected her as she had been.

The thought wasn't just a rationalization. The resemblance was too startling. Despite the heaviness of her heart, Sylvie felt somewhere, in the very center of herself, that Bob had fallen into this affair, made his selection, looking for a Sylvie. Maybe not Sylvie as she was right now, but Sylvie as she had been. Yes. He wanted her. He just wanted the old her.

That idea both horrified and galvanized her. She got up from Reenie's narrow bed and, like a sleepwalker, like Frankenstein's wife, she made her way over to the full-length mirror on the back of Reenie's closet door. She stared at her reflection.

Of course, her hair was wildly disheveled, her eyes red, and her face pale – except for the splotches on her cheeks that she got when she was very angry. Sylvie, in slow motion, began to unbutton her blouse. She dropped it to the floor and then struggled with the too tight button on her slacks. She let them fall to her ankles and stepped out of them, flipping off her shoes. Next she reached behind herself and took off her bra, dropping it to the floor as her breasts dropped as

105

well. Last, she stripped off her panties and stood there, naked except for the little gold cross that she wore around her neck. Then she remembered that Bob had given it to her on their fifth anniversary and she pulled it off too, letting it fall to the floor with the other flotsam and jetsam. It took all her courage then, but she pulled herself together and looked into the mirror.

The light from the window wasn't harsh – Reenie's room faced north – but a clear white illumination. Sylvie looked at herself in her daughter's mirror. When had those bags under her eyes filled in with fat? And when had the two sides of her jaw, each bit beside the corner of her mouth, begun to hang like that? She put her hand up to her throat. When had it gone so soft? She lowered her eyes to her chest. She was covered with little freckles and discolorations all across her breastbone. And her breasts!

Her breasts had never been overly large. She used to really like her breasts. Now she stared and wondered when the nipples had started pointing down instead of up. She remembered the stupid pencil test – the girls in school had always said you had to wear a bra if your breasts hung low enough against your chest cavity so that you could hold a pencil the thickness of a cigarette there. My God! She could secrete a Royal Macanudo cigar and no one would be the wiser. Sylvie continued her examination. Her belly had filled out. She was used to a little round mound, but this was more. When she was younger, even the roundness was cute. Somehow now, the lumpiness and the look of the flesh, her own flesh, was unattractive. And then came her thighs! She looked at the dimpled cellulite. When had she become The Pillsbury Doughboy? Once past the thighs her legs weren't so bad – but as she stared she noticed two or three places where the veins were beginning to come close to the skin. Were they varicose?

She looked down, away from the mirror, directly at her own body. Despite the slight bulge of her stomach, she could see her pubic hair. Was it sparser than it had been? And – oh my god – was that a gray hair among the others?

How had this happened without her noticing it? Had she been too busy with the kids, her music, her students, the house and the garden to notice? She had become a middle-aged woman!

It was, of course, inevitable. She simply had not thought it was going to happen so soon. Forty wasn't old. Somehow she wouldn't have minded so much if she thought she was loved. But now, realizing that Bob had so little interest in her, Sylvie despised what she saw. Ten years ago – even five – she'd been able to hold it together. At thirty she could pass for twenty-two. She'd been carded once when she was thirty-one (and the bar was dark). At thirty-seven she still didn't look her age. But somehow it had all caught up with her. The ten years, or eleven, or whatever the difference was from that other woman were the years where some irreparable change took place, where the rubber hit the road. Sylvie's only comfort was that all of these changes would happen to that hussy too. She would stand before a mirror just like this someday. But, in the meantime, Marla was flawless.

Sylvie looked at herself in the mirror again and blushed. She felt the flush move down her neck and heat her chest. Every time Bob looked at her in the last few months he must have compared her to that other woman, the one with the skin that was still elastic, with the hands that were smooth. How humiliating! Sylvie had to turn away from the mirror.

She took Reenie's old dressing gown down from its hook and wrapped herself in the big flannel robe.

When was the last time she and Bob had made love? She'd joked when she told her mother fifty-six days. But how long was it? She tried to remember. Not since before the children left for school. And she wasn't sure whether they had tried during the summer. Could it be that long? Almost four months? They'd been married forever, and there had been dry spells, but they'd never gone as long as this. Sylvie held her hand out to steady herself against the wall. When would she make love again? Maybe never. How could she possibly ever make love to Bob after this? And she couldn't even think of another man in her future.

In truth, Sylvie had never expected much drama in life. She felt as if she made her own world and was responsible for her own happiness. But she wasn't ready to be counted out. She wasn't ready to give up carnal pleasure or be relegated to the discard pile.

Bob had found somebody new, yet still had all the safety of familiarity. Bob was making love to another woman, a woman who looked just like Sylvie had looked a decade earlier. Bob was turning back the clock.

But for Sylvie, what answer was there?

Sylvie was sitting in Dr John Spencer's office, but she couldn't sit for long. Instead, she began to pace. The usual framed official stuff was on the walls: medical school degrees, awards for community service and the like. There was also a big picture of John's deceased wife Nora and dozens of pictures of the two of them together. Too bad they'd never had children, Sylvie thought. Nora hadn't been able to conceive. John would have been a good father, and if they'd had kids, he wouldn't be alone now. The way I soon will be. Sylvie, still too anxious to sit down, kept pacing back and forth. When John put his head out of the office, she was upon him.

'Sylvie, are you okay? My nurse said—'

Sylvie put up a hand to stop him from talking and shook her head. She was using all of her control not to cry. It seemed to be the only thing she'd been doing successfully lately. He gestured for her to follow him down the hall.

'I need an EKG,' she told John as they entered his office.

He turned to look at her with concern. 'Are you having chest pains? Is this an emergency?'

'Yes. I need an emergency face-lift. And liposuction.'

'A face-lift? Why?' He took her hand. 'Sylvie, what's wrong?'

'Everything. Bob's cheating on me. And I saw her. She looks just like me, but younger. Just like me, but no crow's-feet. Just like me, but without the second chin.'

John sat down heavily in his desk chair and steepled his fingers. 'I'm very sorry, Sylvie.'

Sylvie nodded. 'I'm not even going to ask if you knew about how Bob was spending his free time. You're too good a friend to both of us to have to take sides.' She crumpled into the chair facing John and allowed one tear to slide out of her eye. John got up from his desk, moved to Sylvie, and was about to take her into his arms when she felt him hesitate, just for a second. Sylvie knew about John's deep feelings for her, and it was a comfort. John may have wanted to put his arms around her, but he only touched her in a doctorly way. Now his arms could have been a bulwark against her sexlessness.

'Age just crept up on me, John. I wasn't watching. I didn't know I looked so bad—'

'Are you insane? You need a psychiatrist, not a plastic

surgeon. Are you blaming yourself for Bob's behavior? You are an attractive, vital woman—'

'Last time I was here you told me I had to lose ten pounds,' Sylvie interrupted.

'Well, I didn't *see* it, I was just going by the charts,' John protested. 'To me, you'll always be my prom date. Hey, I'm still upset you didn't accept my proposal.'

Sylvie walked to the window and looked out on the quiet street. 'I couldn't. You were science. Bob was music, and I wanted to play. I thought Bob and I would play together.' She paused. 'We didn't. What happened?' She moved back to John, put her head on his shoulder, and began to cry again. He held her.

'Sylvie, let me speak to you as a medical professional. Occasionally men behave like assholes.'

'You don't.'

'Oh, yes. Even me. Since Nora died, I've thought of every compliment I didn't give her. Sometimes men forget the important things.'

'Oh, John. I'm so sorry for you . . . and Nora.'

'We're talking about you, now. Sylvie, it's not about *you*. It's about Bob. I see this all the time. Forget surgery. A woman suffers a blow to her ego, gets insecure. You're thinking if you looked younger, if you changed your looks . . . but it's not about looks.'

Sylvie had stopped listening. She gestured wildly with her hand. 'You don't understand. This is not the normal situation. She looks *exactly* like me, John. It *is* about looks. About youth. About mortality.'

'No. No . . .'

'You don't understand . . . I could *be* her. She could be me. We could switch—'

110

'Sylvie, most men think they want the comfort of a wife and the excitement of an affair. It's the human condition, the pull between safety and the unknown, but in the end . . .'

But Sylvie still wasn't listening. Her brain was, at last, moving with lightning speed. Realization dawned on Sylvie. '. . . and neither one of us is happy. She wants a marriage. I want . . . romance.'

'. . . no one can have it both ways.'

The blurred image of Marla and herself flashed in Sylvie's mind. How they had stared into the quince-filmed mirror, identical. 'You don't understand,' she repeated. 'I could *be* her. I *could* be her. *I* could be *her*,' Sylvie kept repeating like an actress rehearsing her lines.

12

Sylvie slept — well, she'd pretended to sleep — on the narrowest sliver of the edge of the bed, her back turned to the vast empty space behind her. Eventually — it must have been past midnight — Bob had returned and slipped quietly in beside her. It had been dreadful for her to feel his body lying there, even though he wasn't touching her. Her back felt as if it were a kind of tingling radar; she could feel his slightest movements and kept herself as far away as possible. She'd pushed herself ever closer to the bed edge. She couldn't help having these feelings even though he was late because tonight he actually *did* have his damn Masons' meeting. But the tension in her body was unbearable. If Bob had actually reached out and touched her, she would probably have screamed and begun slapping him. But instead he had fallen into a loud, breathy coma while she lay there awake most of the night.

Each time she did close her eyes her dreams were vivid — and violent. A piece of paper wrinkling, then catching fire and burning down her beloved house. She woke in a sweat, only to sleep and dream again. This time something about that girl moving into her house and Sylvie outside, in the street, peering in the window. They had traded places, or at least that woman had taken hers. Awake, her thoughts would circle and circle among the facts and her options.

And then, like a tremor that started in her head and moved through her whole body, it came to her. The idea that had been lurking just beyond her consciousness sprang clearly into her mind. Sylvie actually thought the bed shook, but it was only her brain moving. Why *not* change places? Sylvie didn't want Marla to replace her – she wanted to take Marla's! Was it possible? People had already mistaken them for one another from a distance. And their smeared images in the mirror were identical. Could it be possible? Last year Bob had finally given in and gotten reading glasses. How misty was his vision up close? And then it had come to her – the culmination of not only Bob's reality, but the advice from her mother and John's view. It had all meshed in a daring, creative way. But, hey, Sylvie told herself, I *am* capable of being daring and creative.

Excited by the plan she'd begun incubating, Sylvie got out of bed and paced the downstairs hall, sipping cup after cup of tea, until she'd thought it all out very carefully. It was wild and complicated and maybe impossible and crazy. But, if she could pull it off, she'd have everything she wanted.

With a little bit of surgery – not much – and the loss of a few pounds (which she'd been meaning to lose anyway), and the lightening of her hair, plus the addition of a lot of what was probably herb-based makeup, Sylvie figured she could take Marla's place. Then she'd not just catch Bob in the act of cheating on her, but she could also make a fool of him, just as he had of her. And, if she chose to, she could let Bob make love to her the way he once had. Be wooed. Romanced. Or she could let him lust and then turn him down flat. Let *him* feel the rejection she now felt.

Of course, to make it happen she'd need some luck, some surgery, and the complete cooperation of the woman she'd begun thinking of as Marla Molensky, N.A.D. (New Age Ditz). But the more Sylvie thought about it, the more she felt the plan was doable. After all, the N.A.D. wanted to be a wife. Let her try it. It made Sylvie think of one of those World War II films her dad always watched where someone like Gregory Peck would have to go behind enemy lines and impersonate the Nazi general because of a coincidental resemblance; then you'd see army intelligence tutoring Peck in German, giving him a dueling scar, and briefing him on all the general's personal habits. Last, they'd tailor a perfect uniform and send Peck off on a mission that was almost impossible.

But he always pulled it off. So why couldn't she? She could learn to speak New Age. Certainly Marla could learn to cook some chicken and be ignored. It would be Twainish – the prince and the pauper – but at this particular moment Sylvie couldn't figure out which of them was which.

The more she thought about it, the more excited she became. The obstacle would be to convince Marla. But Marla was dying to play a wife. She could be persuaded to start with a dress rehearsal. Might as well try, Sylvie thought. I have nothing to lose: if Bob found them out he might be furious at Sylvie's deception but he'd be shamed by his own. At the same time, there was a chance he might look at Marla's complicity as a complete betrayal. Sylvie smiled. That in itself wouldn't be such a bad thing. Sylvie didn't know if she could save her marriage, or if she wanted to, but she was certain that she wanted to break up this little affair. If she forgave Bob now, she'd still be just the wife – the reliable, comfortable, taken-for-granted wife. And she knew her mother was right in one respect – she didn't want Marla Molensky to ever really become the new Mrs Bob Schiffer. Sylvie knew how the water closed over a divorcée's head in Shaker Heights. But worse, her pride couldn't take knowing that she was replaceable, a human lightbulb that was once screwed in but was now screwed out.

Sylvie put down her last cup of tea and got dressed at daybreak, left a note for Bob, and drove through the quiet streets of Shaker Heights. The leaves were at their peak. It was beautiful here in the pink light of dawn. She loved her hometown. She wanted to stay here, but not as Rosalie had. Sylvie wanted to stay on her own terms.

So all she had to do was convince Marla to fall in line. Sylvie knew she'd have to be a little bit duplicitous, but she was capable of it, especially in the face of the duplicity she had just experienced. What she needed to convince Marla was an incentive. Despite her mother's suggestion, she knew money wouldn't work — but she thought she *did* have a way to motivate the girl.

Sylvie drove across the North Woodland Bridge, found a strip mall with a deli that was just opening and had a cup of coffee. She almost bought a glazed doughnut, until she realized there would be none of those until this plan was completed. While she drank her coffee, she stared out the deli window at the water. To her it wasn't Shaker Lakes. She felt as if she had crossed the Rubicon. She got back in her car, fortified by the caffeine, and drove — for the second time — up to 1411 Green Bay Road.

'I have a proposition for you. May I come in?'

'I don't think so. For some reason, we upset each other,' the bimbette said.

'I upset you?' Sylvie asked, as coolly as she could. 'I can't imagine why.'

The sarcasm was lost on blondie. 'Do you have Scorpio rising, by any chance?' Marla inquired nervously.

115

'I haven't a clue, but I promise I'll find out,' Sylvie said sweetly. 'And if you let me in, I promise you'll like what I have to tell you.' Slowly, Marla opened the door and let her in. The girl was gullible.

Sylvie had to explain her idea twice. Maybe it was the early hour, but this girl wouldn't ever win a MacArthur grant.

'That would be *in*-sane,' Marla said once she got it, still wincing in the morning light. She had come to the door in a nylon baby doll nightgown, rubbing the sleep from her eyes, and though Sylvie had brought out two paper cups of coffee and offered one to Marla, she'd refused it. She simply lay down on her sofa, listening and yawning and stretching like a cat. Sylvie had explained everything breathlessly — twice — and was now reduced to standing over Marla, waiting for her to think things out. '*In*-sane,' Marla repeated.

'Think of it as a temporary career change,' Sylvie suggested. 'You wouldn't have to fly the overly friendly skies.'

'Fly?' Marla asked, awake for the first time. 'Oh. Fly. Well, actually, I don't.'

Sylvie paused. 'Didn't you say you were a flight attendant?'

'No. Well, yes. I said it. I mean, I *was* a stewardess. Almost. I got hired and I started stewardess school but . . . anyway, it didn't work out. And my work now is *much* more important.' She tossed her head.

Sylvie marveled at the freshness of her skin, the gloss of her hair, the lies on her lips. Who was this girl? She was fascinating to observe. Sylvie felt as if she were watching an old video of herself. Had only a dozen years robbed her of so much? 'So, what is it that you do? I mean, professionally,' she asked.

Marla sat up, smoothed down the cheap lace of her nightie,

and said, 'I'm a state-licensed professional reflexologist. It's very therapeutic. I'm not defensive about it.' She said it defensively.

'That toe massage stuff?' Sylvie asked. Well, *that* explained the new condition of Bob's feet. Sylvie tried to imagine what it would be like rubbing strangers' insteps all day long. God! Worse than oral hygiene. She felt a little nauseated, but it could have been due to her empty stomach, the coffee, and the lack of sleep.

'You know, the sole is the window to the soul. And I think I have the gift of healing.'

'No puns intended?' Sylvie asked.

'What puns?' Marla responded blankly.

Sylvie, tired of standing or pacing, realized this was going to take some time. Marla seemed to be short on furniture — just the sofa in the living room — so Sylvie fetched a folding chair from the card table in the kitchenette and brought it back, pulling it close to the couch. 'Listen, Marla, think of it as a job change. A promotion. If we change places for a little while, we'd both be happier in our new jobs with Bob. You could see what it's like to be drowning in security . . . and you could learn how to be a good wife. It will help you get a good husband. I'd teach you. Meanwhile I could feel what it's like to have good sex with the man I usually only sleep with.' Sylvie held her breath. The girl hadn't said no. Would she say yes?

'Won't he know that we switcherooed on him? I mean, like, right away?' Marla asked.

'He hardly looks at *me*,' Sylvie admitted bitterly.

Marla considered. 'Truthfully, I think he's embarrassed to look me in the eye . . . eyes. Is it eye or eyes?' she asked. 'I never know. Because you really can't look in both at once.

117

Except for my cousin Dean, my mama's sister's youngest. Him and Sharleen live in Montana now, or maybe Wyoming. Anyway, he had a lazy eye and when he looked at you each of his eyes looked in a different direction. So he could look you in your eyes.'

Sylvie ignored her. It was that or go mad. And Bob *liked* this? 'Look,' she said, 'here's my offer: we change houses, lives, clothes, everything. Just for a while. Say, two weeks.'

'Well, maybe not our clothes. Ya know,' Marla said, squinting at Sylvie, 'I don't think you're an autumn at all.'

'An autumn?' Sylvie asked, her heart sinking. Was the little witch making a reference to her age?

'Yeah. I don't think you're an autumn, so those colors you're wearing are all wrong for you. Even with the mousy hair. I mean, no wonder Bob would . . . you know.' Marla shrugged apologetically. 'You're, like, wearing the wrong season. Which would completely confuse your aura.'

Was there any con this girl hadn't fallen for? Sylvie wondered. 'Are you talking about that color-me-beautiful nonsense everyone was doing years ago?' she asked. Rosalie had tried that as a career after Mary Kaye didn't pan out.

'Oh, it's not nonsense,' Marla Molensky protested. 'I mean, it's really sophisticated. But there's a lot of practitioners who don't know what they're doing, I'll grant you that. I mean, I have a girlfriend who had her colors done by this woman. And she was told she was a spring. So Lynette went out and got all these new clothes. She spared no expense. I know for a fact she went way over her Ann Taylor limit. And then, right after that, her dog ran away.' She paused. 'Animals know more than we think they do.'

'Marla,' Sylvie said gently, 'dogs are color-blind.'

'Oh, are they? Well, maybe. But they're *very* sensitive to

auras. Anyway, Lynette finds out that she *isn't* a spring. Just because she'd dyed her hair and eyebrows, it didn't make her a spring. She was a winter all the time, even with the highlighting. So, you see you have to be really, really careful.'

'Well, I agree with that,' Sylvie said, trying to have the gravity necessary to land the girl on this planet. 'We'd have to be really, really careful to pull this off.' Was it a sale? Sylvie didn't know if it was a yes, but it certainly wasn't a no. And this girl was so . . . addled . . . that . . .

'Oooh. I almost forgot.' Marla Molensky shrugged, got up, and went into the tiny kitchen. Sylvie followed her and watched as she began opening bottles and laying out first pairs and then groups and then dozens of pills. When she started to swig them down Sylvie, amazed, couldn't be silent.

'What are you doing?' she asked. Was the girl a drug addict? No wonder she was so addled.

'I'm taking my supplements. Don't you? You know, that's one of the things I feel I've done for Bob.' She took a few more pills and looked hard at Sylvie, obviously frightened again by what she saw in her own future. 'It's *very* important to supplement your diet. But you have to be careful to use only natural supplements. Some of the other stuff could be really bad for you. You know, you want only natural vitamin C.'

'Then why not eat an orange?' Sylvie asked, annoyed.

'Calories, silly. Plus, this is much more concentrated. As long as it's not synthetic.'

'Marla, Linus Pauling took synthetic C.'

Marla put her hands on her hips. 'You think I take my health advice from a *Peanuts* cartoon?' she asked.

Sylvie took a deep breath. 'What I'm saying is that most people don't need any supplements, and there's no difference between them. John, my doctor, says all it does is get washed out by the kidneys. You're making expensive urine.'

'You're mistaken,' Marla said. 'And doctors don't know most things. Western medicine is very backward.' Despite Sylvie's frown she continued. 'No. It's true. I know this girl whose friend – well, he was her lover at the time but now she's back with her husband. Anyway, this guy works at this company. Like a pill company or something. And *she* says that *he* told her they just use all kinds of really bad things in synthetic vitamins.'

'Like what?' Sylvie asked.

'Spider eggs,' Marla said smugly.

'Spider eggs? What for?'

'They use crushed spider eggs to coat the pills and make them slippery, so you can swallow them easily.' Marla gulped down the last of her pills as a demonstration.

'But, Marla,' Sylvie said in her most reasonable tone, 'where would you find enough spider eggs to coat thousands of vitamin pills? And, anyway, aren't spider eggs natural?'

'Well, they're natural, but they're icky. Plus, they probably have, like, spider egg farms. Forcing them to lay. You know. Like they do with those poor battered chickens.'

'Battery, not battered,' Sylvie corrected, then decided it was best to move back to the real subject. 'I really believe we could fool Bob, if I had the surgery and you . . . didn't talk so much.' She crossed her fingers, keeping her hands in her pocket.

'What if we got caught?'

'So what? He's the guilty one,' Sylvie said, though she neglected to mention Marla's guilt. Well, she had her fingers crossed. 'He lied to both of us. He told you you were one of a kind.'

'That's true,' Marla agreed. 'I mean, it's true he said it, but it wasn't true. We're two of a kind.' She paused, apparently thinking, or whatever passed for it under that Goldie Hawn mane. Sylvie held her breath. Would it be this easy? 'Say, hey! What's in it for me? You love the man and you get to be hot and sweaty with him, while I get the chance to just *pretend* I'm his wife. Where's the security in that? Seems to me I'm, like, just left with this condo.'

'He bought this for you?' Sylvie asked, shocked breathless. The car was one thing but . . .

'No. It's just a sublet, like my whole life,' Marla admitted. She put away her vitamins, walked back to the living room, and collapsed onto her sofa. She pulled her knees up under her chin, and Sylvie couldn't help but notice that her bikini underpants matched her baby dolls. 'I'm twenty-nine years old. Since seventh grade, all I've ever wanted to do was get married. My friends are already having babies.' Marla had begun panting with anxiety. 'Why are you doing this to me? Just when I finally found a really, really nice man. I want to marry him. I want a detached house and kids. I want people to love.' Marla began to sniffle. 'The holidays are coming up. I'm not sure I can get through them all alone.'

Sylvie took a deep breath, thinking fast. She patted Marla's hand. 'You switch places with me and you get to have a family for Thanksgiving. Make the dinner. Have guests. Be the hostess of a big house. Practice. You won't be alone this holiday.'

Marla sat up. 'Wow! I could do the whole thing? Set the table? Have place mats? Wear a Pilgrim hat?'

'Oh, yeah. *And* cook the meal. Soup to nuts, and we'll have plenty at *that* table.'

Marla paused, considering it. Sylvie's crossed fingers ached.

Then, 'You're headed in the right direction, but no,' the girl said.

'Please,' Sylvie begged, then got a grip. 'Let me ask you a question. Do you want to get married to a man like Bob?'

'That's *all* I want.'

'But you don't know what it's *like* to be married to a man like Bob, do you?' She paused and let that sink in. 'I am going to give you the opportunity to see what it's like to be married to Bobby. And, if you like it, and can do it . . . who knows?'

'What? I can have him? That's a little *too* nice, isn't it?' Marla asked suspiciously.

'No. Because I want something from you.' Sylvie paused to muster the strength and courage to continue. 'In exchange for my kindness, I ask that you let me experience what it's like being Bob's little piece of fluff on the side. You can live in my house. You can sit at my table, and you can sleep in my bed, but you can't make love to Bob. That's the deal. Then we renegotiate.'

Marla looked Sylvie up and down again. 'Do you really think you have it in you to make him happy in bed?'

'Who the hell do you think taught him foreplay?' Sylvie asked, her voice getting edgy.

'Sorry. And thank you. He's very thoughtful.'

Sylvie took a deep breath to calm herself. 'Look. I'm suggesting we each, for lack of a better term, test-drive Bob by switching places for a couple of weeks.' Marla didn't say a word, only shifted her position on the sofa. God, her body was perfect. Sylvie tried to remember if she'd looked that good. She thought she had, but she hadn't appreciated it then. 'Listen carefully,' Sylvie told her. 'I tell Bob I'm visiting my sister and having a little plastic surgery. You make up some other excuse. Then we both go away for a few weeks. Together. My treat.'

Marla squinted. 'You're not a lesbian, are you?'

Sylvie rolled her eyes at Marla. The girl shoved herself back in the corner of the couch, as if to protect herself from Sylvie. 'Okay! Just asking.' She stared at the ceiling. 'Well, maybe. But . . . but I wouldn't know how to run a big house. Is there zoned heat? I've never had zoned heat. And I can't iron. I don't know what he likes to eat. Or how to make it. Or, or, anything.'

'Exactly my point. As part of this exchange program I give you a crash course in "Bob: The Husband." And *you*'re going to teach me to be seductive and dependent.'

'That's easy!' Marla cried.

'Great! So, we go someplace where I have everything lifted that needs to be lifted, lose some weight, and blonde up,' Sylvie said. She uncrossed her cramping fingers. Victory! 'Meanwhile, you . . . make yourself look like me. So it's a deal? Move into my detached house for a little while? Really see what married life to Bob is like? And, maybe, win the jackpot. Or the bobby prize.'

Marla seemed to back off. 'I don't know,' she said. 'Maybe it's better if I just steal him slowly.' Marla held up her thumb and forefinger, only an inch apart. 'Mrs Schiffer, I'm this close to getting your husband all on my own. Why would I take a risk? And what if you mess up here, in *my* life? I have a reputation, you know.'

'I'm sure you do,' Sylvie said, but the sarcasm was lost on Marla. 'Look, I won't mess up. I'll learn reflexology. I'll do everything you do. I'll even take supplements. My heart is really in this.' Sylvie crossed her fingers again. 'Come on. Just for a couple of weeks. It'll be fun. Remember, there's Thanksgiving.'

'You have bone china? Place settings that match?'

'Miss Molensky, my home has twelve legitimate dining chairs.'

It was the final inducement for a woman who had no chairs
that didn't fold, not to mention no dining room. 'Wow! All
right,' Marla said, 'I'll do it.' The two women shook hands,
closing the deal.

Sylvie was upstairs packing again but this time all alone,
organized and with a mission. When Bob walked in with the
mail she looked up calmly and managed to smile. She was
afraid that what felt like a grimace on her face might frighten
him, but it was the best she could do. Typical. He didn't seem
to notice. She comforted herself with the knowledge that his
lack of observation would help her plan. She had their next
dialogue all scripted. Sylvie tried her best to keep her voice
normal. 'Hello,' she said, but to her own ears even the single
word sounded like a rebuke. Not to Bob's though.

'Hi, kiddo.' He threw himself onto the chaise by the
window and thumbed through the new *Sports Illustrated*. 'I
missed you this morning.'

'I decided to go back to those early morning yoga classes.'

'Hey, that reminds me. Do we have any more of that
frozen yogurt? The low-fat kind?'

Why did men think their wives had a total mental inventory
at all times of all foodstuffs available? 'Did you look in the
freezer?' Sylvie asked, overly patient. Where else would
frozen yogurt be?

'No,' Bob admitted cheerfully. 'I thought you'd be in the
kitchen when I came home.'

'Really? Why?' Sylvie continued with her packing, stowing
her shampoo and conditioner in a sealed plastic bag. Bob
hadn't even noticed what she was doing. He was engrossed

in the magazine. Sylvie wondered if she left right now how long it would take him to realize she was gone? Five minutes? An hour? Two weeks? Probably not until he ran out of clean underwear, she thought bitterly.

He was engrossed in the magazine. 'It's just that you're always in the kitchen when I come home,' Bob finally responded.

'So this is one of life's little surprises,' Sylvie told him, finishing her packing and snapping her bag closed. 'Any surprises in the mail? Have we won a romantic trip for two to Mexico?' Sylvie almost bit her tongue. Watch yourself, she mentally advised.

Bob didn't rise to the bait. 'Nothing from the kids. They call?' Clearly, he was on automatic.

'Kenny did. He said if I paid for half of his new bass, he'd pay for the other half. I sent him a check.'

Bob finally did look up. 'I got the same call! So I sent him one too. The kid's got himself a free guitar!' Bob shook his head, then laughed. 'He'd make a hell of a car salesman.' He turned back to *Sports Illustrated*.

'We can only pray,' Sylvie said. 'Anyway, you'll have to straighten him out on this double-dipping while I'm away.'

Bob glanced up again from the magazine. He saw the packed valise for the first time. 'You going somewhere?'

'Perhaps you hadn't noticed. In four words, I'm packing a suitcase.'

'I thought you were just re-rolling socks or something.' He stopped, an expression of slight dismay on his face, and looked down at his feet, comfortably propped up on the end of the chaise. 'You know, I didn't notice this morning until I got to work, but I wore mismatched socks all day long. One black, one blue. It seemed to make me limp.'

'Really?' Sylvie deadpanned. He was taking her departure hard.

'Yes. My black foot was heavier than my blue one,' Bob said. He peeled off both socks and dropped them on the floor. Sylvie caught a glimpse of his renovated toenails and turned away before she was arrested for violence with a valise.

'As much as I love a good sock re-roll,' she said, 'my sister is getting a chemical peel and she needs me.'

'Your sister? Ellen? What's a peel?'

'Something I, apparently, haven't had enough of,' Sylvie muttered and slammed the suitcase shut. If only his toes were caught there. Watch it, she told herself. Don't ruin this before it gets started. 'Huh?' Bob said, or something like that. She looked at her husband with a falsely bright smile.

'Nothing. Anyway, a peel is sort of like refinishing an antique car – first you coat it with some chemical that pops off its top layer of paint, then you sand it down gently and hope it looks better.' She paused. 'The point is, Ellen needs me to be there for her. Just until the scabs fall off.' Sylvie looked in the mirror. 'Maybe I'll have something done,' she said casually. 'Since I'm there anyway.'

Bob got up from the chaise and patted her back. It took all of Sylvie's willpower not to dislocate her shoulder pulling it out from under his hand. 'You don't need anything done,' he said. 'You look great.' Then he started off to the bathroom, his face back in *Sports Illustrated*.

'Oh, really?' Sylvie asked, her voice intense. 'I guess you haven't noticed that gravity has visited this house.'

She indicated the mirror over his bureau. Bob looked into it. Sylvie joined him. She stared at their reflections and thought of how she and Marla had stood, side by side, staring into the glass in just that way. Bob looked

126

now too, but only at himself. 'Jowls,' Sylvie said with satisfaction.

'Look at that.' His voice had wonder in it.

'Yes. Look at that. Both of us hang a little lower. Young people must look at us and turn away in disgust.' She smirked.

Bob touched his chin, his eyes scanning his own reflection. It was clear to her that he was more concerned about his own looks than about hers. Good. It would give him something to think about while she was gone.

'Well, I have to go,' she said, sounding cheerful, to herself, for the first time that evening. 'I don't want to be late for the dermabrasion.' Bob continued to study his face, tapping, right under his chin, the little weakened spot that sagged à la Michael Douglas. 'I hate to have to leave you alone,' Sylvie cooed. 'Promise me you won't stay home every night.'

'I'll find something to do,' Bob said, his voice distant with distraction.

Sylvie tried not to sneer. She knew what he *thought* he was going to be doing, but he'd have a surprise coming. 'Maybe you could hang out with John or Phil.'

'Give me a break,' Bob said. 'From the sublime to the ridiculous.'

'Well, then you'll just have to find yourself a new girl-friend,' Sylvie forced herself to laugh.

Bob gave her a look that seemed, well, nervous, but it lasted for only an instant. 'Me?' he asked. 'Who would want me?' Sylvie shrugged. Bob turned back to the mirror. Sylvie nearly laughed. Then she picked up her bag. While he still stared into the mirror she called, over her shoulder, 'I'll be home for Thanksgiving.'

She walked out of the bedroom knowing, if all went well,

that it would be Marla who returned. Sylvie was already going down the stairs by the time Bob scuttled out behind her. 'Well, call me when you get there,' he said. He put his hand on her shoulder as she descended the staircase. 'It'll be nice having the kids back, the whole family together.'

Sylvie couldn't help it. She was safely in front of him on the stairs, and he couldn't see the tear that slid out from her eye as she descended to the bottom of the steps.

Marla was throwing some underpants and a pair of Lycra bicycle shorts into a duffel bag when she heard the knock at the door. She quickly kicked the bag under the bed. She went into the living room, checked through the peephole, and opened the door. Bob stood there, a big grin on his face and a bottle of champagne in his hand, just as if he didn't have a nice wife to go home to. Marla was a bit stiff when he took her into his arms.

'Guess what?' Bob asked as he moved her into the living room, closing the door behind him. Marla had noticed that he didn't like to be seen outside with her. 'My wife is leaving town for a couple of weeks. And you know what that means?' he yodeled, then nuzzled her neck.

'That she's on to us?' Marla asked.

'No, no.' He kissed her tenderly. Marla held her lips firm. 'She's going to visit her sister. But for us it means I don't have to run home at night.' He fetched two juice glasses – all she had – from the kitchenette. 'You know how you always ask me to stay over? Well . . . I'm yours.'

How come she'd never noticed before that he was . . . arrogant. *She* was always doing the waiting, *he* was always giving her his valuable time. But now she smiled. 'Wow!' Marla said. 'You're kidding! Boy, Venus must be in retrograde, because I have to leave town too.'

'What?' Bob asked. He'd been playing with the cork of the champagne bottle and at that moment it popped. The bubbly erupted all over his hands.

'Momma just called to say Grammie's got the cramp again. It's the damp from the river that runs right by the Home. Shouldn't have built a home for the aged in Lowood, I said. Anyway, I've got to go rub her.'

Bob's face dropped. Marla tried to keep hers serious. It was hard to do since her grammie actually lived in Vegas where she worked in a casino as floor security. She watched Bob as he stood there, his dripping bottle of champagne in his hands. 'When will you be back?' he asked, sounding like a boy.

Marla shrugged. 'As soon as Grammie feels better. Probably no time at all. But I *do* have to leave right away. Like, tonight.'

'Tonight? You're kidding!' Bob tried to grin. He put his arm around her. 'Come on. You don't want to waste Dom Perignon, do you? And maybe we have time for a quickie.'

'Oh no,' Marla said, already high on newfound power. 'I never drink and drive.'

13

Sylvie woke up choking and realized two things: she hadn't died under the knife and she was in a stark white recovery room. The surgery was over, then. But something, not the bandages wrapped around her head, not the cold compress on her eyes was . . . smelling. Was . . . worse. It was stinking. Was she infected already? Had her face turned into oozing pus?

Panicked, Sylvie pulled the wet compress off her eyes. Marla's lineless face was directly over hers. 'Well, hi!' she said cheerfully. 'Looking bad. Feeling good?' She didn't wait for Sylvie to answer. 'Wow! You look like my sister Brianna after she had one of her, uh, "little discussions" with Tony. But it's okay. She's got a restraining order now.' Sylvie noticed that Marla was wafting a bandage or some sort of gauze pad around her face. That was the thing that smelled like . . .

'What are you doing?' Sylvie croaked.

'Aromatherapy,' Marla told her. 'Herbal oils to promote healing.'

'God. Get it away! It smells like rotting bananas and something – dead,' Sylvie gasped. 'I think I'm gonna be sick.' She managed to sit up and grab a basin in time, just before she vomited into it. She hoped she wasn't breaking any stitches. She patted her eyes, then her swollen cheeks. Her face didn't actually hurt; it felt numb. She lifted her head up from the nastiness in the bowl.

'Great!' Marla said, as cheerful as a bigot at a Klan convention. 'It's working. You're expelling toxins and poisons already.'

Sylvie wiped her mouth on the cold compress and wondered if she had enough strength simply to strangle her rival. 'Marla, get rid of that rag right now,' she said weakly. Was the girl trying to be helpful or trying to murder her? It was hard to tell.

'Hey! I used this when my mother had her second hysterectomy,' Marla said, sounding hurt. 'It made *all* the difference.'

'Her *second* hysterectomy?' Sylvie asked weakly, falling back against the pillow. She handed the basin to Marla. 'Who needs two?'

'*Exactly*. If she'd used aromatherapy the first time, she wouldn't have needed a second one. That, plus if she hadn't gone to that Filipino doctor. He said he could do the first operation without a scalpel. Come on! You know, just between us, I think my mother's still vain about her body, and she's already forty-seven, bless her heart.' Marla stopped, just before Sylvie was going to try to kill her, and rang for the nurse. 'Personally, I think vanity in old people is very self-affirming.'

Sylvie looked at Marla Molensky through the slits of her eyes. She wondered if the girl sometimes knew what she seemed to be doing so unconsciously. And it seemed as if she lied – a lot. 'What mother? I thought you said your mother abandoned you in Santa's lap.'

'Oh,' Marla said. Her face registered fear for only a moment. She seemed to be regrouping mentally. 'Well, she *did*. For a while. But then she did come back. Meanwhile, Santa asked if he could meet me later, so she reported him to security.'

'I'm confused,' Sylvie said, feeling dizzy.

'Think how I felt!' Marla agreed. 'Listen, you look really pale. Maybe you better rest. Oh! Here comes the nurse.'

A woman in green scrubs had entered the room, holding more cold compresses on a tray. 'What *is* that stench?' the nurse asked. She looked at Sylvie as if she were guilty. 'Your daughter better leave the room while I clean you up a little,' the nurse said. Sylvie groaned. Marla, lucky for her, vanished somewhere beyond the whiteness of Sylvie's bandaged head.

Sylvie was sitting in an examining chair. Marla was pacing the room while Dr Hinkle was cutting off the now stiff bandages. 'I don't want you to be disappointed. It's going to take time for the swelling to go down,' Dr Hinkle explained.

'She didn't use enough ice packs. I warned her,' Marla interjected.

'It's going to take a while for the discoloration to go away,' the doctor told Sylvie, ignoring Marla. 'Remember, what you're going to see today is not the end product,' he reassured Sylvie. She felt so nervous that she almost wished to put off this moment, though she'd spent three days waiting for it.

'Will it gross me out?' Marla asked. 'Because I can't even stand to see a little birdie hurt. You can imagine what big old bloody face stitches would do to me.'

'Your little sister is *very* supportive,' Dr Hinkle said dryly as he removed the last bandage. He gently touched Sylvie's cheek, then examined the incisions behind both ears. He surveyed her face for a few moments while Sylvie held her breath. 'You did very well,' Dr Hinkle said, nodding. 'Not much swelling.'

'He's lying! Get your money back,' Marla told Sylvie. 'You look like a side of raw beef.'

The doctor held up a mirror, but Sylvie turned her head. 'I don't want to look if it's that bad,' she whispered, ducking away.

'Sibling rivalry can affect recovery,' the doctor said. 'Maybe your sister should go home. Anyway, it's not that bad. I do great work. I completely re-did each of my wives.'

In two more days the swelling on Sylvie's face had gone down considerably. The bruises had already lightened from purple to blue. She was up and walking around, though she felt a little self-conscious at first, her head swathed in a sort of Eskimo parka hood, all white gauze. But there were a lot of women at the spa who were wearing worse, including protective cones. A few women also had plastic protectors over their noses, indicating rhinoplasty, and some – whose faces looked just fine – walked with the telltale stiffness that bruises after liposuction caused. So Sylvie fit right in.

She also found there was an unexpected bonus to the operation – she'd lost her appetite since anesthesia. She'd been living on Jell-O and consommé, and she'd already dropped four pounds.

While Sylvie had thus far been recuperating, she and Marla had started what Sylvie thought of as 'the counterintelligence program' to ensure the success of the switcheroo. They'd begun by giving one another general notes about their lives; friends, bureau contents, brand of tampon they used. Now they sat in the bedroom they shared, the sliding glass doors open to the cool air. Outside, fat women in sweatpants were running (or trying to) behind a lithe young female drill sergeant. Ugh! Next week Sylvie would have to start that regimen. She might as well enjoy relaxing now, while she could. She was propped up in bed while Marla sat in a chair beside her, a notepad in her lap, a pink pen with a heart on it in her hand. Sylvie couldn't help but notice that Marla had the awkward handwriting of a fourth-grader. To her own surprise, Sylvie had actually come to like the girl during this week. She was flighty, but there was a sweetness to her that Sylvie – despite herself – responded to. 'Okay,' she said now. 'Bob likes all the hangers in his closet going the same way.'

'Is that because he was in the army?' Marla asked.

'No. It's because he's anal retentive.'

'I thought we weren't going to talk about sex yet,' Marla said, and before Sylvie could respond there was a knock at the door. Marla got up and went to open it. Sylvie was surprised to see her mother standing there.

'Oh my god! Sylvie? . . . What did that doctor do to you?' Mildred cried out to Marla. She put both hands up to her own face. 'I wonder if he could do it to me?' she added. Before Marla could answer, Mildred, in a state of shock, grabbed the hallway service cart for support. None was forthcoming; it merely rolled away. Mildred tried to steady herself, but the cart kept moving and Mildred slowly slid past the door, from vertical to horizontal. From her bed Sylvie yelled out to her mother.

'Mom, are you okay?'

Mildred pulled herself up off the floor and entered the room. She was hypnotized by Marla's face and hadn't taken her eyes off it, even when she had been lowered to the hallway carpet. 'No problem,' Mildred told Marla, her eyes still riveted. 'How do you talk without moving your lips? And who did your eyes?'

'God,' Marla said.

'Dr Hinkle,' Sylvie answered at the same time.

At the sound of Sylvie's voice, Mildred looked away from Marla. 'Oh my goodness!' she said as she finally realized there were two of them. She looked from face to face as her own face turned pallid. Then she sank onto the chair Marla had just vacated, sitting on both Marla's notebook and her heart-shaped pen. Sylvie winced, but Mildred didn't seem to feel anything. Sylvie remembered her own shock when she'd first seen Marla and tried to help her mother get over it. 'Mom, what are you doing here?' Sylvie asked gently.

It took Mildred a few moments of silence to sort things out. She stared at her bandaged daughter. Then she stared at Marla. 'Oh my god!' she said, realization dawning. 'She's the bookkeeper—'

'Yes, Mom. This is Bob's squeeze.'

'But, but . . . how? Are we talking Stepford wives here? Is this a clone? I didn't know they'd moved up from sheep.'

'How did you find me?' Sylvie wanted to know.

'Bob told me that cock-and-bull story about Ellen and an emergency skin peel. Come on! Only a son-in-law would buy it. So I called your sister. By the way, she told me she'd cover for you with Bob and wanted to know how you enjoyed being forty. Anyway, I got your car serial number, looked up your theft locator, and used Bob's computer to find you.' Mildred stared at Sylvie, stared at Marla, and then looked back at her daughter. 'I haven't been watching *Murder, She Wrote* all these years for nothing,' she added. Then she looked back at Marla. 'Extraordinary,' she breathed.

Sylvie smiled. Now, at last, her mother would understand. 'Where are my manners? You two haven't even met yet. Marla, this is my mom. Mom, Marla.'

'Your mother named you *Marla?*' Mildred asked and looked back to Sylvie. 'Perfect name for a . . . bookkeeper.'

'Say, hey! I'm not a bookkeeper,' Marla protested. 'I'm a licensed massage therapist, with a specialty in reflexology.'

'Do you mean you rub men professionally?' Mildred asked, her nostrils flaring.

Marla crossed her arms and made a face that passed – on her – for stern. 'Why do people think that massage therapy isn't a totally legitimate medical service?'

Mildred took in the girl, from the tip of her blonde head, past her adorable shorty top, her flat, exposed midriff, down her long legs in tiny shorts, to her pink, pedicured toes, exposed by her high-heeled mules. 'Gee, I can't imagine why,' Mildred said dryly. 'Blind prejudice, I guess.' She shook her head. 'So, your day job is stealing other women's husbands,' Mildred said. 'Good luck with this one. He'll never leave the lot.'

Marla bridled. 'Firstly, I didn't know he was married. Second, I'm not a thief. That thing that happened with the dress at Target was a mistake. I meant to pay for it. And fourth, when I met Bobby, I just didn't know your daughter was such a giver.'

'She *is* a giver,' Mildred agreed. 'Look how she gave all her wrinkles away.' Mildred stared at her daughter's face. 'It's amazing,' she said. 'You *do* look a decade younger. Did it hurt a lot?'

'Not at all,' Sylvie said and smiled.

'Did it cost a lot?'

'Oh, yeah.' Sylvie's smile widened. 'But I charged it. Bob won't get the bill for a month.'

Mildred snorted, looked back at Marla, and returned her eyes to Sylvie's face. 'It is amazing,' she admitted. 'Not just the surgery, but the resemblance. No wonder it unhinged you.' She took her daughter's hand. 'Thank god for your coping skills.'

Sylvie smiled at her mother. Marla smiled at Mildred too, though Mildred paid her no mind. It didn't deter Marla. Kittenish, she sat down on the floor at the foot of what was now Mildred's chair. 'You are *so* lucky to have a mother like Mom,' she said to Sylvie.

Mildred snorted. 'And your mother would be . . . ?'

Marla's pretty face registered that look of pain.

'Framed by the cops,' she said earnestly. 'There's, like, no way she could have embezzled that money. She wasn't even good at math.'

Mildred's eyes opened so wide Sylvie was afraid they'd need Dr Hinkle for reconstruction if they opened any wider. 'Mom, can we take a walk?' Sylvie asked, attempting to get out of bed. Mildred helped her daughter tenderly, despite shaking her head in disapproval. 'I'm supposed to keep my blood circulating,' Sylvie told Mildred. 'No embolisms for this girl.'

'No. Save them for Bob,' Mildred agreed.

Marla jumped up. 'I'll help you,' she offered.

'Why don't you fetch some water for that plant instead?' Mildred suggested to Marla. 'It looks as if it needs it.' She gestured toward the tired corn plant in the corner.

'Oh, I'm not very good with that kind of thing,' Marla admitted, missing Mildred's point. 'I guess I'm just a green dumb.'

'I think my mom wants time with me,' Sylvie said gently.

'Oh. *Oh.* Okay. Sure. I'll just study my notes,' Marla told them, sounding more than a little crushed, and looking at the equally crushed notepad in the seat Mildred had just vacated.

'Sure. I'll review my notes alone so I know where everything of Bobby's—'

'Bob's,' Sylvie corrected.

'Oh. Right. So I know where everything of *Bob's* is, except for those missing cuff links.' She winked at Mildred. 'Mom, can I expect you for Thanksgiving? It's my favorite holiday. And I can't wait to cook for *Bob*.'

'You're letting her do Thanksgiving?' Mildred asked Sylvie, obviously appalled. Sylvie nodded. 'We're *not* coming,' Mildred told Marla emphatically.

Sylvie led Mildred out of the room and into the hall. Women were walking back and forth slowly, some holding onto the grab rails. They *all* had cone heads. As they passed, Sylvie overheard two talking: 'This one was free because he didn't pull enough the first time,' a middle-aged woman was explaining to an older one. 'Hinkle's good that way. He corrects. Last time he didn't take out enough skin to make a wallet.'

'I know what you mean,' the other said. 'I told him "I don't want to look rested, goddamnit, I want to look *young*."'

Mildred, sighing heavily, shook her unencumbered head. 'I don't know what you're up to, but I know it's no good,' Mildred told Sylvie. 'You're scaring me. Why can't you be like your sister, Ellen? She's accepted the fact that she's growing older and never going to have sex again. Just as I have.'

'*You're* scaring *me*, Mom.'

'No. You're scaring me. What is this, Sylvie? I admit, the girl's a dead ringer for you. It's shocking. It . . . it . . . obliterates you. But what are you trying for? A ménage à trois? Because I simply can't condone—'

'Mom, please. I've got everything under control,' Sylvie

said, and then explained the entire plan – how it could work, and if it did how she'd get everything she wanted: Bob making love to her *and* being made a fool of. 'Then I'll be able to dump him,' she said. 'Or maybe I won't; I'll just dump Marla.'

'Sylvie, it was the inside, not the outside, of your head Dr Hinkle should have operated on. Aren't you scared about letting another woman into your home? Into your *bed*? How can you trust her? A shoplifter, the daughter of an embezzler? Have you made her take a blood test? You've lost your mind, and next you'll lose your marriage.'

'I don't have it now. I know it's a family tradition, Mother, but I'm not going to be celibate for the rest of my life.'

'And what if Bob falls in love with her?'

'Love? Don't be ridiculous. He's going to think she's his wife.'

Mildred paused for a minute, blinked, shook her head and then laughed and hugged her daughter.

Sylvie was sitting at the piano in the spa lounge playing 'If They Could See Me Now.' It was one of Lou's favorites, but he played it like a dirge. Marla was supposed to be trying to act the teacher's part. She had her hand under her chin, and kept nodding. She was also keeping time – off the beat – with her foot. Even Lou, depressed and talentless as he was, would notice *that*. Sylvie shook her head. Whatever other talents Marla Molensky had, she was not musical. She knew nothing about classical music, couldn't play any instrument and, apparently, couldn't even sing. Sylvie purposely made a couple of horrendous flats, but Marla kept moving her head as if the music was played perfectly. Finally Sylvie stopped, but not before she banged her fist on the keyboard. 'Marla!

Listen! I told you! You're supposed to interrupt a student when you hear mistakes.'

'I will! As soon as I hear one,' Marla promised cheerfully. Then she dropped her voice. 'I'm not really that good at confrontation, though.'

Sylvie sighed. Well, few of her students seemed to listen to her comments anyway, so she guessed Marla could fake it for a week or two before the holiday.

The two of them were having lunch, or something that passed for it. Sylvie was only being given a protein-rich diet drink while Marla would get a feast. Both had pads and pens next to their plates. They were at one end of a long communal table, simultaneously talking and writing, cross-instructing. Marla, not yet served, watched Sylvie sip her drink, trying to make it last. 'Sylvie, stop! You don't need all that,' Marla said.

Sylvie looked down at the pathetic diet glass, only half empty. 'Marla, I—' but before she could finish, something else had caught Marla's attention.

'Oh my god,' Marla said, pointing to the plate of the woman beside her. 'What are you doing?'

The woman looked down, a guilty expression already on her face, though all Sylvie could see on the dinner tray was the prescribed diet meal: a butterless baked potato, a single small skinless chicken breast, and some shredded cabbage salad that passed for coleslaw. 'I wasn't going to eat the whole potato,' the woman said defensively.

'Oh, you can eat the potato,' Marla told her, 'but you can't eat it with that animal protein. Do you want to kill yourself? Starch and proteins just do *not* combine. Do you know how long they will lie in your stomach and rot?' The woman shook her head. 'You know, in nature, animals eat only one kind of food at a time,' she continued. 'You don't see a cow eating grass and then fruit and then protein, do you?'

By now, the whole table was looking at Marla. 'Are you calling me a cow?' the woman asked, her face flushing with anger. She was a bit bovine, Sylvie noted. 'Who died and made you dietician?' the cow demanded. 'I don't even know why *you're* here.' Several of the other women at the table nodded. 'You're thin enough. In fact, you're perfect. What's your goal? To be anorexic?'

Marla reached her hand down the table and gently took the heavy woman's in hers. 'I'm just trying to help,' she said. 'There are simple rules about food combining that make *all* the difference. You can eat all you want — you just have to be careful not to combine it with the wrong things.'

'And don't you eat at all?' asked a chunky middle-aged brunette. She looked Marla over. 'I'm Brenda Cushman from New York City, and I know about diets.'

'Oh, I eat. I'm just waiting for my tray,' Marla told her.

Sylvie figured she better jump in before there was a revolution. 'Marla, everyone eats protein with a starch. Chicken with rice. Meat and potatoes. Tuna noodle casserole.'

'Well, everyone is wrong. That's why they all look so bad. If you eat protein, you can only combine it with green vegetables. Or you can have fruit with vegetables, but never fruit with protein.' She looked at the rest of the table. 'And remember, ladies,' she reminded them all, 'a tomato is a fruit, not a vegetable.'

The Brenda woman glared at Marla. 'I'm only here because my daughter Angela's getting married and I'm not going to be a fat mother-of-the-bride in front of my ex-husband Morty.' Then she turned to the heavy woman beside her. 'She's a fruit,' muttered the Brenda Something as she motioned toward Marla with her head.

'No, a nut,' added a woman Sylvie had noticed earlier. The poor thing was thin from the waist up but had a huge behind and deeply dimpled thighs.

'Oh, nuts are something you have to be *very* careful with,' Marla said to Dimples.

'Don't I know it,' agreed Sylvie. She could see that revolution was about to erupt. Marla was too young, too slim, too pretty, and too annoying to be popular here. Then, for her to have the nerve to give advice – and such wacky advice at that – was . . . 'Marla, I'm not sure if everyone is interested,' Sylvie warned.

Marla shrugged. 'Well,' she said cheerfully, 'it's their funeral.' She turned to the table at large. 'You're just digging your graves with your teeth.'

The New York woman looked up from her cantaloupe and cottage cheese plate. 'That's an attractive image at lunch,' she snapped.

Marla looked in her direction. 'Oh, no!' she exclaimed. 'You're eating *cheese* with that cantaloupe? Don't you know what we say? Melon: eat it alone or leave it alone.'

'Leave *me* alone,' the woman from New York snapped and very deliberately took a big scoop of her cottage cheese, mixed it with a chunk of melon, and chewed it with her mouth open.

At that moment one of the staff arrived, at last, with Marla's own tray. There, steaming, in front of everyone, were three thick slices of meat loaf, a big portion of macaroni and cheese, and a salad swimming in oil. To top it off, there was also a slice of banana cream pie. Sylvie looked up longingly from her protein-and-wheat-grass-juice. All of the other women stared.

Marla looked down at the plate. She shrugged apologetically. 'Well,' she said, 'I'm here to try and look like her,' and she gestured to Sylvie with her fork before she took her first bite. Then, her mouth full, her face became blissful. 'I never knew you could eat like this,' Marla crooned. 'Being a wife is a wonderful thing.'

Sylvie was having long, fake talons applied to her fingers by someone called a 'nail technician' while Marla, sitting beside her, was getting her own nails clipped, which proved to be a traumatic event for her.

'My hands look awful now,' she moaned. 'Even if I get an engagement ring, I couldn't show it off with these little M&M's at the ends of my fingers.' She stretched out her hands mournfully.

But Sylvie felt as bad, or maybe worse. 'No wonder you can't play the piano,' she exclaimed. 'How could you massage feet or do *anything* with nails like these?' she asked, extending her own hand and staring at her new Anne Rice vampire look.

'It's something you just know from birth,' Marla said smugly. 'And when I hit those acupressure points, believe me, people stand up and take notice.'

'How can they stand up if you're massaging their feet?' Sylvie asked.

'I was speaking metabolically,' Marla told her. Then she stood up herself, with as much dignity as a woman whose name ended with an 'a' could muster. 'And now,' she said, 'I have to go and tinkle.'

They were eating again, if you could call it that. Their meals with the other spa guests were, in Sylvie's opinion, getting dangerous. All the other women, cranky from food deprivation, envied and despised Marla. Some snubbed her openly. And all of them wanted her food, which Marla ate with gusto and speed, though she complained that since she'd been declawed she was having trouble using her fork. Sylvie had finally been taken off the protein drinks and was now being served a tiny salad, a bit of fish, and three small cooked carrots. The group of women at the table invariably talked about food; what they'd like to be serving for Thanksgiving – or wanted to have on their plates right at that moment. Sylvie tried not to listen – their talk made her stomach rumble.

'I'm going to lose four more pounds,' said the chunky woman from New York. 'Then, when I get out of here, I'm going to eat an entire pumpkin pie from the bakery on the way home.'

At the other end of the table a newcomer was giving advice. 'If you put sugar in the stuffing, they'll come back for more,' she counseled the woman next to her.

'They're not fooling me or anyone with that spaghetti squash. If that's pasta, I'm Kate Moss,' the brassy blonde next to Marla was saying to anyone who was listening. Sylvie was amazed at how obsessed they all were with food. Was she? The woman next to Sylvie looked over at her, trying to involve her in the conversation. 'You know what's good for Thanksgiving? Candied yams, but topped off with a pound of whipped cream instead of marshmallows.'

'Really?' Sylvie tried to act surprised. She'd eat a foam cushion if it was topped with whipped cream.

As all of the women were chatting, each of them continued to look at Marla's plate. A few newcomers elbowed one another. Marla was the only one who had tempting food mounded high. And she was eating maniacally while everyone else pushed their carrots around on their plates. She might have food theories but she was eating like a trucker at the last good diner before the turnpike. Marla finally looked up from her feeding frenzy and motioned for the server to come over. 'Can I have more butter?' Marla asked.

'How does she do that and stay so thin?' Dimples, at the end of the table, dared to verbalize, as if she were the spokeswoman for the whole group.

The brassy blonde leaned forward. She had introduced herself, but maybe because Sylvie was lightheaded from hunger or maybe because she wasn't interested, she couldn't remember the woman's name. 'What are *you* in for?' the woman asked Sylvie, as if this were a prison. That must mean my bruises have healed, Sylvie thought, so she gave a noncommittal answer. Then the woman turned to Marla. 'You must be here just to keep your twin sister company,' she said. Enviously, she eyed Marla's plate. 'But if you keep eating for two, you'll be back alone soon enough.'

Sylvie took that in. She'd gone from being mistaken for Marla's mother, to her older sister, to her twin. Marla and Sylvie exchanged a look. Perhaps it made the brassy blonde feel left out, because she raised her voice. 'Hey, I've got a joke for ya,' she blurted, breaking the silence with volume. Sylvie and Marla both looked up at the woman. Heartened, she continued, 'A big millionaire has three girlfriends, all about the same, and he has to decide which one to marry.' Now everyone was listening. She leaned into the table and lowered her voice. 'So he gives each one a million dollars to spend any way she wants. The women don't know it, but this is how he's going to decide which one to marry.' Sylvie and Marla stared at the woman, who went on, 'The first one, she goes out and blows the whole thing shopping. The second one takes it to the bank – she *saves* it. The third one, she invests it and doubles the million. So which one do you think he chooses?'

Sylvie and Marla looked at each other. 'The investor?' Sylvie guessed.

'No, silly,' Marla said with superior wisdom. 'The one with the biggest tits!'

14

Bob didn't remember ever eating this badly — not in college, not at summer camp, not even in the frat house. When, during the last ten days, had he eaten anything green, except for that leftover tuna salad, and he hadn't noticed the mold until he'd bitten into it late last night. Tonight he and John were on their way out to dinner. Bob was driving Beautiful Baby despite John's discomfort in it. John was too tall and gangly for such a small car, but Bob couldn't take any more change — with Sylvie away and Marla out of town he'd had his whole life disrupted.

'So, you want Italian?' John asked.

'Nah. I don't. I had Italian for breakfast.'

'Who has Italian for breakfast?'

'Italians,' Bob told him, grim. 'Look, I'm living on takeout. This morning I had two cold slices of pizza. I'm doing my own laundry. I can't even get my socks to match.'

'All of this because you cheat on your wife.'

'No I don't. Not now.'

John brightened. 'Oh. You broke it off with P and N—'

'Almost.'

'Almost? What does "almost" mean? This is binary. You're on or you're off.'

'Not necessarily,' Bob admitted. 'She's away. You want Chinese?' Bob asked as they drove past Beijing Palace. He paused. 'Nah. Forget that. Since they went from Peking to the new spelling the food's gone downhill.'

John shook his head. 'Fella, you should be more worried about your marriage and less about your diet.'

'Of course I'm worried about my marriage.'

'Which is a marriage you never should have had in the first place. If you had stayed away in our senior year, *I'd* be married to Sylvie now.'

'That would be terrible,' Bob admitted. 'She's been gone for almost two weeks. The house is in an uproar. I miss her.'

'Do you miss her when you're visiting Pink and Naked?'

'I don't think about anything at her place. Thinking is not what she's about.'

'Well, I think it's my turn to step up to the plate,' John said. 'Maybe I can appreciate what you don't. I picture Sylvie lonely at night. She could be spending that time with me.'

Bob looked over at John, his knees pushed up high by the low seats. 'In four words or less, would you tell me if you're trying to steal my wife?' Bob asked him.

'Goddamn right, buddy,' John snapped back. 'And that's only three words. Anyway, it's not stealing. She was mine first.'

They drove in silence for a few moments. 'Hey! How about steak?' Bob asked, swerving in both the conversation and the highway lane. He pulled into the Hungry Heifer restaurant parking lot.

'Marbled fat flesh? You better come in for a cholesterol count this week,' John said as he unfolded himself from the car, a kind of human origami in reverse. John patted Bob's shoulder as they walked toward the restaurant. 'You're *really* living dangerously,' he told his pal.

Bob fell into bed, his stomach distended. He couldn't have

eaten the whole porterhouse. Lying down, he struggled out of his pants, but left his shorts on. He was even too tired to take off his polo shirt. Well, he could sleep in it – if he *could* sleep. He hadn't been sleeping well lately – and couldn't remember the last time he'd slept alone for this long. Not since college, he guessed. And he didn't like it. The whole bedroom – usually a haven – had become uncomfortable. He hadn't made the bed in a week, and the sheets were wrinkled, the blankets pulled into ropes. Piles of his clothes lay, like drifts of dirty snow, around the room. Newspapers and junk mail were taking up both nightstands and there was a lot of other stuff on the floor that he couldn't identify without a closer look. Sylvie would faint if she saw all this. Tomorrow he'd have to get organized, he thought. If he could get through the night. He groaned and turned on his side. He wouldn't be sleeping on his stomach, if he slept at all.

Just as Bob reached to shut the light the phone rang. He put his hand out, but the phone wasn't in its usual place. It took him a minute to find the phone – he had to follow the wire to locate it – almost under the foot of the bed. He got to it by the third ring. Who would be calling him at this hour? It had to be Sylvie. He lifted up the receiver and fell back into bed, relieving the pressure on his stomach by lowering the band of his shorts. 'Hi, honey, I'm home,' he said. And from the other end of the line he was rewarded for his trouble by Sylvie's giggle.

'You are now. I tried to call earlier but you weren't in. Out with a girlfriend?' Sylvie asked.

'Out with your boyfriend,' Bob grumbled. 'John made me take him to the Hungry Heifer and spent the night telling me how perfect you are.'

'Gee, I think I detect two lies in that sentence,' Sylvie

teased. 'John *made* you eat a porterhouse? With your cholesterol levels? I doubt it. And I'll bet he didn't spend more than twenty or thirty minutes talking about me.'

'Right on both counts,' Bob laughed, rubbing his belly with the hand that wasn't holding the receiver. It felt better already. It was good to be understood. 'You got me,' Bob admitted.

'Do I?' Sylvie asked.

Bob stopped for a moment and didn't respond, at least not quickly enough. Sometimes, lately, it seemed as if Sylvie was . . . He'd just let it drop. 'So how's Ellen?'

'Ellen? Oh. Ellen is fine. She's doing great and so am I.'

'I thought you said there was a problem with her scabs,' Bob complained. 'If she's fine, come home.'

'Well, not *quite* yet,' Sylvie said. 'See, it's not just Ellen. I had a little tiny nip and another tiny tuck.'

'You're kidding!' Bob said, almost sitting up until his belly rebelled. 'You didn't need anything. You look great.'

'Well, now we both look great,' Sylvie said. 'But I don't think Ellen's going to make it to our house for Thanksgiving. Hey, did you hear from the kids?'

Before Bob could answer, he heard the call-waiting tone. 'Hold on a second,' he said. 'I have another call.'

'At this hour?' Sylvie asked.

'It's probably one of the kids,' Bob murmured, though he doubted it.

'This late?' Sylvie said, concerned. 'They never call at night unless it's an emergency.'

'Hold on,' Bob told her. He clicked the phone.

'Hi, Cookie Face,' Marla's voice cooed in his ear. 'I snuck out of Grammie's and walked all the way down to the 7-Eleven to call you.'

'Marla.' Bob paused. 'I've missed you. I can't believe your grandmother doesn't have a phone.' Bob felt his upper lip break out in beads of sweat. Sweat, or maybe pure grease from the porterhouse. 'Hold on a minute, babe,' he said. 'I have another call.' He clicked back to Sylvie. 'Sylvie?' he asked. Then, for a horrible moment, it occurred to him that it might still be Marla, but, thank God, Sylvie's voice responded.

'Yes. Was it Reenie? Has she switched her major again? Is everything okay?'

'No. No. I mean, yes. It wasn't Reenie.'

'Was it Kenny? Is he still having trouble with the room-mate?'

'No. It was just one of those sales calls. You know. A veteran who wanted to sell me lightbulbs. Oops, could you hold for a minute?' he asked without giving her time to respond. He had to find out when Marla was returning. But he couldn't put off Sylvie.

'Hello,' he said into the phone tentatively.

'Say, hey! I'm not going to have enough quarters to pay for this,' Marla's voice told him. 'You know I'm too smart to call your house collect.'

'Look, I can't talk now,' Bob told her. 'When are you coming home?' His stomach was really beginning to bother him, and now his forehead and his upper chest were also covered with sweat.

'I walk all the way down here in the dark, where they don't even have streetlights, and you tell me you can't talk? Bobby, have you got another girlfriend?'

'Oh, babe, believe me, one's enough.' Bob realized the tone his voice had taken and tried to lift it. 'You're all any man would ever need. Listen, I have to—'

'If I'm all any man needs, how come you're still with your wife?' Marla asked.

'Hold on a minute,' Bob said and clicked back to Sylvie. 'Hello?' he said and paused. He waited to hear whether Sylvie would respond. Sometimes the button on the phone didn't work and you had the same person on you'd had on before you clicked. It would be bad to call Marla 'Sylvie,' but it would be fatal to call his wife by another name. As fatal as this porterhouse which, at the moment, seemed to be sitting not only in his belly but on his aorta.

'Bob? Who *was* that?' Sylvie asked.

'Oh, it was the damn veteran again. He had to tell me how he was in a wheelchair. You know, it's probably a scam but I bought a dozen bulbs. But, anyway Syl, honey, I don't feel well. I think – well, let me just say that this meat hasn't gone down well. In fact, it may come right back up.'

'Oh, baby,' Sylvie cooed, 'I'm so sorry. I wish I was there to hold your head.'

Bob figured he could escape on that line and find out when Marla returned. 'Hey, I've got to go. Love to Ellen,' Bob said, and just barely waited for his wife's response before he clicked back to his waiting girlfriend. But when he got on the other line he heard only the buzzing of the dial tone.

Marla had hung up.

The next morning Bob, in recovery, was sucking on a couple of Tums as he carefully washed down Beautiful Baby. There was something calming, something almost sensual about sudsing her fenders. Washing your car was one of those few acts in life that deeply satisfied because, if you took pains, you could do it perfectly. As he rinsed the soapy sponge, Bob spotted his brother-in-law Phil coming across the lot. Bye-bye serenity. As he got closer Phil started to speak. 'Is Pop here today?'

'It's Wednesday. He's golfing.' Jesus, after five years of his father golfing on Wednesdays Phil still didn't get the schedule. Didn't he pay attention?

His next question proved the answer to be no. 'Hey, where's Sylvie been? I stopped by the house earlier and she wasn't there.'

'Wake up and smell the anesthesia,' Bob said, looking up. 'She went to your sister's for a few days. Ellen's having something "done."'

'Oh, she's always redecorating. No kids. Gives her something to do.'

'No. I mean elective surgery. You know, cosmetic.'

'Yeah? What? A hooterectomy?' Phil probed, obviously deeply interested. 'I tried to give a boob job to Rosalie on our last anniversary.'

'Maybe that's why it was your last,' Bob commented, shaking his head. His mood, his entire meditation, was ruined by this clown.

'You've heard the one about the guy whose fiancée was perfect in every way? You know, gorgeous, young, rich, and sexy. Just one thing wrong: she didn't have big knockers. You heard this one?' Phil asked.

'No, Phil. I don't believe I've heard this one,' Bob answered, turning back to his car. Rubbing it would bring him peace. He'd ignore this mosquito buzzing. 'Can you give it to me in four words or less?'

Phil put a hand on Bob's shoulder, stopping him from buffing. 'So anyway, of course he's hesitant to marry her. I mean, no bazookas. But one of his friends says, "Are you crazy? You'd give up a beauty like that just because she's a little titularly challenged?" "But I like 'em big!" the guy says. "So I got the solution," says the other one. "Just have her pat them with toilet paper three times every day. Before you know it, she'll be Pamela Lee." "You're kidding me," the guy says. "Toilet paper? This works?" "Sure," says his buddy. "My wife's been wiping her butt with it for years and now her ass is bigger than a house."' Phil fell into hysterics. 'Hey, you hear the one about the millionaire with three girlfriends?'

Bob, unmoved, looked at Phil and answered simply, 'Phil, you're a throwback. So out of date: it's not Pamela Lee anymore. She's Anderson. They got a divorce.'

'Oh yeah? Now she and I have something in common.' He shifted on his feet, but didn't offer to help Bob with the car.

'So have you heard from Sylvie?'

'Every day, but those telephone conversations are never enough.'

'Are you kidding? Women can kill you on the phone. I kept telling Rosalie I didn't need details. I know more than anyone needs to know about her mother's . . .'

Bob looked over at his brother-in-law. He sounded so bitter. 'So you don't regret . . . ?'

Phil was silent for a minute and looked away, across the lot of empty models. 'Sure I do. I haven't had a solid bowel movement since Rosalie the Vindictive threw me out. Sicilian girls! They live for vendetta, but they sure can cook.'

'And Sylvie made a hell of a pot roast,' Bob agreed nostalgically, as if she'd been gone for two years instead of only two weeks. With that, he got into Beautiful Baby, wet as she was, and drove off the lot.

15

Sylvie had already been to her yoga class when she met Marla for breakfast — such as it was. Marla had a loaded plate with toast and eggs and peanut butter and sliced bananas, along with a bowl of yogurt covered with the delicious, high-calorie granola. Sylvie sat opposite, sipping her soy and melon concoction. She'd need the protein to get through aerobics.

Marla was spooning yogurt into her mouth and giggling. 'So when he put you on hold, who did he say it was?' she asked again.

After the two women had admitted that they were thinking of secretly calling Bob, they'd decided to call him simultaneously. 'He said you were a disabled veteran,' Sylvie said.

'Well, that isn't true,' Marla explained. 'I was never in a war.'

'Only if you count the battle of the sexes,' Sylvie told her.

'I can't figure out why you walk like a boy,' Marla was saying later, as the two women were working together in a long, deserted spa hallway.

'Maybe because I had an older brother,' Sylvie suggested. 'Phil was an athlete. Very butch.'

'Hey, I had an older brother named Butch too,' Marla said. 'Well, he was a stepbrother. Or maybe a half stepbrother. What a pig! He made a pass at me when I was eleven.' Marla was on the floor, taping paper spa shoes to the carpet. It looked a lot like a foot diagram from Sylvie's days at Miss Walker's School of Social Dancing. 'Okay. Now try,' Marla said, getting up off her hands and knees. Was it Sylvie's imagination or was the girl's face a little fatter? When Marla bent over, it became clear that her butt was. Thank god for mashed potatoes and butter, Sylvie thought, and smiled to herself.

'Okay. So walk in my footsteps,' Marla commanded. Shrugging, Sylvie placed her feet, one by one, on the places Marla indicated. It made her almost cross one leg in front of the other, throwing her pelvis from side to side.

'That's it!' Marla cried, watching Sylvie from behind.

'Marla, this is ridiculous,' Sylvie said, turning around. 'It's a hooker's walk.'

'I never got paid for it in my life!' Marla said hotly.

'What I meant was, this isn't the way *you* walk.'

'It is when there's a man behind me,' Marla told her. 'Do it again.' Sylvie obeyed and managed to 'walk the walk' without toppling like a fallen tree.

Sylvie sat on the toilet, the seat down, and squirmed. For what seemed like an hour she'd been trapped here, being made-up by Marla.

'Come *on*,' Sylvie said. 'My behind has gone all pins and needles.'

'Speaking of needles, you could use some electrolysis,' Marla commented as she picked up yet another brush and tickled Sylvie's chin. The girl had more colors and brushes than Rembrandt. 'Blend, blend, blend. It's the secret to a perfect face,' she confided.

'Would you just stop?' Sylvie asked. 'I mean, what's the point?'

'Ta da!' Marla said. 'Just gorgeous. *That's* the point.'

When Sylvie looked in the mirror, 'Oh dear Lord!' was all she could manage at first. 'This is what I waited so long for?' Marla had used a heavy base to cover Sylvie's few remaining yellowish bruises, then painted a whole new face on the blank, poreless canvas.

Sylvie pursed her glistening cherry lips, which now extended below her lip line on the bottom but were drawn in smaller on the top. Below her eyes there were pink streaks on her cheeks, then brown streaks below that, approximating cheekbones and hollows. Her eyes – well, they weren't *her* eyes, they were the eyes of Nathan Lane in *The Birdcage* – were shaded with three colors and then outlined in black and fringed with lashes that resembled fat black centipedes.

'I look like Norma Desmond,' Sylvie whispered.

'Yeah. But remember, Norma became Marilyn Monroe.' Marla looked at Sylvie's face in a dispassionate but critical way. 'It is a little bland. I could touch it up,' she promised.

That night, charley-horsed and exhausted after her two sessions of water aerobics, Sylvie fell into bed feeling as if her car had landed on her in the spa pool. Everything hurt, but she had to admit she was tighter and firmer than she had been in years. Marla, meanwhile, was sprawled on the armchair watching a movie. 'What are you watching?'

'It's the latest Elise Eliot. I forget what it's called.'

'Isn't she wonderful?' Sylvie asked.

'I really don't know. I've never met her.'

Sylvie was too tired to even grin at Marla's response. She hurt everywhere. 'God, I'm fried,' she groaned as she pulled the blanket up with her aching arms.

'I'm hungry,' Marla said. 'I'd like something fried. Chicken, or maybe mozzarella sticks.'

'How can you be hungry?' Sylvie asked. She hadn't had more than a lettuce leaf and a sliver of fish for dinner, while Marla had devoured a steak, roasted potatoes, and two ears of corn, along with an enormous salad drowned in enough dressing to make each woman at the table raise their eyebrows.

'That's the trouble,' Marla said. 'What did I tell you? Once you start to eat you can't stop. Eating just makes you want to eat more. I wish I had a Three Musketeers,' Marla said.

Sylvie just groaned again and turned on her side. She hadn't had sugar for two weeks, and anyway, she was too tired to chew.

She lay in bed in the dark until she heard Marla's snores. Sylvie smiled. Bob may have done everything else in bed with that girl – but he had probably never spent the night with her, so he didn't know the kind of noises that came out of that adorable nose. In fact, there were dozens, now maybe hundreds of things she knew about Marla that Bob did not.

And it was odd, but the more she knew, the more Sylvie liked the girl. Oh, she was a ditz and not very bright and a bit of a liar, but none of that was her fault. Sylvie actually felt a lot of sympathy for her. What would she have done if she'd been born into a family as dysfunctional as Marla's seemed to be? What if she hadn't been bright, and if she hadn't had musical talent? And their age difference made a crucial economic difference as well. Nowadays, with fewer and fewer opportunities, not to mention her lack of education, Marla wasn't fit for much. If she hadn't been pretty, she could have wound up with a permanent job at the fry station in Mickey Dee's.

How terrifying to be without resources.

It was hard to find your niche in the world, Sylvie thought, and even harder for a woman than for a man. There were still fewer opportunities, and the jobs paid less, yet men no longer possessed the old chivalry that had protected wives and single women. Sylvie knew that having a comfortably well-off family, with a father who had paid not only for her education but for her prom dress and piano lessons and every kind of sports equipment she ever wanted was an enormous luxury. What would it be like to have no one to provide you with those things? What would it be like to have no one to fall back on in case of an emergency? She thought of Marla and how frightened she must sometimes feel.

Sylvie had been so lucky, and she knew it. But what would happen to Marla? Sylvie could imagine the nurturing part of Marla as being good as a mother, but her impracticality, her lack of logic — well, to be honest, her idiosyncrasies and crazy belief system — would make for a really weird upbringing for her child, if she ever had one.

Who would love and commit to a girl like Marla? She was so easy not to take seriously. When Sylvie thought about it, she felt sad and angry on Marla's behalf. What Bob did was wrong — not just a wrong he'd committed against her but a wrong he'd committed against Marla. Sylvie knew he wasn't going to take care of the girl, not in the way she needed. He was using her, just as he was using Sylvie. She thought of the old army doggerel: 'This is my rifle, this is my gun. One is for shooting, the other's for fun.' Marla was the gun and — unless she was very wrong — Sylvie figured her husband would sleep with Marla, give her some money and some attention, but never really commit to anything. He needed Sylvie to be his rifle, a tool to keep his life orderly. Bob liked things orderly.

And even if Bob did – god forbid – decide to leave Sylvie for this girl, Sylvie knew that he would never, ever consider having children with her. Where would that leave Marla, who craved them? The more she thought about it, the angrier Sylvie got. Until she realized that it was crazy to feel this kind of outrage on behalf of your husband's mistress.

They were back in the lounge, Sylvie again at the piano. She had briefed Marla on all her students, their personalities and their skill levels. But though Marla had memorized Lou's and Honey's and Samantha's and Jennifer's current exercises and name and favorite songs, she still couldn't identify a sharp from a flat. Sylvie was playing the end of 'If They Could See Me Now.' Marla was, as usual, nodding her head, off tempo. 'Yes, yes,' she murmured. In desperation, Sylvie made a big, obvious mistake, and she made it loud. Marla looked up and, tentatively, shook her head no. At the no, Sylvie jumped up from the piano stool.

'Good! Good!' she cried and hugged Marla.

'I think you've got the wrist action on that. Now the back of the heel. How strong are your hands?' Distastefully, Sylvie was doing as she was told, but the act struck her as obscene and more than a little ridiculous. Plus her hands were getting tired. How long would she have to keep this up? As if she read her mind, Marla said, 'Reflexology is ninety percent strength and thirty percent technique.' Sylvie refrained from mentioning that those percentages added up to much more than a hundred. 'Hold my foot in your left hand as you work with your right,' Marla instructed.

Sylvie sat, Marla's feet in her lap, practicing her new 'profession.' She had a look of disgust on her face and plenty of disdain in her heart. Sylvie hadn't expected the whole process to be that difficult but she was finding out that there was more involved than she'd thought.

'I guess I never knew this about myself before, but I can't stand touching anyone's feet,' Sylvie said with a grimace.

'Jesus didn't mind,' Marla said in a superior tone. 'Anyway, it's just because you don't understand them. They don't call what you walk on "soles" for nothing, you know. Why do you think people say, "Bless my soul"? Feet that hurt are a misery. Plus, they say "the foot is the window to the soul."'

Sylvie looked at the girl as if she were mad. 'No they don't,' she told her. 'You already said that the sole is the window to the soul. And they don't say that either. It's the *eyes* that are the window to the soul.'

'Whatever,' Marla said and Sylvie tossed her heel. 'Ouch. Hey! Be careful. Doing that could permanently hurt a person's instep for a long time.' She pulled her right foot off Sylvie's lap and rubbed it. 'Anyway, once *you* respect the foot, you'll get over that sick feeling. Except, of course, if the feet are dirty or they have those big, hard calluses. Oh, by the way, Simon Brightman likes hot pink nail polish by Clinique,' Marla told Sylvie. 'I don't think it works with his skin tones, but let him have his poison.'

'Simon? A guy who *wants* polish on his toenails?' Sylvie asked, disbelief on her face. Sylvie was sitting at the foot of Marla's lounge chair with Marla's right foot propped up on her knee. 'Wait, I have to write all this down,' Sylvie said as she reached over for her notepad.

'That's not all they want,' Marla said. 'One of my regulars insists I wear pumps that show toe cleavage.'

'What's that?' Sylvie asked, queasy.

'Oh, you know . . . when a shoe is low cut and a little

tight and it makes your foot crease between your big toe and your index toe. He just loves to look at it. And get this: some of them want to suck toes.'

'What? You've got to be kidding me,' Sylvie said, squealing. 'What do you do?'

'I'm a professional,' Marla answered without hesitation. Sylvie wasn't sure if that meant toe sucking was in or out. She gagged.

'The deal was that you would be doing your special customers,' Sylvie said.

'Yes, but what if there's an emergency call and Bob doesn't want me to go out in the middle of the night? I'm not gonna let you lose any of my regulars.'

'What the hell is an emergency pedicure?'

'Well, okay. It's not *just* pedicures. I'm more, like, a therapist. See, my clients feel they can call me any time – night or day.'

'So it's not just feet?' Sylvie said, pouncing.

'It *is* feet. You know very little about people.'

'Marla, are you a hooker?'

Marla sat up. 'Now that was cruel. I have never – ever – gotten paid for sexual intercourse. My specialty is . . . well . . . foot fetishes.'

'You mean you actually put it in your mouth?'

'No. Usually I let them suck mine, though. Men love that. The royal family is into it big time. I've seen pictures.'

'That is gross. That is *disgusting*.' Sylvie shivered visibly. 'You do that with Bob?'

'Of course. He's a Sagittarius on the Capricorn cusp. That's a very sensual sign. It's also probably why his toenails are so hard.'

162

'I knew there had to be a reason for it. But he *likes*
. . . sucked?'

Marla didn't speak, she merely licked her lips and nodded
her head, giving Sylvie a cat-that-sucked-the-canary look.

'I don't care,' Sylvie said, rebelling. 'He doesn't deserve
to have his toes sucked. Or any other part of his body. And
there's *no* way I could suck strange men's toes.' Sylvie shut
the light and turned her back on Marla.

'Fine. Then we'll call the whole thing off and I'll get Bob
the hard way.'

The salon was crowded. Each client lined up in one of the
chairs before the mirrors, no matter what her age or coloring,
was going blonder. They all had blue cream on their roots or
foil in their hair. Sylvie was doing both: blonding her hair *and*
getting streaks. That was nothing. A chubby dark woman in
shorts was going platinum.

'Are you sure I'm going to be Gwyneth Paltrow blonde?'
Sylvie asked her beautician, Leonida, nervously.

'Absolutely. A Hollywood friend of mine swept up some
actual samples after her last trim. I can show them to you if
you like.' Sylvie shook her head. She thought of the medieval
reliquaries that housed saints' fingers and shank bones and
teeth. Were movie stars the saints of our day? Saint Gwyneth.
'Maybe if it was Mozart's hair,' she murmured. 'Otherwise,
just make me look good.'

'No problem,' Leonida assured her. 'It's your sister I'm
worried about.'

'Do you believe in fate?' Marla asked.

Sylvie's ears were burning and her upper lip was dripping
from the heat of the dryer. She adjusted the cotton. She'd

been in the salon for more than three hours. How long did this transformation take and how much upkeep would it require? 'Hate?' she said. 'Of course I believe in hate. Right now I hate my husband for making me go through this pain.'

'Who doesn't?' asked the newly platinum woman. She was under the next dryer. Both Sylvie and Marla ignored her.

'Fate, I said. You know, destiny.'

Sylvie shrugged. There was a thin line of brown dye slowly moving down Marla's forehead. It looked sort of like the letter 'J.' It looked *very* dark. Sylvie wondered if it might mark the younger girl's skin permanently. Too bad it hadn't dripped into an 'A.' 'I don't think so,' Sylvie said.

'Oh, I do. Like, totally. See, I think I'm fated to be married to Bob.'

'You do?' Sylvie swiveled her head so quickly she nearly severed her ear on the hot rim of the dryer. 'Why?'

'Well, for three reasons. First because my mother, she once had her fortune told by this woman whose cousin was married to a gypsy. And she even said to my mother that she was going to have trouble with me but then I was going to settle down. She also said my mother's ringworm would go away and it did, once my stepdaddy killed the cat.'

Sylvie couldn't help but be fascinated by this logic. 'What are your other proofs?' she asked.

'Well, once we were in Atlanta, my girlfriend Tonya and me, and we threw money in the fountain at the Hyatt hotel. It's, like, a really good hotel. Anyway, so she wished that Buddy — that was her boyfriend, now he's her husband, well, actually, they've been separated for the last year and she served papers. But, anyway, back then Tonya wished that Buddy would give her an ankle bracelet and, like, just four or five months later, at Christmas, he did. So I wished that I'd get to marry a nice guy like Bob. I mean, I hadn't met Bob yet but I figured I would meet him *someday*. So that's another reason. And then the last reason is because when I called the Psychic Friend's Network, Hoshanna – she channels an Indian spirit – told me everything was going to work out really great.'

Sylvie took a deep breath. If she spent a lot more time with Marla, one of them would wind up in a mental institution. It was just a question of which one. Marla was looking down at the pedicurist, who was busy painting the large toenails of the platinum woman. 'Oh, no,' she said. 'No. You should *never* start with the big toe. It blocks the energy from the kidney and liver. It's, like, really, really bad.'

The pedicurist and the woman both looked up.

'When you start at the pinkie, it gives time for the negative ions to move to the larger toes and be released,' Marla explained matter-of-factly. 'Otherwise you just wind up with a lot of yang energy trapped in the ball of your foot.' She shook her head, a warning look on her face. 'And you know what *that* feels like.'

Marla was on the chair next to Sylvie. The hairdresser just finished blowing out Marla's hair. It had been turned mousy brown, and was in the nonstyle that Sylvie wore. Marla turned her eyes from the pedicure and stared at her image in the mirror. She made a whimpering sound. Then she hung her head and covered it with her arms. She was clearly depressed.

Up and down the row of chairs, women leaned in to look. 'What did I do?' Marla cried.

The hairdresser, patting her shoulders, tried to console Marla. 'I know, I know. It's very difficult to go from light to dark. Why did you do it?'

'*She* made me,' Marla said, pointing a finger at Sylvie.

'You don't have to do what a younger sister tells you to,' the newly platinum woman told Marla. 'She's probably jealous.'

'Not anymore,' quipped the woman from New York. Sylvie, her hair now a streaked blonde mane, sank into her chair.

'When I went from honey blonde to just a light brown, I needed massive doses of Zoloft,' another customer added. 'I was on anti-depressants for months.' Marla burst into sobs.

Trying to comfort Marla, Platinum patted her shoulder. 'Winona Ryder is a brunette,' she said, 'and she had Johnny Depp.'

'For a while,' added the New Yorker.

'And look at Princess Di. Where did blonde get *her?*' a third woman chimed in sadly. 'It doesn't look so bad.'

Marla moaned and got into a deeper and deeper funk. Finally she got out of the chair, strode over to Sylvie, and pulled her down the aisle, past the other women and outside.

'It's off. The whole thing is off. What an idiot I am! I didn't really realize after all this that I was going to actually look like you.'

'Did *I* look that bad?' Sylvie asked, surveying Marla. Her hair was not only brown but bowled around her head. Without makeup and without the height her mane gave to her face she looked a lot like a Doberman.

'Worse! You looked like this with wrinkles. This deal stinks.' Marla turned to the wall and hit it. 'God, I'm always getting suckered! I've put on thirteen pounds. And how are *you* supposed to get me a man when you couldn't even hold on to your own?' Marla turned and started walking to their room. 'I'm out of here.'

Sylvie, panicked, followed her and desperately tried to calm her down. 'Marla, come on. You can go back to blonde in two weeks. You'll get back in shape.'

'But I really, really *like* eating now. I mean, I hadn't eaten in *years*. Food is addictive. Last night I dreamed about macaroni and cheese. You know, in a casserole with crunch bread crumbs on top.'

'Well, at least that's starch with a starch. According to your theory, isn't that okay?'

'Ha! You think I can just go cold turkey? Oh god, I'm talking food again.'

'Well, it's almost Thanksgiving.'

She wasn't listening. 'I'll end up being alone, fat, drab, and unmarried for the rest of my meaningful years.'

'Marla, calm down. This has just been a shock, but it's not so bad. Marla, there are benefits to this. Really. Remember how you wished Bob would sleep over? He'll sleep over every night now.'

'So what? We won't *do* anything.'

Sylvie was thinking as fast as she could. They'd come so far. She couldn't let the scheme fall apart now. One of the exercise instructors was walking by. She smiled at Marla. 'Got to make a few more classes, Sylvie,' she said.

'I'm *not* Sylvie . . .' Marla began, but the woman had passed them. 'Oh my god! She thinks I'm you,' Marla whispered. 'It's worked. It's really worked.' Marla began to sob.

It had, Sylvie realized. She grabbed Marla by the shoulders and tossed her mane of hair.

'Listen to me. It's not so easy to wind up secure. Finding a man, a family, is a big thing. You need help. Everyone does.'

'They do?' Marla said, though she kept weeping.

167

'*You* do. It takes a village, or at least a cul-de-sac. I could teach you how to be a good wife so you'll get another man. I'll be the role model you never had.'

'Thanks, anyway,' Marla said, pulling away and wiping her nose with her hand. She began to walk away.

Sylvie was desperate. 'I know every rich, single man in the area. I'll help you get a husband.' Sylvie brightened. 'How about if I *guarantee* you a husband?'

Marla stopped. 'How about I don't leave your house until you do?'

Sylvie considered, then decided to go for broke. She nodded her head. 'It's a deal. I'll find you someone.'

'Good. Because otherwise I'm keeping Bob.'

Sylvie tried not to hear that. 'Marla, listen. You have no idea how much respect a wife gets no matter *how* she looks.' Sylvie pulled Marla toward the reception desk. 'I want you to get a taste of what it feels like. Watch this.' Sylvie took Marla by the hand, led her back to the salon, and approached the reception-ist. 'Excuse me. Mrs Schiffer would like to pay our bill now.'

The receptionist found the bill immediately. 'Color. Color. Cut. Cut. Full-head highlights. Blow dry. Blow dry. That will be $357.00. How would you like to pay, Mrs Schiffer?' She looked at Marla.

'She would like to pay with her Mrs Schiffer Visa Gold card.' Sylvie passed a credit card to Marla. Marla looked at it, smiled wanly, and handed it over to the receptionist.

'Thank you, Mrs Schiffer. Would you like a cappuccino or espresso, Mrs Schiffer?'

Marla broke into a broad grin. Holding her heart, she murmured, 'Mrs Schiffer. Mrs Robert Schiffer.' Marla was clearly overwhelmed; Sylvie was simply relieved.

* * *

Marla and Sylvie were lying down, Sylvie because she couldn't stand up after her last abs of steel session and Marla because in their last days she'd packed on every ounce of fat she could. No more leg lifts.

Now Sylvie had her pad in her hand. It had been almost filled by the notes on Marla's life though, sadly, it seemed that there wasn't a lot in it: some girls she knew at her gym, a neighbor with a cat, and her folks whom she'd rarely mentioned. 'What if anyone in your family calls?' Sylvie asked.

'Oh, they never call. But if they do it's always collect. Just don't accept it.' Marla didn't seem upset, but it had to bother her. 'Oh, and be sure not to promise them any money. They call if they need money.'

'I'm so sorry,' Sylvie said, trying to show support.

'*You're* sorry?' Marla asked. '*I* used to send it.'

Sylvie decided to move on. 'Okay,' she said, instructing Marla. 'I always sleep on the right. Please don't forget where right is . . .' She took a breath. This was the last part she hadn't had the courage to address before. But now, with her youthful face and flat tummy, not to mention the wheatfield of hair on her head, she thought she could handle it. 'Now tell me what you and Bob do in bed.'

'Ha! You're gonna need a lot more paper than that,' Marla said, laughing, and she pulled a list out of her pocket. 'Here. I figured you'd get around to asking. I prepared some notes. I wrote them up while you were doing squat thrusts.'

Sylvie looked at Marla's papers and got very scared. 'Talk about squats and thrusts! You've done *all* this? Are you sure?'

'I'm really, really positive,' Marla said. 'Don't tell me you've *never* done those things.'

Sylvie cleared her throat. 'Of course I've done . . . some of them.' She looked at the notes again. 'Actually, some of these were the very first things Bob and I did. But – I don't know – over the years we stopped exploring . . .' Sylvie tried to explain. 'Maybe there was just no more unexplored territory. We went for comfort over novelty,' Sylvie admitted. 'And it seems like a lot of trouble. Plus, it could throw Bob's back out.'

Marla shook her head, took out a few more sheets of paper from her pocket. 'Sketches,' she said. 'Just in case.'

Sylvie glanced at, then studied them. She tried not to let her eyes widen. 'You could have at least indicated "This Side Up." I'd need an open-book test to pass this!'

'Hey, it better come naturally to you because he'll come to you first when we get back,' Marla warned.

'No he won't. He'll go to his wife first,' Sylvie said. If after almost three weeks away he didn't, she'd kill him.

'Wanna bet?' Marla asked, raising her brows. 'Look, I used to be his mistress. I *know* he'll come to me – I mean, you,' Marla said. Her eyes narrowed. She looked down at Sylvie's hand. 'What do you want to bet?'

Sylvie looked down at her ring. Bob had given it to her on their fifteenth anniversary. It came from Cartier and was the most beautiful ring in the world. It was three separate rings of gold: white gold for friendship, yellow gold for fidelity, and pink for love. 'Well, I know you like the ring,' she said.

'Like it? I love it. What do *you* want?'

'You mean, aside from Bob?' Sylvie asked. 'I want everything he's ever given you, including the car, returned.'

'Well, he didn't actually *give* me the car. He just leased it for me.'

'Forget the car. I want all the little knickknacks. The

170

lingerie, the necklace, the dead flowers. Every single little thing.'

'*Everything*?' Marla whined.

Sylvie nodded and held up the ring. The different golds shimmered in the sunlight.

Marla rose, went to the foot of Sylvie's bed, and spoke in a strict voice. 'Fine. You're on. Meanwhile, you've got to be serious about this, Sylvie. When he comes to you, be ready. Sexual energy is at the very center of our being. It's like a vitamin rush. Our yin and our yang. It's the most important thing. If you mess up with Bobby, you'll never get to know what good sex is like with him again.'

'Well, spelling is important too,' Sylvie said defensively. 'And grammar. I can't even understand some of these notes. You can't be a good wife if you can't communicate in writing.' Sylvie knew her defense was weak, but she was flustered, even shocked by the pages she held in her hand. 'Oh. Never let Bob see your handwriting. It's awful. And you have to do something about your grammar, though I know what a pain in the neck grammar is.'

'My gramma isn't a pain in the neck. I mean, she *had* a pain in the neck, but since her cramp cleared up she's fine. Anyway, we're not talking about my gramma.'

Sylvie silently nodded assent to that. 'Well, you spelled "oral" wrong. It's with an "a" not an "e,"' she said primly.

'Well, I might not know how to *spell* it, but I know how to *do* it. Men don't send roses to stiffs. Rigid is frigid.'

'Did he say I was frigid?' Sylvie demanded with heat.

'No. No. He never talks about you,' Marla assured her. 'I just figured he wouldn't be looking for hamburger if he had steak at home.'

171

Sylvie looked at the sexual menu spread before her. Her face flushed.

'I'm going to do *all* of this,' Sylvie said with new determination.

'Good girl,' Marla told her. 'Oh, and don't forget: he yells in bed when he climaxes. Don't get scared.'

'I *know* he yells,' Sylvie said resentfully. She paused, her pride fighting her curiosity. 'What does he yell?' she asked.

'I'm dying! I'm dying!' Marla howled in imitation.

Sylvie tried not to change her expression, and if she had she wouldn't have known whether to laugh or cry. 'Okay, I haven't heard *that*,' she admitted. 'If I had, I would probably have called 911.' Sylvie tried to take all of it in.

There was something here so serious, so intimate and so very real that Sylvie felt both physically sick and hurt. She was hurt all over again, as hurt as when she'd first realized Bob had cheated. But now, sitting there, she no longer had her anger to mask her pain. She actually lost her breath and felt a constriction in her chest. *Not as if my heart is breaking*, she thought. *But like it's hardening and shrinking*. The pain was actually physical. She could feel it below her sternum and her right breast. She pressed her hand to her chest and had to look away from the pages in front of her.

What did Marla understand about this? She seemed to look upon sex as a healthful aerobic activity. Did Bob whisper how much he wanted her, as he used to to Sylvie? The yearning in his voice had always brought tears to her eyes when they made love. Now tears filled her eyes for a different reason.

There was a silence in the room. Bob had actually done these things — these intimate, complicated, sexual things with a stranger. All her strategizing had led her to this. Her manipulations had brought her this visceral pain. Suddenly

172

the game, the fun of what they'd been up to drained away; all that was left was the ugliness of betrayal and adultery.

Marla, with a sympathetic look, reached across the space between them for Sylvie's hand. Sylvie let her hold it. She lay in the silence, feeling the pain.

Sylvie finally spoke. 'Can I ask you something . . . and will you tell me the truth?'

'As close as I can get,' Marla said.

'What is your story? You really are a nice person. You don't really steal. Why did you try for other women's husbands?'

Marla shrugged. 'I want to get married. I'm like every other girl, but I got confused. Guys my age I date are phobic about commitment. I got tired of wasting my time. I just figured married men were the kind who get married.'

Sylvie lay silent.

Both Marla and Sylvie's luggage was being loaded into two identical silver BMW Z2 convertibles. Every once in a while, the wrong piece was put into the wrong car, partly because the bellman wasn't too bright and partly because Marla and Sylvie kept getting confused. They both kept watch, rescuing stray pieces to get them into the right identical car trunk. When the bags were finally loaded, the two women faced each other.

'Well, I guess this is it. The acid test,' Sylvie said. 'Are we interchangeable parts or not? And can we get away with it?'

'You know what?' Marla said. 'I'm going to really miss you. It's, like, you're part of my family or something. Well, not *my* actual family. I mean, forget about *them*. I mean, like . . . well, like a good sister who's, you know, not always borrowing my personal hygiene products and getting hair on the deodorant ball. Which is a totally new feeling.'

'I'm going to miss you too,' Sylvie said, surprised that she meant it. 'And don't you worry, I'm there if you need to ask me anything. No question is too small.' She paused. 'Just remember not to talk too much – he doesn't listen anyway – and *don't* write him notes. He knows my handwriting.'

The women hugged and, for a moment, it felt to Sylvie as if they couldn't leave each other, either out of mutual affection or mutual fear. They took two steps away from each other and Sylvie remembered one last thing.

'The oven is slow,' Sylvie called out.

Marla, almost to her car, turned around. 'It's okay. So am I,' she said, and they both laughed. 'Say, hey!' Marla walked toward Sylvie. 'We forgot. Here are my keys. We have to switch. Can you drive a standard?'

'Not well,' Sylvie admitted, handing over her car and house keys. 'Oh, wait,' she added. She took out her wallet. 'I guess we should exchange these too.'

Marla opened up Sylvie's wallet. '*Gold* Visa *and Gold* MasterCard?'

Marla dug into her purse and handed Sylvie something. It was Marla's wallet. Sylvie looked through it. 'I don't see a license here.'

'Oh, that's because I don't have one,' Marla explained. 'I didn't want to get points or anything.'

'You don't have a driver's license? Marla, that's a crime.'

'No it's not. It's a crime if you get a ticket. I just haven't complied with the law.'

'What if I get stopped by a cop?' Sylvie asked.

'Do what I do. Try to date him. They're all babe hounds. If that doesn't work, call Bobby.' Marla laughed. Sylvie shook

174

her head, laughed, and then the two women hugged each other again. They walked off in opposite directions. This time they got only four steps apart.

'One more thing . . .' Sylvie said. Marla spun around. The moment to Sylvie felt important, ceremonial. They stood facing each other, reflections that had stepped out of each other's mirror. 'You should have this,' Sylvie said. Slowly she pulled her wedding band off her finger. She hadn't removed it since Bob had put it on her on their wedding day. She extended her hand, giving the band of gold to Marla, who just stared at it.

'I can't. It would be like stealing from the poor,' Marla said. Sylvie wasn't sure how to take that remark but she let it pass.

'Bob's wife has to have a band,' Sylvie said. 'Fair is fair.'

Marla was overwhelmed. She didn't move. Sylvie waited, then took the ring and put it on Marla's finger. Marla took a deep, almost shivering breath. 'And soon I'll win the Cartier!' she added.

'No you won't,' Sylvie assured her, but good-naturedly.

'If this doesn't work we have only one person to blame, and that's each other,' she said. Sylvie laughed and they hugged for the last time.

'In the meantime,' Sylvie said, 'you wear the Cartier ring. Focus on the white gold: that's for friendship.'

Marla didn't need to be asked twice. She slipped the graceful gleaming gold around her finger. 'Yes!' she breathed. She held her hand out full length away from her body and admired it. Then she looked back at Sylvie, her eyes wet. 'You know, this isn't girlfriend jewelry. It's serious. I feel married.' She looked at her hand again. 'Real Cartier,' she said.

PART 2

Switch

16

Marla pulled up to the house, her head practically hanging out of the window of the convertible. For some reason the car smelled like mildew, and she was very allergic to mildew. She'd sneezed most of the way home. But now, at last, she was here – at Mr and Mrs Bob Schiffer's residence. She pulled into the driveway, hurried out of the car, and ran up the steps. She fumbled with the key to the door. Then she had trouble with the security system. Sylvie had told her exactly what to do, but somehow, she'd punched the code in too soon or too late, started it beeping, and had to beg it to be quiet. At last she got the all clear and entered.

'A foy-aie!' she breathed.

Spread before Marla was her new domestic wonderland: a large entrance hall, a high-ceilinged dining room to the left and the arch to the living room on the right. Marla took a map out of her purse and was careful to check where she was on it. She walked to the center of the hall, checked again, and slowly spun around, her arms out.

She followed the map into the living room, turning on all the lights as she went – overhead chandelier, table lamps, floor lamps. She'd never had so many lighting fixtures in her life!

She was drawn to the fireplace. Over it hung a big portrait of Sylvie (clearly at a younger age) with the twins as young children. Marla pressed another switch and the portrait was illuminated.

'A picture light!'

She took out her compact, checked her image, and then checked it against the painting. She was amazed all over again at the likeness – the portrait was *her*, if she'd organized her life a little better. She looked at the kids – *her* kids. She felt tears rise in her eyes over 'her and the children.' But she got distracted by the shelves on either side of the fireplace. She moved to one of the bookshelves, and ran her hand over the books. So many of them! Had Sylvie or Bob read them all? Marla had only three books at home – *The Celestine Prophecy*, her Herbalife manual, and a book she'd never been able to get into, one about bridges of some town or something.

She felt intimidated by all the books, so she let herself wander away, over to the silver-framed photos on a side table, she picked one up and pointed to the individuals. 'Reenie, Kenny, Phil, Ellen, Bobby – er, Bob – and . . . me. Easy!' she said aloud, really proud of herself and, still testing, she moved to another shelf and another photo. 'Jim, Bob, Phil, me . . .' she paused, sentimentally putting her hand on her heart, 'and Mom.' She thought of Mildred. She seemed like the kind of mother who had had lots of fresh aprons instead of fresh boyfriends. She sighed and turned again to look at 'her' family. There was another, larger photo of just two people. 'Bob . . .' she paused, unable to identify the older man, '. . . and some geezer,' she finished lamely. Enough of pictures.

She turned and began to leave the room, but as she exited she noticed the television remote, picked it up, and punched it on. TV had always kept her company. She surfed. Boy, these guys must have a satellite – there were dozens and dozens of stations. She kept going until she hit a shopping channel. '. . . QVC!' she cried, greeting it like an old friend.

Then she noticed an empty silver candy dish. She picked it up. Engraved across the bottom was: 'Grow old with me. The best is yet to be.' Marla stared at the words, her face mirrored back by the silver. Tears were reflected in her eyes. Who would she grow old with? She held the dish to her chest and hugged it. Maybe Bob. Maybe. Finally she put it down and, following the map, she walked toward the kitchen.

But she'd never been good at geography. She had some trouble. First she walked into a closet, then out the back door, thinking it was the kitchen. But, finally, she got there.

And it was worth it! It was her dream kitchen. She couldn't cook, but she'd always believed if she had a bigger, nicer place to cook in she'd know how. This was the place. She walked to the counter at the center and put her cheek lovingly on top of the granite. 'An island!' she breathed.

It was paradise. Like a child in a playground, one thing after another caught her eye. She opened the freezer and checked out all the food. 'Stouffer's!' she cried. (Only the *most* expensive frozen brand.) She went through the dozens of boxes and bags of vegetables, pizzas, potpies, and poultry. Only when she herself started to feel frozen did she close the freezer and open the refrigerator, also filled with food. She checked the cottage cheese date. 'Unexpired!' she cried. It all seemed too good to be true.

There was a gleaming white microwave with a complex array of buttons. She pushed the controls, but it made a few noises that sounded threatening. She pushed a few more, but it didn't shut off. Marla wanted it to be quiet. 'Please! Please stop!' she asked it.

She backed away and bumped into a small TV. Well, she knew how to work that! It would cover up the clicking and beeping of the microwave. She turned it on to QVC. All was well. She was thrilled with her new life.

There were at least two dozen lit candles around the room. Sylvie, in *her* new life, was wearing white stockings, a white lacy garter belt, and was struggling into a bustier that just barely closed. She pulled in her stomach, took a deep breath, and checked herself out in the full-length mirror. It was obvious that the transformation had been wildly successful. She looked ten years younger and fourteen pounds thinner. But would she pass as Marla? Sylvie wasn't so sure. You're insane, she told herself, and this is both crazy and demeaning. When did you, where would you, ever dress up like a tart and deceive someone? Who was she?

Sylvie got very scared, ran for a terry cloth robe to put over it all, but then was drawn back to the mirror. She realized immediately that the terry cloth look was not working. The robe came off slowly. Seeing herself, one feature at a time, was easier.

Then the phone rang. Sylvie jumped and ran for the phone, but as she was about to answer she became too scared to pick it up. She reached for it, but the bustier moved, exposing part of her breast. She panicked again and, as if she could be seen, blew out several candles before she picked up the receiver.

Sylvie tried imitating Marla: 'Hello,' she purred. She heard heavy breathing, and didn't know what to do. 'Bob? . . . Bobby?' she asked.

'No,' someone whispered.

'Is this a pervert call?' she asked. 'Because I have a whistle here—'

'No. Don't whistle. It's me. Mrs Bob Schiffer,' Marla said,

her voice still breathy. 'What's up? Did I win my — I mean your — ring yet?'

'Well, I'm having an anxiety attack, and Bob hasn't even arrived. He called and he's coming to me first, not you. Can you believe it?'

'Sure. I won the bet.'

'You sound out of breath too.' Sylvie was hurt by that, but so excited and nervous she didn't have time to register it. 'What are you doing?' she asked.

'I opened all the bedroom closets and drawers,' Marla said. 'I can't believe it. Your house is beautiful. It's like TV people live here. But not the *Married . . . with Children* kind of TV. Like *The Cosby Show* kind. I mean, all your underwear is so . . . cotton.'

'Say, hey! I found a pair of *your* underpants and they have no crotch.'

'I'm a busy person,' Marla said defensively. 'Some things you got to let go of.'

The doorbell rang. Sylvie immediately panicked. 'Oh my god, it's Bob! . . . This is scary.'

'The first time always is,' Marla said, trying to reassure her.

'What if I'm not perky? What if he knows right away? What if I'm not sexy enough?' Sylvie thought of the diagrams, the instructions Marla had given her. 'What should I do?'

'Just pretend you're me being Sharon Stone. That's what I do.'

There was another ring. 'I gotta go. He's knocking again.' They both hung up.

It was the moment of truth: Sylvie wanted to run and hide. Instead she blew out yet more of the candles. She took a deep breath, lifted each breast and pulled it farther forward into its brassiere cup. Then she used that old female trick: she squeezed her arms together, producing cleavage. Holding herself that way she headed toward the living room and the front door.

Sylvie continued blowing out candles as she went. By the time she opened the door she was in semi-darkness. Bob was standing there with two dozen roses and a big, lustful smile. Seeing him, knowing that he was about to cheat on her, Sylvie took a deep breath (unaware that she was helping her cleavage mightily) and tried to stop herself from being too emotional. This was *her* plan, *her* scenario, and she'd control herself, Bob, and her future. She was in control here, she told herself.

'Flowers?!' Sylvie managed in a Marlaesque voice.

'All for you, baby,' Bob said, stepping inside and sweeping Sylvie up in his arms.

The flower cellophane got in the way of their first embrace and Bob let the roses drop to the floor. Sylvie felt his arms around her in a different way than usual. But she pulled away. Sylvie bent over, beginning to pick up the flowers until she remembered that her derriere was the least successfully transformed part of her body. She stopped, bent her knees instead of her waist, and tried to reach for the fallen roses without showing her butt. Awkward in the high heels, she got down to the carpet in an ungraceful squat, still focused on gathering up the roses. But in reaching she lost her balance and sprawled gracelessly.

'Oopsy daisy . . .' she said in a Marlaish voice. 'I mean, oopsy *roses.*'

Bob reached out his hand to help her up. 'Come on. Forget the flowers. Bobby's here.' He took her hand and began to pull her into the bedroom. 'I missed you,' he said, his voice husky with . . . was it lust? Sylvie wondered. *She* hadn't heard that tone. Not in years, if ever.

Sylvie realized with a shock that she might actually get away with this charade. He wanted her, whoever he thought she was. And she felt a stab of pain. 'Oh, really?' she asked, and she couldn't contain the edge in her voice. 'Did you miss your wife too?'

'Didn't we agree we weren't going to talk about my wife?' Bob asked. He put his arms around her again. His cheek felt so smooth, so good. He started to whisper. 'You're so pretty,' he told her. 'So, so pretty.'

Sylvie felt herself melting. This was the homage she had craved and worked for. Tears filled her eyes. Was this all it took? To be told you were so, so pretty? She was luxuriating in the new feel of his arms, then pulled back. He was not hugging *her*, after all. He was hugging another woman. 'Why do you come here, Bobby?' she asked.

'To see you.'

Sylvie felt her anger rising. Control yourself, she thought. Be Marla to him. Don't blow this now. 'For love? Or just for sex?' she asked.

'God, you're really beautiful when you're angry,' he said in a joking way.

'God, you're really trite when you're horny,' Sylvie retorted, then realized she wasn't being Marlaish. 'Really, really trite,' she added with a smile, then said, 'But that's a good thing.'

'You know you love me,' Bob said, caressing her cheek. Sylvie couldn't feel it because of the nerves that had been cut when the face-lift had been done. They would regenerate, she'd been told, but it was unnerving. She took the petting for a moment, then pulled away.

185

'But do I mean it?' she asked teasingly. Sylvie let Bob take her hand. But then, to her surprise, he swooped her up and began to carry her toward the bedroom. Without thinking she warned, 'Be careful of your back.'

Bob laughed. 'I can handle it,' he said, and nuzzled her neck. 'I can handle you.'

'Because you're a big, strong man?' Sylvie asked to make up for the wifely question.

'Because you make me feel that way,' Bob whispered, and his breath in her ear affected another part of her anatomy. He thought she was sexy. It was just what she wanted.

But oddly, though she'd lost her beautiful ring over it, Sylvie didn't want to hear it just then. She thought about her lost ring – friendship, love, and fidelity. He'd given that ring to her. Ha! She pulled out of his arms. Bob lost his balance and they both nearly fell. She regained her footing, but he staggered against the wall. He took the weight on his elbow – the one he'd hurt playing tennis. He screeched for a moment, then recovered himself and began to rub the joint.

'You're making me . . . *in*-sane,' Sylvie said, and, not knowing what to do, began to pick up the scattered flowers.

'Ouch. Wow. This hurts,' he said. 'I wonder if I chipped the bone.' Then he looked down at her.

'Marla, what's going on?'

Sylvie had to use all her willpower not to jump to Bob's aid and call John for a quick X ray. Instead she kept picking up flowers, the first ones he'd brought her in . . . she couldn't remember. They were what she'd longed for. Flowers. Compliments. Attention. But . . . 'Nothing . . . something. I wanted to be here with you so badly, but . . .' she trailed off.

'But?'

Her anger at him boiled up, curdling the way milk did when it boiled over. Clenching her teeth, she replied, 'I just have to arrange these goddamn flowers.'

17

Marla was lying in Sylvie's bed wearing a pair of her very unattractive
flannel pajamas – red-and-black plaid, with pockets – and was
on the phone. She had a bowl of Ben & Jerry's Phish Food
resting on her tummy and was eating it slowly with a soup
spoon. 'Yes, Saturday night,' she mumbled through the ice
cream. She swallowed. 'A table for two. For Mr and *Mrs*
Robert Schiffer,' she managed to say, clearly proud.

Marla hung up. A jewelry show was on QVC and she turned
her attention to it. But they had already sold out the zircon
pendant and Marla didn't want the earrings. Anyway, now
that she owned the gorgeous Cartier ring in three colors of
gold, she didn't crave cubic zirconium – well, not as much.
She clutched 'her' Visa card in her left hand and continued
eating with her right. Then she began working on a bag of
Milano cookies along with the melting dish of ice cream. Sylvie
had better find her a husband, fast, because soon she'd be too
fat to get or keep a boyfriend. God, once she'd started eating
she couldn't stop.

The phone rang and Marla hesitated. This was the aphid
test. She got her notebook ready before she answered. 'Hello?
Could you hold for a second?' Marla started looking through
the book, then realized she hadn't asked who was calling.
Well, she could fix that. 'Hello. Mrs Sylvie Schiffer here.
Before you hold again, could you tell me who this is?'

'It's John. Welcome home.'

Marla sighed with relief. 'Oh, John . . . I'll be right with you.'

Marla quickly paged through the notebook to an entry that was headed 'Friends and Family.' She found the thumbnail description of John. '*Good friend, doctor. Has had a crush on me since high school.*'

'Hi. So, John, how do you like being a doctor?'

'Uh . . . fine.'

'Good. We had fun in high school, didn't we?'

'Yes. Sure. Hey, Sylvie, are you okay? Have you been drinking?'

'No. Just eating,' Marla told him.

'I heard you had . . . work done while you were away. Did you really think that was necessary? Even with elective surgery, there are risks.'

'I might of had a little something done, but I'll let you be the judge,' Marla giggled.

'Well, it wasn't necessary. You were perfect.'

'Don't be silly. Of course I wasn't perfect. Nobody is . . .'

'What does Bob think?'

Too cheerfully she responded, 'Bob? He's not back yet.'

'He hasn't come home? Where is he?'

'Maybe off with his girlfriend—' She realized suddenly that she shouldn't talk and certainly not joke about that, so she added, 'I'm trying to adjust. It's hell.'

'Sylvie, how about having lunch with me tomorrow at the club?'

'Lunch? Yeah, that would be great.' Then Marla sat up in bed, startled, and pointed toward the television with her spoon hand. 'Wait! There's that Diamonique "Y" necklace that I've been waiting for. It would look great with my ring! Cathy swears it's going to sell out.' Sweetly she asked John,

'Will you promise not to stop having a crush on me if I put you on hold for a minute?'

Marla bought the necklace, charging it, and had it sent to Mrs Robert Schiffer, even paying extra for overnight delivery. After all, she wasn't sure how long this gig would last. Still, a week ago she was the kind of girl who didn't have any gold. Now she had three colors! Plus more – cubic zirconiums! When she got back to John she was filled with the energy of a successful purchase. 'So, I'll see you tomorrow,' she told him. 'You'll know me because I'll be wearing my new "Y" necklace.'

John laughed. 'Bob told me you had something done. Is the change that dramatic? I'd still know you anywhere, Sylvie.'

'Good, then you'll know me tomorrow.' She hung up and then wondered how she'd recognize him. She pulled out the photo albums she considered her homework. Maybe John was in one of these pictures. A picture stopped her. She looked up a number in the spa notebook. She put on the speaker phone and punched a number in.

'Hello.' Mildred's voice, so deep and sure of itself, crackled over the speaker.

'Hi. This is your daughter, Sylvie Schiffer.' Marla lowered her voice. 'Not really. It's sort of Marla.' Then she raised her voice again. 'I'm sorry to bother you, Mom, but who is the geezer with the bald head in all our family pictures?'

'Bob's father. *My* family has hair,' Mildred told her.

Marla tried to figure it out. 'So, he would be my . . .'

'Father-in-law, if he were alive.'

Marla's voice went low, respectful. She always tried to be respectful about those who had moved on to another plane of existence. 'Oh. When did he pass on? Were we close?'

'I don't think you should worry about it tonight, Mrs

Schiffer.' Mildred's voice sounded a little — well, a little short. 'It's already past eleven. Isn't Bob home yet?'

'Nope,' Marla said. She looked down at the ring that was now hers to keep forever and licked the very last bit of melted ice cream off the spoon. 'But that's okay. He's been getting me a Cartier ring right this minute.' She grinned and held out her finger, admiring it.

'My god. Shouldn't he be with his wife tonight?' Mildred paused. 'Well, I guess he is. But he doesn't know he is. I'm *so* confused.'

'Now you know how I *always* feel.'

'Well, keep yourself busy and out of trouble.'

The phone beeped. 'Oops. I have another call. Can you hold for a minute?' Marla asked, and before Mildred could answer she hit the flash button.

'Yo, Sis! You're home? How was the boob job?'

Marla paused. Who could this possibly be? He'd called her Sis. That wasn't her name or even Sylvie's name. Was 'Sis' short for Sylvie? But maybe it meant he might be her real brother. Not *her* brother, Sylvie's brother. 'I'm talking to my mother,' Marla said. 'She's on hold.'

'Well, she's *my* mother too. How does Ellen look? Did she get rid of those acne scars?'

'I have to say good-bye to Mom, Phil,' Marla said proudly because she'd solved the puzzle. I could have been a spy, she thought, if reflexology wasn't so important.

'Phil is on the other line, Mom,' Marla reported. 'I have to go. But maybe I'll see you tomorrow at the club. I'm having lunch there with John. That should keep me busy.'

'You are?' Mildred didn't sound pleased.

'Yep. Do you think I can wear a jumpsuit?' Marla asked.

Mildred sighed. 'No, but what do I know? I just sell pots.'

'One of my stepbrothers got busted for doing that,' Marla warned. 'You better be careful.' She punched off the flash button and was back to Phil. 'So, Phil, isn't it great that we have all these memories?'

'Which memories, Syl?'

'Oh, you know,' Marla said vaguely. 'The childhood ones. When we were kids together.'

'I remember when I accidentally broke Ellen's nose, that time we were playing Red Rover.'

'You did?'

'Yeah. By the way, did she get that fixed too?'

Marla gulped. She and Sylvie hadn't covered this. 'I'm not telling. You call her.'

'Very funny. You know Ellen and I haven't spoken for the last six years.'

'Oh, yeah. I just forgot that for a minute.' Marla paused, curious. 'And I forgot why too.'

'Because of that food fight Rosalie and I had at Thanksgiving at her house. That's why she won't spend the holidays with us anymore. You remember.' He stopped talking. 'Hey, Sylvie, was it really cosmetic surgery they did on you or was it shock treatments?'

Bob and Sylvie had gotten as far as actually lying on the bed; she'd arranged the flowers and then made up with 'Bobby.' Now he was kissing her. Really kissing her. 'God, it's been so long . . .' he breathed.

'You have no idea,' Sylvie told him.

Bob had been a good kisser, Sylvie remembered, he hadn't practiced on her in a long time. In fact even when they'd had sex he hadn't kissed her much in the last few years. Now he kissed Sylvie tenderly, his hand cupping her face. His lips were firm, his hand gentle, yet it pulled her to him. Sylvie felt herself responding, but then she couldn't help but pull away and ask, 'Do you think I'm special?'

'*Very* special,' he whispered and started kissing her again.

'Who else is special?' she asked. God! She could bite her tongue, if Bob didn't.

'Nobody . . .' He kissed her more deeply. Sylvie felt herself letting go, enjoying this. It was what she wanted. It was what she *needed*, and she felt a tug at her groin as she let herself move into that place where you floated into foreplay. 'Nobody . . .' Bob repeated.

Sylvie put her arms around him. He rolled onto her and moved her legs open with his knee. It gave her the shivers.

'Oh, Bob . . . Bobby.'

'Oh, Marla.'

Sylvie stiffened. Without thinking, she pushed him away.

'What?!' Bob said. He sat up, clearly irritated and confused.

Sylvie rolled to the other side of the bed, her back to Bob. She pulled her legs into a fetal position, with a pillow cradled at her stomach. *What was she doing?* Encouraging her husband in infidelity? Playing out some kind of charade? How was this going to help her, either with revenge or happiness? She began to weep.

'Marla, is something wrong?'

'Stop saying that!' Sylvie cried.

'What? I just asked if something was wrong,' Bob said.

Sylvie was out of control, sobbing by now. She couldn't keep this up. It had all been a terrible mistake, a stupid, foolish idea. 'I'm not Marla.'

'Oh, Cookie Face. Do you want to be someone else tonight?

I love when you do that. Are you the French maid? Who are you?'

Sylvie cried as if her heart would break.

Marla surveyed the bedroom — her bedroom with Bob. A bedroom they would sleep in every night, together, once he got home. She looked at the four-poster, the window across from it draped in a cheerful chintz, the dressing table against the bathroom wall, the crammed bookshelf, and shook her head. People were so ignorant! No wonder poor Sylvie had trouble keeping Bob! The feng shui of this room was *all* off. It was clear to anyone with the slightest common sense that energy traveled right through the window and out the door, missing the bed completely. No wonder Sylvie's sex life had suffered.

Marla had read two books on feng shui, not just one, so she knew that a lot of changes had to be made and how to make them. Plus, this was *her* room in *her* house now and she could do what she wanted. She went to the radio, turned it on to a rock-light station, and surveyed the room again with narrowed eyes. She wished she had some of her New Age music, but she'd have to make do with the Eagles. She sat down on the floor, in the very center of the room, and pulled her legs up into a half lotus. She tried to meditate on where the furniture should be located, but she kept being distracted by the vision of another dish of Ben & Jerry's Phish Food. That stuff was addictive. In addition to the marshmallow, she loved the little tiny chocolate fish that crunched when you bit into them. Anyway, she didn't need to meditate. She stood up. She crossed to the chaise, then decided instead on the ottoman and piled the latter on the former. She pushed them over to the other side of the room, near the bedroom door. She separated them, moved to the bed, and surveyed what she had wrought. It was a start. She noticed the floor lamp, which had been beside the chair in the corner. She got up and moved that next to the bookshelf. The bookshelf could stay where it was, but the bed absolutely would have to be moved.

It was heavy, and she could only push it by lying on her back and putting her feet against first the side, and then the headboard, and pushing. Inch by inch, she managed to move it into the proper energy flow. She was hot by then, and exhausted, but at that moment 'Our House Is A Very, Very, Very Fine House' began to play on the radio.

Marla knew it wasn't just a coincidence. It was what that Jung guy called 'synchronicity.' It was a sign. She smiled radiantly, got up on the bed – now situated in the middle of the room – and got into a full lotus this time. She tried to feel the energy as it coursed through the room and knew immediately that this was a big improvement. But then she noticed the bureau, blocking the energy release. Marla shook her head. A woman's work was never dumb! She would have to move the bureau.

She got up, crossed to the other side of the room, and began to push the enormous dresser, her skin radiating a New Age Martha Stewart flush. All she had to do, she thought, was get this dresser moved and then light some incense. She was exhausted, but it would all be worth it. Wait until Bob came home! What a transformation!

18

Bob left Marla's frustrated and exhausted, on top of feeling guilty
about having gone there instead of home in the first place. He
was trying to ease his frustration by listening to WMJI-FM. It
wasn't the usual nighttime deejay, and it wasn't time for John
Lannigan and Jimmy Malone's morning show, but Bob was
grateful for the company even if it was just a voice. He had
just gotten off the North Woodland Bridge and paid the toll.
But then, like an itch that couldn't be scratched, he'd realized
he had to clear his mind, see Marla again, and find out what
was wrong. He swung Beautiful Baby into a U-turn and had
to pay the toll again. The female toll taker recognized him.
This was not the first U-turn he had made that night. 'Nice
car,' she said. Bob merely nodded an acknowledgment and
accelerated, then punched a number into his car phone.

'John, it's me again. Will you bear with me?' Bob asked.
'I've already given these toll people seventeen bucks! I don't
know if I'm coming or going. I wanna be with the naked one,
I wanna be with my wife.'

'I may be your closest friend but I can't tell you what you
should do for the rest of your life,' John said.

'You don't get it, do you?' Bob whined. 'I know what I
should do. But I'm a worm without a conscience.'

'Grandiose again,' John commented. 'You're just an aver-
age adulterer. Are you going to give P and N up?'

'Yes,' Bob said firmly and pulled another U-turn. Then,

somehow, his assurance faltered. 'I don't know. It's not me going to that woman's house.' He raised his voice at his friend. 'Explain who's doing this – in four words or less.'

'It's your evil twin?' John suggested.

By now Bob was back at the toll booth, confusing the toll taker yet again. He spoke to the toll taker and John simultaneously. 'You know, I never believed in the devil before, but in me he's found a home for the nineties.'

Marla was back in bed, her flannel pajamas a crumpled mess, the sheets pulled up to her neck. She looked over her work and found it good. The bedroom made no sense, but she was deeply satisfied. She was also worn out and looked at the clock, now perched all the way across the room on the bureau. It was past midnight. What was he doing out this late? He never stayed with *her* till twelve.

She must have dozed for a while, because the next thing she heard was the sound of Bob's car pulling into the driveway. Marla went to the window. He had not only gone to her house first but he had stayed longer than usual. That should make her feel good, and had won her the gorgeous three-gold ring, but instead she felt bad. From upstairs she saw Bob enter the house. Marla made a few last adjustments to the room, rearranged the pillows, and quickly slid into bed, pretending to be asleep.

Bob opened the bedroom door. He tiptoed in, trying to see by the light from the window, but tripped over the ottoman, upsetting the floor lamp, which crashed into the bureau. Marla sat up, concerned. 'Are you all right, Bob?'

'I think so.' He had one hand on his elbow, rubbing it, the other on his foot. 'Why was an end table in front of the door? I just hurt my ankle. Yeow!'

'And your arm?'

'No. I hurt that . . . at the lot.' Bob got up and stumbled to the bed, limping only a little. But the bed was only halfway across the room, so he smacked into it, hard, with his shin. 'Oooh!' He literally fell into the bed. 'What happened in here? And what is that smell?'

Marla realized, too late, that Sylvie wouldn't have used any incense. 'It's my new perfume,' she ad-libbed. 'Elaine gave it to me.'

'Elaine? Who's Elaine?'

'My sister.'

'Ellen? I thought you said Elaine.'

'No. I know my own sister's name,' Marla said, defensive. Distraction was the best move. She gestured to the room. 'My face isn't the only thing I redecorated, Bob.' Marla turned on the lamp, angling the shade so that the room was softly illuminated. 'So, what do you think, *Bob?*'

He stopped rubbing his ankle long enough to look up. 'You moved the furniture,' he said as if it were the dullest fact in the world.

Marla, more than a little disappointed, turned the light off.

'Sylvie, I'll look at it closely tomorrow. We'll talk about it . . .,' he said with a hint of guilt. He started undressing, reached across the bed, and kissed her on the cheek. 'Look. Let's start this over. Welcome home. I'm glad you're back.'

'You are?'

'Of course I am. How is your sister? In four words or less.'

In four words or less? That was impossible. Or maybe he was testing her, Marla thought. Unsure of how to respond, she talked as if she were answering a drop quiz. 'Six years older, but her face looks good. We don't get along. Never wants to live anywhere near the family.' She'd counted off the first four responses on her finger, then paused, trying to remember the last one. 'Her therapist supports her decision!' she added proudly as it came to mind, and triumphantly pushed down her thumb.

'I'm glad she's . . . the same,' Bob said. He got into bed. 'I really missed you,' he told her, and put his arm around her shoulders.

Marla was truly surprised. He'd never seemed to miss his wife when he talked to Marla about her. 'Why?' she asked.

Bob tried to manipulate Marla into a spooning position, but she was resistant.

'Why did I miss you?' he asked as if it was an unreasonable question. 'Because you were gone. What do you mean? You're my family.'

'I am?' Marla felt tears well up in her eyes but didn't know why.

'Come on, Sylvie,' Bob said. 'Let's get into our positions.'

Sex. Uh-oh. She'd promised Sylvie she . . . not only that but while she'd gone over sex with Sylvie, Sylvie hadn't gone over sex with her! Marla cocked her head. 'Tell me just once more what our positions are,' Marla murmured.

'Sylvie, are you all right?' Bob asked, sitting up. 'We've been falling asleep the same way for twenty-one years.'

Oh, *that* was what he was talking about . . . sleeping. 'Boy! You forget one little thing—' Marla began.

'We spoon,' Bob continued.

Marla got it. Bob spooned up against her. She cuddled her back into his belly. They lay beside each other in the darkness. Marla felt herself relax. This was what marriage was like.

Night after night. She liked it. She knew she would. But it was so new that she wanted to talk, to connect more with her husband. 'Bob, I'm sorry about your father,' Marla said.

'What about my father?' Bob asked drowsily.

'Being dead and all.'

'Sylvie, are you all right?' Bob asked, rising on one elbow. 'Did you hit your head when you moved all this stuff? Who's the president of the United States?'

'Like you don't know.' Marla smiled and pulled the blankets up to go to sleep, a man beside her for the whole night.

19

There were definitely some advantages to sleeping alone, Sylvie thought as she stretched out diagonally across Marla's bed. She didn't have the whole bed to herself, however. Sylvie looked at the roses, now badly wilted, lying in bed next to her. It was silly, sentimental, but she had slept with them, a symbol of her victory to come. She was still wearing the ridiculous Marla nightwear – the girl didn't seem to have a single pair of comfortable pajamas. Sylvie had felt foolish in the baby dolls and her after-face-lift chin strap, a charming combo. It was something she'd never let anyone, much less Bob, see her wearing in bed.

But she'd woken up with a bad anger hangover. The problem was that she didn't know if she was angry at Bob or herself. After all, she had orchestrated this switcheroo, and though it hadn't worked exactly the way she'd planned, she had definitely pulled it off. Yet she didn't like it.

Firstly she couldn't get over the fact that Bob had come to her – Marla – first. She'd lost her bet with Marla, but there was more than her precious ring at stake. There was an emotional backlash to be paid for, a very real cost.

And if she'd gone this far, shouldn't she have gone all the way – in both senses of the word? Shouldn't she have snagged Bob? Shouldn't she have grabbed the chance to be Bob's lover and prove to him – and herself – that she could do it?

Sylvie lay there, confused and miserable. She didn't know

what to do. What she needed was some time at her piano. If she could sit down and play some Bach or maybe Mozart's Sonata No. 23 she'd be able to order her thoughts. Then it hit her: No piano. She hadn't thought about how she'd live without a piano, even for a week. Right now it seemed impossible. What could she do? She couldn't think of a single thing, so she called her mother. 'I'm back,' she said.

'And where are you?' Mildred asked. 'At the bimbo's?'

'Watch what you call her, Mom. She may be a bimbo, but she's my bimbo.'

'Oh my god!' Mildred snapped. 'It's the Stockholm syndrome. Sylvie, you're identifying with the enemy.'

'No, Mom. I *am* the enemy. And Bob came over here to me last night.' Sylvie thought she was happy, but then, to her surprise, a sob escaped her.

'That's a pretty sad statement after more than twenty years of marriage.' There was a pause. 'I'm sorry, Sylvie,' Mildred said. 'People we love hurt us. It's a terrible thing. Should I come over?'

'Yes, please,' Sylvie said.

Marla had awakened at dawn, thrilled to find Bob gently snoring beside her. It was so homey to wake up next to a man. Inspired, Marla had slipped into a fluffy robe, donned warm slippers, and crept down to the kitchen. Now, at 7 A.M. she was putting happy faces on freshly baked cookies. As she frosted them, each smile got bigger and bigger. The phone rang and she happily picked it up. 'Schiffer residence . . . hi. How was last night?'

'Confusing as hell,' Sylvie's voice told her.

'Say, hey! Me too. And it's good to have a reason for it.' She continued to decorate the cookies.

'Was Bob happy to see me?' Sylvie asked.

Marla felt a pang, and not sure if it was guilt or pity, decided to lie. 'Oh, yeah. A big fuss. Well, not too big. You know, he was really, really tired. So, was it good?'

There was a momentary pause. Marla, holding the phone under her chin with a hunched shoulder, opened the oven and pulled out another batch of cookies. 'Don't you worry,' Sylvie's voice said in her ear. 'It was all good. Wonderful, terrific.'

'How would you describe it?' Marla asked, truly interested. Again, there was a pause. Marla looked for the spatula. Flour, cookbooks, dirty bowls, the sugar bin, measuring cup, and butter dish were all hiding the spatula. Baking was very messy. 'How would you describe the sex?' Marla asked.

'Uh, I would describe it as "sexy,"' Sylvie said. It was kind of disappointing, but that was the least of Marla's problems right now. She just had to find the spatula.

'I bet he was real hot for you . . . I mean, me. It must be why he was so tired. He's still sleeping.'

'He's sleeping?' Sylvie asked. Marla could tell she was shocked. 'Bob's always up at a quarter to seven. He's always at work by eight exactly.'

'I think I know where my husband is,' Marla said. 'He was sleeping so deeply I turned off the alarm.'

'Oh my god,' Sylvie said.

'Don't you think it'll put him in a good mood? A little extra sleep always sets *me* up,' Marla said.

'Hey, it's your problem,' Sylvie responded. 'By the way, I did remember to tell you how cranky Bob is in the mornings, didn't I?'

Marla acknowledged that; then they hung up. Marla decided to stop with the cookies. She doubted that Bob would mind the extra rest, especially if she made him a good breakfast. She took down the last clean bowl, threw four eggs into it, and began to beat them. Then she went to the freezer and took out the bacon. She put coffee on, using the fancy coffeemaker that only nice suburban women had. She set the table for two.

It was 8:41 on the microwave clock when she heard Bob limping down the stairs. 'My god, Sylvie,' he said. 'What the hell happened to you? What happened to the alarm? I woke up, it was past eight o'clock, and you weren't there.'

'Did you miss me?' Marla cooed. 'I was cooking you breakfast.' She poured two cups of coffee and waited by the window. She'd defrosted the frozen Stouffer's croissants. She'd cooked bacon. And the eggs were still hot.

Bob approached the table. 'What's this?' Bob asked.

'What does it look like?' Marla responded.

'Croissants? Butter? You made bacon and eggs?'

Marla nodded, trying not to look too proud. She'd hoped she'd gotten all the shells out of the eggs. 'Are you trying to kill me?' Bob asked. 'You know how high John says my cholesterol level is.'

Marla blinked. She tried to decide whether she should be upset because he was an ungrateful Neanderthal or whether she should try to cover up her errors. She decided on the latter. Her eyes were drawn to the lawn, its drifts of leaves and the big mud ruts that ran through part of the yard. 'Have we got moles?' she asked. 'Or is it voles?' Marla had once seen a nature show that showed those little creatures with nasty pink tips digging tunnels.

Bob was gulping his coffee, putting change in his pocket, and looking for his car keys. 'Voles?' he asked. 'What are you talking about?'

'The ruts,' Marla told him. 'What loused up the lawn like that?'

'The crane did that, Sylvie.'

'I didn't know that birds could mess up a lawn. Was it a herd?'

'A flock,' Bob said, putting down his coffee. 'A group of birds is a flock, not a herd. Are you trying to be funny this morning? The crane that pulled your car out of the pool ruined the lawn.'

'Carpool?' Marla asked.

'Look,' Bob said, putting his coffee cup down on the one bit of available counter space. 'I don't have time for jokes. I'm really late for work and I have meetings tonight.' He turned and started walking for the door.

'Haven't you forgotten something?' Marla asked, trying to keep her voice sweet. The least he could do was kiss her before he left.

'Oh, yeah,' Bob said. He grabbed the garage door opener from the ring at the side of the door. 'I'm outta here,' he told her, and he was.

After Sylvie got dressed, she went into the kitchen to get something for breakfast. She opened the refrigerator, but all she found there was expired yogurt and bottles of vitamins. She started opening cupboards, one after another. They were loaded with bottles of food additives, food replacements, and food supplements, but no food. Sylvie *had* to have some food and coffee. She'd have to go to the supermarket.

Sylvie was lying across the bed again when her mother rang the doorbell, though she now had Bob's roses on top of her in a funeral position. She laid the flowers aside and ran to the door. Mildred was standing in front of her with two Styrofoam cups filled with coffee. 'Bless you. You always know what I need,' Sylvie said as she reached out for a cup. Then she brought Mildred quickly into the bedroom. Mildred looked around with distaste at the dusty fake ficus tree. She picked up a pillow shaped like red lips. 'So this is how a mistress lives now? Your father's chippie did better.'

'Nothing is easy for women anymore,' Sylvie said.

Mildred opened a jewelry box on the bureau and distastefully lifted out a cheap pearl choker from the tangle of costume junk. 'This is not the jewelry of a successful mistress,' Mildred said, sniffing.

'She's hidden the cubic zirconium in the freezer,' Sylvie said in a depressed tone.

'Well, I suppose we should be grateful,' Mildred said. 'Bob's obviously not embezzling.' She turned to look at her daughter. 'Come on, Sylvie. You dreamed up this crack-brain scheme. At least enjoy it.'

'Oh god, Mom! I can't. I'm so . . . torn. Marla – I mean, *me*, as Marla – couldn't let Bob touch me last night.'

'Good girl! I knew I raised you right,' Mildred said brightly. 'So now go back home, throw her out of the house, and that's that.' Since there was no chair in the bedroom, she sat at the edge of the bed.

'I can't do that. I would *never* get what I wanted.' Sylvie sat up and took her mother's hand. 'Mom, last night I got a glimpse of the old Bob. I remembered what it felt like . . . to be desired.' Sylvie paused, remembering. 'It was so good. And I realized how long it's been since I had those feelings.' She let go of Mildred's hand and stood up. 'Oh, Mom! I wanted to hit him for depriving me of what I married him for.' Sylvie stifled a sob as Mildred patted her shoulder. Sylvie picked her head up and looked at Mildred. 'Do you think he'll call again or come over?'

'Wait a minute,' Mildred snapped. 'Now you're hoping that your husband will come back to his mistress?' Sylvie nodded. 'Women! We deserve what we get,' Mildred said.

Just then the doorbell chimed. Sylvie sat up straight, a gleam of hope in her eye. 'Maybe that's Bob!' Sylvie looked around. 'God! You've got to hide. He can't see you here.'

'Well, then he's blind,' Mildred said.

'No, Mom, you've got to hide.'

'Sylvie, I have gone as far with this as I am going to go. I am not hiding from my son-in-law.' The doorbell rang again. Mildred smiled. 'Just don't open up. Or tell him I'm Miss Bimbo's mother.' She paused. 'Say my name is Deirdre. I always thought I looked like a Deirdre.'

'Mom, stop it. Stay in here.' Sylvie closed the bedroom door and ran across the tiny living room. 'Who is it?' she called out.

'Pete.'

'Pete?' Sylvie asked. She'd studied Marla's notes. There was no mention of a Pete.

'Probably another boyfriend. Maybe you'll like *him*,' Mildred said from the bedroom doorway, her arms crossed over her chest.

Sylvie gave her mother a dirty look, made sure the safety chain was on the door, then opened it cautiously. There in front of her was an enormous flower arrangement with legs. 'Ooooh!' Sylvie cooed. She unlocked the chain and opened the door wide. The flowers filled the doorway and, she supposed, it was Pete's legs that brought them in. Sylvie turned to Mildred, her face radiant. She reached for the card.

Pete staggered into the living room with the flowers. 'I think the best place for these beauties is on the box next to the couch. It'll balance out the room,' he offered from behind a spray of gladiolus.

'Deliveries *and* decorating advice,' Mildred commented. 'Not that anything could balance this decor, except a psychiatrist.'

Sylvie read the card, then looked up joyfully at her mother. 'He can't give me up. He wants to see me again tonight.' She looked at Pete. 'Thank you,' she said. 'You've made me very happy.'

'Hey. Is this your mom?' Pete asked. He turned to Mildred. 'Your daughter is a really friendly person.'

'My daughter's a romantic fool,' Mildred told Pete, handing him a tip.

Marla was in the music room giving a lesson. Jennifer was at the piano. She was playing the *MinuteWaltz*, but doing it in thirty seconds.

Marla felt very professional, very teacherly. She was a true authority figure to this little girl. 'That's really good, sweetie. Even I can't do it that fast,' Marla said, smiling and patting the girl on her shoulder. 'Try it once more, even quicker. I bet you can do it.'

A look of confusion flooded Jennifer's face. She started over and played even faster. Marla nodded, an encouraging smile on her own face.

Pete had gone and Mildred was preparing to leave too when the phone rang. Without thinking, Sylvie lifted the receiver. 'Hello,' she breathed in the sexiest voice she could. Mildred rolled her eyes.

'Hi, it's Eena. I'm really in a crisis here. You were gone for months.'

Who was Eena? What was her crisis about? Sylvie hadn't a clue, didn't remember anything from the notebook, so she ad-libbed in the way she thought Marla might. 'Wow!' she said.

'Anyway, I'm in the new place in Highland Hills, right off Chagrin Boulevard. Could you come over this morning? My feet are really in terrible shape.'

'Um, okay,' Sylvie said. 'Should we say in about two hours?'

'Fine, let me give you the address.' Sylvie jotted it down and Eena, whoever she was, hung up.

Mildred raised her brows. 'So you have a date with Bob while Marla has a date with John?'

'That wasn't Bob, it was a female client. And what date with John?'

'I spoke to Marla last night. *You* didn't call, I noticed. Anyway, she said she was having lunch with John.'

'That's impossible. She never even met him. She just got home last night.'

'She's a fast little worker, that girl,' Mildred said. 'Can you imagine her at the club?'

'At the club? They're having lunch at the country club? What possessed her?'

'What possessed *you*? Sylvie, you have opened Pandora's box here, or haven't you been listening to anything I've said? I know I'm just your mother.'

Sylvie turned to Mildred. 'Okay,' she said. 'I admit this is a glitch. You have to help me. I'll call Marla and tell her the lunch is out of the question but you go to the club, just in case. If I can't get to her you'll have to keep an eye on her.'

209

'Why bother? Every woman in Shaker Heights who's there will be keeping both eyes on her – I mean, you. I don't think they're going to believe you – I mean, her – when she says all she's done to herself is had "a nice little rest."' Mildred paused. 'You'll be the Cher of Shaker Heights by tomorrow. And do you think she knows a salad fork when she sees one?'

Sylvie looked at her mother beseechingly. 'Please, Mom.'

Mildred picked up her purse, shrugged, and then nodded. 'What the hell,' she said. 'It'll be the best floor show at the club since Dick Edenboro joined AA.' Mildred kissed her daughter, shook her head, and departed, taking her Styrofoam cup with her. Sylvie turned back to the bare apartment and dialed her home phone number. The line was busy. But as soon as she hung up, the phone rang again. Before she lifted the receiver Sylvie took out her reference notebook. Then, poised to research, she answered the phone.

'Hullo. Oh, Mr Brightman.' Checking her notes, her face registered who Mr Brightman was and what he expected. She couldn't read some of it. Sucking? Was this guy the . . . ? 'Today at two-thirty?' Oh no. He could forget about that. Sylvie paused, but conscientiously said, 'Yes, Mr Brightman.'

Then she hung up and panicked. Okay, she'd rub an instep, massage an ankle, but she drew the line at sucking a toe. This was a job for a professional. She immediately tried Marla. No answer at first, then her own voice greeted her on the answering machine. Sylvie wondered what she should do. Well, she'd dress and go to Eena's first. Meanwhile, she'd keep trying Marla. She got off the bed and began to go through Marla's closet. All of the clothes were cheap and flimsy. What do you wear for your first toe job? she wondered.

On her way to Eena's Sylvie picked up her car phone – Marla's actually – and dialed her own car number. Maybe she'd catch Marla in transit since she wasn't answering at the house.

'Mrs Sylvie Schiffer,' Marla's voice said.

'Sorry. You have to be yourself for an hour. Where are you?'

'I'm in the car.'

'This I know. But where *is* the car?'

'I'm not sure. I just passed Canterbury Road, but I'm trying to get to Courtland Boulevard.'

'You are right where I am. I'm surprised I can't see you. Are you heading north or south?' Sylvie asked.

'Straight,' Marla said. Sylvie sighed and shook her head. 'Look, Mr Brightman's office called. He wants "a complete treatment," whatever that is, at two-thirty. I'll do Eena this morning, but *you're* doing Brightman.'

'I can't. I'm having lunch with John at the club,' Marla said airily. 'Anyway, Eena doesn't pay. She just gives me cellulite treatments in return. You can forget her,' Marla said. 'Hey! John really, really likes you. He's a bright man. Is he cute?'

There was bad static, or interference, on the cell phone. Sylvie only heard part of the question. 'Brightman?' Sylvie asked. 'How would I know?'

'No, not Brightman! Dr John.'

Sylvie tried not to sound annoyed with the girl. 'I don't know if he's cute, but he's smart.' She needed Marla's cooperation on this. She'd be a reflexologist for some woman masseuse, but she wouldn't play footsie for money with some old crook. 'So, John's not going to think you're me in person. Not in daylight. *He* actually looks at me. We're not married. You can't have lunch with him.'

'That's not fair. I'm not having fun,' Marla pouted. 'What's the use of being a wife if I can't go out to lunch at the club *and*

I have to do Brightman's feet?' She paused. 'Hey, where's this club anyway? I can't find it.'

'Wait a minute,' Sylvie was telling her. 'It's Wednesday, John's day off. It's the only day he drinks at lunch.' Maybe they *could* get away with it, Sylvie thought, if Marla didn't talk too much. John would like to believe in the wonders of modern surgical science. 'Okay,' Sylvie agreed. 'Here's the deal: you'll have lunch with John, I'll do Eena. Then you have to cut out early and do Brightman's feet.'

'But what are *you* doing? It's not fair! I still have to shop for the Thanksgiving groceries,' Marla whined into the phone.

'Do it later. And be careful with John. Don't drink and don't talk. We'll both be dead if you make a mistake. Then do Brightman'

'But I don't have my equipment!' Marla whined. 'My oils or my incense or my aromatherapy.'

Sylvie pulled up to a stoplight. On her right was a black sports car. She couldn't help herself. With her younger look Sylvie felt a whole new confidence. She lowered the passenger window so she could see more clearly. The noise made the man turn his head and he looked at her. He was nice-looking, with a mustache. But he didn't smile. A look of utter confusion, or even horror, crossed his face as he turned his head from one side to the other. Then he closed his tinted window. When the light changed, his sports car burned rubber. Only then did Sylvie see Marla in the far lane. The guy had been sandwiched between them! They'd been stereo for him. Someone behind her honked, and Sylvie put her foot on the gas, then turned left while Marla, not noticing any of this, turned right.

'Well, if I do Brightman, you'll have to do the laundry,' she was saying. 'There's just so much. I can't get the machine to turn on. And I don't have time for every-thing.'

Sylvie sighed. Bob probably hadn't done a load since she left. 'Okay, it's a deal. I go to Eena's, just to get some practice. You do John, then come and meet me at Brightman's. I give you the oils and your bag. And while you do Brightman, I'll do the laundry. But be quick, and be careful with John. He's a very smart doctor.'

'I've done doctors before,' Marla said, sounding insulted. 'Where is this . . . ?' She apparently still couldn't find the country club.

'What? Can't hear you, I'm in a tunnel.'

'I'll be fine with John,' Marla shouted. 'You meet me at Brightman's. If I'm late, just go in. I'll take over. His office has an outside door. And then *you* can go do the laundry.'

20

The Shaker Heights Country Club had all the brick, ivy, and curved driveways it could possibly need. It was done inside in the rich deep blue and green and wine that meant 'class' to Marla. The walls were hung with pictures of people on horseback, and other pictures of dead birds and dead rabbits. She'd once worked in a restaurant like this as a hostess. The people who eat here ride and shoot animals, she thought. Weird that they love to sit on some while they kill others. Stuff like that confused her. Perhaps that distraction was the reason she didn't plan this out better. As she entered the dining room it occurred to her for the first time that she didn't actually know what John looked like.

The dining room was large, and as most of the tables were already occupied by groups of women, it made it easy to rule *those* out. Then there were tables of men. Tables of women, tables of men. It was interesting, Marla noted, that there were no men and women sitting together except for one very, very old couple, and it looked as if that man was more dead than alive. He was in a wheelchair, so maybe even *he* didn't want to be eating with a woman but he couldn't get away. She scanned the room for John. There was a man sitting alone, but he was pretty elderly. He was looking at the menu, but as if he felt her eyes on him, he dropped it and looked up. From across the room he smiled and winked. Marla couldn't believe John would do that. But this man did look familiar.

God, was he a client? Anyway, this guy was too old – a real geezer, though not bad-looking for a geezer. She could wink back . . . but she decided to pointedly ignore the geezer. She wasn't going to do any flirting with anyone except John.

Then she saw the only other man alone, seated at a corner table, and she was glad she'd resisted her first temptation. He was tall – she could tell that even though he was sitting down – and staring out the window at the golf course. Was he John? Marla figured that if he saw her and waved or stood up or something she'd know. But what should she do? Shout out 'Is there a doctor in the house?' Other people might be doctors, though. Just then Marla felt her arm taken by a bony hand. Before she could protest and tell whoever it was not to throw her out, that she was Mrs Robert Schiffer and a member here, she turned and realized it was Mildred behind her. 'He's the one in the corner,' Mildred hissed.

'Mom!' Marla said and gave Mildred a big kiss. 'What are you doing here?'

'Don't overdo it, dear,' Mildred said, pecking her cheek, 'and sit with your back to the rest of the room.' Then she nodded to the geezer. 'Did you say hello to your father?' she asked.

'That's my dad?' Marla whispered. 'I thought he was . . .' She stopped before she got to the wink and how she'd snubbed him. Marla stared at the man, who was back to looking at the menu. When he looked up again she said, 'Oh! I have his eyes.'

Mildred rolled hers. 'A quick hello and then get over to John. And make *that* quick too,' she warned.

Marla walked across the carpet to her father. She'd never known her real father before and, even though she reminded herself that this really wasn't him, it *might* have been him, or somebody who looked exactly like him. She felt herself choking up. There was something so solid about him – his thick thatch of white hair, his clean, very clean, sun-speckled skin, and the tweed sports jacket with the Oxford-cloth blue shirt. He looked like a perfect dad. Much more solid than Mike Brady on *The Brady Bunch* or even Charles Ingalls on *Little House* – although Pa Ingalls was definitely hotter. 'Hi, Daddy,' she said in a soft voice.

'Oh, *now* you say hello! Three weeks away, not a call, not a word!' He looked her over. 'I gotta say, you're looking a treat, Sylvie. That dip in the pool must have done you some good.' He patted her head. 'I think the chlorine lightened your hair.' Marla thought of how much lighter her hair had been and sighed. 'But I didn't know you were going to have lunch with us,' her dad was saying.

Marla felt an odd lump in her throat. 'I'm not,' she said. 'I'm . . .' But she really wanted to. She realized that more than anything she wanted to sit down here with her nice clean daddy.

'She's lunching with John,' Mildred said. 'Get on over there,' she told Marla. And, before she could burst into tears, Marla turned around and made her way across the dining room to the corner table.

John, still gazing out the window, must have sensed the attention because he turned, spotted her, and stood up. Marla's mood instantly brightened. She could see she'd made a good impression on him because his mouth hung open. Even with the brown hair and extra pounds she guessed she could still look okay – at least to this guy who expected frumpy Sylvie. 'Sylvie, sit down,' John invited, holding the chair for her. 'Do you want some wine?'

'Sure,' Marla agreed. 'Do you want to meet my mom and dad?' she asked.

He looked up from pouring her wine. 'Meet them? I've known them all my life,' John said.

Marla, flustered, took a sip of her wine. 'Of course you have. Silly me.' She smiled to cover up her slip. Then she started to run her hand suggestively up and down the stem of the glass.

John, marveling, watched her hand, then moved his eyes up to her face. 'You look . . . beautiful.'

'Well, this is the new Sylvie,' Marla said, smiling.

John laughed. 'As a philosopher, I have to say I have problems with cosmetic surgery. As a professional, I just have to tell you that whatever you did to yourself, you look terrific.' He lowered his voice. 'As a man, I want to tell you that you look better than terrific.'

Ah, this was more like it. Marla gave John a look from beneath her lids. 'What's *better* than terrific?' she urged.

'I would say it's in the range of breathtaking,' John said, and then looked down at his drink. He seemed to blush.

'Why, Dr John! You are a flirt!' Marla said, finishing the wine. She should have eaten some breakfast. 'You really, really should have asked me to marry *you* before Bob did.'

'I did,' John said.

Marla, confused, stopped for a moment. 'Which is why I respect you so much,' she told him, recovering.

'I respect you too, Sylvie.' He reached out and took her hand.

Marla deeply enjoyed hearing that. Men had adored her, had lusted after her, had courted her. But respect? 'I don't think I've ever heard that word before . . . applied to me.'

'I can't believe that,' John said. The waiter came to take

their lunch order, and John pulled his hand back, breaking the mood. When the waiter left, John seemed to get serious. 'You said you had something urgent to tell me.'

'I do, but you may not respect me when you hear it,' Marla said, hanging her head.

'Try me.'

Marla thought she would like to, but used her better judgment and didn't tell him. She looked down at the glistening Cartier ring gleaming on her finger – now hers forever. She took a deep breath. Now *she'd* get the chance to be a victim. 'Okay, John. You'll have to get this the first time. It is *so* painful that I'll never be able to say it aloud again. Not even to you, my best friend.'

'Go on. You know you're always safe with me.' John took Marla's hand again.

Marla took another deep breath, drank down the glass of wine, and looked deep into John's eyes. 'Bob is cheating on me,' she announced. She exhaled loudly. 'There! It's out in the open now. I feel much better.'

John looked more confused than concerned. 'Sylvie. You already told me about that,' he said gently. 'Before you left, you told me.'

Marla panicked for a moment, but then pretended to remember. 'Oh, right. Well, then it's old news.' She gulped her wine. 'So I went away, thought about it all, and just decided it was nobody's fault but blame itself. And I'm going to live by those words.'

'I don't understand,' John said.

'Thank goodness!'

The waiter returned with their order and poured the rest of the wine. Once again John pulled back his hand. 'Let's have lunch,' Marla said brightly. Then, when they were alone again, she smiled seductively at John. This time *she* reached out and took *his* hand. John did not look unhappy that she did so.

Sylvie was sitting in the reception area waiting for Mr Brightman. She had recuperated from the shock of Eena's place — a tiny garden apartment filled with cats, crystals, dying houseplants, and some of the dirtiest throw rugs Sylvie had ever stepped on. When Eena had lifted her feet up, their bottoms had been absolutely black.

And Eena hadn't just expected to have her arches rubbed: she'd wanted a reading. She needed to know whether it was her bladder or her kidneys that were acting up, because she wasn't sure which healing crystal to use. Sylvie had faked it as best she could and then, when Eena mentioned that there was blood in her urine, Sylvie strongly suggested that she call John for an appointment.

She'd washed her hands five times since then; twice at Eena's, then with Handi Wipes in the car, again at a gas station rest room, and here at Mr Brightman's.

Apparently, though Marla had called him a crook, Brightman was actually the president of some kind of trucking company. Men moved back and forth across the green linoleum of the office, talking about depots and weigh stations. Each of them managed to look her over, most of them either averting their eyes or winking. She sat there, as primly as she could, in a pair of Marla's skintight blue leggings and a yellow sweater, feeling like she was a child in school waiting to see the principal.

'Mr Brightman will see you now. He's sorry you had to wait so long,' the receptionist told her with a smirk.

'That's all right. I can wait longer,' Sylvie replied nervously. Where was Marla? She'd promised she'd come.

'He can't. He has a three-thirty.'

'I could come back tomorrow,' Sylvie offered. Where the *hell* was Marla?

'He specifically said he needed to be relaxed *now*. He's all ready.' The receptionist held up Mr Brightman's shoes as if they were a pair of dead fish. Sylvie felt as if she might faint.

'Right. Absolutely. Now.' Sylvie forced herself to rise, then started to walk toward Mr Brightman's office. The receptionist stopped her, redirected her to another door. 'You know he likes it in there,' she said.

God, what was 'in there'? Marla didn't tell her about *this*. Was this something more than . . . playing footsie? 'Oh, right. I don't know where my head is today,' Sylvie murmured to cover up her mistake.

'That's okay. You never did,' the receptionist said, so it was clear that Marla had on this been truthful – she was a regular.

Sylvie, slowly and hesitantly, moved to the door and entered. It was, thank god, not a bedroom. It was, instead, totally empty except for wall-to-wall pink carpeting, pink velvet drapes, and a black leather chair and ottoman placed in the precise center of the room. Mr Simon Brightman was sitting in the chair. Sylvie saw that he had his feet naked and ready for her. He was portly, with thinning gray hair and a round face that seemed to be missing a chin. He wore a wrinkled plain gray suit and a white button-down shirt with the collar open, his blue tie loosened. But it was his feet, naked and propped up on the ottoman, that Sylvie couldn't avoid looking at. His feet were tiny for a man his size, and sprouted enormous tufts of hair on each toe knuckle. The hair was almost long enough to braid, not that Sylvie wanted to get close enough to do that. The bottom of each foot was yellow with thick calluses, and the tops, up to the ankles, were covered with a road map of distended, ropy veins. Most disgusting of all were his toenails – painted a Molly Ringwald pink. Sylvie thought of Eena's black-bottomed feet. Now these. Of all the feet in all the world she had to start with these?

'There you are!' he said. 'Why didn't you come in the side door?' He indicated a door at the back of this room, almost hidden by the velvet drape. 'You know I don't like you to be in the main reception area.'

'Oops, sorry. But here I am,' Sylvie said, trying to sound as cheerful and dotty as Marla normally did. 'Wow!' she said. 'You have a really, really great aura today.' Sylvie opened her bag, took out a bottle of oil, some incense, and Marla's aromatherapy kit. Getting closer, Sylvie recognized that Simon Brightman's feet could use some therapy in the aroma department. *Where was Marla, damnit!* Sylvie fiddled with a match, lit the incense, and wondered whether her evil twin was still at the club with John.

'Go on, baby. Do me,' Brightman said and winked.

Sylvie almost fainted. Desperate, she vamped for time. 'You'll have to excuse me for a minute,' Sylvie said. 'I have to tinkle.'

Brightman sighed heavily. 'I don't have much time,' he said. 'Make it quick.'

Sylvie left the room and closed the door behind her. She leaned up against the wall long enough to regroup her thoughts. She had to find Marla, and fast. Otherwise she was just walking out. Sucking those feet was too disgusting for words. Sylvie headed toward the reception desk. She was about to ask the receptionist for permission to use the phone but then she spotted a pay phone in a small alcove. Of course she didn't have any quarters. Sylvie began punching an endless stream of numbers into the phone. Calling cards were convenient, she supposed, yet what a nuisance. Who can remember all these digits when they're under stress? She misdialed her own car phone number and had to reenter everything one more time. All she could think of were Brightman's feet, waiting for her. Thank god Marla picked up on the first ring. 'Where are you?' Sylvie demanded.

'I've been caught!' Marla said, sounding frantic.

'What!?' Sylvie's stomach did a flip. Had Bob figured it out? Were they busted? Her stomach lurched and she thought she should have made love to him last night while she'd had the chance.

But, 'I'm caught in a loop,' Marla was saying. 'How do I get out?'

'What are you talking about?' Sylvie snapped, relieved but confused. Maybe they hadn't been busted.

'I left John at the club but I can't seem to find my way to you. I've wanted to live in a place like the Heights all my life, but now I can't get out! How many cul-de-sacs are there in this place? I've passed our street four times already. Oops. There it is again.'

Sylvie tried not to implode. She had to be patient to get Marla here. Then she could kill her.

'You know, our husband has to mow the lawn,' Marla was saying. 'Say, hey, people around here are so rude! This lady that lives two houses down just flipped me the bird. Boy, does *she* give off bad karma. I can feel it from here and I'm protected by steel and glass.'

It must have been Rosalie, Sylvie realized. Marla would need lead to protect her from poor Rosalie's 'karma.' 'Just get on Lee Road to the bridge and get over here,' she said, sounding as desperate as she felt.

'Lee Road? I'm *on* Lee Road. Or I was. I know I saw it,' Marla said. 'Say, hey, your brother called. He called me here on the car phone. He said his nosy ex-wife saw me driving in circles and thought I might be looking for another pool to drive into.' Marla giggled. 'He's really sweet, isn't he? He was worried about me.'

'I'm more worried about me,' Sylvie snapped. 'Simon Brightman's feet won't last forever.'

'I'm just lost. I can't get past Eaton and Carlton roads, and I've got to get out of here. People are looking. Please, be my control tower.'

'All right. Calm down,' Sylvie reassured her. 'Take a right at Carlton and a right on Eaton. Two doors down you'll see a duck mailbox. Take a left. Go through two lights and you'll see the shopping center on the right.'

'You don't really, really mean to go *through* the lights?' Marla asked. 'What if they're red? You'll have a pimple on *your* license, remember?' Marla paused. Sylvie was silent. 'I'm trying to be funny,' she explained.

'And I'm trying not to laugh,' Sylvie said bitterly, drumming her fake nails against the phone. She waited.

'I've been through four lights and I still don't see any ducks,' Marla told Sylvie.

'I said *two* lights,' Sylvie snapped, desperate. 'Two.'

'Okay. Okay!' Marla said. 'I'll hang a U-ee.'

At that moment, Mr Brightman stuck his head out of the door and looked around. He spotted Sylvie and motioned for her to rejoin him. He pointed down at his watch. Sylvie smiled and nodded.

'Hurry up, Marla. Mr Brightman's getting really impatient,' Sylvie begged. 'And what's "the full treatment," anyway?'

'I'm out! I'm out!' Marla cried triumphantly. 'I see the

bridge. I'll be there in four minutes. Boy, I'd hate to have to try to get out of the Heights in an emergency.'

'This *is* an emergency!' Sylvie said with clenched teeth, and hung up the phone. She started back to the room and Mr Brightman. As she approached him Sylvie shrugged and smiled, Marlaesque. 'I'm sorry about that. I was getting bad vibes about my sister and I just *had* to call her.' She sat on the stool at his feet. 'Uh . . . your toes look particularly adorable today.'

Mr Brightman leaned back and closed his eyes. 'That's what I like to hear. Change the polish. I want something . . . youthful.'

'Well, you've come to the right place. I mean, I have. Come, I mean. I mean, come here.'

'My insteps are killing me. Why don't you give them a try? But first put on new polish. You know I like a *lot* of color.'

It took everything Sylvie had to get even her hands and his toes in close proximity. She had Marla's kit, but it wasn't a pedicure kit . . . it had essential oils and cream but no Revlon Fire and Ice. Sylvie took out some massage oil and dripped a little onto Simon Brightman's foot.

'Haven't you forgotten to take something off?' Mr Brightman asked, his voice low.

'Take something off?' Sylvie inquired, staring at his horny toenails. It seemed to her that it wasn't just his nails that were horny.

'My old polish. *And* say the poem. I want the full treatment. Are we playing coy? Please, Miss Molensky, I'm losing patience. I've got only twenty minutes left.' Sylvie, not knowing what to do, started to rise. Enough was enough. She simply couldn't do this. She'd leave.

'Go behind the drapes, like you always do,' Mr Brightman

said, his voice commanding. Without thinking about it, she did. She'd stood there for a moment, almost in tears, when she heard Marla dance into the room from the outside door. Sylvie peeked out from behind the velvet curtains.

'One little piggy goes to market,' Marla cooed to Mr Brightman, 'one little piggy stays home.' Marla ducked behind the other drape, pulling it in front of her while she searched her bag for something. She pulled out a Day-Glo-pink Hard Candies nail polish, which she held out from behind the curtain with a practiced stripper's gesture and shook before she tossed it across the room. Mr Brightman groaned. 'Oh, yeah!' he said. 'It's perfect. You little tease!' Marla danced out from behind the curtain. 'Go out the side door. Now,' Marla whispered as she passed the drape that Sylvie still clutched in front of herself. Marla retrieved the polish and squatted at Mr Brightman's feet. He closed his eyes and Sylvie slipped gratefully out of the room.

21

Sylvie pulled up to her house, parked the car, and looked around the cul-de-sac, checking it out through her rearview mirror. She certainly didn't want her neighbors, including her mother and Rosalie — above all, Rosalie — to see her. Bob had always complained about the garage being separate from the house, but this was the first time that Sylvie herself minded making the walk from the driveway to the back door.

She stepped in through the French doors to the music room. She froze, then gasped. The disorder was amazing. Her beloved sheet music was spread in messy piles on the settee, on the window seat, with the biggest pile on the floor, far too close to the fireplace. Some of those arrangements were irreplaceable, done by her professors at Juilliard, long dead now. Didn't that girl know anything? Aside from the music morass there were two or three half-filled mugs and an empty soda-water bottle sitting on the end tables but, worst of all, there was a vase full of dying chrysanthemums and lilies — a vile combination — on the piano. Sylvie couldn't tell how long it had been there, but the flowers were drooping and, when she rushed over to it, Sylvie could see the fetid water within the vase. Yellow-brown pollen from the stamens of the lilies blotched the surface of the baby grand. Holding her breath, Sylvie lifted the vase. Thank god, there was no water ring under it, but somehow she was sure that wasn't because of Marla's care. Sylvie caressed the unblemished smoothness of the top of the piano. She'd missed playing almost as much as she'd missed Bob. She wished she had the time right then to sit down and play – even for just a few minutes – but it was a luxury she couldn't afford.

Sylvie tried to remember the last time she'd gone this long without playing. Maybe right after the twins were born, but not since then. Reluctantly, she forced herself to leave the desecrated music room as it was but she *did* carry out the vase. She'd have to tell Marla – if she hadn't told her already – *never* to put anything on the Steinway's ebony lacquer.

Sylvie walked through the dark hallway. She felt like a ghost, haunting her own home, carrying the dying white mums and lilies before her. She walked by the bookshelf and noticed a photo at eye level. She stopped. Bob stood with the twins on a beach in South Carolina. The photo was in an old silver frame that Sylvie had been given by Bob's mother just before she died. No one looking at the picture, except for her and Bob, would know that she had snapped the photo, or that just minutes before Kenny had been caught in an undertow that had nearly pulled him out to sea. Sylvie had seen it happen, quick as a flash, and screamed: Bob had raced into the waves, crossed the current, and managed to pull Kenny along with him. Now Sylvie looked at the children's smiling faces. They were completely unruffled but, despite Bob's tan, Sylvie knew he had been, at that moment, pale beneath the sun's ruddiness. Her finger had trembled on the shutter, and when they had gotten the photos back both of them had looked at this one together silently for a long time. Then Bob had mouthed her thought: the picture on the roll before this one might have been the very last one of the twins together.

Sylvie clutched the dying flowers to her. She didn't want

227

to lose Bob. It was more than just love and it was more than lust and it was more than pride. He shared memories and experiences of her whole adult life, things she would never be able to share with anyone again. She wanted to get to keep her life and his reflection of it, just as she was willing still to reflect his. If her marriage ended, Sylvie knew she would never marry again. Not because she would continue to love Bob and moon over him, and not because this possible dissolution would turn her into a man hater, but because if this union failed, she would know that all unions could fail. She would never want to go through another, a false union doomed to disappoint and unravel. Rather than that she would turn to God, a love that would always be returned. That or she would get those golden retrievers.

She pushed open the swinging kitchen door with her hip and stopped dead in her tracks. Every surface of the kitchen – the counters, the table, the island – was covered with food. It looked as if Marla was about to open a farm stand at the back of Sylvie's home. Pumpkins were set on the table, tomatoes lined the windowsill, an entire net of garlic – at least a two-year supply – hung from the pot rack, and three sacks of potatoes were leaning against the basement door. There were also cans of baked beans, bowls of yams, boxes of Pepperidge Farm cookies, a huge pile of Indian corn, two or three tins of anchovies, a tray of baked cookies . . . just doing an inventory would have taken Sylvie all day. What in the world was Marla doing?

Sylvie was a fanatic for putting things away and keeping her kitchen cleared and organized. She didn't go as far as alphabetizing the canned goods, but she did keep them stacked, with the soonest expiration dates in the front, the later purchases in the back. She put down the vase, having to push over a stack of mail to find the counter space. Then she took a deep breath and scratched at her inner elbow. This chaos was enough to give her hives. And Bob hadn't even noticed? Didn't the man have eyes? Sylvie wondered for a moment why she had bothered fighting the daily tide of entropy for the last two decades. Certainly the kids had never minded disorder. Apparently Bob didn't either. Had she been doing it all for herself? Sylvie thought of those hours – hundreds of hours – of unpacking and folding grocery bags, organizing and putting things away. She could have spent the time playing the piano. She could have spent the time with the children. Or exercising and having her hair streaked blonde. Maybe, if she'd spent the time on her appearance and with Bob instead of working in the house, she'd still be in this house, happy and loved.

Sylvie looked up at the kitchen clock, a clock that had measured out her life for almost twenty years. She didn't have much time, and thought it best to not even look at whatever other changes Marla had wrought. Instead, Sylvie just turned and opened the door to the laundry room, shutting it behind her and simultaneously turning on the light.

She almost screamed. Here, confronting her, was the most enormous pile of laundry she'd ever seen, except maybe for that time when the kids came home from camp on same day Bob came back from a business convention. But this wasn't just kids' T-shirts and shorts. There were sheets and towels from all of the bathrooms. There were Bob's sweaters, his polo shirts, his chinos and socks. There were dishcloths and washcloths, dress shirts and her cloth napkins. The biggest pile had obviously towered too high on the counter and had fallen onto the floor, creating a cloth swamp. Worst of all, there was no separation between the delicates and the permanent press, hand washables, or even the whites and colors. It was a stew.

With a sigh Sylvie cleared the top of the washer so that she could at least begin the first load. As she pulled open the top the mildew smell that came from the darkness of the washer's hold nearly knocked her over. She looked inside, her heart sinking, knowing what she'd see. A wash – god knew when it was from – was still in there, along with plenty of old water. Sylvie looked up at the control dial to discover that it was on the presoak cycle. God! How was she going to get the heavy, wet clothes out without touching the slimy soap-scummed water? Sylvie looked around the kitchen and managed to find her long-handled wooden spoon. She was curious as to why it would be in the pot cupboard when it belonged in the utensil drawer, but she couldn't help but be grateful that whatever Marla's housekeeping habits, she'd managed to find the thing.

Sylvie pulled out nasty sopping rags for ten minutes and piled them next to the sink. Then she put the machine on the spin cycle to drain it while pulling out all the whites she could find. She began throwing sheets, towels, and the like into the now drained machine. She grabbed a pair of Bob's briefs and then, beside them, a pair of her panties. They were panties that Marla must have worn. Sylvie stopped dead. Holding both pairs of underwear in her hands, Sylvie knew in a more visceral sense that Marla was not just in her shoes or in her house, but in her bed, on her sheets, and in her panties. It seemed, all at once, way too much for Sylvie.

What had she done?

Her hands began to shake. She threw the underclothes into the washer as if they were contaminated. The tears that trembled on her lower lids were hot. She bent down to gather more clothes, coming across her blue silk nightgown. What was *this* doing here? It needed to be dry-cleaned, not washed. Sylvie never wore that unless . . .

No way, Sylvie told herself. Bob was too occupied with her – the faux Marla – to even *think* about having sex with his wife – the real Marla. Right? Right! Sylvie tried to shake the thought out of her head but the fact that she – as Marla – hadn't made love with Bob yet didn't make it any easier for her. Would her hesitation and teasing him cause him to have sex with his wife – faux Sylvie? Perhaps not; Sylvie couldn't remember Bob coming home to her in the past few months after 'a meeting' and being interested in sex. Now that Sylvie thought about it, he always just opted for a shower.

With tears now running down her cheeks, Sylvie finished loading the machine, added the detergent, and closed the lid. She felt more pathetic than Cinderella, but she continued to sort the remaining dirty clothes into their respective piles, automatically emptying the pockets of Bob's chinos, wiping away her tears as she went. I wonder, she thought, how many women are weeping in laundry rooms all over this country right now.

She put her hand in all the pockets. She found the usual: change, crumpled dollar bills, business cards, and gum wrappers. Then, in the last pair of pants, she felt a larger object, almost billfold size. Bob normally carried his wallet in his jacket pocket; she put her hand into the slacks and found a tightly folded color pamphlet. Probably specs on a new car at the lot, Sylvie thought.

But as she unfolded the Hawaiian brochure she couldn't help but notice the colors. 'Oh my god!' Sylvie said out loud. The crumpled bit of paper, which had been delivered only weeks ago, reminded her of how simple things had seemed and what a simpleton she'd been. Sylvie had thought Bob loved her and that the two of them would find their place in the sun. Now she found a place on the floor amid the drift of dirty laundry and, clutching the crumpled brochure in her hand, she wept aloud to the hum of the washer.

22

Marla was prepared to get prepared for Thanksgiving. She had a
list. She'd used Sylvie's cash card and had loved it — it was
like going to Las Vegas and winning a jackpot every time.
Now, with several hundred dollars in her purse, plus the tip
from Mr Brightman, she entered Food Universe. It was one
of those stores with giant everything; there were mayonnaise
jars the size of coffee tables. Marla wasn't even used to regular
supermarkets — she bought all her stuff at either the Vitamin
Cave or the 7-Eleven.

Marla was already pushing two huge carts and was only
halfway down her list. She had institutional-size cans of cranberry sauce, a huge box of stuffing, and sweet potatoes. She
stared at a gigantic bag of marshmallows that could supply a
university. What was that about? Luckily, an employee passed
her and she stopped him. 'Excuse me. I would like to see
something smaller in a marshmallow.'

'Sorry, that's the only size we have.'

Marla threw the huge plastic bag into her cart and continued down the aisle of the supermarket. She was searching out turkeys. She felt like a hunter. She was going
to get the best, biggest bird for her family. She rounded
the corner and was forced to steer her cart to the left
to avoid running into the back of a lady waiting in line.
It seemed they'd been there a long time. They were all
talking to help pass the time. 'Last year they ran out, just

fifty people ahead of me,' the woman in front of Marla said.

'Me too. And all the supermarkets were out too. I had to go to the children's petting zoo and kidnap one,' a red-headed lady admitted.

'You kidnapped a turkey?' another asked. 'Then what?'

'I was ready to wring *somebody's* neck,' the redhead said with a laugh. 'So it was the turkey's.'

Marla started to sweat at the thought of not getting a turkey for her family. She tried to sneak up the line, and got four or five places up, but an angry woman saw what she was doing. 'Line cutter!' the woman yelled. All the other women caught on to what she was doing and pushed her all the way back to the end of the line.

'You don't understand!' Marla cried, 'It's my first Thanksgiving. I'll do anything to get a turkey. It's worth cutting in or strangling your own bird. Because when the table is set and beautiful, and the whole family sits down, they're going to be really, really grateful for all the work I did.'

Every woman who heard her started to laugh. They looked at Marla as if she were insane.

Marla managed to finish all the shopping and leave the store, exhausted but with no major injuries. She hadn't had any idea that shopping could be such an aggressive sport. There were so many bags that she filled up the huge cart and the shelf under it. The parking lot was a nightmare of angry women and beeping horns. Then, when she got to the car, she realized how small it was. She managed to pack the trunk and stuff the rest of the groceries in the tiny backseat. She stepped back and felt proud of herself for her accomplishment. As she turned back to the cart to put it in the storage area, she remembered the huge turkey on the bottom. She'd almost forgotten the main course! And after what she'd gone through to get it!

She had trouble lifting it, and once she'd hefted it up she realized she had no place to put it, at least not in the trunk or the tiny backseat area. So, with difficulty, Marla pushed the turkey into the front passenger seat. It barely fit because she had already moved the seat up to make room for the bags in the back. She strategically angled the frozen, slipping turkey, then put her foot on the corner of the passenger seat, pushing down the upholstery. There was just enough space for the turkey to pop into place but she was afraid it might pop out if she stopped the car short. God! Her turkey through the windshield! So lovingly, she fastened the seat belt around it. 'Good boy,' she cooed, and patted the frozen carcass.

Marla had been very, very lucky. When she'd gotten back to the house and begun unloading, a woman who called herself Rose offered to help. After her shopping experience, she didn't think she had the strength to pretend to be Sylvie in front of anyone, but this woman seemed nice, so it couldn't be a relative or the nutty witch Sylvie had described as her sister-in-law. Rose seemed like a nice woman and had offered to help her carry the endless groceries into the house. Now everything was in the kitchen – except for the huge unmovable frozen turkey, still strapped in the passenger seat of the car. There were huge bottles, bags, and cans everywhere. Marla and Rose had to roll in the huge jar of olives. The stuff overwhelmed even the enormous kitchen, not to mention Marla herself. 'Really, really, thank you for helping. I couldn't have gotten all this in here without you.'

'Neighbors have to help each other.' Rose paused for a moment and peered more closely at Marla in the kitchen light. 'You look great. That spa visit really paid off. Where was that place?'

Marla knew the spa wasn't going to help Rose, so she pretended not to hear and lifted the gigantic bag of marshmallows, putting one part on her shoulder. But the other half of the bag swung up, hit her in the face, and lodged on her other shoulder. Rose helped pull the bag down. 'Thanks on both accounts,' Marla said. 'Boy, they should have warning labels on this. It could suffocate you. It would have been really, really embarrassing to die in a topping for sweet potatoes.' Marla reached for the bottle of olives. Where would she put *them*? 'This is even harder than I thought it would be.' Marla remembered then that she was supposed to be experienced in all this. 'I mean, I've done it a million times, but each year it gets harder,' she said to Rose.

Rose pulled over a stool and sat down, clearly tired. 'Each year you get older. Not that you look it. And no one ever appreciates it.'

'No. But the whole family is grateful for the wonderful job you've done . . . right?'

'Oh yeah. The applause is deafening,' Rose said sarcastically.

'Then it's all worth it,' Marla said cheerfully, not getting the sarcasm.

Rose meanwhile stared at Marla. 'Boy, you really are different. Was it the spa, or did you hit your head when you went into the pool?'

'I never swam at the spa,' Marla said, folding the paper grocery bags.

'Well, *something's* different,' Rose said.

'I guess I have the holiday spirit.' Marla smiled as she headed back out the screen door. She'd always figured she must be nicer than Bobby's wife. 'Can you give me a hand with the bird?'

'Sure,' Rose answered as she followed her out.

When Marla opened the car door, Rose gasped. 'Is that a turkey or an ostrich?' she asked, then cackled. 'Ah, gee, is it enough? How many platoons are coming to your dinner, anyway? While I eat alone.'

'So far just the usual family.' God. Marla felt sorry for a woman alone out here in the boonies. What had happened to this poor thing's family? Maybe some younger woman had stolen her husband. Guilt swept over her. She had been the cause of at least one . . . marital problem. 'Say, hey, you want to come too?' she asked.

'Are you kidding?' Rose asked. 'No, you're not, are you? Will everyone be there? I'll be there with bells on. But, in the meantime, how are we going to get this ostrich in the house? You'll need another crane.'

'It's not a crane or an ostrich,' Marla said, annoyed. 'It's a turkey. The best, biggest one the store had, and I got it.' She looked around and noticed a red Radio Flyer wagon in the garage. She brought it to the car, and Rose helped her align it against the open door.

'Remember when Billy pushed Kenny down the hill in this?' Rose asked.

'Not really,' Marla answered, distracted and trying to slide the turkey carefully into the wagon.

'At the time, you acted like the world was ending. You would think that the scar above his eye would be a constant reminder.'

'Out of sight, out of mind,' Marla chimed back.

'Does it bother you, not having the kids home?' Rose asked in a sad tone of voice. By now they had the turkey in the Flyer and Marla was trying to pull the wagon up the walk.

'Sure it does. And with Bob gone so much I'm starting to feel like I'm single.'

'At least you don't feel divorced. *That's* hell,' Rose said.

The old man – Lou was his name – sat hunched over the piano. He was playing some corny old song, and Marla could tell he was not playing it well. She wondered why he was stooped over that way – he wasn't that old – but his posture and his attitude aged him. She came up behind him and put both hands on his shoulders, gently pulling him back and leaning into him so that his spine was straight. Lou's hands slowed, then trembled, and at last he stopped playing.

'To play well, you have to sit well,' said Marla, mustering up her professional voice. 'Do you think Beethoven slumped?'

'I think he did,' Lou answered. 'At least in all those pictures he looks humped over.'

'My god, Lou. These muscles are so tense!' Gently Marla pushed her thumb into the space between the tendons on Lou's shoulder.

'Tense? Yeah. I'm worried I might live another day.'

'Lou! What a terrible thing to say,' Marla said, sincere and shocked. She dug her fingers deeper into Lou's shoulder. How could she help him, she wondered. 'Lou,' she said with new determination, 'take off your shoes.'

'What?' he asked. 'Is my pedal foot too heavy?'

'No. No,' she reassured him, 'I think this attitude of yours needs an adjustment, a confrontation. And it begins with your feet.'

'Believe me, Mrs Schiffer, no one wants to confront my feet. Trust me on this.'

'Don't be silly,' Marla said as she knelt and began to untie his lace-up shoe. Suddenly a smile, as wide and bright as a rainbow, spread across Lou's face. 'What is it?' Marla asked.

Lou looked away, as if he was embarrassed. A hole in his sock? No. Marla looked back down and pulled the sock off his foot. She looked up again at Lou's gleeful but abashed face. Then her eyes moved back down, but this time stopped at his lap. There, under his old man's trousers, was a very visible boner. Marla smiled up sweetly at Lou. 'You see?' she asked. 'Reflexology cures everything.'

23

Sylvie lay with her eyes closed, not quite asleep, not quite awake, but in that gray zone of nodding contentment. Along her right side she could feel Bob's warm body pressed against hers. His arm under her neck and around her shoulder gave her a feeling of such peace and contentment that she was tempted to slip back into the twilight of satiation she'd been in, while at the same time she wanted to wake so that she could consciously savor this moment. The draw of the coma of pleasurable afterglow was difficult to ignore. Sylvie sighed. She couldn't remember the last time she'd felt this good.

After luxuriating for a few more moments, she made the supreme effort and opened her eyes. Bob's profile was beside her on the pillow, and though most of the candles had burned out there was still enough light to see him. He really was a beautiful man, she thought, even after all these years. His head, pushed back on the cushions slightly, was noble and – from this angle, with his neck stretched back – his jawline looked as firm as it had twenty years ago. His lashes, so very dark, threw a shadow onto his cheekbone and the slight flush and sheen of sweat on his face gave him, at least temporarily, the dewy skin of youth.

Sylvie wanted to kiss him – on his cheekbones, on his eyelids, and on his full, slightly open mouth – but she was afraid to move, afraid to wake him and break the spell. Because, right now, at this very moment, Sylvie was perfectly happy:

no matter what, she loved this man beside her and now she knew that he loved her with a passion perhaps even deeper than her own. She'd finally succeeded. She was having an affair with her own husband, and it had all the edgy appeal of the forbidden. But – for her – there was also the depth that their combined history and her knowledge of him added.

As if he felt her gaze on him, Bob's own lids fluttered. Catlike, he opened his eyes slowly, turned his head on the pillow, and looked at her. For a moment they said nothing, but the look said it all. Then he gathered her closer to his side. Sylvie felt safe, protected in the circle of his arm.

'I'm glad you called me. I'm very glad I came over,' Bob whispered. They stared again at one another. She could feel him searching for words. For a moment she was tempted to put her hand over his lips. Words could only spoil this perfection, but before she could gesture he had already continued. 'That was . . . wow . . .' He blinked. Were there tears on his lower eyelids? Sylvie knew Bob's pauses were as important as the words he spoke. '. . . powerful,' he finished.

She was flooded with pleasure. She had not been wrong. The magic was not in her imagination. 'For me too,' Sylvie whispered back, but didn't move. She wanted him to touch her again. She needed him to make the first move.

Bob, as if sensing this, reached over and stroked her hair. He did it gently, almost worshipfully. Then his face changed: he looked confused. 'Something's different. Really different,' he said. 'You've changed.' For a moment Sylvie became frightened. Maybe now, at last, he'd realized the trick she'd pulled on him. Maybe she'd been caught. And maybe that was good, maybe that was what she wanted.

Bob looked at her, *really* looked at her. Sylvie didn't shrink away. She could see the confusion in his eyes, but met it calmly. Bob tried to speak again. 'Tonight our lovemaking was . . . it was deeper than ever before . . .' He stopped. Then, instead of using his lips to speak, he kissed her. It was a movie kiss, a Warren Beatty–Natalie Wood–*Splendor-in-the-Grass* kiss. 'I think going home to visit your Grannie was good for you. It grounded you, or something. Meanwhile I can't seem to let you go,' he said.

'So then I guess you'll have to keep me,' Sylvie said. She shivered and Bob reached for the sheet to cover her. For a moment Sylvie – always the good homemaker – wished for the pure cotton damask from her own bed instead of this scratchy, wildly patterned permanent-press fabric. Her skin – well, all of her – felt so tender now. But bed covers, *things*, were no longer important. They could be lying on animal skins in a cave, or on hay in a barn loft. She felt Bob inhale and then release a giant sigh. She stiffened. She knew, as if by osmosis through his skin into hers, that he had just thought of going home.

Then, for the first time since they'd begun making love, she remembered that she wasn't Sylvie. Bob hadn't made love to her. She was Marla right now. Bob loved Marla while poor Sylvie was being betrayed. After what had just gone on between them, she knew now that she wanted Bob, and wanted him desperately. But who did Bob want? The woman he had just made love to, or his mistress at home in his wife's bed?

As if in answer to her question Bob lifted himself on his uninjured elbow and looked at her. 'Marla, I want to keep you. Forever. To tell you the truth, I was going to break up with you before you went away.'

'You were? Really?' Sylvie said, her voice cheerful. Then she realized both the past tense he'd used and that she – Marla – should be sad.

'Yes,' Bob said. 'It's not that things had changed with my wife, it just seemed—'

'What do you mean, "things had changed with your wife"?' Sylvie asked.

Bob rolled onto the other elbow, then winced in pain. 'It's not about my wife,' he said. 'It's that your . . . uniqueness grows on me,' he said.

'Really, really?' she asked, almost a parody of Marla. She couldn't control herself. 'Promise me I'm not like anyone else you've ever known.'

'Are you kidding? That's an easy promise,' Bob said, laughing. Then his face grew serious, his voice husky. 'You're not like anyone else,' he whispered, his mouth against her ear. 'And tonight your uniqueness took a giant leap forward.'

'One step for a man, a giant leap for womankind,' Sylvie said, sitting up abruptly. The man had no idea she was his own wife's twin. God! He was so blind, so stupid . . . and so adorable. Remembering that she was Marla had made her decide that it was time to torture Bob.

'Wasn't it new and special tonight?' Bob asked.

'Sex with you *always* feels good to me,' she purred. 'You are a really, really good lover. One of my best.'

For a moment Bob's face froze, his mouth trapped in an unattractive gape. He turned on his back, sank back down onto his pillow, stared at the ceiling, and didn't say anything. Maybe she'd gone too far, Sylvie worried. She lay down again too, quiet for a moment, and, when he hadn't spoken or moved for a little while, she rolled onto his chest and pinioned his wrists against the mattress. 'What was different?' she asked. 'There were less acrobatics than usual, right?'

'Huh?' Bob came back from wherever he had gone away to. 'Less acrobatics?' he repeated.

Guiltily, Sylvie said, 'I'm sorry. I was tired.'

Bob shook his head. 'No apologies. It was perfect. You're perfect.' He paused, and the spark had returned. 'I loved it. I love *you*,' he told her and then kissed her.

'You *love* me?' Sylvie repeated.

She could hear Bob calibrate the importance of what he'd just said. She waited to see if he'd back off. 'Sure,' he told her, but 'sure' was surely too casual a word.

'What kind of love?' Sylvie asked. 'The love a man has for a woman?'

'Yes. That one,' Bob said lightly. He looked at Sylvie and pulled her down to him. 'You're trembling.'

How could he betray me like this? Sylvie thought. How could he tell Marla he loved her? 'I'm cold.'

Tenderly he tucked a blanket around her. They lay silently for a while, until it became clear to Bob — the lunkhead — that her coldness was not only physical. Then Bob's wristwatch alarm went off, breaking the silence. 'I'm afraid time's up. I better get going,' Bob said.

He had set his alarm? Sylvie couldn't believe it. He'd set a limit on their intimacy, their pleasure. Oh, it was he who was cold. When had he done it? 'Oh, no . . . not yet,' Sylvie pleaded. 'Please . . .'

Bob took her by the shoulders. 'Stop,' he said. 'You promised we weren't going to fight anymore about me going home.' He kissed her on the cheek. 'This isn't easy for me.' His voice sounded husky, and so sincere. Was he lying to her? Should she tell him he didn't have to go – not to please his wife, anyway.

'Please stay, Bobby,' she whispered. 'Just a little longer.' She paused. 'That wasn't fighting. It was begging.'

'It's hard enough for me, Marla . . .' He paused.

'But how can you just go? Especially after what we just had together? Besides, the candles haven't completely burned out. And you *said* it was deeper.' She paused. 'Deeper than with your wife?'

'No more questions,' Bob told her, putting his legs over the side of the bed. Sylvie could tell he was trying not to sound annoyed. 'I don't have answers for any of them.'

Bob struggled into his trousers and began tying his shoes. Sylvie, hurt and more confused than ever, turned her back on him and pulled the sheet up all the way over her head. It was a childish gesture, but she felt like a child.

'Who cares about her anyway?' Sylvie said childishly.

'I do.'

Sylvie rolled over, pulled down the sheet, and turned back to Bob, now hopeful. 'You do?'

'She's the mother of my children,' Bob said flatly.

'Is that it?' Sylvie spat out. She couldn't believe he'd said that. What was she as a wife, some sort of brood mare? Wasn't she a woman to him at all? 'Maybe that's not all she is. Maybe she'd be more if you did the things you used to do with her. Things like what we did tonight.' She realized, then, what she was doing and cut herself off.

'What did you say?' Bob looked at her, his face even more contorted with confusion than her own.

Sylvie pulled the covers up higher. 'Nothing,' she said and forced out a Marla giggle. 'Bobby, you know we never know what I'm talking about.' Sylvie got up on her knees and put her arms around Bob's waist. 'I know I'm under your skin. And once I had chiggers, so I know how that feels! You'll *always* come running back to me.'

Marla and John were sitting, eating and drinking wine. 'I'm glad you came over, Johnny, because otherwise this whole dinner would have gone to waste. Again.' Marla sighed, and pouted her lips as prettily as she could, but only partly for effect. 'I'm still going to make Bob eat it when he gets home. If he ever does.' Had Bob *really* spent this much time at her apartment before the switcheroo?

The table was completely set for Thanksgiving. Actually, it was overset. Dishes, silverware, Pilgrims' hats, pumpkins, a huge cornucopia, and fold-out paper turkeys took up the entire surface, along with the two dozen or so place settings. The whole lot was swathed in dry cleaner's polyethylene, reminiscent of Miss Havisham's table. Or maybe it was more like the Mad Hatter's tea party, since only a corner of the vast table had been cleared for the two of them.

'Bob never comes home for dinner. He hardly comes home at all. I don't think it was just because of the shrimp.' She looked up at John. 'That was an accident.' He nodded. 'Anyway,' she said, 'I cooked it, he said he'd be home, and then he couldn't make it. Meanwhile, children are starving in India. So I called you.'

'And I was very happy that you did,' John said. 'I hope it wasn't just so the food wouldn't be wasted.' He lifted his glass.

'Uh-uh,' she told him, and took a sip of her wine. 'It's to confess. John, I've done something awful,' Marla began. 'I think it's really going to affect my karma.'

'What?'

'It's so bad I have to whisper it,' Marla admitted and leaned forward. John averted his eyes from her cleavage but also leaned in toward her, until her mouth was almost touching his ear. 'I've put Nair in Bob's shampoo,' Marla whispered.

John laughed for almost five minutes. 'God!' he managed to gasp. 'He told me about the hair loss. I said it was all in his head.' He started laughing again. Every time he almost stopped, he'd look at her and start over. 'Well, I can tell you something *I* did that wasn't good for *my* karma, as you put it,' John said when he could finally talk again. 'Remember, back in our junior year of high school, the night you dragged me into Cleveland to that Swedish movie and made me see it twice?'

Marla hadn't a clue. 'Wait. Let me think . . . oh, of course I remember. What happened?'

'I told you I loved it as much as you did.' John paused. He looked at her blank face. 'You don't even remember, but it's bothered me ever since. That I lied,' he admitted.

'And all these years I never knew.' Marla leaned over and took his hand. 'Know what? I didn't really like it either.'

They smiled at each other intensely enough for them both to avert their eyes.

24

Bob was just getting home from Marla's apartment. He looked at his watch by the light of the oven door. It was almost one o'clock. He shouldn't have stayed so long again. He started climbing up the stairs. Sylvie must be asleep by now. But before he'd gotten past the third (always creaky) step, Sylvie's voice stopped him. 'Hey, mister. Where are you going? I made dinner for you.'

Bob turned around, walked down the steps, through the hall, and looked in the dining room. There, in the light of two guttering candles, sat his wife. 'Honey, you didn't have to wait up. And I'm not hungry.'

Marla narrowed her eyes. 'It took me all afternoon to make this. And I've been waiting all night to eat it. You have two choices: eat it or wear it.'

'Oh. Okay, I'll have it now.' Bob slipped into his seat. The table was set and a sad, wilted salad sat in front of him. He looked at Sylvie. Maybe it wasn't hormones. Maybe she was mentally . . . upset. He picked up his fork. 'The salad looks good,' he said.

'I'll get the entrée,' Marla said, but she pronounced it 'entry,' like the doorway. She stomped out of the dining room. Bob wondered for a frightened moment whether she was on to him and his . . . situation. He didn't think so, but it was best to be conciliatory.

Marla stomped back in, two plates in her hands. She

slammed Bob's down on the table in front of him, then threw herself into her chair, picked up her fork, and stabbed at her food.

Bob picked up his own fork, lifted up what looked like some sort of rice, and took a bite. 'Umm, good,' he said, though it tasted fishy. He chewed and swallowed it anyway and took another mouthful. Sylvie glared at him. 'You're angry, aren't you?' he asked. Sylvie didn't answer but just put another forkful of food into her mouth. 'I'm sorry, Cookie Face,' Bob said nervously.

Marla narrowed her eyes. 'Cookie Face? Who's Cookie Face?' she asked.

Bob was completely flustered. 'Nobody,' he said. 'I mean, you are.' He felt his throat close and picked up his water glass. He gulped a mouthful, but it was white wine. He managed to choke it down. He broke out in a sweat. 'Nobody,' he managed to repeat.

'It better be *exactly* nobody. Because if I'm spending my life taking care of you and . . . you know . . . those twins, and you're running around on me . . .'

Bob felt so dizzy he could hardly hear her. Something was very, very wrong. Bob clutched the arms of the chair. Even his hands were sweating. 'I can't breathe,' he whispered, because all the air was gone.

'See what happens when you do something wrong? God punishes you,' his wife said and marched out of the room.

Bob looked down at his plate, dizzy and breathless, shock running through him. He couldn't believe this was happening. His chest was so tight. He reached in his jacket pocket and pulled out his phone. He had all he could do to focus on the numbers. He needed help – medical help. He punched in John's home number and prayed he wouldn't get the service.

After what seemed like a lifetime, the phone was answered and he heard John's voice. 'It's Bob,' he gasped. 'Shrimp,' he said, and then he blacked out.

'You'll live. Only the good die young,' John said as he threw away the disposable syringe and pulled up Bob's shorts.

Bob couldn't exactly remember John's arrival or the first adrenaline shot. He remembered a weeping Sylvie and John putting him face down on the sofa. Now Sylvie was sedated, sleeping upstairs. Bob turned over and tried to sit up. 'She's trying to kill me,' he croaked to John.

'Don't be ridiculous,' John said.

'It isn't ridiculous. Either she's trying to kill me or she's got Alzheimer's. She forgot she put the car in the pool. She didn't remember the crane. She made me bacon and eggs.'

John nodded soberly. 'Bacon and eggs will kill ya,' he agreed.

'I'm serious,' Bob said.

'No, you're a narcissist,' John responded. 'Sylvie was hysterical over her mistake. But mistakes happen. I work at a hospital. Trust me. I made her take an Ambien so she would sleep. She feels terrible.'

'*She* does? *I* almost died.'

'People forget things, Bob. They're distracted or unhappy – and maybe they have every reason to be – so they get forgetful. Or they're full of rage and simply not aware of it.' John closed his bag and rolled down his sleeves.

'Wait. Before you go, can you take a look at this rash? It's driving me crazy.'

'Do I have to?' Bob pulled up his shirt. John leaned over him. 'That's just your nervous rash. You had it the day the kids left for school. Use the smelly cream.'

John picked up his winter jacket and started to leave. 'Wait,' Bob said. 'That's not all. When I shampooed this morning, there was hair in the drain. More than usual.'

John stopped in the doorway. 'Hair loss, huh? I don't see it.' He shrugged. 'In my medical opinion, it's caused by the mess you're making of your life.'

And all Bob could think about was getting to Marla's side as soon as he could.

25

What she needed, Sylvie decided — aside from a complete psychiatric appraisal and the appropriate pharmaceuticals — was a close girlfriend. Since Gloria had moved to Kansas City, she really hadn't replaced her with a friend of equal depth. But she just *had* to talk to somebody about making love to Bob — otherwise she would burst. She couldn't talk to John, close as he was. To him she liked to complain about Bob, not praise him. So the only person left, inappropriate as it was, was her mother.

Sylvie got into the car and drove over to the strip mall. She had a key to the service entrance of Potz Bayou and parked her car back there. If anyone saw it they would just think it was her car, not Marla's. Maybe that was why Bob had given Marla the car. She shook her head. Sometimes it was hard to tell if Bob was a genius or a moron.

She snuck into the back room, where the plaster casts, extra enamel jars, and brushes were kept, along with the detritus that collected in any storage room. Over by the coffeemaker were a bunch of mugs that had been abandoned by customers who had left them to be fired and never picked them up. Sylvie lifted an aqua one with little angels and the name Nan painted on it. Whoever Nan was, she couldn't paint angels for shit, Sylvie thought. Sylvie filled the mug with coffee and picked up the receiver on the wall phone, using one line to dial the other. When she heard Mildred's voice, she felt better. 'Mom, could you come back here and meet me?' she asked. There was a moment's pause.

'Sylvie?' her mother asked in a hesitant voice.

'Of course it's Sylvie,' she almost snapped. 'Do I sound like Phil?'

'Well, actually, you and Miss You-Know-Who sound a lot alike.'

'Could you please just come back here?' Sylvie asked.

'Back *where*?'

'Mom, I'm in the storeroom.'

'What storeroom?' Mildred asked, exasperated.

'*Your* storeroom,' Sylvie said, even more exasperated.

'Oh, for heaven's sake!' Mildred exclaimed and, moments later, walked through the doorway. She went past Sylvie, giving her a peck on the cheek *en passant*, and picked up a mug. She began to fill it.

Sylvie stared down moodily into her own coffee. 'Who's Nan?' she asked.

Mildred glanced at Sylvie's mug. 'Some jerk,' Mildred said. 'She ran off with her contractor and never came back for the mug.' Mildred glanced at her daughter and raised her brows. '*She* wasn't smart enough to leave her marriage alone either.'

'Oh, Mom. Don't scold me now,' Sylvie begged. 'I admit there's something seriously wrong with me. I was only trying to get back what I once had.' She looked over at her mother. 'Look, I had the old Bob but now I have this new Bob, who is like Bob used to be. Not like the old Bob, like the young one, if you know what I mean.'

Mildred squinted her eyes. 'Are you really Marla?'

'Mom, he made love to me and it was . . .' Sylvie couldn't go on. She stared into her coffee cup again and a little shiver ran up her back. 'Oh, you don't remember what it was like.'

Mildred patted her arm. 'I remember,' she said, her voice softer. 'Your father was a very passionate man.' They both stood there for a few moments in silence. 'You love him, Sylvie?' Mildred asked.

'With all my heart,' Sylvie said. 'He's so beautiful.'

Mildred rolled her eyes. 'Your late grandmother loved like that. Thank God it skipped a generation.'

'Mom, this plan isn't working,' Sylvie said. 'I mean, I got what I wanted, but now I'm so afraid I'm going to lose it. I'm really scared.'

'What's new? You were born scared. All women are. Remember, this is a man who cheated on you and is cheating on you right now.'

Sylvie panicked. She immediately felt her skin go clammy. 'He's sleeping with Marla? She told you that?' she asked.

'No! He's sleeping with *you*. *You* are Marla.'

'No, *I* am Marla,' Marla said from the doorway.

Mildred looked up. 'Is this a scene from *Spartacus*?' she asked.

'What's a spartacus?' Marla asked.

The two older women ignored the question. 'You're not supposed to be here. We can't *both* be here at the same time,' Sylvie hissed.

'Well, *you're* the one who isn't supposed to be here,' Marla pointed out. 'I can visit my own mother if I want to. I don't have anyone else to talk to. The kids are away and Bob's never home.'

'Tell me about it,' Sylvie said tartly, 'after you've lived it for six months, not six days.'

'I don't get it,' Marla admitted. 'It's not like you're a

good sex partner or anything. You're living on borrowed time.'

'I *am* a good sex partner,' Sylvie snapped, then shivered with the tactile memory that flooded her. 'The sex hasn't been this good since before we were married.'

'Before?' Mildred asked. '*Before*? When I think of what your father and I spent on that white wedding—'

'Come on, Mom. It was the seventies,' Sylvie said.

Marla put her hands on her hips and walked over to the coffee machine. 'I was born in the seventies,' she reminded them.

'That's a lie,' Sylvie shot back. 'Admit it. You're over thirty.'

'Girls, girls. Stop it,' Mildred said, pouring a cup of coffee for Marla and handing it to her in a green mug that said 'Kiss Me, I'm Irish.' 'Solidarity, please. I thought this whole plan was supposed to be two women against a common enemy,' Mildred reminded them.

'She started it,' Marla snapped.

'And I'll finish it too,' Sylvie said. 'Right now. I just want to go back to being his wife *and* have great sex with him. Is that too much to ask?' Sylvie asked, turning to her mother.

'Yes,' Mildred told her. 'You want it all.'

'If she has it all, I want it all too!' Marla whined. 'Marriage, medical insurance, puppies that you have to buy.'

'Look. Get this straight, the two of you: no woman has it all. Romance and marriage? No. Excitement and stability? Uh-uh. Not together. Pick one and shut up.'

'But this terrific sex thing isn't enough. I need to be with him more,' Sylvie whined.

'*More*? He's practically living with you. I mean, me.' Marla put down the coffee mug. 'Listen to me: my kids are coming home the day after tomorrow and I expect to have a good family holiday. He *never* comes to see me – you – on holidays or weekends. So I want him home. If you want out, you have to wait until then. We don't tell him until after Thanksgiving. And I could still sleep with him, you know. I could try to make him remember why he married you in the first place.'

'You said you wouldn't. You promised,' Sylvie said, frightened again.

'So what? What about me? You promised that I would come out of this with a husband. You make noises about it but – excuuuuse me? I don't see a groom.'

Mildred went to the door and closed it. 'All right. Stop it. Both of you,' she said. 'Sylvie, Marla is right. It was a hell of a stupid promise, but you have to come through.'

Marla smiled tremulously. Sylvie could see that she was thrilled by Mildred's protection. 'Thanks, Mom,' Marla said. She turned to Sylvie. 'What about John? What about him as a husband?'

'John? John's in love with me! You can't have John.'

'Oh, forget John. He was born to be a widower. It's his pain that makes him so attractive,' Mildred told the two of them.

'John will never marry again, and he doesn't want children,' Sylvie told Marla.

'He never told *me* that,' Marla retorted.

'Yes he did, about three years ago. You just don't remember,' Sylvie snapped.

Mildred interrupted again. 'It would probably be a good idea to come up with a specific man,' she told Sylvie. 'Why should Marla have to cope with an abstraction?'

'Yeah,' Marla agreed, 'whatever that means.'

'Okay,' Sylvie said, putting down her empty mug and

holding her hands up. 'Okay. It's not as if I haven't been working on it. I've been thinking about giving her Phil.'

Mildred dropped her own coffee mug then which was, luckily, almost empty. When it hit the floor it virtually exploded into a million bits. Despite the mess around her feet, Mildred didn't move. 'Oh, you broke the mug!' Marla, ever obvious, said, stooping and picking up the pieces. 'I'll make you a new one.'

Mildred ignored her. '*Our* Phil?' she croaked.

'Who is Phil again?' Marla asked.

Mildred looked at Marla. 'She's talking about your brother, my son. Sylvie, are you out of your mind? This isn't ancient Egypt and he's not a pharaoh.'

'You mean I could be in the family?' Marla asked, child-like.

Sylvie nodded, avoiding her mother's eyes. 'You'd be my sister.'

'In-law,' Mildred added. 'Sylvie, this is ridiculous.'

Marla looked to Mildred for confirmation. 'No, it would be great. You'd let me call you . . . Mom?'

Mildred shook her head. 'He's my own son, but . . . well, he deserves love . . . on some level,' she added. She eyed Marla. 'Sylvie, this is ridiculous. It's out of the question. I—'

'He's nice-looking, he's single, and he's got a job,' Sylvie said to Marla. 'And she'd be better than the last one,' she added to Mildred.

'I would be? Great! I take back all the bad things I said about you. You know, now I remember Phil spoke to me on the phone. He was worried about you. He's very protective. I like that in a man.'

'Before you two buy the ring, you might want to check

in with Phil about this,' Mildred said. 'He might have a few reservations about incest. Meanwhile, I wash my hands of both of you.'

'You can check him out at Thanksgiving,' Sylvie told Marla, who clapped her hands like an excited child. 'Make a good meal. He loves to eat. Then we'll both keep our promises. And don't touch Bobby,' she sang out.

'Don't see him over the holiday,' Marla sang back. 'And get me married. By the way, I invited one of the neighbors for Thanksgiving. She helped me roll in the olives. She's very nice, Rose.'

'Rose? Who's Rose? You mean, Ros*alie?*' Sylvie asked.

'Happy turkey day,' Mildred exclaimed and walked out.

PART 3

Which?

26

Bob and Marla were standing on the front porch as the entourage of college kids arrived in cars. The fall air was crisp but not cold. The leaves, now down from most of the trees, lay in drifts on the still-green lawn. It was like a scene from a made-for-television movie, Marla thought, feeling deeply sentimental. This was what she had shopped for, worked for, what she had expected. Bob's arm was around her shoulders and the sun was shining, glinting off all the BMWs in the driveway. It was a perfect Kodak moment. Marla thought of her perfectly set table inside the perfectly arranged dining room inside the perfect house. Yes, this was what she wanted for herself. Stability. Organization. Routine. Ritual. People who loved her, who'd take care of her and who she could take care of. It would all be perfect as long as neither of the twins ratted her out.

Marla tried to cover part of her face with her hair so the kids wouldn't see her too clearly. She watched a boy and girl as they jumped from two of the cars and immediately recognized Reenie from the family photos. They were both carrying huge duffel bags. Reenie was hanging on to the arm of the guy, and Marla noticed that she didn't even look toward her parents because she was so absorbed in looking at him. Good. Maybe she wouldn't notice the switcheroo. Marla smiled tensely, then waved. But Reenie didn't notice Marla then, so she now stretched out her arms as if she'd been waiting for this moment her whole life.

'Hi, Daddy,' Reenie called out. 'This is Brian. Hi, Mom. This is laundry.' Reenie bounded up the steps of the porch, quickly kissed Marla, then put the duffel bag in her 'mother's' arms.

'It's very open of you to accept me for the holidays,' this Brian person said to Bob and Marla as he shook their hands.

'Another guest?' Marla asked under her breath. She thought of her table. Well, if she added one more place on the far side she might squeeze him in.

'You should have let us know, Reenie,' Bob said, but his voice was indulgent.

'So? Guess who Kenny brought home?' Reenie demanded in a childish voice. 'His whole soccer team.'

Marla held in the yelp rising in her throat. Kenny got out of the car then with four big guys. Marla stretched out her arms again. 'Not the whole team, I just brought you the defense,' he shouted, correcting his sister. He ran up to the porch, threw a fake punch at his dad, and dropped a huge duffel bag. 'I brought you my laundry too. Thanks in advance, Mom.' He gave her a hug – but not the long, warm one Marla had imagined and wanted – then ran back to the guys.

Marla faintly murmured, 'More people?'

'Yeah. Devon, Alex, Simon, and Hugh.' The boys waved. Then one of them – the handsomest – said something, the others laughed, and Kenny responded. There was another outbreak of laughter. It made Marla, suddenly, feel very left out and . . . old. Clearly the kids were more interested in their friends than in their parents. And even though those young guys weren't that much younger than she was, when they grabbed their gear and walked up to the door they said brief hi's as if she were invisible and then rushed into the house.

Bob turned to Marla and looked at her fondly. He pecked her cheek. 'It's good to have the family together, isn't it? The family and John. He would have been all alone this Thanksgiving.'

'John. Right. And Rosalie says *she's* bringing a date. That's roughly . . . what?' said Marla, weakly counting on her fingers. 'Twenty-nine?'

The table had been perfectly set – flowers, pumpkins, Pilgrim figures, candles, and all. Marla went into the dining room, sighed deeply, removed the dry cleaner's plastic covering the perfectly set table and started squeezing place settings together.

Bob had taken the kids to the mall. Kenny needed new Reeboks, and Reenie, as always, thought there was just one more pair of shoes somewhere that would make life perfect. Alex, Devon, and Hugh hadn't joined them – they were playing one-on-one at the high school basketball court. But Reenie's boyfriend, Brian, and Kenny's friend Simon had come along, and so had Jim – as if Bob needed to spend any more time with his father-in-law.

'Hey, Dad. How's business?' Kenny asked. Before Bob could open his mouth Kenny added, 'In four words or less, of course.' There was a laugh from the peanut gallery in the backseat.

'Not good enough to let you keep the car, I'm afraid,' Bob said, but Kenny didn't even blink at the bluff.

'Hey, give him a new model if he wants it,' Jim said, as usual, playing king of the lot. Bob tried to keep himself from being annoyed. 'You okay way back there?' he asked. Reenie was lying down in the back of the station wagon with that . . . that annoying guy. Bob craned his neck to get a look at them in the rearview mirror. Was he groping her?

A horn blew and Bob stopped short. Traffic was awful. They crawled to the mall and, once he parked, Bob told the kids to follow the family's usual mall procedure – Kenny and Simon were going for the two-hundred-dollar sneakers and checking out the action at Sports Authority, while Brian and Reenie and Bob would also split up, all rejoining at the food court. 'In an hour. In front of the potato skins counter,' Bob reminded them all. God knew what Jim, the indulgent grandfather, would do. Bob figured he was on his own.

After potato skins, the kids had more plans: Brian wanted to check out the Rock 'n' Roll Hall of Fame. Bob had begged out but had to pick up some cumin – whatever that was – for one of Sylvie's recipes and so the group separated in front of the Ritz Carlton, planning to hook up again in two hours. Bob couldn't help but watch Brian as he and Reenie walked toward The Gap. He had stuffed his hand in the back pocket of her jeans and Bob felt an almost irresistible urge to run over and smack his hand away. He turned and leaned on the railing that overlooked the central fountain of the mall.

Tower City was crowded. When the place had first been converted from the old RTA railroad station and been renovated, the kids had liked nothing better than to come here, eat junk food, and watch the dancing waters in the choreographed fountain. Every half hour music was piped in and the show began: water spurted in coordinated runs to the sounds of Tchaikovsky and John Philip Sousa. Sylvie despised it, Bob enjoyed it as just kitsch, but the kids had once thought it was magical. Now they ignored it completely, walking by the large reflecting pool as if it didn't exist. As the program began Bob watched the fleeting silver arcs of water that made the milling crowd below point and ooh. For some reason he thought of Marla, and the beauty and depth of their lovemaking last night. It had shaken him. He had meant to end this thing but, god, she was under his skin. He wanted to hold her, to feel her skin against his. Then he wondered if Reenie was sleeping with that Brian kid yet. If not, she would be soon. The idea made him a little queasy. What would it be like for her? It was hard to believe his baby was that old. Where had the time gone?

The music changed tempo and the water arcs below started breaking into moving dotted lines that completed their flight and disappeared back into the pool, more graceful than flying fish. Some of the people in the crowd clapped. Who were they clapping for? Bob wondered. The music recorded years ago? The programmer who had designed the computer-controlled fountain performance? The engineer or architect who'd conceived of the plan? Or maybe the applause was for the water itself?

Somehow their disassociated clapping made him feel . . . strange. Lonely. He wanted Marla beside him. Bob shook that idea out of his head. He knew he ought to get moving and get over to the specialty gourmet shop, but he stood for a moment more, away from the crowd, above it. His ankle was hurting from all the walking and it seemed to throb to the rhythm of the cascading water. But his real problem was that he realized he was lonely. For almost twenty years he'd been the center of Kenny and Reenie's life, the center of Sylvie's. Now, with Sylvie at home in a frenzy of table setting, and Reenie and Kenny back, but not really with him, Bob, all at once, felt such a sense of uselessness and isolation that he had to clutch the railing for a moment. He'd been a good husband, an involved father, and a capable businessman, but what had it added up to? He'd done a lot less than the pianist — perhaps dead now — who was playing the music, less than the computer programmer. No one was clapping for him. No one knew he was there. He thought of calling Marla, because the way they had been . . . with her . . . well, he hadn't felt lonely. It was crazy to call her — she was nothing but pressure for him, especially on a holiday, but somehow, something that had only been a physical thing had, just the other night, turned into . . .

But this was a family holiday. A day to take stock and be grateful. Bob was not a religious man, but he was aware of his blessings. His kids were healthy. He had never meant to cheat on Sylvie. He really had never meant to. Marla had just shown up and . . . He'd felt flattered by her interest. He hadn't taken her seriously. He knew he loved Sylvie. What he didn't know, what he couldn't remember, was exactly how the affair with Marla had started. Had she made the first move? Had he? What he did know was that he had never meant for this to happen. What would Kenny think if he knew? What would Reenie . . . His mind jumped away from that. It was unthinkable. Bob knew, now that the children were home, that he had to end this double life. Only a fear of hurting Marla — that and a little lust — had kept it going. But the damned thing was that just in the last week or so, just since the other night, he'd realized he had . . . well, a lot of feelings for Marla. Being with her, making love with her, had felt too much like love. He'd even *called* it love.

To make it worse, since Sylvie had come back from her sister's — especially in the last few days — being with her had also been different: it had been too much like work. She was more dependent, while simultaneously self-absorbed. She seemed addled, and the house, except for the dining room table, was a mess. Bob sighed.

He looked down and noticed Brian coming out of the bookstore below. He was carrying a bag and talking to a young girl. Bob thought he recognized the girl from Reenie's carpooling days. Jenny — a real little flirt even then. He watched as Brian took her hand and she pulled away, laughing. Then Brian spoke earnestly to her for a few moments, and at last she reached into her purse, took out a pen, and wrote something down on his bag. Jenny flung the boy a pouty look that was as good as a promise before she flounced off.

Bob could hardly believe what he had just seen. Maybe it was innocent, he told himself. Don't jump to conclusions. Don't project. But it seemed to him that the sensitive little son of a bitch his daughter was obviously besotted with had just taken Jennifer Hill's phone number. Outraged, he spun around, ready to confront the bastard. Then he stopped himself. The two kids would work out their own future. The question was, what the hell was he doing? Brian, the little scumbag, owed his daughter a lot less than Bob owed Sylvie.

And it was all so odd. He could have sworn that just a few weeks ago he would have been able to break up with Marla effortlessly. It was only now that something had gone terribly wrong. After last night his world had been shaken. He realized that he loved her. It wasn't just sex, or his protective instincts. It felt like love. He wasn't sure if he could bear to give up that love. His life would feel too empty without it. He had never expected this to happen. And he didn't have a clue as to what he should do.

Jim came up behind him and put his hand on Bob's sore

elbow. Bob jumped, both from the pain and the guilt. 'Oh, sorry,' Jim said, leaning on the railing and putting his hand to his back. 'You're getting almost as decrepit as I am,' he said. 'You've got that bum ankle, and now your elbow. You've got a rash all over your neck too,' Jim observed. Then he moved in a little, straining his eyes. 'And is your hair starting to thin?'

Bob reached up to his hairline self-consciously. He thought so too, but he wasn't going to admit it to Jim. 'I might have a couple of good years left in me,' Bob told his father-in-law.

'Well, spend them wisely,' Jim said. Bob looked at him. Was there a warning in the old man's voice?

Bob wondered who he'd spend his last years with and, turning away from the railing, began limping over to fetch the cumin for Thanksgiving dinner.

27

Marla woke up and turned the alarm off so that it wouldn't wake Bob, snoring beside her. She pushed herself out of bed. She checked the clock — 4:45 A.M. She threw on one of Sylvie's terry robes and thick socks, then — after splashing some water on her face — she stopped in the laundry room.

She looked around. It was beyond her. Though Sylvie had done it earlier in the week, now again there were piles and piles of nasty, dirty, bits of clothes. Socks, sweat bands, jockstraps. There were T-shirts in tatters, and at least a hundred pairs of jeans.

Marla looked at the dials on the machine that hated her. Cold/Cold, Warm/Cold, Hot/Cold, Warm/Warm . . . Why so many choices? And load size. How should she know what was normal? None of this was normal for her. Not to mention all the other dials. What did *they* do?

After getting nowhere for ten minutes, Marla simply picked up an armful of stuff and threw it into the gaping washer's mouth. She closed her eyes, turned the dials, and hoped for the best. Marla staggered to the kitchen. It was 5:10 already. She was behind schedule! She reached up and turned the oven to 350, then went out the back door and dragged the enormous turkey in. It didn't seem as if it had defrosted at all, because the weather must have gotten colder overnight. There was frost on the lawn. Marla put the turkey on some aluminum foil, because no pan was big enough to hold the sucker. She opened the oven door, but then couldn't carry the turkey to it. She looked around. At last she leaned the ironing board against the oven, and pushed the turkey up the board and almost into it. At the mouth of the oven, though, it soon became very clear that the turkey was too big to fit inside. Way too big. No matter what she did, she couldn't get it in.

Marla was about to cry. She pushed the damn bird back down the ironing board and managed to get it onto the kitchen island. Next she tried to cut it in half, first with a knife, then a saw, then an ax she found in the garage. She hurt her arm but didn't put a dent in the carcass. It was frozen, rock hard. Forty-four pounds of turkey and no way to cook it.

Nothing worked.

Marla pulled up to the parking lot just as the sun rose. Despite the time of the morning, the twenty-four-hour supermarket was filled with dozens of zombie women who all had one mission in mind: to pick up the single crucial thing they had forgotten to buy. The problem was that all the crucial things — cranberry sauce, sweet potatoes, boxed stuffing — were long gone.

Marla approached the butcher counter. It was decimated. Not a bird was left, only piles of dirty ice and blood from the carcasses. It looked like a deserted battlefield. A butcher, obviously a casualty of shell shock, was sitting there, legs sprawled.

Marla knew she didn't look her best. Her hair was still uncombed, her face bare of makeup, and she was dressed in baggy sweats. But she had to get this man to like her, to come to her aid. She began to blather out her tale of holiday hell. '. . . so it doesn't fit. And it's still completely frozen,' she finally ended with. 'Help me,' she said to the butcher. 'I need a new bird.'

'It's kind of late, lady. We don't have anything left,' he replied, his eyes glazed with exhaustion.

'But you have to do *something*,' Marla cried, on the verge of hysteria. She couldn't do Thanksgiving without a turkey! They'd all be so disappointed she'd be found out as a screwup. She never got things right! 'Can't you make me one?' she begged, desperate. She fluttered her eyelashes. 'You can probably do anything.'

'Lady,' said the butcher, 'only two turkeys can make another turkey.'

At that very moment – 7:21 A.M. to be exact – Sylvie was in the same supermarket, but over in the frozen food aisle. She had a Hungry Man turkey dinner in one hand, a Lean Cuisine in the other. She was reading the nutritional information on each, judging her options. She was not happy. This was not the day to wake up early, but she had in spite of her plans to sleep for most of the day. Since the previous evening, she'd done nothing but think about Bob, Reenie, and Kenny, united without her. She'd become sadder and sadder. She'd been a fool to give up her family for even a minute, much less for the whole holiday. When she saw a box boy unloading a new case of frozen creamed spinach she went over to him. Poor kid, he had to work on the holiday.

'Hi,' she said, trying to cheer him up. 'I was just wondering which one of these you would recommend for an appropriate Thanksgiving dinner for a . . .' She paused. Her voice had become shaky. 'For a woman who gave her husband and children away?' she said.

'Uh, it's a matter of taste,' the boy said.

271

Sylvie could see the kid didn't want to talk to some middle-aged crazy but she couldn't stop. 'I have a son around your age. He's tall and—'

'That's nice,' the boy said, trying to cut her off. But since he continued to load the freezer case, Sylvie babbled on. 'He's a twin, you know. Fraternal, not identical. The younger. Such a gentleman; he let his sister out first.'

'That's real nice,' the boy said, finally looking up. Then Sylvie could see the sympathy in his eyes. No, it was pity. She was pitiful to a box boy.

But, she realized with horror, she had no pride. 'People ask me if they're identical,' Sylvie added, despite the kid's obvious boredom and pity. She was too needy to stop talking.

While Sylvie was breaking down in aisle 14, Marla was desperately pawing through the butcher's bloody ice. Her tenacity was rewarded: buried deep in the Arcticlike waste she discovered some very little birds.

'You do have turkeys,' she said with assurance to the butcher. 'Baby ones.'

'No. We don't got a single turkey.'

'Okay, then what are these?' Marla demanded, holding up a small frozen corpse triumphantly.

'That's squab.'

'They look like little turkeys, don't they?'

'Not even close,' the butcher told her, his contempt obvious.

'Well, they do to me. I'll take twenty-eight,' Marla said.

Sylvie was pushing her cart containing the Lean Cuisine dinner, a small cantaloupe, a plastic bag of prewashed salad greens, an opened Kleenex box, and a bottle of wine. She headed toward the express checkout lane. There she stood behind an older woman who had *exactly* the same cart contents, though her Kleenex box was unopened. Sylvie put her hand to her mouth. She thought of Marla's half-furnished, empty apartment, the Macy's Day parade blaring on the TV, and the endless string of football games to come — programs she'd never watched at home because she'd always been too overwhelmed with dinner preparations and family talk to have the time to watch.

Now, despite Bob, despite what had happened between them the other night, Sylvie felt a loneliness that was almost unbearable. The cashier totaled up her purchases and Sylvie paid, walking out with her single pathetic bag of a single person's Thanksgiving. As she walked out the double doors she didn't notice Marla at another checkout counter, a huge pile of rock-hard little dead birds in front of her.

28

Sylvie checked the clock on Marla's refrigerator. It had taken Sylvie less than four minutes to unpack her groceries. That made it 8:14 A.M., which meant she had only fifteen hours and forty-six minutes more of Thanksgiving to get through alone. Sylvie sat down on the uncomfortable wire-backed chair at the tiny table that passed for a kitchenette set in Marla's cramped kitchen. The trip to the supermarket had been unbearable, and this day didn't seem to hold any promise of deliverance from her mood.

Why was it that today, a day she planned to ignore as a holiday and spend luxuriously, even self-indulgently, napping and giving herself every single one of Marla's herbal beauty treatments, was the one day she woke up at 5:41? It was clear to Sylvie that, once her eyes popped wide open and her anxiety adrenaline began pumping, there was no way she could possibly relax or sleep. Had twenty-one Thanksgivings with Bob programmed her on some kind of annual calendar? Was she nothing but a preprogrammed clone? Had her marriage done that to her? The idea made her angry.

But despite her anger, she couldn't keep her brain and her body from flashing back to her time with Bob — Bobby — the previous night. Thinking about it sent a hot flush to her face. He had held her and kissed her and thrilled her in a way she hadn't felt in a decade. It had done something to her. When she closed her eyes she could replay it: she could hear his breath in her ear, she could hear the words he murmured. Oddest of all, it was as if she could feel his hands on her again, as if each touch, each caress, had been imprinted somehow on her body. Was there a part of the brain, dead in her for years, that had suddenly been reactivated?

Sylvie put her head in her hands, her elbows on the tiny table. She felt a shiver down her back, and a flush rose again. She felt alive, more alive than usual, alive all the way through her body. It was in the way that music made her more alive.

This, she realized, was an almost irresistible feeling. It was why people craved sex and craved love – to feel like this. It probably had something to do with endorphins or hormones but it felt like love. She did love Bob. And her body missed his body. She wanted him all over again. And again.

Sylvie lifted her head and opened her eyes. She had to come back to reality, and reality was brutal. Bob had not made love to *her*, he had made love to his mistress. Now, as his mistress, she was abandoned, sitting alone in this tiny closet of a kitchen with nothing but a thousand bottles of vitamins and food supplements, no way to mark the holiday, and no family around her to mark it with. Was that Bob's love? Sylvie, greedy as we all are, wondered why she couldn't have it both ways. Why couldn't she be married to Bob and in love with him too? Why couldn't he love his home life *and* her body? All at once she was swept with anger and a loneliness so fierce that she couldn't bear to sit there any longer. She had to get up and move.

She also missed her children. She missed all of her family, but especially Kenny and Reenie. She'd been an ass to trade Thanksgiving with Marla. She'd had no idea what the day felt like when it stretched, this long and this empty, in front of you. What did orphans do? What did unmarried, childless orphans do? That was how she felt, like a UCO. Were there UCO meetings in church basements today, the way there were AA gatherings?

Sylvie decided she had to see the kids. If she saw them, she could get through the day. She wanted to see them see each other again. They'd never been separated for this long, not since they were born, even including summer camp. Sylvie looked at the clock again. It was now 8:16. If she called her house, the chances were good that everyone but Marla would still be sleeping. She told herself that if anyone else answered, she could just hang up. She had to. She didn't know what good it would do, but she had to do it. She dialed her number and held her breath until the phone was answered – before the first ring had ended.

'Hello,' Marla's voice snapped. It wasn't her usual space cadet voice. Marla actually sounded anxious.

'Marla, it's me, Sylvie. Tell me what's going on. Are the kids all right? Is anybody up?'

'*Everyone* is here. They're in sleeping bags and on sofas all over the house,' Marla whispered fiercely. 'Anyway, you can't call here now. We have a deal. It's *my* holiday.'

'I had to,' Sylvie told her. She knew what she needed and had to get it. 'Marla, I have to come over.'

'Are you out of your mind? I *told* you. Everybody's already here, except Mom and Pop and your brother. I have salad to make. And succotash. Come over? What are you talking about?'

'I didn't know I'd miss the children this much,' Sylvie said, hearing the tears in her voice. She knew she sounded pathetic. Well, she *was* pathetic.

'Sylvie, you're acting really, really crazy,' Marla told her.

276

'How could we both be here at once? Did you forget? I'm supposed to be the dopey one, not you.'

'Marla, I have to know how they are. I have to,' Sylvie repeated. She paced the tiny kitchen's floor.

'They're fine. Trust me.'

Sylvie thought that was the last thing she'd do. 'I need to see them to know that. I need to touch them.'

Marla paused for a minute. 'I don't think my mother ever felt that way about me,' she said. 'She hasn't called today, by any chance, has she?'

'No, but it's early yet,' Sylvie told her gently.

'Early or late, she won't call,' Marla said. 'Not unless she needs money or her boyfriend's left her.' Marla sighed. 'Okay. I'm wearing black leggings and a black sweatshirt. Put on a hat and my sunglasses. Come over to the kitchen window. You know, the one with all the shrubbery. Knock on it. Showers are on. It sounds like they'll be down in the next half hour. You'll see them then.'

'Thank you, Marla,' Sylvie breathed, truly grateful.

Sylvie, her hair stuffed into a knit cap, was standing in the rhododendron bed, peeking in her own kitchen window watching her family having breakfast. Reenie lovingly served a dark young man a perfect plate of eggs. (She gave the ones with the broken yolks to her father.) Sylvie thought of Bob's cholesterol level, but bit her lip. Kenny, meanwhile, was opening a gigantic bag of marshmallows and he and his buddies began throwing them at each other, trying to catch them in their mouths. Marla was ignoring it all – she seemed to be working on her pumpkin pies, missing all the fun. How many pie crusts were laid out there? A dozen? More? Sylvie tapped on the window a few times and, when Marla at last glanced up, Sylvie signaled for her to come out. Marla nodded, giving her a look that told her to be careful. She inclined her head to the back of the house, and Sylvie snuck out of the bushes, then went behind the garage and into the farthest corner of the yard.

Sylvie and Marla sat in the little grove of evergreens in the backyard, facing away from the house.

'I just don't get the kids thing,' Marla said, wiping her floury hands on a dish towel. Sylvie saw that the beautiful Cartier ring was now breaded. She almost told Marla to take it off while she worked in the kitchen, but what was the point? The ring, like her family, wasn't Sylvie's now. 'You work your ass off, and for what? They barely kissed me. They didn't even notice I'd – you'd – changed.'

'They're kids,' Sylvie said and shrugged. 'They don't act-ually think of me as a person, not exactly. I've been nothing but a breast to them. You can't be in it for gratitude. I'd still willingly come between them and a bullet,' she admitted. 'So, give me a clue as to how they are.'

'The girl—'

'Reenie. Short for Irene,' Sylvie interrupted.

'Right,' Marla agreed. 'Anyway, she tells her boyfriend she loves him about sixty times an hour. Didn't you teach her anything? She's degrading herself.'

'No she's not. She likes him. It's sweet.' Sylvie smiled to herself. 'You know, she was shy in high school. Her brother got her a date for the senior prom. She doesn't have much experience with boys.'

'Ha!' Marla barked. 'She drools over this guy. I hate to be the one who breaks the news, but she's no virgin.'

'Yes she is!' Sylvie protested. 'I mean, she was when she

left for school. And she wouldn't make a decision like that without talking to me about it.'

'Denial . . .' Marla sang out. 'Think what you want, but I know the truth. Anyway, the boy – Kenny – well, you didn't tell me he was homosexual.'

'A homosexual? What? Are you crazy? He's not,' Sylvie said.

Marla raised her brows. 'Look, all I know is he brought home four friends. Two couples. They eat together, sleep together . . . well, you get the picture.'

'Marla, they're his *team*,' Sylvie exclaimed. 'He's a soccer player! He's been part of teams his whole life!'

'Just an excuse to hang around in locker rooms with undressed men,' Marla said and nodded her head knowingly. 'Anyway, his aura is lime green. Another sign.'

Sylvie felt a knot forming in her stomach. 'I have to see them. I have to talk to them.' She paused. 'I have to hold them.'

'Don't you think we're pushing the antelope?' Marla asked. 'I mean, we've come so far. You got what you wanted, but *I* want Thanksgiving, and a husband and family; I haven't gotten anything.'

'Please, Marla . . .' All of Sylvie's need was in her voice.

Marla sighed. 'Okay. I'll take a shower. I'll send them out here for something. You got half an hour. Then disappear. And keep your yellow hair under your hat.'

Sylvie nodded and made sure her hair was tucked in. It was good of Marla to allow this, and Sylvie was grateful – an appropriate feeling for the holiday. Her heart beat hard as she waited, down near the garage. Sylvie watched from behind the garage door as Reenie and Brian came out the back door, walked to the wood pile, and attempted to bring in firewood. They each picked up a log. Then they stopped and kissed, then Brian picked up another log while Reenie dropped hers and put her arms around Brian. They kissed again. To have his hands free, Brian threw the logs he was carrying back in the pile and held Reenie in his arms. Then he put his hand inside Reenie's jacket. Deep into her jacket. Sylvie turned her face away. Please, God, she prayed, don't let any boy ever hurt Reenie the way Bob has hurt me.

Sylvie waited a decent interval, then approached them casually. 'Hey, you two lovebirds,' she said. 'Time to go in the house and have a nice innocent cup of cocoa?'

'Mom! You just asked us to come out here for wood. Now it's inside for hot chocolate?' Reenie asked. She squinted at her mother. For a moment Sylvie thought she was nailed, but she'd forgotten the narcissism of children. 'Were you spying on us?' Reenie demanded.

'Of course not,' Sylvie said as nonchalantly as she could manage. 'There's nothing to spy on, is there?'

Reenie and Brian exchanged a guilty look, then shared a laugh. It was an intimate laugh. Sylvie, more nervous than ever, moved closer to Reenie. She put her arm protectively around her daughter. She meant to do it casually, but once she felt Reenie's young body she squeezed her breathless. 'I've missed your hugs, Mom,' Reenie said.

'I love you, Reenie.'

'I love you too,' Reenie said. Then she pulled back. 'Plus, it's very important to me that you accept and love Brian.'

'Well, of course it is.' Sylvie noticed that Brian looked away as Reenie said this. 'I'll try to, though it might not be the exact same way I love you, toots.' Sylvie paused for a moment. How could she possibly explain to her beautiful daughter the consequences of trusting the wrong man? 'Love is very serious. It takes time and trust. I hope that you try to stick to the values that I've taught you.' Sylvie turned and smiled brightly at Brian. He was paralyzed. Reenie, though, was unfazed.

'In addition to your values, Brian and I are adding some of our own,' Reenie said.

'Like?'

'Oh, we've decided we're not going to hold ourselves responsible for our actions,' Brian said, speaking up for the first time. Sylvie's face registered the shock she felt, until she realized the boy was joking.

Reenie began laughing hysterically. 'Oh, Mom. Don't you love it? What you've just experienced is Brian's so-called sense of humor.'

'Deeply amusing,' Sylvie said and was shocked to hear her voice sounded exactly like Mildred's. 'Brian, could you excuse us for a moment?' Sylvie asked. He nodded, picked up some wood, and moved to the house. Reluctantly, Reenie watched him go until Sylvie pulled her away. They stepped into the garage. Sylvie looked at her daughter's beautiful, trusting face. Where should she begin? 'Enough with the jokes. What have I always told you?' Sylvie asked. 'Sex is so much better when there's love.'

Reenie made a 'duh' face. 'Sure. I brought Brian home because I want to see if I *do* love him. Don't worry, Mom. I'll let you know the second we have intercourse. I'll bring my cellular, along with condoms, and call you from bed.' Sylvie stood there for a moment, her mouth open, and then she and Reenie both burst into laughter.

'Okay,' Sylvie said, 'I'll simmer down.' She hugged Reenie again until the girl broke free, eager to hurry back to Brian.

When Sylvie came out of the garage, Kenny and the other

boys were playing soccer on the back lawn. Sylvie watched for a moment. She thought of Marla's comments about his sexual orientation, but Marla was crazy. Lime green auras. Come on! To Sylvie it seemed the guys were healthy and sportsmanlike, even when they patted each other's butts.

'Kenny! Can I see you for a second?' Sylvie yelled out to her son.

Kenny left the pack and came over to his mother. He was flushed and out of breath. 'Is this important, Mom? 'Cause we have a big game next week and we need the practice.'

'I just wanted to hug you and tell you how much I miss and love you.' Sylvie paused. 'That and to ask you if soccer is considered a contact sport.'

Kenny, not getting the question, said, 'I missed you too, Mom. Don't worry. I won't get hurt.' He paused, looked around the garage for a moment, then lowered his voice. 'Don't tell anybody, not even Dad, but . . .' Sylvie held her breath, '. . . there are times when I really get homesick.'

Sylvie smiled at her son, the boy who towered over her. More than anything, she wanted him to be happy. She figured he had a better shot at it if he didn't have to trust a man. Let him find a girl to adore him, and if he betrayed *his* wife, she'd come after him with a hairbrush. 'That's the sweetest thing I've ever heard,' she told him, and patted his arm. 'But you have your . . . friends. And you all seem very . . . close.'

'It's more than close,' Kenny said.

'As a group, right?' she asked.

'Yeah.'

Sylvie felt relieved. Not that she would really, really mind, as Marla might put it, but . . .

'Most of the time,' Kenny said. 'But Hugh and I . . . we're really close. By the way, Mom, you're looking good.' He looked at her appraisingly. 'Maybe we could go downtown, get you some really cool outfits.'

Sylvie was worried by that, but Kenny ran off. Sylvie shrugged. She'd accept him any way he was. Slowly, she walked away, her half hour over.

Marla had showered, changed, and was now frantically rummaging through the cupboards. The kitchen looked like a war room operating theater, with buckets and bowls and instruments and pans on every surface. It was past two o'clock, but she was only up to . . . up to no good, Marla thought. She did have the pies done, the potatoes peeled, the yams almost ready, but the green beans were already limp and the little turkeys didn't seem to be cooking. She had them lined up in the oven like the Rockettes at Radio City. She also couldn't find the egg beater, or the measuring cups, though her recipes called for both. The pressure was killing her. Her feet ached, right on the balls of the feet, which meant she was having heart problems. Probably she was having a heart attack and only her feet knew it! In desperation, Marla picked up the phone and called Sylvie.

Sylvie was watching the end of the Macy's Day parade. She was trying to decide if she should put her TV dinner in yet or not. The phone rang and she was relieved to answer it. Even talking to Mr Brightman was better than the feeling she had now of being entombed. She put the phone to her ear. It was Marla, whispering, 'Okay, where the hell is it?' Marla asked.

'Where's *what*?' Sylvie asked. 'Anyway, *you're* the psychic, not me.'

'The turkey baster,' Marla said, still whispering.

'God! I don't know. I haven't used it in years. Anyway, I *told* you to get a self-basting one,' Sylvie reminded her.

'I think one of them is. But you can't expect it to baste all the others,' Marla whispered louder.

'The others? What others?' Sylvie asked. 'How many turkeys do you have? What's going on? Things were fine this morning,' Sylvie said, her eyes on the TV screen. The mute was on. She wondered what had gone wrong from the time the Popeye blimp had gone by to now, when the Hercules balloon was being marched down to Herald Square.

'Nothing's fine now. The natives are restless.' Marla had forgotten to whisper. 'Come over. Please. I need your help.'

'Now? The two of us in the same kitchen?' Sylvie asked. 'Are you *in*-sane? We already took too much of a chance this morning.' Still, Sylvie sat up, feeling a little jolt of adrenaline. Maybe she *wouldn't* have to face this impossibly empty day alone. 'Do you want to quit? We could exchange places in the next ten minutes.'

'Forget about that!' Marla snapped. 'I want to get the thanks and appreciation after all this work. I just need a little assistance here.'

Sylvie was tempted but said, 'Marla, come on. We can't both be in the same place at the same time. Everyone might ignore middle-aged women, but not when they clone right before their eyes. Why don't you just call my mother?' Sylvie asked. 'She'll help.'

'I already did,' Marla admitted. 'She is helping, but I need you. I'll never do it alone. They've already finished *all* the chips, the cream cheese-stuffed celery, and even most of the olives. Do you know how many olives that is? Can people overdose on olives?' Marla asked. She did sound desperate.

'Plus, Phil just tried to eat the pumpkin centerpiece. You know, we have to have a little talk about Phil. I'm not so sure he's husband material. And speaking of husbands, it isn't helping that your husband is serving a lot of booze.'

'He's *your* husband today,' Sylvie said bitterly.

'Yeah, and he's not pitching in,' Marla admitted, sounding equally bitter. 'I thought Thanksgiving was a family holiday.'

'Wake up and smell the pumpkin pie. Wives do it solo. It's just the way it is,' Sylvie said. She suddenly, clearly, remembered all the frenzied preparations she'd been through in the years before and smiled. Maybe this alone-on-the-sofa deal wasn't as bad as she'd thought.

'Well, Bob is busy doing one thing: he's topping off drinks. He and Phil and John and Jim – I mean, Dad – are all here, and they're drinking,' Marla said. She paused. 'They're probably seeing double already. If they haven't figured us out so far, they really, really won't now.'

Sylvie was torn, and said, 'I want to come.' She thought of the empty day stretching in front of her. 'Frankly, Marla, right now I'm not happy with your life.'

'Like *I* like *yours*,' Marla said and snorted.

Sylvie pulled up and parked around the corner from her cul-de-sac. She figured the best way to get into her own house was by going through the Beyermans' yard. She certainly didn't need two identical BMW convertibles parked along with the rest of the Bavarian convention in her driveway.

It seemed as if the Beyermans were away for the holiday. At least that was what she thought until she got to the rhododendron wall that separated her yard from theirs. At that point Ching, their nasty black Pomeranian, darted out at her, barking furiously as he did virtually all day, every day. But now he sank his little pointed teeth into her ankle. Totally surprised, Sylvie shook him off, dove through the rhododendrons, and they yelped simultaneously as they hit the dirt, she in her territory and Ching in his. Crouching and limping, she managed to sneak around the garage, up the back steps, and then peeked, for the second time that day, through the kitchen window. Marla, still dressed pretty much as Sylvie herself was, in black leggings and a black sweater, was looking for her. She opened the door. From somewhere – Sylvie couldn't even imagine where – Marla had gotten an apron. It wasn't one of those practical Williams-Sonoma ones, it was a little number Betty Crocker might have worn in 1954. Sylvie limped into the kitchen. If she hadn't already been breathless, the scene here would have taken her breath away. The place was more of a disaster than ever. Sylvie had never seen such disorder. 'Hello, dear,' Mildred said. 'Welcome to bedlam.' Amid the bowls, pots, spatulas, and pans her mother had found just enough room to lean her elbow against the counter.

'Quick! Get in here,' Marla whispered to Sylvie. 'You have to help with this meal. *And* you have to get me a different husband. I don't want Phil.'

'Join the club,' Mildred said dryly. She sighed. 'The middle-child syndrome,' she said, shaking her head.

Sylvie glanced around. She couldn't begin to take it all in. Not with it being almost three o'clock, no smell of food cooking, and the totality of the chaos surrounding her. She looked at her kitchen island, almost sunk by the flotsam and jetsam. 'Four whisks? I didn't even know I *had* four whisks.' She lifted one. Some unidentified liquid dripped from it. 'And you've used them all,' she added faintly. 'Didn't your mother teach you to clean up as you went along?'

'The only thing my mother taught me was French inhaling,' Marla snapped. 'But it hasn't been useful since I quit smoking.' She wiped her hand across her apron. 'Does anyone have a Marlboro?' she asked.

'I hope not,' Sylvie said. She looked over at her mother, who simply shrugged. 'Truthfully, is *anything* ready? Where are we?'

'It feels like Rwanda,' Mildred piped up.

'Nowhere,' Marla said simultaneously. 'The desserts are finished, but I burned the potatoes, and I haven't made the salad. I can't get the electric can opener to work, so I don't have the cranberry sauce out. And what are you supposed to do with this winter squash, anyway? How do you expect me to work with all this protein and starch? You know how I feel about mixing these together. I just can't . . .' Marla stepped back from the counter and pulled off a shoe, rubbing her foot. 'I think I'm having a heart attack,' she said, staring at her heel as if it mattered. Mildred gave Sylvie a quizzical look. Marla then turned to the stove top where all the pots were starting to steam. She was glaring at them so hard, it was as if she were trying a Yuri Geller, attempting to move them with telepathic powers.

'What are you doing?' Mildred asked.

'A watched pot never spoils,' Marla said, still staring at the pans.

Sylvie shook her head. 'It's not like you got here yesterday. What have you been busy with all this time?' she asked.

'Setting the table,' Marla told her.

'She sets a nice table,' Mildred confirmed. 'The calligraphy place cards are a very personal touch. And I love those turkey napkins. Too bad there's no turkey.'

'So where is everybody?' Sylvie whispered.

'Watching the game,' Marla said. 'Everyone but the kids is drunk,' she added. 'At least one thing here is like back home.' Then she turned to the window, pointed, and gasped. 'Uh-oh! Benny and his friends are back from the park and looking this way.'

'*Kenny*, not *Benny*!' Sylvie corrected as she squatted down out of the line of sight. She rubbed her own heel while she was down there. She wondered idly if she needed a dog-bite shot. Tetanus or rabies? Meanwhile, the boys were in a noisy group, coming up the driveway. If they came in the kitchen door she and Marla were dead. They were coming toward the back door. 'Marla, get lost! Quick,' Sylvie gasped.

'Where should I go?' Marla whispered, panicking. 'I better get out of here. Too many cooks saves nine,' she intoned, looking around frantically for a place to hide.

'Into the laundry room. Hurry!' Sylvie told her.

'No,' Marla said. 'I'm afraid of those machines. They hate me. *You* go.' Before Sylvie could strangle her, the boys drifted off behind the garage. Sylvie stood up. 'I think they're smoking joints back there,' Marla told her, looking out the window.

'What?' Sylvie asked, shocked. 'Did you see any of those kids—'

'I didn't see anything, but it's what *my* brothers always used to do behind the garage,' Marla admitted. 'Say, hey! I wouldn't mind a hit myself.'

'Don't you even *think* about it,' Sylvie warned.

Marla sighed. 'Who has time? A woman's work is never fun.'

Before either Mildred or Sylvie could react to that, Phil's

and Rosalie's voices were heard in the dining room. 'Jesus, would you look at that table!' Phil was saying as he pushed open the kitchen door. 'It looks like a scale model of Epcot Center. What's all that about?' Sylvie ducked in time, hiding behind the island.

'Your sister put in a lot of time planning for this dinner,' Rosalie snapped. 'Not that you deserve it. She wanted to make it nice for the twins and all.'

'Whatever. Where the hell are the pretzels?' Phil began opening cabinets, moving around the island. Sylvie, on her hands and knees, scurried in a circle like the dog that had bitten her, just managing to keep out of sight.

'Why don't you ever close a door? Check in the cabinet near your right foot,' Rosalie suggested to her ex.

'Speaking of foot, what the hell is it with your boyfriend? That Mel guy. He says he's missing some equipment.'

'Hey, he can't help it if he's not all there,' Rosalie snapped. 'Neither are you. And the equipment *you* were missing wasn't just a toe.'

'Yeah, I know. I'd lost my balls, but I got 'em back now.' Phil gestured to his crotch with one hand, pulling out the pretzels with the other.

'Phil, please,' Mildred said. 'This is a kitchen.' Neither her son nor her ex-daughter-in-law heard her.

'Really? That's not what your dad says. Anyway, it's not Mel's *toes* that I'm interested in.'

'Spare me the details,' Phil begged, and they both walked out of the kitchen as they had come in, sniping away. Sylvie realized that the two of them were perfect together.

'It's always amazed me that those two can be in a crowded room and never know it,' Mildred said as she helped Sylvie up off the floor.

'Turkey time!' Marla cried. She opened the oven to reveal rows of Cornish hens, or something, in the oven.

'That isn't turkey!' Sylvie yelled.

'It's *almost* turkey. I think of them as "turkey light,"' Marla said defensively. 'The butcher swore they could be stuffed,' she added.

'With what? A tweezers?' Mildred asked.

'Marla, you can't serve the kids these. They won't eat squab. We've always had turkey. I mean, it's Thanksgiving, isn't it?'

'What do you want me to do?' Marla whined. 'The really, really turkey didn't fit in the oven. I tried, I really tried.' She began to sob, her shoulders shaking, her nose running almost immediately. 'I'm just not cracked up to be a wife. See? I can't do it. I can't even take care of myself, let alone a soccer team. No wonder Bob doesn't want me. Nobody does.'

Mildred stepped forward and put her arms around the girl.

'Look, you set a lovely table,' Sylvie said, trying to comfort Marla.

'Two days ago. But there keep being more people. I can't keep up!' Marla burst into tears again. 'We need two more places.'

'I'll do that. You slice the carrots.' Sylvie looked over at Mildred. 'Mom, you're just going to have to go out and buy a cooked turkey.'

'I find that very embarrassing. Anyway, nothing is open.'

'Be embarrassed. It won't kill you. And go to a restaurant if you have to. Order à la carte.'

Sylvie had to get all this under control. Poor Marla. Just as Sylvie had expected, she'd been undone by the holiday. But instead of feeling glad, Sylvie felt guilty and sorry for her rival. She'd at least give Marla the holiday meal she craved. Sylvie snuck in to the dining room with Mildred following, still protesting. When Sylvie saw the table, she gasped. It looked like someone's model railroad – there were miniature Pilgrims, a couple of teepees, and – for some weird reason known only to Marla – a little covered bridge. They had started to move things around, eliminating some of the centerpiece, when Bob walked into the room. Mildred and Sylvie froze. Sylvie's heart began to beat harder, but Bob went directly to the liquor cabinet.

'Do we have any more scotch?' Bob asked as he started rummaging through the cabinet. 'It seems to be the drink of choice. Your father and John are actually giggling. Phil seems even angrier than usual.'

'Damnit!' Marla hollered from the kitchen.

'Rosalie is too,' Sylvie said, quickly covering and heading for the kitchen. 'Sssh!' she scolded. 'What happened?'

Marla held up her hand. She was bleeding. She'd obviously cut herself chopping the carrots.

'Run it under cold water,' Sylvie said as the door swung open.

Rosalie had come back into the kitchen, this time with her date. Sylvie couldn't make it over to the laundry room door so she wedged herself beside the refrigerator. She was surprised to find that she fit. She really had lost weight!

'Sylvie, this is Mel,' Rosalie said to Marla. 'I've told her nothing but good things about you,' Rosalie murmured.

But Marla was paying no attention to anything but her little cut. 'Ouch! Son of Sam, I could have cut off a finger. I'd be marred for life,' Marla cried.

Rosalie shot Marla a poisonous look. Hugging her date,

she said, 'I think the number of fingers or toes a person has means nothing! Nothing!'

She stomped out of the kitchen, followed by the now morose Mel. Sylvie was just squeezing out from the space beside the refrigerator when John entered. He nearly saw her, so she jumped out the back door and stood in the cold, peeping in the steamed-up window. John was listening to Marla, and seemed very solicitous, if a tiny bit high. Sylvie was wondering if she could somehow ask him to look at her Ching bite when she saw him take Marla's hand out from under the running water. Leaning over Marla, he kissed her finger to make it better. Sylvie couldn't believe her eyes. John had better be dead drunk! She watched as he lovingly applied a Band-Aid and put his arm around Marla. Sylvie's breath clouded up the window. Then the two of them left the room together. Sylvie cautiously went inside. As she entered the kitchen, John came back in. Surprised, but obviously high, he blinked, confused, and came toward her. 'Why are you wearing that hat?' he asked, his voice slurred. 'Are you better?' He picked up her cold hand. He was obviously surprised by the temperature. He looked down at it and was more surprised to see that the bandage and the cut were gone. 'My god. What happened?' he asked.

'You kissed it and made it better,' Sylvie said sweetly. She'd like to really confuse him and pull off her cap and let her blonde hair fall down. Let him think his kiss did that!

John was confused. Thank god for alcohol, Sylvie thought.

Jim and Mildred were sitting at a table in the Hungry Heifer. Patiently, Mildred was repeating their order. 'That's right. Turkey for twenty and two glasses of water,' Mildred told the waiter, who left, confused but willing.

'Mildred, this is painful,' Jim said. 'How did Sylvie manage—'

'Oh, it's a long story,' Mildred said, leaning into her husband. She had unfastened the top two buttons of her blouse and she hoped he noticed. Her chest was spotted now, and the flesh at her cleavage had the pleated look of wrinkled silk, but still, cleavage was cleavage. 'You know, Jim . . . your eyes look very blue tonight.'

'Mildred?' Jim said in a tone of voice that asked a lot of questions.

'They do,' Mildred averred, staring into his eyes. They had seen her, years ago, as a young, desirable girl. They were the only eyes left on the planet that had. 'Jim, I don't want to go to my grave never having made love again,' Mildred said.

Jim's blue eyes blinked. And it seemed to Mildred that he might be interested.

All the men except Brian were watching football. They were huddled tensely, watching an important play. Sixth down, ten to go, or something like that. Marla never understood the rules of football, or what the excitement was about. The guys with the big shoulders looked good and all, their butts tiny in comparison, but she knew it was all padding. She stepped over to Phil.

'Can I refresh your drink?' she asked in her best hostess voice. She felt a little better. Sylvie had taken over in the kitchen, dinner was almost ready, and Marla had hidden in the upstairs bathroom, cleaning herself up and calming down. Maybe she could become a part of this family, she thought. They looked cozy, all of them huddled over the TV like cavemen crouched around the fire.

Maybe she could like Phil. Maybe he could be her very own caveman.

At that moment a touchdown was scored, or something. Everyone, except Phil, yelled. Marla jumped. Phil screamed. He'd missed it.

'Sylvie, can you get your ass away from the television so a man can see? I got a spread I got to cover,' her caveman barked. Marla stepped back, offended. 'Women!' Phil said, looking up. 'Any word on dinner?'

'Just one: choke.' Marla left, stricken. She walked into the kitchen.

Sylvie was almost finished with the potatoes. Mildred had come back with the turkey. 'It's a go,' Mildred said, looking at Marla. 'Boy, you've pulled yourself together.'

Marla ignored the compliment. She stared at both women. 'I thought you were nice,' she said. 'Not the type who would let me marry a woman-hating moron.'

'Phil?' Mildred asked and sighed. 'I was really hoping you could straighten him out. I know he has love in him . . . somewhere. And, truthfully, you're a nice girl.' She paused. Marla felt her heart soften. She would like to be part of all this. 'You know,' Mildred was saying, 'all men take a little shaping up.' Mildred was still in her coat, her cheeks pink, her eyes sparkling. She looked good for an old lady, Marla thought. She looked as if she had a secret. Marla tried to focus on what her mom was saying. 'One of the great ironies of life is that when men and women marry, the man is hoping his wife will never change and the woman can't wait to start changing him. Of course, they both wind up disappointed. The woman always does change. The guy never does. Look at Phil as a fixer-upper.' Mildred smiled. 'Jim is still my work in progress, but I'm beginning to see some improvement.'

She took off her coat. 'Let's serve dinner together. I'd like you in the family,' Mildred said sincerely to Marla.

'Really, really?' Marla fell into Mildred's arms. Sylvie took the opportunity to leave.

29

Sylvie, all alone, stood across the street from her own house. It was twilight. All the other houses on the cul-de-sac were dark: her mother and father and Rosalie were out, across the street, inside her home, and the Brennans always went to his parents in Arizona for the holiday. She was alone. A wind had come up and, although it wasn't really cold yet, the dampness and the wind made Sylvie shiver. She was still in her black leggings and sweater, but she'd only taken a denim jacket with her and it wasn't really enough to keep her warm.

Once she got into her BMW she'd put the heat up full blast. At the thought, she shivered again. She hesitated to double-back through the Beyermans' yard – not because she was afraid of Ching, though her heel still smarted – but because she just couldn't take her eyes off the lit dining room window of her house. There, inside, was the happy, quintessential family scene. Norman Rockwell, as American as pumpkin pie. Kenny, Reenie, her mother and father, her brother, her husband, and her friends. Even she was there. Right now she was spooning mashed potatoes onto John's plate. It seemed that everyone was busy passing food, eating turkey legs, or laughing. It was a little bit like Huck Finn at his own funeral. No, it was as if she didn't exist. Sylvie thought of the movie *It's a Wonderful Life*. But in that film Jimmy Stewart realized he was irreplaceable. He saw the impact his life had on others.

Standing there, in the deepening dark, it was as if Sylvie was completely replaceable. She didn't need to exist.

The table had been cleared with the help of the kids, who had then all left to go out somewhere. Somewhere fun, Marla thought. There had been no standing ovation. There had been no applause at all. The only thanks she had gotten were the polite ones from Benny's friends, who had just murmured 'Thanks, Mrs Schiffer' as they bussed their plates to the sink. The kitchen was a mess. Marla surveyed all the wreckage. She thought that shopping and preparing had been the work. Somehow she hadn't imagined this. She couldn't *believe* the enormous task ahead of her. The thought of all the mixing of proteins and starches, and having fruit touch vegetables, was just too overwhelming for her. 'The aura's still not right in this kitchen, no matter how hard I try,' Marla said aloud to herself, feeling her eyes well up with tears. Was this what family life was supposed to be like? Or had it become this because of Bob's affair with her? Marla wasn't sure if she felt sorrier for herself or for Sylvie, but she decided on herself. Then the kitchen door swung open. For a moment she thought Bob might appear, ready to hug her and tell her how great dinner had been. But it wasn't Bob. It was John, clearly woozy, and Mildred, giving him a hand to help him into the room. 'Jesus, I drank too much.'

'"Jesus" is right,' Mildred said, looking around at the incredible mess. 'Martha Stewart definitely doesn't live here.'

John blearily surveyed the chaos. 'Hey, can I help?'

'I think what you need to do, Doctor, is lie down. That's an order from Dr Mom,' Mildred told him. 'I'll stay and help Sylvie.'

'No, you've done enough, Mom. My husband should help,'

Marla said. At that moment Bob did come into the kitchen. Maybe it would end all right. Marla smiled. Now she would get some appreciation, and in front of John.

But Bob said, 'I'm going out for a little while; I left a few things on the lot.' He picked up his car keys and jingled them, then turned to get his coat. Marla narrowed her eyes. She knew he wasn't going to any lot. She knew exactly where he was going. He had his nerve! Who did he think he was, and who did he think she was? Some galley slave? Some cleaning lady? Marla looked at the stacks of greasy plates, dirty bowls, blackened pans. There were the dishes waiting to be scraped into the disposal. This marriage ought to go into the disposal as well, she thought, and deliberately swiped her arm across the island, sending dishes crashing to the floor. Bob turned back around.

'What broke?'

'A marriage?' she asked. She picked up a tray, still holding some candied yams and the damned melted marshmallows. She flung it in his direction, missing him but almost hitting John.

Mildred propelled John out of the room. 'I don't think we're needed in here,' she said.

Bob had ducked but now rose and looked at the tray smashed against the door, along with the sweet potatoes that had ricocheted onto his corduroy cuffs. 'Sylvie! Stop it. Are you crazy?' Bob asked. 'What's this supposed to mean?'

'It doesn't mean anything because . . . it means everything's off balance because the starch touched the protein . . .' Marla sputtered. She wanted to tell him who she really, really was, and what he was as well. But she had promised Sylvie. 'This isn't really a marriage. I mean, you're married but . . . anyway, it's not what a marriage is supposed to be,' she said.

'You don't want to make love to me. You don't want to take care of me. I have a house. I have kids. Big deal. I have to do everything.'

'Sylvie, I—'

But Marla wasn't going to listen to his lies. She was exhausted, and her disappointment was so deep she felt as if something inside her chest was cracking. 'Shut up! You think it's easy being *your* wife? I'm not just the cook, the cleaner, and the woman who watches you leave, ya know.' She began to cry, but she didn't want to. She was too angry, and too proud. Bob made her feel like some kind of neutered dog or something, some animal that didn't even have a sex. 'Do you know how hard I worked on this meal?' she asked. 'How hard it was to not mix the wrong fruits and vegetables together? Do you know how long it took me to organize it? And now you think you're going to go over to some other . . .' She stopped herself. She thought again of Sylvie. If this was the life that Sylvie had been living, Marla understood why Sylvie had pulled the switcheroo. Sylvie ought to have the right to tell Bob about the switch, right before she castrated him.

Marla watched as Bob bent down and tried to brush the marshmallow and yams off his corduroy cuffs. Then he turned to her, as if she were the most important thing in the world to him – right after his car and his cuffs. 'I appreciate you,' Bob said, coming toward her.

Marla couldn't take it. She picked up a bowl of stuffing and flung it at him, but she again missed by a fraction of an inch. The stuffing exploded on the wall above the broom closet. 'I don't want to be appreciated. I want to be loved, and undressed, and not necessarily by you. Why don't you just get out! Get out and go to your girlfriend!'

'What?'

'You heard me!' Marla threw another dish, and another. Bob, a look of real fear on his face, ducked, turned, and began to back out of the room. Marla emptied the island with both arms, throwing everything onto the floor. Then, after she'd realized what she'd done to all of the beautiful dishes, Marla screamed and ran out the back door into the dark.

30

Sylvie, alone and exhausted after her bizarre Thanksgiving Day, had put on yet another uncomfortable sexy nightie and had just decided to go to bed even though it was only a little after eight. She was glumly brushing her teeth when she heard the doorbell. Mouth foamy, toothbrush in hand, she made her way to the door and cautiously looked through the peephole. Seeing Bob, she quickly pulled herself together, spit the toothpaste into the pot of the silk ficus tree, and opened the door.

'Bobby? I don't remember you ever visiting me before on a holiday,' she said. Then she wondered if perhaps he *had* come to Marla after every family event. She stood there, loving him and hating him. She wanted him to come in, to hold and comfort and love her, but fair was fair. What about Marla? She needed her 'husband' with her now. 'You should be home,' she forced herself to say.

'Home?' Bob echoed. To his credit, he looked like a shock victim. His eyes seemed glazed, or else he was on the verge of tears. 'I don't know what's happening,' he said. 'I'm starting to think of you . . . this . . . as home.' Bob hugged her and she hugged him back, feeling the cold that still clung to his jacket. He buried his face in her hair. 'You smell like turkey,' he murmured. She stiffened for a moment, but she couldn't help holding him — he felt too good to her. His arms, always muscular and long, felt like her husband's arms, and her lover's.

The thing was that Sylvie knew he loved *her*. He just didn't know that she *was* Sylvie. 'Every time you leave, I think I'm never going to see you again,' she admitted, and felt truly sorry for Marla.

Bob stroked her hair. 'I'm not going anywhere,' he promised.

Bob was sleeping, and Sylvie propped herself on one elbow to watch him. Making love had been even better than before – they'd fallen on each other hungrily, and they'd made love until they were both exhausted. Now Sylvie pulled the sheet up over Bob's bare shoulder. She loved the way his skin, darker than hers, looked against the pillow.

As if he could feel her eyes on him, Bob's own lids fluttered and he woke up. 'You watching me sleep?' he asked, stretching his arms out to the headboard.

'I have for years,' she admitted.

'I've only known you since July.'

Sylvie remembered her role. 'Oops! Well, it *feels* like years.' Sylvie tried a Marlaesque giggle. 'You know how bad I am with months and numbers.'

Bob smiled. 'It does feel like we're old friends. Well, not so old in your case.' He reached for her hand. He looked deep into her eyes from his place on his pillow to hers on her own. 'I love you. I really do, Marla.' He looked almost as surprised as she felt, hearing this.

Sylvie felt so happy and so sad all at the same time. Somehow she knew that if there was a time to end this road show, to prove her point and push her advantage, it was now. Go for it, she told herself. 'Then you should marry me,' she said. She kept looking into his eyes. She felt she could lose herself in them. How could someone look at you so deeply and then go and lie to his wife? She wouldn't let him off the hook. She'd make sure he'd learned his lesson. She'd made him love her — Sylvie — and now, after he lost Marla, she'd decide if she'd have him back or not.

Bob sat up. He'd lost his flush. In fact, he looked pale now. 'You knew from the beginning that that wasn't in the cards, Marla. I told you I was married. That I couldn't bear the thought of breaking up my home—'

'You just said *this* was home,' Sylvie reminded him.

Bob got up and looked out the window into the dark street. He sighed, very disturbed. For a moment Sylvie felt sorry for him, but not enough to save him from wriggling on the hook a little longer. 'Look. The truth is, Sylvie seems to have gone crazy,' Bob admitted. 'And it's my fault. I've made her angry and miserable. We're two people standing in the cold. We don't seem to make each other happy anymore but neither of us is capable of taking the first step forward.' Bob turned and looked at Sylvie, then bit his lip as if he might actually cry.

'Maybe she didn't invite special things in,' Sylvie suggested, testing him.

'No. Sylvie was — is — a pure romantic. I've neglected that. She has music in her soul. I've lost mine.' He sat down heavily on the side of the bed. 'The holiday's been a fiasco. She's been cold to the kids, angry at me, and obsessed with the table decorations. The other night she served me shrimp, even though I'm allergic to shellfish big time. Did you know that? Then tonight we had a scene and she walked out on me. If she knew about us, she'd never forgive me . . . and she shouldn't.'

'I'm sorry, Bobby,' Sylvie said, hardening her heart. 'I understand how loyal you are and how difficult it must be for you, but I've made a decision. I love you, but I can't spend another holiday alone. If you don't want me full-time, I don't want to see you anymore.'

Bob sat very still on the side of the bed. Sylvie held her breath. He turned to her, finally deciding. 'Marry me,' he said.

Sylvie burst into tears. This was it. She'd won! She'd gotten what she wanted, if she still wanted it. Yet she couldn't have been more confused. 'You'd leave your wife?' Sylvie asked, shocked to the core. 'Really?' Then, 'Really, really?' she added.

'Yes. This last week . . . I guess I've just realized how happy I am with you. And . . . I don't know. Maybe Sylvie needs a chance at love.' He embraced her gently. 'I love you,' he said. Sylvie couldn't stop crying. She held Bob, hugging him so tightly he could hardly breathe.

31

The door opened slowly. Marla, sad and disheveled, entered the bedroom. She couldn't believe the mess she'd made of everything — not just the kitchen but her whole life. No wonder she didn't have a real family. She couldn't handle one. Now Bobby was off with Sylvie, the kids were out, and she — like always — had ended up alone. Too tired to even don a nightie, she stripped off her filthy food-stained clothes and got into bed. Once under the blankets, she wished she could go to sleep and never wake up. She stretched out, in the center of the huge king-sized bed, and it was then her foot felt something warm beside it. Her foot told her someone else was there.

Marla, grateful, whispered softly, 'Bob?'

But it was John who put his head up, groggy. 'Sylvie?' he asked. 'What are you doing here?'

'Sometimes I wonder myself.'

John, slightly more conscious, looked around. 'Jesus, I'm at your house.' He shook his head as if to clear it. 'This is why I'm not a heavy drinker. I'm *so* sorry.'

'You don't have to apologize,' Marla said. '*I* screwed everything up.' She covered her face with her hands. 'I always do. No wonder I don't have anyone or anything.' She began to sob.

John put his arm around her. 'You do. Of course you do.'

'I don't!' Marla insisted and bent her head. 'You don't

understand. Oh, John, I made a huge scene. I probably broke every dish in the house. Sylvie will be furious.' She realized, too late, what she'd just said but John seemed to think it was okay.

'I think Sylvie is furious right now,' he said, taking her hand. 'Don't disassociate. You can acknowledge your anger. Especially with me, Sylvie. Maybe Bob can't hear it but I can,' he told her, then sat up. 'Where is Bob?' he asked. 'Where is everybody?'

'The kids went to the movies,' Marla said. 'They just don't want to be with me. Not to mention Bob. He was gone when I got back. We know who he's with.'

'The bastard.'

Marla began to weep again. 'I never knew a wife could feel like this. I'm so sorry. And ashamed.'

'You have nothing to be ashamed of,' John said. 'It's Bob who should be ashamed.'

Marla looked up at him. She began to cry more loudly. 'You don't understand,' she said, 'it's my fault.'

John put his arm around her, kissing the top of her head. Then the blanket fell from her shoulders. He stopped. 'Sylvie! My god! You're . . . all pink and naked.'

Marla nodded, shrugged, and lifted her face to his kiss, but just on the cheek. He smelled good – a healthy smell of sleep mixed with scotch seemed to envelop her. Without thinking, her kisses moved to his eyes and – finally – to his mouth. John groaned. For a moment he resisted. She could feel his lips held tight. Then his mouth relaxed and opened. She knew he'd waited a long time for this kiss and she made it a good one. When he could, John stopped, but only when both of them were breathless. Gently he pushed her away. 'This isn't right,' he said.

'But it's not as wrong as you think,' Marla assured him. She held her face up to his. He could not resist. They kissed again. Gently, the way you would move in the presence of a woodland deer, she put her arms around John's neck. With her right hand she tugged very, very gently at his hair. He groaned again.

'Sylvie. Oh, Sylvie,' he whispered, 'please stop. Bob, your marriage . . . oh, Sylvie.' Marla could feel him give up. He wrapped his arms around her, low on her naked back, and she felt him trembling. Then the two of them disappeared under the blankets.

When Bob went into the bedroom, he felt heavy, full of his bad news. The room, like the rest of the house, was a disaster, the bed lumpy and unmade, Sylvie nowhere around. All the way over, on the now too familiar drive across the bridge from Cleveland, he had been thinking and rethinking his decision. He was a man who tried to please others, and a man who liked and needed order in his life. Right now he was pleasing no one and his life – as they said in twelve-step programs – had become unmanageable. His home life was over, and a new chapter could open, but why did he feel like such a slimeball? Perhaps it was because Sylvie had always been so good, so perfect. He sat heavily on the edge of the bed, slowly stripped off his clothes, and too exhausted to bother with pajamas, pulled up the duvet. Only then did he notice the big lump in the middle of the bed. Poor Sylvie. After her outburst she must have crawled into the fetal position there. As gently as possible, Bob leaned over and patted the lump. 'Sylvie, we have to talk. Now. About our marriage.'

Marla felt someone patting her awake and sat up, clutching

the blanket to her chest. 'Excuse me?' she said. Bob was there beside her, and for a moment Marla became deeply confused. Hadn't it been John who'd just . . . of course it had. She put her hand under the blanket and felt John's silky hair beside her hip. Now she remembered everything. It wasn't a dream. She loved John and he loved her. Unless, of course, he loved only the real Sylvie, but she didn't think so. Not after what they'd just shared in bed. Now, however, she had Bob to deal with. 'Excuse me?' she said again.

'Look, Sylvie, I'm sorry. I'm very, very sorry. But we have to talk. We've shared a lot but——' At that moment John sat up too.

'No more sharing?' he asked.

Marla watched Bob's face as he realized that his 'wife' was in bed with someone else. Well, now she'd get to see how he felt about sharing. She'd had to share him for the last four months. But, to be honest, Bob didn't look as if he was in a sharing kind of mood. He pulled away from her, grabbing at the blanket. John, on the other side, pulled back. All three of them were covered by nothing but the duvet. Marla could honestly say that John had more to hide.

Bob's mouth had dropped open. His eyes went from one to the other, the way people on TV watching tennis ricocheted during a volley. Bob took in the scene, but slowly, as if he couldn't believe it. 'John?' he asked. 'Sylvie?' Marla figured he was batting five hundred but she didn't have to tell him that. 'How could you?' he asked. The full horror of it hit him, and even in the semidarkness Marla could see him pale. 'My god, how could you betray me like this?' Bob demanded.

'Betray *you*?' Marla asked in return. 'How could I betray a man who's already sleeping with another woman?' It seemed like a reasonable question to her, but it shocked Bob to the core.

'You know?' he asked.

'Oh yeah,' she answered.

Bob turned to John. '*You* told her!' he cried, as furious as a naked, guilty man in bed could be. 'I sell you a BMW at cost and you . . . you . . .'

'*Me?*' John asked. 'I didn't tell her anything. She knew. She came to me. And *you* were the one cheating on your wife.' He turned to Marla. 'Cheating on my best friend,' John added.

'*I'm* your best friend!' Bob exclaimed. He was furious. But Marla didn't even turn to look at him. She kept her eyes on John. She could hardly believe her ears.

'I'm your best friend?' Marla asked John.

In answer, John put his arm around her. 'Yes, Sylvie,' he told her.

'Really?' she asked, hardly daring to believe it.

'Really, really,' John said. Marla blushed, then smiled up adoringly at John.

'You're mine too.'

'You take that back!' Bob demanded. '*I'm* your best friend.'

'I don't think so,' Marla told him.

'Bob, you don't have to leave your wife for me. Because I *am* your wife . . .' Sylvie said out loud, trying to prepare herself for her speech to Bob. She turned left on Courtland and tried again. 'Bob, I know you love me, but do you know how much you love your wife?' she practiced, then giggled.

Sylvie, feeling totally victorious, pulled into the driveway of her home. She'd figured it was time for the charade to end, that she'd better follow up with Bob, cushion the blow for Marla, and – not to put too fine a point on it – make sure

Bobby — Bob — lived up to his word. She braked and turned off Schubert's Ninth Symphony, which she'd been blasting on the stereo.

She ran up the front walk, into the hall, and up the stairs. She could hear Phil and Rosalie, still fighting as they cleared up the wreckage in the kitchen. Those two could not give each other up. On the landing she met her mother. Mildred was sitting on the lower two steps, her chin on her hands. 'I figured you'd come back,' Mildred said. 'I took the kids to the movies. I sent their pals to a hotel for the night.'

'Thanks, Mom. Where's Bob?' Sylvie asked. Mildred motioned with her head toward the second floor. 'He proposed to me,' Sylvie said, beaming.

With an effort Mildred pushed herself up off the steps. She sighed. 'So let me get this straight: he's leaving you for . . . you?'

'Right!'

Mildred sat down again. 'Well, congratulations, I guess. You're the first woman in all recorded history to have it both ways. Romance *and* security.' She looked at her daughter. 'But your father won't pay for another wedding,' she added. 'And there could be a few surprises for you up there.' She motioned to the bedrooms above.

Sylvie giggled again and quickly ascended the remaining steps, Mildred following. Sylvie felt great, better than if she'd won the lottery. But when she entered the bedroom the first thing she saw was Marla, naked and in bed with Bob.

'Oh my god!' She paused, looked at the two of them and then around the room. 'And who rearranged my furniture?'

'What are *you* doing here?' Bob asked Sylvie.

'I'm here to hear you tell her,' Sylvie said.

'Tell me what?' Marla asked.

'I can't, Marla. I just can't,' Bob said to Sylvie.

'You can't what?' Marla asked from the bed.

Sylvie couldn't believe what she was hearing! He was backing down? After what they'd shared? And what had he just been sharing in her bed with Marla? 'What!' Sylvie cried. She felt she'd go postal right there; if she'd had a machine gun there'd be blood on the walls. 'After tonight? After . . . you promised?' Of course, she reminded herself, Bob was saying that he wouldn't leave her, his wife, but . . . Sylvie stood at the foot of her own bed, so confused and frustrated that she almost screamed.

'Marla,' Bob said to her, 'seeing Sylvie in bed with someone else . . . well, I realized the truth. I love her. I love my wife.' Bob looked at Sylvie. Then he turned to Marla. 'I do love you, Sylvie,' he said. He turned to Sylvie and shrugged apologetically. 'I love my wife.'

'I *am* your wife, you idiot!' Sylvie screamed, stepping up and slapping Bob across the face. She stepped back again and turned to Marla. 'And who were you in bed with, you tramp?'

At that moment, Phil, Jim, and Rosalie entered the room. 'What the hell is going on up here?' Jim asked. 'The kids are really scared. I think that you should go down and talk to them . . .' He paused and saw the two Sylvies. 'Hey, what gives?'

'I'm not sure, but it's better than TV,' Mildred commented.

Bob was rubbing his reddened cheek. 'I know I deserved that,' he said.

'I can't believe the two of you would do this to me,' Sylvie said to Marla and Bob, ignoring everyone else in the room.

'But this isn't what you think,' Marla protested.

Bob stared at Marla, beside him in bed. 'Why are you apologizing to her?' he asked Marla. Both women ignored him.

'Oh. You're naked in bed with my husband and it's not what I think,' Sylvie said to Marla.

Only then did the blanket move. Cautiously, John raised his head from under the blankets. Jim, shocked, turned and left the room. Sylvie nearly passed out. John looked from Sylvie at the foot of the bed to Marla beside him. 'Oh my god! I'm sober and I'm seeing double. What the hell is going on?' John asked Marla, then looked again at Sylvie. 'Who are you?' he demanded. He looked back at the woman beside him. 'Or, who are *you*?'

Sylvie, totally shocked, stepped away from the bed filled with this loathsome ménage à trois. As if they were vermin that could bite, she jumped onto the ottoman. John was in her bed. *John.* He too looked shocked, the loathsome lizard. He stared at the two women. Then John looked at Bob. 'You never told me your girlfriend was a dead ringer for Sylvie.'

As if a light had gone on upstairs, Sylvie watched as Bob finally began to realize that something . . . something was very, very wrong. 'What the . . .' He turned toward Sylvie. 'Marla?' He spun around to the bed and looked at Marla beside him. 'Sylvie?' he asked her, his voice growing faint.

'Try again,' Sylvie said coldly from the foot of the bed.

'My god,' John whispered.

'What the . . . you two . . .' Bob stammered.

'Deception. Women are nothing but deception,' Phil said.

'This from a man who tells women they could only test-drive a car in the backseat with him,' Rosalie snapped back.

'I heard that!' Jim called out to his son from the hall. 'That's it! You're off the lot!'

'Fine. And what about perfect Bob?' Phil asked. 'Your golden son-in-law is doing a Marv Albert impersonation in there!'

Bob gulped. 'I . . . I didn't know . . . John, meet Marla . . . but I'm not forgetting *you* thought she was my wife,' Bob said. He turned to Sylvie. 'And I'm forgiving you, Sylvie. You made me love you all over again.'

Sylvie couldn't believe her ears. *This* lizard was talking about forgiving *her*? He was insane. Meanwhile, the other two asylum inmates were busy. Marla had extended her hand to John. 'Hi! Nice to make your acquaintance.'

John took her hand. Instead of shaking it, he simply held it. Sylvie wished she lived in some Arabian country where a man's hands were cut off. He was gazing at Marla – Ms Alternative Medicine – with adoration. 'Marla? Your name is really Marla?'

'Actually, it was Susan. I changed it to make it sexier,' Marla admitted. 'But that was before Donald dumped her,' she added.

'Your name is Susan?' Sylvie snapped at Marla. 'Don't you tell the truth about *anything*?'

'Yes. From now on I want to be honest. I don't want to tell any half-truths – unless they're completely accurate,' Marla said.

'You could have told me,' John said, his voice soft. 'I would have understood.'

'Sorry. I wanted to have . . . something really, really real,' Marla told him. 'Is that so wrong?'

'My god! What *is* this?' Sylvie cried.

Mildred, who couldn't restrain herself any longer, shrugged and turned to Sylvie. 'It's certainly not your traditional Thanksgiving,' she said.

'You didn't know? Are you blind or stupid?' John asked Bob.

'The answers to those questions are yes and yes,' Sylvie said. 'But, John, what are you? How could you? How could you sleep with . . . me?'

'I've always loved you, Sylvie,' John said simply. Then, confused, he turned to Marla. 'Uh . . . Marla?'

Sylvie now focused her rage on the lying, cheating little bimbo. 'It wasn't enough that you slept with my husband? You had to sleep with my best friend?' she demanded.

'He's *my* best friend!' Bob shouted over Marla's head.

'Not anymore!' John shouted back.

'Listen. There's a simple explanation,' Marla said, cringing between them. She looked at Sylvie. 'Bobby wasn't sleeping with me. I had to do something.'

Sylvie turned to Bob, who by now was immobilized, his jaw permanently unhinged. She hated him. He was despicable, the lowest form of life. '*You* are the villain here. I wanted you, but you didn't reciprocate. When I found out why——' She pointed to Marla, '——*I* didn't sleep with John.' Sylvie then turned and focused on Marla. '*Or* the rest of the men of Cleveland, Ohio,' she added.

'All right. I did everything wrong, as always,' Marla said. She began to weep. 'I'm going to jump off the bridge.' Marla got out of bed, trying to take the duvet with her but not quite succeeding. Bob and John, stripped of their cover, clutched pillows to their privates.

'Wait. We have to talk,' John said to Marla as she walked, her duvet like a lumpy bridal train behind her, across the room.

'Okay. Listen up. Here are all of your orders,' Sylvie said, trying to gain control. 'Marla, get out of here. Not for sleeping with my husband, for sleeping with John, my friend, my doctor, and my backup in case Bob left.' She caught her breath. 'And don't jump off the bridge.' She turned to John. 'You too, you traitor,' she said.

'I wasn't going to jump off the bridge,' Marla said.

'Well, maybe you should think about it! Anyway, I just meant you should go.' She spun around and faced her mother. 'Show's over. You were right, as always. Now would you all please go downstairs?' Sylvie came down off the ottoman, but not her high horse. She stood there, her arms crossed. They might as well be double-crossed, as was the rest of her.

Mildred gave her a hug and a look, then walked out the door. Marla scrambled for her clothes and, clutching a sheet to her chest, approached Sylvie. 'Here,' she said, and handed Sylvie back the Cartier ring. 'Thanks,' she said. 'But I'll get my own now from John.'

John pulled the duvet around himself and left without looking her in the eye. Only Bob was left, naked on the bed, a pillow over his crotch.

'Sylvie? What about me? I know I've done wrong, but you've woken me up. That was passion, it was love we felt.'

Sylvie walked up to him and pulled away the pillow fiercely. 'It's not as if I haven't seen Little Bobby before,' she said nastily. 'You weren't so modest an hour ago. You're out of here.'

'Out of here? Out of the house?'

'Out of my *life*. I gave, Bob . . . my whole life with you was about me giving.'

'And I loved it. I love you. I just . . . forgot.'

'Until just now,' Sylvie said, turning her back on him.

Bob scrambled into his chinos, stood up, and approached

her. He put his hand on her shoulder, but she flinched away. 'So, I lose everything I love because I had an affair?'

She nodded, keeping her back to him. 'That's the way I see it.'

'You just said you'd marry me,' Bob said, sounding desperate.

'That's when I was her,' Sylvie reminded him. She turned to face him. 'Hey, don't worry. She probably still would.' Bob's face had turned a ghastly white, his few freckles standing out starkly against his livid cheeks. He had been obliterated. Her plan had worked. He was a fool, a clown, a liar. He could say nothing. Sylvie managed to look calm, not to move or speak or even take a breath until he left the room. Then she threw herself across the bed, collapsing.

32

Hours later the family, by now all conscious of the crisis, were gathered in the dining room. Their student guests had taken off, at Mildred's suggestion and with extra carfare and motel money supplied by Jim. Now the twins and the rest of them sat hunched over the Thanksgiving table. It was as decimated as they were. For the last hour or so they had been eating pumpkin pie, since Marla seemed to have left an endless supply of it. All of the family was there, except, of course, for Bob and Sylvie. She had stayed in the bedroom for the last two hours. Now, though, they all paused, forks suspended, hearing her on the stairs. When Sylvie entered the room she was still wiping her puffy eyes.

'Is there any pie left?' she asked quietly.

Wordlessly, Mildred cut Sylvie a large wedge while Jim pushed over his plate. 'Here, honey,' he said, 'finish mine.'

Wordlessly, Sylvie sat down and picked up a spoon. After all, she thought, what was left at this point but combining fats and carbohydrates? Her life was ruined. All eyes were on her. Obviously the twins knew something was up, but thank god they'd been spared the details. 'Thanks, Daddy,' Sylvie said, and patted her father's hand.

'Mom, did you and Daddy—' Reenie started to ask, but was interrupted by Kenny.

'They'll still love us, and they'll both come to our graduations and weddings . . .' he said in the falsely sincere voice of an actor from an after-school special. 'Just . . . separately.'

'Oh, kids . . .' Sylvie said, about to reassure them, but then she realized she didn't have anything to reassure them about.

'I could never figure out, where does love go when it goes away?' Reenie asked. 'I mean, Brian said he loved me, but—' She stopped. 'I loved him yesterday.'

The phone rang. Phil jumped to answer it, Rosalie at his elbow. He started murmuring to his ex-wife. Sylvie could hear their whispers turn fierce. 'Don't tell her,' she overheard Rosalie insisting.

'She'll want to know, Rose.'

'Go ahead, then. But she won't talk to him. And if she does, she's a wimp.'

Mildred finally spoke up. 'Who is it?' she asked, but Sylvie knew.

'It's Bob,' Phil volunteered, his voice falsely casual.

'Hang up on the son of a bitch,' Jim snapped.

Mildred raised her brows and looked at Jim, who paused for a moment, glanced at his daughter and grandchildren, then hung his head and shut up. Mildred calmly looked over at Sylvie and her look said, 'Watch it.' Meanwhile, Kenny and Reenie hadn't taken their eyes off her. Sylvie wondered what lesson her actions right now would teach them. What should she do?

Mildred stood up and took her arm, leading her into the hallway. 'Sylvie, just because your father is angry with Bob is no reason for *you* not to forgive him. You've more than made your point, I think. Now the question is: do you still love him?' Mildred asked.

'I've always loved him,' Sylvie admitted. 'I was ignored by

318

him, but I loved him. I was angry with him, but I loved him. I was betrayed by him, but I loved him.' She looked at Mildred calmly. '*That* was never the question. The question was: did he love me? I don't want him back to be his mother, to feed him, to do his laundry, or keep his goddamn cuff links organized. I only want him back because he loves me. Big time.'

'Hey, I got a guy on hold here,' Phil yelled.

Mildred shrugged. 'He'll keep holding,' she yelled back to Phil. She turned again to her daughter. 'Remember, Sylvie, men aren't the same as we are. They're not exactly human. They're . . . well, let's say humanoid.'

'That's not true, Mother,' Sylvie said. She walked out of the hallway and stopped to kiss Kenny on the top of his head.

'Sylvie?' Phil asked, motioning to the phone.

'Your call, Sylvie,' Mildred told her daughter. 'Do you want me to take it?'

'I'm okay,' Sylvie reassured her mother. 'I'll take it in the music room,' Sylvie told Phil.

Bob was sitting at the wheel of Beautiful Baby. He was holding the mobile phone to his ear and, because of the dropping temperature, he had clouds of smoke coming out of his nose. He'd wet the receiver with his breath and he was shivering. He'd been sitting in the cold for a long, long time. But he could afford to hold on for as long as it took. It had given him time to think.

He couldn't believe how stupid he'd been. What an ass he was. He'd already tried to work up some anger over Sylvie's trick or, if not anger, at least a little righteous indignation. But it wasn't going to work. He guessed he should be proud of that. Maybe he wasn't such a complete, irredeemable asshole if he could acknowledge that he was a complete, irredeemable

319

asshole. He'd been caught lying and he couldn't condemn Sylvie for outlying him. He began to replay the events of the last few weeks and the blushes actually sent a wash of warmth over his icy face and neck.

He shook his head and wiped off the receiver again. How could he not have noticed that Marla and Sylvie were doubles? How could he not have noticed the switch? And how could he have been so stupid and so blind as to risk his marriage and his family for a quick fling with youth? The fact was, he was forty-four years old. No younger woman would change that – except in his own pathetic mind. He was no longer young, he was middle-aged. After this he would be old. Then he would be dead. That was the way it worked. Contrary to popular opinion, denial did not stop the aging process.

He shivered in the dark interior of the convertible. The cloth roof gave no protection against the night chill. Why had he so carefully restored this car, and why did he insist on driving it? It was all part of the same syndrome: the look-I'm-still-young-and-potent disease. He'd seen it hit Phil and wreck his life.

Bob sat in the ridiculous, tiny, freezing-cold car and thought about how much he loved Sylvie and how he had forgotten to appreciate their life together. Sylvie hadn't grown middle-aged, he had. She was still spontaneous, still loved her music, was still ready to travel and do vibrant, crazy things. Even the switch she'd pulled on him showed how creative, how talented she was. Alone, in the darkness, on hold, Bob blushed again. He thought of the secrets he'd kept from her that she now knew. He thought of making love to her at Marla's, how exciting and how moving it had been, and how stupid he was to not know her then. Didn't the Bible use that expression – Abraham 'knew' Sarah – when it spoke of sex? He hadn't known her. And he'd probably ruined his life irrevocably. He looked down at the telephone receiver and, unworthy as he was, said a prayer.

Sylvie walked into the music room and closed the door behind her. She was in no rush. After all, what could she possibly say? And what could Bob say that would make everything all right? She flipped on the exterior lights but left the room dark. Outside, the view through the French doors was magical. Frost had whitened the lawn, glowing now in contrast with the ink-dark evergreens. Sylvie sat down at the piano, as she always did in times of joy or misery. She began playing a nocturne. After a few moments Sylvie took a deep breath and then lifted up the telephone.

'What exactly is it you want?' Sylvie asked.

'Sylvie?' Bob's voice sounded surprised, as if he hadn't expected her to be there. Well, why should she?

'Yes. It's me,' she said and, holding the phone between her ear and shoulder, returned to playing the song, more and more slowly and with heavier chords. 'What do you want?' she repeated.

'I want you,' Bob said. 'I know that's an outrageous thing to say, and probably impossible, but you asked and I told you.' Bob's voice sounded thick to her, as if he had been crying. Well, she'd cried plenty, Sylvie thought. 'Sylvie, now that I'm losing everything, things are very clear,' Bob's voice said.

'I guess they always are at the end,' Sylvie told him.

'I didn't love her, Sylvie. I didn't even know her.'

'Except in the carnal sense,' Sylvie reminded him. Her fingers stumbled over the keys. The phone was hurting the crook of her neck.

'I know now that what I loved was my past, the time that I had with you, when we were young and it was fun,' Bob said. 'I wanted that, not her.' He paused. 'Sylvie, I didn't even notice the resemblance. Not consciously. I know it's unbelievable. But I think it was—'

Sylvie heard the two beeps of call waiting. 'Could you hold for a minute?' Sylvie asked and pressed the flash button without waiting for Bob's answer.

'Sylvie? It's Marla. I mean, Susan.'

'What do *you* want?' Sylvie asked.

'I just wanted to thank you. And to let you be the first to know: John and I are engaged.'

'*Engaged*? What about Nora?'

'Who's Nora?'

'Never mind.' Everyone was insane, Sylvie figured, herself included. 'Best wishes,' Sylvie managed. John was going to marry that girl? He was welcome to her. Maybe her mother was right – men were only humanoids. 'Congratulations to him,' Sylvie continued.

'You're the only person in the world who's ever kept her promise to me,' Marla – or Susan – said.

'Well, let's hope it's the start of a trend,' Sylvie told her. 'I gotta go.' She punched back to Bob.

'Sylvie? Are you there?' he asked.

'Yes.' This was all she would say; she'd let him do the talking.

'Sylvie, you have to hear this,' Bob continued. 'I've always loved you. I admit that I forgot it for a little while, but it's true. We should have played together more often. Music, and other things. We once made a good team, didn't we?'

She nodded, though she wouldn't acknowledge it with her voice. They were both silent for a few moments.

'You gave. I can give too. I could sacrifice anything for you, Sylvie.'

'Somehow I doubt that,' Sylvie told him, allowing just one tear to roll down her cheek. She'd already cried enough over this, but it seemed as if the one tear had all of her pain and bitterness distilled within it. It tickled her cheek, but she wouldn't wipe it away. 'You really hurt me,' she whispered. 'It wasn't a nice thing to do.'

'I know. You're right. You did better than I did,' Bob acknowledged. 'Forgive me.'

He was incredible. All men were. Couldn't he understand? 'Look,' Sylvie said. 'You've destroyed my trusting you.'

'But I . . .'

Sylvie wouldn't let him say a word. Not until she got this out. Because even if he couldn't get it he had to hear her aching. 'You made love to your mistress. You cheated on me and I was there. I was *her*. Remember your hands on the back of my neck, and the way you held down my shoulder? That was *me* you were holding, me you were kissing.' A tiny pain noise escaped her, but she wouldn't cry.

'Sylvie, I didn't know, I . . .'

'Bob, there's so much you didn't know. You didn't know Marla was my double. You didn't know she was a real person, and how you were hurting her, cheating *her*. You didn't know you still loved me. You didn't know how I wanted you. You also didn't know I could make love like that. It was perfect. The two of us were perfect. Except you didn't even know it was the two of us. You've underestimated me for a long time. I'm not some suburban laundry expert, some genius with the Electrolux. I wasn't just the mother of your children and the keeper of your house.' Another gasp of pain came out of her, but she managed to continue. 'I'm an imaginative, adventurous, passionate woman, and you took me for granted. You . . . you . . . oh Bob, you're a fool.'

'I have no excuse,' he said. 'I'm a jerk. But . . . I made other mistakes that hurt me. And I didn't know that either. I gave up my music,' he said. 'I think I started to resent you. I started to blame you, the kids, Jim. But it was me, Sylvie. I chose as I did. I was safe in my rut. Resentful, but safe.' Sylvie heard him choke up. She wondered where he was calling from but wouldn't ask. 'I've never been as open, as true to myself as you,' Bob continued. 'I didn't know my limits and I didn't know my strengths.' There was a long silence. 'Sylvie? When will you let me try to make it up to you?'

Sylvie stood up, stepping away from the piano bench, turning her back to the rest of the room. What could she say? She stared out the window into the empty backyard. Bob was a desperate man right now. Wouldn't he probably say anything? How long would *that* last? 'I don't know. Maybe when you've learned that vaginas are connected to hearts. Unlike dicks.' She paused. 'I may never be able to trust you again,' she admitted.

And yet her heart yearned for him, for the man who had held her and loved her so tenderly – in another woman's bed. But Sylvie wasn't going to make it easy for Bob. She wasn't going to be weak. He'd promise much now, but what would he really give up for her? How could he make this up to her? Would he ever change from the compulsive, closed man he had become with her? Sylvie didn't want to go on alone. She didn't want to break up their family, but she wasn't willing to go on in the way she had been. 'Good-bye, Bob,' she said and hung up.

Sylvie stood in the darkness of her music room with the dead receiver in her hand. Was her marriage over? If it was, she would be alone without someone to love for the rest of her life. She wouldn't go through this again. Would she give up her history and her marriage? Did she have a choice? What Bob had done was agonizing and humiliating to her. But Sylvie had heard what he said and knew, perhaps from her own wisdom, perhaps from her mother's, that she shouldn't take his indiscretion personally. Not because she was a wimp, nor because she was too 'nice' to keep him on the hook, not because it was more convenient to forgive him. Not even because she wanted those moments of passion again – though she did. She realized she could forgive Bob because he, like many men, often had very little idea of what he was doing until it was actually done. She believed he hadn't meant to hurt her, and that picking someone who looked so similar to her had, more than anything, been a way of recapturing their past. Okay, it was a stupid, ridiculous way and it hadn't worked. It almost ruined both of their lives, and maybe had perhaps scarred the lives of their children, but he hadn't meant for it to happen.

Bob was not really a conniver or a manipulator. If anything, he was an emotional dunce and, she decided, she could forgive him for that. Almost any woman was smarter about her feelings than the very smartest man was about his, but since she preferred living and sleeping with a man she would have to accept men's limitations. He had hurt her, he'd been foolhardy, but he certainly wasn't going to do it again. Maybe she could forgive him. She wouldn't take it personally; she'd take it as a group.

Just then, a bouncing light against the wall caught Sylvie's attention. Was it a flashlight? What was . . . She turned around, expecting to see Rosalie outside the French doors. But it couldn't be her. She was in the dining room. Sylvie flipped off the outside lights in the hope of getting a better idea of where the spots were coming from.

'Oh my god!' she cried. Headlights were coming at her. The hall door flew open. Everyone ran in from the dining room.

'I can't believe it!' Reenie said.

Sylvie and the rest of the family went to the French doors.

'Oh lord!' Mildred exclaimed.

'Go, Dad!' Kenny cheered.

'The car! The car!' Jim shouted in horror.

Sylvie stood completely still, a radiant joy filling her. She held her breath. Would he do it? Would he go all the way for her?

Mildred flipped on the pool lights. 'There is a God,' Mildred said, 'and She is good.'

Sylvie watched as Beautiful Baby approached the brink and, without slowing down, without even a moment of hesitation, was driven over the edge and into the pool. The twins screamed. Jim groaned. The family began as one to move outdoors, but Mildred wisely restrained them.

'Let your mother go alone,' she told the twins.

Sylvie stepped outside and began to run across the patio, then through the yard, toward the pool. Bob emerged, climbing the ladder just as Sylvie got to it. He was already shivering with the cold. 'I'd do anything for you,' he gasped, and Sylvie stood there for a moment, hesitating on the brink. 'Please, Sylvie,' Bob begged. 'Forgive me. Let me try again. Let's play duets again.'

'I don't know. It would take a long time to trust you again.'

'I'll give you all the time I've got left. We'll go on a cruise.

We'll dance, alone at home, to the radio.' He looked at her, obviously desperate. His teeth were chattering, his lips blue from the cold. 'We'll get that bus and drive cross-country.' Sylvie only looked at him. 'Say something,' Bob begged. 'Anything. Tell me you'll consider it. Tell me there's even the smallest chance you'll forgive me. Please, Sylvie. Tell me what to do.'

Sylvie smiled wickedly at the only man she'd ever loved. He'd really have to work hard. And even then . . . But in the meantime she'd have more of that great sex. She'd be adored, and if he stopped admiring her, if he took her for granted, well . . . 'Please, Sylvie. Please. Just say something. Give me a clue.'

'In four words: take me to Maui,' she told him.

As Bob put his arms around her she gasped, from both the cold and from his warmth. He kissed her, hard and deeply. Behind her she could hear the twins, Mildred, and even her father, clapping. But soon, as Bob's cold lips pressed against her warm ones, she heard nothing but their heartbeats.

Acknowledgments

Thanks to Barbara Turner for continuing to be my sister; Dwight Currie because, no matter what, he will make me laugh; Paul Mahon for not being there when I needed him the most; Rachel Dower in memory of our 'Clueless Goes to College' marathon; Diana Hellinger for remembering who I am when I finally call; Larry Ashmead for the books, laughs, and zinnias; Jerry Young, who can recite all the lawyers he works for – in ascending order of skill; Amy Fine Collins for your patience and reciprocal love and admiration; Pat Rhule because you always take my calls and almost always make me laugh; Linda Grady for her continued loving support; Bob Bookman with the hopes that this season you snag a ball in Dodger Stadium; Kelly Lange for your endless hospitality. I still have your keys; Steve Rubin and Ed Town for keeping a candle in the window for me; Jody Post with apologies for not sending this book in draft; Nunz and Rose Nappi with thanks for a great Thanksgiving and the best of friendships; Amy Baer for leaving the baby to come see me; Walter Mathews for the great conversations and the window shopping in Hudson; Kathi Goldmark for letting me perform 'Book Tour Blues' in public; Melody Smith for her selfless concern; Sherry Lansing for starting off everything; Ben Dower in the hopes that this book will get you your next set of clubs; Gerry Petievich, my writing brother on the West Coast; Neil Baldwin, whose work at the National Book Foundation continues to inspire me; Richard Saperstein for 'getting it' and then buying it for New Line Cinema; Ali Elovitz for hanging with me despite my snoring; Beth Dozoretz for being such a kind friend and an inspiration to me; Michael Kohlmann for keeping up with all my madness; Jim Robinson for all the technical assistance a writer girl could ever ask for; Jennifer Perini, the only young, tall, thin blonde I truly like; Michael Elovitz for lending me his room while I wrote this book; Andrew Fisher for passing the bar; Gail Parent for teaching me her immortal ode: 'Oh, Hollywood, Oh, Let Me Go'; Lorraine Kreahling for those weekends in Greenport, Lorrie Sue; Jack Rapke because I'm nuts about you, okay? To all my contractors, for finally getting out of my house; Howard Schwartz for doing what you do so well; Anita Addison for her total understanding of women in the media; Anthea Disney for continuing to laugh at my jokes; Ruth Nathan, best friend a writer girl could have; New York Society Library for their unfailing assistance; Cindy Adams for the drycleaning advice; Paige Rense for understanding my love for my house and Michael Wollaenger for not cutting any of my 3,456 words about the love; Chris Robinson for always being my boyfriend (so far); Harold Wise, even though you haven't shown me your manuscript; Bruce Vinokour with thanks for putting up with me; Marjorie Braman for the great edit and insistence on 'Marjorie Moments'; Lynn Phillips for her insights and the informed reads of my draft; Dalia Rabinovich for listening to her mother; Adam Schroeder and Scott Rudin for making me a household name; Louise Schmidt for her endless pillow making on my behalf; Brenda Segel for the gorilla stories; Keith Gregory at Southern Methodist University for their inspirational attention to new novelists; Storyline Entertainment for giving me work; Jeffery McGraw for your endless enthusiasm and equally endless patience; Chris Patusky for not taking me out; Anita Gates for getting my jokes and allowing me to praise writers publicly; Tyrone D'Brass for inviting me to decorate his palace in Rajasthan; Bert Fields for the superb representation; Ron Fried for still thinking I'm so nice; Martine Rothblatt for all her excellent advice; Nick Ellison, with thanks for our fabulous dinners; Chris Lee for really listening to me; Helen Breitwieser Katleman, with best wishes and congratulations to Mr Right; Michael Chinich for the Polaroids – oooh, Michael! Was Morgan naked in that picture?; Liz Ziemska, in awe of your wisdom and professional knowledge, not to mention the new haircut; Bill, Ann, Kip, and Steven for taking loving care of Matilda; Jacki Heppard for her short stay but lasting impression; Donna Langley for her suggestions, patience, and good humor; Beaver Hall for the gnawing, lodging, and tail slapping; Michael Barnathan for the beautiful bouquets – you make me so happy, Michael; Lucy Hood for the brave attempt at synergy; Susie and Joe at Misakiya for feeding me daily; Phyllis Levy for our shared love of cats; Cathy Cavender for giving me a difficult assignment and helping me get through it; Dan Melnick for being my older, male, more brilliant twin; Hugh Wilson for keeping in touch; Gladys Sanchez for taking care of my house and my office; Beth Arky for letting me walk the line in *TV Guide*; Akiko Wied for your patience and hard work; Patricia Martin and Leif Zurmuhlen for keeping me on the Right Side of Forty; Kitty Kelley for the open invitation; Joe Kiener for being simultaneously so tall and so smart; Jerry Leed at Fashion Award for helping me clean up my act; Leonida Karpick for knowing how to sell my books; Jennifer Blum for being the brains behind the operation; and Nan Robinson for finally showing some enthusiasm.